Karren Brady is the first woman ever to be appointed Managing Director of an English football club, First Division Birmingham City. She runs the business side of the club and took it from loss-maker to profit in her first year in charge and in 1997 successfully launched it on the stockmarket. She is now the youngest MD of a publicly listed company in this country. Karren lives in a small village outside Birmingham with her footballer husband Paul Peschisolido and her children Sophie and Paolo.

Also by Karren Brady

UNITED

Trophy Wives

KARREN BRADY

WARNER BOOKS

A *Warner* Book

First published in Great Britain in 1998 by Warner Books

Copyright © 1998, Karren Brady

The moral right of the author has been asserted.

Although some of the footballing fixtures in this book
are real, for dramatic purposes the characters and
situations portrayed are fictitious.

A CIP catalogue record for this book
is available from the British Library.

ISBN 0 7515 2245 7

Typeset by Palimpsest Book Production Limited,
Polmont, Stirlingshire
Printed and bound in Great Britain by
Clays Ltd, St Ives plc.

Warner Books
A Division of
Little, Brown and Company (UK)
Brettenham House
Lancaster Place
London WC2E 7EN

For Paul, with love.

With thanks to Jason Bennetto, Jonathan Doherty, Derek Douglas, Sharon Kelly, Jane Turnbull.
A very special thanks to Vikki Orvice – a mine of information as always.
And to Jo O'Neill whose constant support and encouragement (and occasional lunch) made the difference.

Prologue

A crowd of unholy angels had descended on Heathrow's Terminal 2 to await the arrival of Iberian Airways flight 202 from Tenerife. All of them female, all of them blond and all of them far, far smarter than they would ever let on.

At first glance they appeared interchangeable – Versace dress, Marbella tan, breasts on Amex and hair on permanent hold. It was a blueprint drawn up by their men – the boys of Notting Hill Football Club – and few dared deviate from it. Lacquered, polished, slicked and primed, they were the Trophy Wives.

On a second glance, a handful of these women, while not escaping the mould entirely, was different enough to merit attention. The first was the skinny but gorgeous honey blond in the white, barely-there mini-dress with the spaghetti shoulder-straps. She was standing by the Arrivals gate surrounded by a horde of adolescent boys demanding her autograph. This was Loulou Lamb, girlfriend of the team's star striker, Andy McKay.

Loulou knew she was different from the others.

Accent alone saw to that. Estuary English was the lin-
gua franca of the footballers' wives but Loulou spoke
in the crisp, cut-glass voice of a well-travelled woman
used to underlining her Englishness. At twenty-four,
her star shone as brightly as any of the members of
the West London Premier League team.

Infamous for the activities of her youth, the former
wild child was now on her way to semi-respectability
as the presenter of *Sorted!*, a late-night youth programme on Channel Four. Although the show had
attracted much criticism for its low-brow content,
Loulou had attracted an army of loyal male fans
bewitched by her stunning azure eyes and unattainable
beauty.

Today as the fans jostled her, clamouring for her
attention, she looked serene and relaxed. With her
green-rimmed sunglasses perched on her head, casu-
ally sweeping her glossy, immaculately contoured hair
away from her finely etched face, which was free from
all but the most subtle make-up, she proffered a cheek
for their kisses, knowing the moment would fuel their
fantasies for months to come.

But inside she was seething. The other women
were glaring at her with ill-disguised hostility, clearly
annoyed at the attention she was receiving. Had she
not been the focus of so much scrutiny, she would
have returned their animosity in spades. But as a
professional she knew what she had to do, and she
turned her dazzling smile on brighter.

There was one other woman present who outdid
Loulou in newspaper column inches, but she had
made herself practically invisible. Tanya Barry sat
quietly away from the others, her platinum blond curls

buried behind a magazine and her famous body hidden behind a shapeless black jumper and leggings.

Tanya was currently the number one Page Three girl in the country, but when she wasn't in front of the camera, she sought anonymity. Although the cockney glamour model/professional footballer interface was a well-worn cliché, the twenty-three-year-old from Bethnal Green brought a breath of fresh air to Notting Hill, for behind the celebrated 36DD breasts beat a heart that was totally without guile.

She refused to indulge in the constant bitchiness that preoccupied most of the other women, shrugging off the endless innuendo and slurs about her supposed sexual easiness. David Ashby, captain of the team, was the only footballer she had ever dated and only the third man she'd ever slept with. And he was the man she dreamed she would one day marry.

Along with fidelity, a practical, down-to-earth wisdom was one of Tanya's strongest attributes. Knowing her limitations had given her a sure-footed confidence about her place in the world. She wasn't beautiful like Loulou, but her round, open face responded extremely well to the camera lens and she was proud that she'd managed to mix this quirk along with *those* breasts into a successful career.

As two small children, one boy one girl, ran past her pretending to be aeroplanes, Tanya looked up from her magazine and smiled at their harassed-looking mother following along in their wake. Rachel Black, wife of mid-fielder Robbie, smiled back weakly before resuming the chase.

Rachel had none of the career aspirations of Tanya or Loulou. With two out-of-control children, Demi and little Robbie Jnr, and a husband to take care of, her time was totally swallowed up by her family. Aside from being a blonde – admittedly her hair was mousy and cut in a nondescript bob – she had little in common with the other Trophy Wives.

It wasn't the way she wanted it but her dreams of glamour were cut short by the realities of her work-day life. The limp Laura Ashley dress she wore was stained with Demi's Ribena, and though she'd have liked to have looked special for Robbie today, getting the children ready had dominated the morning, allowing her only a brief moment to hastily apply a bland pink lipstick to her thin lips.

The wives who didn't bitch about her pitied her, which was worse. Poor, downtrodden Rachel. Sadly, she saw herself in the same light, and buried her dreams for a different kind of life deep inside. At twenty-six, the only time she had ever felt even the remotest bit glamorous was the day she'd been mistaken for Lisa Leeson in Sainsbury's.

Rachel chased the children into the airport bar but was too slow to stop Robbie Jnr from falling and banging his head. As she carried out the screaming child, she was sure that all of the customers were shaking their heads in disapproval. Wife and mother was all it said on her CV, and she didn't feel particularly adept at either.

The woman with the bottle-blond crop perched on a stool at the bar hadn't noticed her at all. This probably had something to do with the Manhattan in front of her, her fifth of the morning. Jenny Waite was the daughter of the legendary Bernard Dorning, the man who had started Notting Hill, and the estranged sister of current chairman Clive. In her spangly Versace cat-suit, the forty-year-old was the club's Queen Bee, both an inspiration to the younger Trophies and a warning of how it could all go terribly wrong.

She had been beautiful but the abuses she had inflicted upon herself were legion, and a life filled with pain had left its mark on her face in deeply etched lines, which disappeared every now and then with a nip and a tuck. On the rare occasion she was sober enough to study her face in a mirror, the word that came to mind was leathery. Like a worn-out handbag.

'Punchbag' would have been closer to the truth. The source of much of her anguish was her husband, Michael Waite, the team's psychotically violent defender, and the trials of their tempestuous marriage had sent her scuttling to substance abuse for refuge.

As the fifth Manhattan merged into the sixth, she realised that life would be easier if she just stopped counting. Stopped counting the drinks, stopped counting the years. The first was easy but the second impossible, married as she was to a man almost fifteen years her junior.

The thought of those fifteen years terrified Jenny, and she stumbled to the toilet to reapply her make-up. War paint, that's what they called it, and Jenny was in no doubt she was at war: with the elements, with the men in her life and, most critically, with herself.

She'd been too drunk to notice the woman who had been studying her every move – Carla Ryman, Trophy-wannabe. Carla desperately wanted what Jenny had and tried hard to emulate the older woman's trash with flash style. The problem with Carla, a barmaid in Notting Hill's players' lounge, was that she was working with a dramatically tighter budget.

Tighter trousers too. Whereas Jenny's excesses at least kept her thin, at twenty-two, Carla was already running to fat, and the white leather pants she was wearing left her no place to hide. The matching waistcoat, worn without a blouse, was equally unforgiving, but she wore her clothes with a lewd self-awareness that appealed to the baser instincts in many men. For the past three weeks she had been dating mid-fielder Stu Williams, but, like the many, many men before him, his interest in her had quickly waned once she'd given him what he wanted.

Today's inches of bare flesh and the new blond streaks in her nicotine-coloured hair were an attempt to revive his passions, but if that failed then Carla had something else up her sleeve. For she had discovered something about Stu that nobody else knew. Something she was sure he wouldn't want getting out.

And so the Trophy Wives waited for their men. Or, more accurately, they lay in wait.

Pin-up boy Andy McKay pushed past Michael Waite to be the first one through the Arrivals gate. The handsome twenty-seven-year-old hated his team-mate with a passion and the two men had come to blows several times. They were complete opposites – and, in this case, opposites didn't attract.

Whereas Andy was tall, blond, middle class, university educated and at the pinnacle of his career, the compact, stocky, dark-haired defender had learned everything he knew on the streets and was staring professional oblivion in the face. Their clashes were frequent and violent, quickly moving from the verbal to the physical – and not once had Andy come off better.

Spotting the assembled newspaper men, Andy pushed this unwelcome thought out of his head as he strode purposefully over to Loulou and swept her into his arms. The cameramen loved it, calling for the couple to repeat the moment. True professionals, they willingly obliged. The perfect couple.

As Loulou and Andy arranged 'exclusives' to talk about their burgeoning relationship with various newspapers, David Ashby walked by unnoticed. Coming to the end of his playing career and hoping to make a quiet transition into management, he had none of the stellar qualities that made Andy so irresistible to the press. At thirty he was starting to lose his hair and, prone to deep introspection and worry, his rough-hewn face was rarely seen breaking into a smile. Except around Tanya. He spotted her reading, waved and pointed towards the airport exit, happy for their reunion to be in private.

As they walked away hand in hand, they passed Rachel struggling to carry Robbie's luggage while holding on to the two children, as her short, baby-faced husband signed autographs for a group of girl fans.

What the fans didn't know was that simply writing his signature was a struggle for Robbie Black. From as far back as he could remember football had been his life and his education had been totally sacrificed so that he could pursue his dream. But his illiteracy didn't bother him at all. He'd made it in the game and people thought he was a nice guy. Robbie was everybody's best friend.

Especially Michael's. Robbie hero-worshipped the bad-boy player and now, spotting his idol, who had clearly taken full advantage of the complimentary bar on the plane, he abandoned his struggling wife to offer a supportive arm to his team mate. Together, they set off in search of Jenny, finally locating her at the bar, where she'd fallen into a drunken sleep. Robbie made a quick exit, knowing that a row would ensue.

Michael shook his wife, who slid unsteadily to her feet. Although barely able to stand himself, Michael launched into a stream of slurred invective as they made their way to the car. Jenny gave as good as she got but was relieved when Michael produced a wrap of coke; at least that would keep him quiet for a while.

The final person to emerge was the red-haired midfielder Stu Williams. He had deliberately dawdled in baggage collection, unable to face Carla. The weekend in Tenerife had been a nightmare, with the other guys endlessly ribbing him. This was his first season at Notting Hill and he hadn't known until too late that bedding Carla was a team ritual: it was all right to do it with her – but only once.

As he walked through the gate she was the first person he saw – no one could miss her in that get-up. She looked like the Michelin man. It was no good. She would have to go.

Chapter One

Clive Dorning flicked through the creased and yellowed pages of his Bible until he found his favourite passage. Silently, his thin lips mouthed the words that had come to mean so much to him: 'The Devil is come down unto you, having great wrath, because he knoweth that he hath but a short time . . .'

Life, he knew, was a constant battle against evil, and sometimes, just sometimes, it seemed like the devil was winning the war. Satan wore many disguises, some too attractive to resist. As he beseeched the Lord to wash away his sins, his thoughts, as always, turned to his sister, a sinner if ever there was one. He prayed every night that she would, like him, find Jesus. But she stubbornly hung on to her Catholic faith, if only by threads.

On being born again, Clive had adopted the extreme beliefs that Catholicism was little above paganism and that the present Pope was the Anti-Christ.

If it wasn't for the memory of their father and because Clive took his Christian duty seriously, he would have long ago kicked Jenny's no-good husband off the team. Not that she ever appeared grateful. In fact, she had scarcely spoken to him in the last ten years, unless forced to by circumstance. What had happened to that very special bond they'd shared when they'd lived together?

The phone rang. 'Amen,' he muttered, rising from his knees and walking through to his office. 'This better be important, Margaret,' he barked at his secretary. 'OK, put him on.'

'Reverend,' Clive said in a tone Margaret would never have recognised. 'No, no trouble. What can I do for you?'

It was in the Reverend Peters' church, an unattractive Victorian building in a little village near Edinburgh, that Clive had found Jesus. From Saturday night to Monday morning Clive lived in a large farm nearby with his wife and two daughters. The rest of the time he lived in a flat 'above the shop', as he liked to describe the two rooms next to his office.

While listening to the Reverend, he absentmindedly picked at invisible specks on his immaculate, double-breasted, dark grey suit. Clive rarely wore anything else, even when he was relaxing, which wasn't often. The only incongruity to this image was the garish and startling rings worn on nearly every finger. There was a large, ugly sovereign, a wide-band wedding ring, a signet ring and three specially commissioned rings bearing religious motifs.

'I'd be honoured to prepare Sunday's lesson.' His quiet voice belied his stature. At six foot three he was an imposing man, and with his silver-grey hair, steely blue eyes and angular jaw-line, the word 'patriarch' was often used by journalists when describing his looks. The only flaw was his caterpillar eyebrows, which looked as if they were having a fight above his nose. He wore an expression that brooked no argument and most who knew him feared him.

Clive went back to his bedroom, his eyes barely registering the hastily made bed. Most of the decor and furnishings, including a battered leather settee and a cracked glass coffee table, were the legacy of the previous chairman – a sweet reminder of Clive's victorious court battle twenty years before. It had been a bitter fight, but Clive had managed to oust all those who had run the club after his father's death. Since then his reputation for hard-headed shrewdness had become legendary and he was one of the most respected football club owners in the business.

Looking out of the bedroom window he surveyed all that he owned. His father might have started Notting Hill but it had been Clive's input that had made it one of the most financially successful clubs in the country. He had just spent millions expanding the stadium to hold over fifty thousand fans.

From his position on the sixth floor he could see beyond the stadium to the elegant terraces of Notting Hill. He hated the houses' inhabitants, with their constant whinging letters to the *Notting Hill Gazette*. They were always on the same themes – the fans caused too much noise, left too much litter and they couldn't park their Volvos when a match was on.

Sitting down on his bed he looked around. Only a few carefully selected people ever visited the flat, and those who did were sinners. He wondered what he should say for the Sunday lesson. Some kind of metaphor involving football always went down well.

Glancing at his watch, he realised there wasn't time to think about it now; the press conference was about to start.

Stefan Lohmann blinked as the camera lights bounced and glided off his glasses. He shifted in his chair, uncomfortable at being the cause of so much attention.

Outside a thin drizzle dulled the light. England looked exactly how he had pictured it – grey and unwelcoming. But if this was the only way he could realise his dream of playing in the World Cup, so be it. Like Klinsmann, he had transferred to an English club in order to play enough first team matches to qualify for his national squad.

The room was becoming hot and humid from the lights and crushed bodies. He tugged on his goatee, nervous and agitated, wondering what Paula, his fiancée, was doing back in Germany. He already missed her and he'd been here only one day. She had told him that without a job she wouldn't come over, and so far no English PR company had been willing to take her on.

The media circus quietened down and Stefan looked round to see his new boss, Clive Dorning, arriving. This would be only the second time they had met. He stood as Clive approached, Clive gave a brief nod, and they both sat down and faced the crowd.

'Thanks for coming today,' Clive Dorning announced to the reporters. 'As you know, Stefan Lohmann is our latest recruit and a very valuable one at that. All the team are glad to have him, especially as it's going to be a demanding year. But, God willing, Notting

Hill will be bringing home a lot of silver. Now, any questions?'

The room erupted.

'One at a time,' Clive shouted, pointing to the woman at the front.

'Vikki Orvice, *Sun*. Stefan, why have you chosen Notting Hill? Is it because of the money? How much are—'

Clive cut her off in mid-sentence. 'I don't think, Miss . . .'

'Vikki Orvice.'

'I don't think, *Miss* Orvice, that's relevant. Stefan is here to answer questions on his contribution to a first-class team. Harry, what's your question?' he said, moving on to the *Gazette* reporter.

Stefan soon realised that other than yes and no Clive didn't want him to speak, which suited him fine; his English was far from perfect. As he listened to the chairman, he was surprised at how many times the help of God was invoked on behalf of Notting Hill. If God was listening they should win all the cups effortlessly.

At last the questions dried up and the crowd moved en masse to the foyer, where more photographs were to be taken. Stefan saw Clive motion to two men.

'Andy and Michael need no introductions. They insisted on welcoming Stefan personally. How about some photos of all three?' Clive asked the bank of cameras.

There were nods and yeses, and once again Stefan looked like a rabbit caught in headlights as his two team mates threw their arms around his shoulders. Dwarfed and swamped by their large bodies pressing

in on either side of him, he felt self-conscious of his
much smaller physique, although he knew that it was
precisely this that made him so quick on the pitch.

Twenty minutes later, when the last of the press had
left, Andy and Michael walked away. Not one word
had passed between either of them or Stefan.

'Andy, I need to see you,' Clive said, catching hold
of the footballer's sleeve.

'Can't it wait, Clive? I'm late for an interview.'

'It won't take a second. Up to my office.'

Andy followed slowly, his good looks marred by
his sulky expression. He could guess what this was
about.

As they entered Clive's office Margaret rose from
her chair, a pile of papers fluttering in her hand. 'Not
now, Margaret. And no phone calls.'

Andy was repulsed by the middle-aged woman's
plump, trembling lips. He would never understand
why Clive had an old dog like that for a secretary.
She certainly didn't reflect his usual taste.

'Close the door and sit down.'

Andy did as he was told, glancing at his watch.
Loulou was going to kill him. Clive paced behind
his large oak desk while Andy slouched in the chair,
feeling like a schoolkid summoned by the head-
master.

Determined not to be the first to break the silence
Andy gazed at the desk in front of him. It was covered
with stacks of papers, press cuttings and photographs
of Clive's absent clan. Andy's mouth twisted into
a sneer as his eyes alighted on the largest happy
family snap.

'I need you to get me another one,' Clive said finally, 'the last was hopeless.'

'Look, it's becoming more and more difficult. I just don't—'

'Aren't you forgetting something, Andy?' Clive snapped, leaning across the desk.

'No,' Andy replied, wanting to add, 'As if you would let me.'

'I spent a lot of time and money clearing up—'

'She was lying!'

'So you say. Anyway it's quid pro quo and I need another one. ASAP. That's all.'

There was no point in arguing and it would only make Andy later. 'OK. I'll get on to it.'

Chapter Two

Loulou winced at the bitterness of the coffee. Anna, her new Filipino housekeeper, still hadn't worked out the right proportions for the Gaggia. Poor coffee-making wasn't Anna's only failing. Judging from the phone bill, any kind of housekeeping was relatively low down on Anna's list of priorities compared with keeping in touch with her family in Mindoro. Still, the way she insisted on wearing a traditional black and white maid's outfit was quite endearing. It looked good and, for Loulou, that was more than enough.

Loulou rested the tiny cup back on its saucer but just as she did so, she lost her grip.

'Shit!' she screamed as the warm liquid spilled into her lap. Leaping up from her seat, brown flecks spattered the cream calico cover of the sofa. 'Shit! Shit! Shit!' Mira Ramirez was going to be there any second with a photographer. It was bad enough that Andy hadn't returned from the club. 'Anna! Would you get off that bloody phone and come in here and clean up this mess.'

Loulou looked down at her white shift dress. The coffee stain spread out from the crotch area and she knew the garment was ruined beyond repair. Still, it was a freebie from a designer she didn't much care for and she would take great delight in giving it to Anna to use as a floor cloth.

Thankfully her shoes were unmarked. They were her favourite pair, white mules with an impossibly high but incredibly sexy heel, and the sound they made as she ran across the polished silver-birch flooring of the living room made her feel in control once again after that momentary loss of composure.

The double-height living room was galleried along one wall, the mezzanine reached by a banister-less staircase that followed the contours of a gently curving wall. Although the house was, from the outside, a traditional Notting Hill five-storeyed Georgian terrace, few of its original interior features remained. A fortuitous fire had gutted the whole building, allowing Loulou's architects and interior designers to circumvent the tightly enforced rules regarding alterations to listed buildings, and they had created what was almost a temple of stark monastic futurism. The colour scheme, a series of neutrals, reinforced the feeling of quasi-religious calm, and Loulou had noticed, on more than one occasion, that guests seemed to drop their voices, as though entering a church.

Loulou allowed none of the clutter of day-to-day living to be on display. Everything was concealed behind invisible cupboards or false walls. Everything, that is, other than the film script she had deliberately left on the low, layered glass table for Mira's benefit. Not that the reporter would need prompting.

Aside from Mira being almost a friend, *Vita* magazine was famous for the easy ride they gave their interviewees and the piece, featuring a photo-spread of Loulou at home with her famous boyfriend, had been specifically arranged to promote her upcoming Hollywood début.

The film, called *Coast to Coast*, was a road movie to be directed by Parker Gooch, one of the biggest names in Hollywood, and although Loulou's part wasn't much of a stretch – she would be playing a nineties 'It' girl – she had fought very hard to get it. It had definite star-making potential.

Loulou glanced at the script and then ran up the stairs, calling after Anna again before going into her dressing room and pulling the sodden dress over her head.

The replacement dress she chose was nearly identical to the one that now lay in a ball on the floor. Loulou's clothes matched her house, pared down, neutral, expensive and designed not to deflect any attention from herself. As she shimmied into the new outfit, she kicked the old dress into a corner. Standing before a full-length mirror, she briefly cast an approving eye over her reflection, then ran back down the stairs to find Anna crouched over the sofa with a cloth.

'Has Andy called?' she asked the housekeeper.

'Good as new,' Anna said, standing up and admiring her work. 'No, Miss Lamb.'

Irritated, Loulou picked up the phone and jabbed at the buttons. The call went straight on to his answer service.

'Where the fuck are you? You know *Vita* is doing us this afternoon,' she shouted and then slammed down the receiver. She hated it when people didn't answer their mobiles.

'You wan' more coffee?' Anna asked. 'I make fresh.'

Loulou shook her head and glanced at her watch, muttering threats under her breath.

The housekeeper scurried off as Loulou sat down in an armchair and began a deep-breathing exercise. Soon she had blotted out all unpleasant thoughts about her boyfriend.

By the time Mira Ramirez was sitting on the sofa opposite her, taking her tape recorder from her Chanel handbag, Loulou was in a state of total calm.

'You didn't miss anything last night,' Loulou laughed. 'The champagne ran out at eight, the guests at five past. The only fun to be had was guessing how much weight she'd put on. It was more like a ship launch than a book launch. I suppose it's from all that sitting around typing.'

'I'm sure she doesn't care,' the reporter replied. 'She's just sold it to America for a million. That'll pay her Valerie's bill for a while. Where's Andy?'

Loulou's composure remained fixed. 'I didn't want him around for the interview. We'll be talking about Oran and you know what Andy can be like – the testosterone surges and he comes over all mannish. It's better if he stays out of the way.'

'As far as I'm concerned,' a look of delight spread across the reporter's face, 'that boy's testosterone can surge away as much as it wants to. Normally I'd say dating footballers was a bit too "Essex" for me but that one . . .' Mira fanned herself, her hot pink Hard Candy nails fluttering in front of her face. 'Now, I know I know all the bio stuff but can we just run through it quickly for the tape? Gives the girl who transcribes it something to do aside from e-mailing her Romanian girlfriend.'

'Sure,' Loulou smiled, switching to auto-pilot.

The details of her life were familiar from any number of tabloid stories. Her father was Harrison Lamb, the sculptor, while her mother, Laura, was Britain's answer to Joan Baez, and the couple had stood at the swirling, psychedelic centre of the late-sixties counterculture.

Brought up in an atmosphere her parents had believed to be creative free expression but which she felt was closer to neglect, Loulou had run riot, her schooling a blur of expulsions, her home-life a whirl of infamous parties, where the great and the good descended upon the Lamb household to sample the drugs *du jour* and more often than not sleep with either of the hosts.

It was at one of those parties that Oran O'Keefe had first left Laura Lamb's bed and climbed into Loulou's, though Loulou wasn't sure whether Mira needed to know the exact details. Somehow or other, her mother's affair with the rock star had never made it to the papers.

Although Loulou felt little but contempt for her parents, she didn't really want the world to know that her affair with Oran, and subsequent marriage, had been engineered by her father who, despite his many protestations about free love, was insanely jealous of his wife's relationship with the rock star. Harrison had practically opened Loulou's bedroom door and told Oran to fill his boots.

To tell Mira all this would confuse the story. She wanted to make sure Oran was the real villain of the piece. Despite the divorce settlement, she still felt she owed him one.

'So you were actually having sex with him at fifteen?' Mira asked, clearly unable to believe her luck.

'Yes,' Loulou said softly, then she bowed her head, biting the inside of her lip to prevent herself from laughing.

Although there had been much press conjecture at the time, and a certain amount of police interest, Loulou had never admitted that she had had underage sex with O'Keefe. The official line had always been that the couple had waited until their wedding night, two days after Loulou's sixteenth birthday.

Loulou wondered whether this revelation might provoke the police to re-open their inquiries, and the thought made her want to laugh even more. But just then the photographer sidled up to capture this moment of revelation, and she remained sad, slightly ashamed and the perfect victim.

'Is that when you started taking drugs? Oh, Loulou, it must have been awful for you. You were a child.'

Loulou kept her head bowed. 'It was all consensual, I was never forced. I wanted . . . well, I wanted what he wanted. And I took drugs of my own accord.'

At seventeen, she had checked herself into a rehab clinic. The marriage was on the rocks and Loulou was said to be suffering from nervous exhaustion. When the drug rumours started, Loulou did nothing to deny them. Her wild-child image had been truly established so addiction was felt to be par for the course. But drugs weren't the problem.

Sure, being around Oran had meant that there were drugs on tap. Occasionally she'd dabbled, but she hated the sensation of being out of control. People were, in the main, dribbling bores on drugs. It wasn't a good look. But anorexia was a worse look and that, for a while, had been Loulou's real problem. But that was all in the past, and again the disease was something Mira didn't need to know about.

'I really loved him,' Loulou said, looking up, and for the first time in the interview she was telling the complete truth. She *had* loved him, with all of her young, stupid heart. 'I thought it was a lifetime deal.'

'Marriage never is,' Mira said, currently on husband number three, 'but the right divorce settlement can be.'

The statement was a clumsy nudge to get Loulou to talk figures, which she never had. She didn't want anyone to know that she'd actually walked off with far less than the millions bandied about in the papers. Oran's lawyers had represented their client well, and although he had gone on record saying that she was a mercenary little tart, she had felt that it was a better image than a duped naïf.

'You know I won't talk about that. It was part of the divorce agreement.'

'Then tell me about his hair. Did you really do it?'

'Mira, you've heard this a thousand times.'

'But I love it!' she squealed, clapping her hands.

'Oran was screwing two of his backing singers. In his words, when it came to big-titted black chicks, he just couldn't help himself. I'd always known about it, I didn't really care.'

In fact, it had hurt her dreadfully, and it was then that the anorexia had started.

'I just felt the *Morningstar* cover was rubbing my face in it.'

The album cover had shown Oran in bed with the

two naked singers. It was horribly sexist, racist, and a tired old cliché; gratifyingly the album had bombed.

'The night I saw the proof, I waited until he was asleep and I cut off all his hair. What more can I tell you?'

There was a lot more she could have told. When she had taken the shears to the bedroom, her intention had been to cut off more than his hair . . .

'He's lucky,' Mira said, interrupting her thoughts. 'I would have cut off something else.'

Loulou winced. 'I cut off all his hair, hence the cover for *Shellfish Dreams*.'

'"The Hat Album"!' Mira laughed. 'So did he—'

'You know all this,' Loulou repeated. 'I thought you were meant to be asking me about the film.'

Mira picked up the script. 'I know all about that too. Every Tara and Tamara from Portobello to Kensington would have given their eye teeth for the part. If not their Prada handbags. You must feel a little bit of sweet revenge.'

The remark was an unintentional knock. When the papers had compiled their list of the 'It' girls a year or so before, Loulou hadn't quite been in their league. The ascendency of her star had happened only over the last ten months because of the runaway success of *Sorted!*.

'Not really, I was too young to compete with the real "It" girls.' Loulou smiled sweetly, knowing her reply would ruffle a few exquisitely appointed feathers.

'Has your mother given you any advice on acting?'

Laura Lamb had appeared in several films, including

Andy Warhol's *Chelsea Girls*. In that, as in every other
film, she just stumbled on screen stoned, then wobbled
off again. It wasn't the direction Loulou was planning
to take.

'I don't see her that much any more. My father has
his studio in Ibiza.'

'And she's with him?'

'On and off. You know what she's like. She's there
when she's not saving the planet.'

'What about your brother?'

'What about him?' Loulou's voice was icy. They
were straying too far off her chosen territory. Any
talk about Dexter made her feel uncomfortable.

'I mean, who does he live with?'

'My mother, mostly.' Loulou worked hard at keeping any emotion out of her voice. 'Did I tell you that
I've said no to another series?' Loulou wished she
could withdraw the words as soon as they'd left her
mouth.

'Really?' Mira said. 'This is *such* a scoop.'

A feeling of panic began to stir in Loulou's stomach.
Negotiations were under way for the new run of
Sorted!, and as far as the producers knew, she was
still keen. She would just have to use this story as a
way of upping her fee. *Sorted!* without Loulou Lamb
. . . well, it was *the* girlie show.

'I've been talking to a couple of American networks
about a Ricki Lake kind of thing.'

Mira made approving noises, then began searching
in her handbag again. 'I wrote down some ideas for
the photo shoot somewhere.'

Just then, Andy appeared behind the journalist,
looking breathless and dishevelled.

'Sorry!' he mouthed silently.

Loulou shaped her fingers into a gun and aimed at him. His body flinched and, staggering back, he clutched his hands to heart. Then he planted a kiss on the journalist's head. Surprised, Mira looked up and practically swooned.

'Hang on to your gussets, girls, it's the thinking-woman's crumpet,' Loulou said, sarcastically referring to the name given to him by the women's pages of the tabloids. 'Mira, you know Andy, my *ex*-boyfriend.'

'I'm really sorry. I got tied up at the club.'

'Now there's a picture,' Mira said.

'Don't I get a kiss?' Loulou asked. Andy walked over and planted a long, slow kiss on her lips to the accompaniment of the photographer's flash. 'Urgh! You're really sweaty. Go and have a shower.'

'Oh to be a bar of soap,' Mira sighed as he left the room.

Andy reappeared twenty minutes later, his hair still slightly wet, wearing an outfit Loulou had picked out for the shoot. Over a pair of cream linen trousers, he was wearing a loose-fitting, stone-coloured, open-necked shirt.

'I've always had a thing about men's feet,' Mira said, looking at his Birkenstocks, 'especially when they're tanned. What do I have to do to get myself a man like this?'

Wash your hair, lose twenty-five pounds and get yourself a personality, Loulou thought, beginning to tire of the way Mira was fawning over Andy.

But instead she said, 'Oh have him. Footballers are just so . . . Essex.' She glared at Andy, but then the glare broke into a smile. He *was* gorgeous. She put her arm around him, feeling a surge of excitement as she felt the hardness of his body. 'On second thoughts, I'm not quite finished with him yet.'

'Shame!' Mira booed.

The shoot lasted for over three hours and required several changes of clothes. Mira had the couple posing all around the house. She suggested a shot of Andy preparing a meal for Loulou, but neither Andy nor Loulou had a clue where anything was in the industrial steel kitchen, so Mira had to settle for a shot of Andy pouring Loulou a glass of champagne. They finished off with a series of shots in Loulou's Japanese-inspired garden against the backdrop of one of her father's bronzes.

'Honestly, that woman,' Loulou said, as she closed the door behind the journalist. 'She was practically rubbing herself against the furniture.'

'I thought she was your friend,' Andy said, finishing the last of the champagne.

Loulou's eyes narrowed. 'There are no such things as friends in this business. Only the useful and the useless. Make sure you remain in the former category. One more stunt like today and—'

'And what?' Andy asked, pulling her towards him.

'Get your hands off me. I'm not interested.' But even as Loulou protested, every bone in her body disagreed.

Andy sensed her need, and in one swift move, he picked her up and threw her over his shoulder. Showing no signs of exertion, he raced up the stairs, taking her into their bedroom and throwing her on to the bed.

The windows were open and a gentle breeze caused

the muslin curtains to billow. Loulou lay back on the bed, her hand already between her legs as she watched the footballer step out of his clothes. Once naked, he lifted the hem of Loulou's dress over her stomach and pressed his face between her thighs.

'You're creasing my dress,' Loulou gasped, not really caring, aware now only of the sensation of Andy's tongue moistening the soft lacy fabric of her knickers.

'Do you want me to stop?' Andy asked, looking up at her, a mischievous smile on his flawless face. Not waiting for an answer, he hooked his thumbs under the elastic of her underwear and pulled them down over her ankles.

Loulou sat up and slipped out of her dress. Then, grabbing Andy by the hair, she forced him back down between her legs. Andy's tongue drove into her and Loulou tightened her grip. Her free hand slid across the bed searching on the bedside table for the one thing that would make this moment perfect. Knocking over a glass in the process she found the remote control, pressed it and, behind Andy, the large video screen flicked into life.

Suddenly the screen was filled with the image of Loulou spreadeagled on the bed, with Andy preparing to take her. Around the room were several strategically placed video cameras. For Loulou and Andy, life was never so real as when it appeared on screen. And how the cameras loved them. Both had known what the photo-shoot would do to the other. It had been three hours of the most exquisitely torturous foreplay. They were a couple of media sluts.

'Fuck me,' Loulou screamed, as the television showed Andy's rock-hard cock almost pressing against his six-pack stomach. The footballer grabbed hold of her ankles and obliged.

Chapter Three

Rachel opened her legs a little wider, allowing her husband to push deeper into her. She sighed, more from boredom than pleasure, and tried to imagine she was a tempestuous heroine from one of the romances she was continuously reading – a ripped bodice, long, raven hair ... Before she could picture a different Robbie, she heard him grunt.

'Thanks,' he murmured into her neck before rolling off her. The second his head hit the pillow he began snoring.

What was wrong with her? she wondered, staring at the ceiling. Why, after nine years of marriage, had she still never experienced an orgasm? As far as she could tell, she'd never even got close to one. Yet she loved Robbie and had done since the first time she saw him at the school bus stop. Both sweet sixteen and never been kissed.

Rachel looked across at her sleeping husband and smiled indulgently at the dribble trickling down his chin. Orgasms aside, Robbie had a lot going in his favour, she told herself. He was a good father and, unlike most of the other players, if the stories she had heard and read were anything to go on, a decent, faithful husband. Perhaps he drank too much sometimes but nowhere near as much – or as often – as his team-mates.

Asleep, Robbie looked even more baby-faced than ever. Rachel propped herself up on her elbow and stole a closer look at him. He wasn't exactly good-looking, well not in that Heathcliff way of her fantasies. He was just ... sort of ... ordinary, sensible. The type every girl's mother would like. A bit like herself really. Rachel knew she was no Cathy, with her mousy blond bob and plain face. Her pale lips were too thin and her eyes, a watery blue, too close together.

But their lack in the looks department did not explain the lack of passion in the bedroom. Rachel tried to think back to the beginning. Had sex been any different then? She couldn't even remember back that far. Had she changed? Had he? She turned over and tried to stop herself thinking. She needed to sleep.

'Mummy! Mummy! Robbie Jnr's broken my dolly.'

'Whaa ... ?' Rachel looked at the green neon light of the bedside clock. 'Sweetheart, it's six o'clock. It's Saturday. Daddy's playing today – we all need to get our rest.'

Demi's bottom lip began to tremble. Knowing her five-year-old daughter was capable of producing a scream that would put Violet Elizabeth Bott to shame, Rachel jumped out of bed, groped for her floral dressing gown and meekly followed the tiny tyrant out of the room.

The shriek that escaped Rachel was louder than Demi's. Rachel couldn't believe the havoc her four-year-old son had managed to wreak in her usually spotless house. Between bouts of uncontrollable howling, Demi showed her mother the decapitated Barbies.

'My Barbie Spice Girls are dead,' she sobbed.

'You're a very bad boy,' Rachel said, as evenly as possible, having read that losing your temper was a sure way to make your child a delinquent. But she wasn't convinced. Most of the time her children took no notice whatever child-rearing method she used.

'*You're* bad. I hate you!' Robbie Jnr screamed, pushing past his mother and knocking his sister over in the process.

Ignoring Demi's bawls, Rachel walked around the room collecting her far-flung thimble collection, and painstakingly arranged each one back on the sideboard.

Next she picked up the swan plant pot and scraped the earth back in. Getting on her hands and knees she looked around until she located her mother-in-law's tongue under a nest of tables and shoved it back in the pot. The plant was her own private joke; it reminded her that however bad things felt, at least she wasn't living with Robbie's dreadful mother.

She drew back the flowery curtains and plumped up the sofa's matching cushions. She could hear Demi and Robbie Jnr arguing in the garden and decided that now she was up, Robbie asleep and the kids outside, she might just as well clean.

The feather duster flew across the mantelpiece, where family photographs vied with miniature collectibles for space. Rachel picked up one of the pictures, which had been taken outside their first home in Wigan. Robbie had just joined the town's reserves and they were struggling to manage on his wage of £80 a week. There was no struggling now. She had a lot

to be grateful for, not least this four-bedroom house.
It was a palace compared to their previous home.

'Can't you ever shut those two up?'

Rachel let out a yelp of surprise. 'Sorry they woke
you, love. But kids will be kids. Like a cup of tea, my
old grumpy?'

Robbie allowed her one of his 'I know I'm being
unreasonable' smiles as he hoisted himself up on to
a breakfast-bar stool. While filling the kettle Rachel
watched Robbie's reflection in the kitchen window.
Unconsciously, her fingers tightened around the handle
as she saw his slow progress reading the *Sun*'s three-
word headline. Pity fought with annoyance. For her,
printed words had become a lifeline and more and more
Rachel used fiction to escape real life.

What future did her illiterate husband have after
football? He wasn't management material, that was for
sure. Rachel couldn't bear the thought of scrimping
and saving again, or worse, she shuddered, ending
up living with his mother, as in their early years of
marriage.

'You all right, pet?'

'Of course,' Rachel replied, feeling treacherous. Who
was she to criticise Robbie? She'd be nothing without
him. Just plain Rachel Williams, probably working in
a mundane job. Instead, she was married to one of the
top players in the country. Count your blessings, she
told herself, not for the first time that day.

An-dy! An-dy!' the crowd chanted, their feet stamping a tattoo of Andy McKay's name. Robbie watched
as Andy, playing to the fans, twirled and pirouetted
in a virile ballet with Aston Villa's John Brentwood.

However, over confident, he soon lost the ball to Brentwood.

The score was two-two and there were ten minutes left, but Robbie hardly had time to turn on his heels when he heard the referee's whistle.

'Schizo! Schizo!' the crowd hissed.

It was obvious from the booing that Michael had once again fouled the opposition. Robbie found it strange that the defender took such pride in the nickname Schizo. The referee was as unimpressed as Villa's fans and he promptly showed Michael the red card. The away fans began to chant 'Cheerio, cheerio, cheerio' to the tune of 'Here We Go', while the home fans responded with 'The referee's a wanker.'

As Aston Villa's Danny Ross placed the ball on the penalty spot, the crowd could feel the pressure building on the Notting Hill goalkeeper. Not all of it was coming from the pitch. David Ashby's name was being linked with a number of player-manager jobs up and down the country. And at that very moment representatives of several different clubs were evaluating his play from the executive boxes.

David always had a knack of making himself look bigger than the goal by emphasising his bulk, standing up tall and rounding his arms. Ross took three steps back and aimed at the top left-hand corner of the goal. David sprang into action, diving sideways and blocking the penalty.

The crowd erupted as David punched the air with elation, chanting 'Ash-bee, Ash-bee.'

David knew that with five minutes left they could still win the game. He managed to kick the ball

almost to the halfway line where Robbie was waiting.

Robbie had gone through the youth system but even
at an early age he had shown the skill and speed that
would make him one of the most exciting players in
the country.

As he now wound in and out of the Aston Villa
defence he lived up to his reputation for brilliance.
Off the field he was a clumsy oaf but on the pitch
he was transformed into a creature of grace.

Robbie passed the ball to Stu then glanced up to
the Players' Enclosure where Rachel was talking to
his mother. Seeing them together made Robbie feel
sure that he had made the right decision in inviting
his mother to live with them.

Stu scored. Notting Hill beat Aston Villa by three
goals to two.

'Come on then, Ma, we'd better get the kids home,'
Rachel said, placing her hand on her mother-in-law's
back to speed up the older woman's progress.

'Don't push, Rachel,' Mary snapped. 'What's the
hurry?'

Rachel looked furtively around to see if any of the
other wives had heard Mary's belligerent tone. It was
because of her mother-in-law's attitude towards her
that Rachel wanted to leave quickly. She knew Mary's
caustic and sarcastic remarks could only add fuel to
an already well-lit fire, and she'd be handing the other
wives ammunition if she allowed them to hear.

Rachel had hoped that their relationship would
improve with the birth of Demi. But her arrival had
made things even more fraught. The placenta was

barely cold when Mary started criticising Rachel's mothering skills.

'Bye, Rachel. See you Wednesday.'

Rachel turned quickly, surprised to hear her name. She located the speaker. It was the Page Three girl. Tanya, that was it. Rachel remembered that she had been the only one to give her a smile at the airport. Despite this Rachel gave Tanya only a quick nod, embarrassed by the girl's enormous bosom. And although the offending breasts were hidden under a discreet black top, as far as Rachel was concerned Tanya still looked as though she were dressed for a nightclub.

Still, that was how most of the wives dressed. Every match, come rain or shine, it was always a fashion parade. A parade Rachel knew she couldn't march in. As if she needed proof, she glanced down at her M&S beige slacks and the embroidered T-shirt Robbie had brought back from Tenerife.

'Rachel. Are you coming? First of all you get me and the kids to move like there's a fire, now you're just standing there with your mouth open catching flies.'

'Sorry, Ma,' Rachel sighed.

'God, have you seen what she's wearing today?' one of the wives giggled.

Rachel bowed her head as tears stung her eyes. Sometimes she felt so lonely it was almost unbearable.

Chapter Four

The way Jenny's hands were shaking made it difficult to undo the small pearls that were the blouse's buttons. When she finally managed to get the blouse off, she threw it on the floor, where it lay next to a mound of similar-looking tops.

Her reflection in the mirror stared back at her accusingly, leaving her to conclude that her newly cropped, newly peroxided hair only exaggerated the effects of too many pills, too much coke and definitely too much booze.

With her forefinger she traced around her latest eye tuck, the bruises that had kept her hidden for several weeks were now healed. The surgery gave her only an approximation of youth; the ageing process just a millimetre away behind the stretched skin.

But underneath her eyes, her lifestyle had left the tell-tale signs of dark shadows, and she deftly painted on foundation until they disappeared. To cure her trembling hands, she swallowed a couple of diet pills, then she slipped back into her week-old Versace mini-dress and finally felt ready to face the assistant hovering outside the door.

She handed the woman the pink creation, choosing it more because it matched her nail varnish than from any real preference. As the woman slowly folded and wrapped the blouse, Jenny impatiently drummed her fingers on the counter. She didn't even notice the £800 price tag as she handed over her gold Amex.

She threw the straps of the Versace bag over her shoulder, where it joined five other bags. Shopping, she knew, had become just another drug, albeit a legal one, to help her while away the empty hours. But after the high there was always the low, and Jenny couldn't wait to leave the shop and its immaculate, overbearing assistants.

Jenny flew down the marble stairs to the entranceway, where the doors were opened by two large, dark-suited doormen who, with their earphones and mikes, looked more like they were planning a military oper-ation than greeting the shopping élite.

Bond Street was full of black cabs disgorging the privileged and Jenny jumped into the first one that crossed her path.

Spotting Carla, Jenny stifled a shriek. It didn't sur-prise her in the least that the restaurant's *maître d'* had sat Carla at the very back of the room. She was a sight to behold. Stretched across the girl's pendulous breasts was the tiniest piece of spandex material and between this and a red imitation leather mini-skirt leaked Carla's pale, flabby midriff. The *coup de grâce* was the bare, mottled pink legs and the six-inch black patent stilettos plonked on the end of them. 'Two vodkas. Fast,' Jenny hissed at a passing waiter.

As she sat down Jenny forced a smile. 'Hi, Carla,' she said.

'I'm glad you agreed to come.' Carla looked up gratefully. 'You're not stuck up like the rest of them.' A waiter placed two glasses on the table and Carla knocked back her vodka in one go. 'I think you and me are alike. We even dress the same.'

Jenny managed to swallow her drink. Just. What was this girl on? The same? The waiter returned to their table but by now Jenny's diet pills had had their desired effect, causing what little appetite she'd had to disappear. Carla readily agreed to a liquid lunch. They both lit a cigarette and there was a few seconds' silence as each woman inhaled the smoke and exhaled with pleasure.

'So you're seeing Stuart at the moment; that's nice,' Jenny said, attempting to find something they could talk about. That she was here with Carla only served to underscore how alone she was in the world.

'I suppose. What's Clive like? He seems a bit scary,' Carla giggled. 'Of course, I'm just a barmaid – why would he waste time talking to me?'

'You don't know how lucky you are,' Jenny replied, the mere mention of the man's name making her head spin. She discreetly swallowed a couple of Valium with her drink to banish all thoughts of her brother.

'What do you mean?'

'Look, Clive's boring. Let's talk about you. Your accent says you're from London.' Jenny only half listened as Carla spoke about her childhood in Hendon. The thought of childhood had sent her memory reeling back to a period she spent most of her time trying to forget. She was only fourteen when her parents – an unloving, authoritarian father and a docile, meek mother – died in a boating accident. After that she went to live with Clive. She would have been safer on the streets.

'Has old Clive always been religious?'

'No!' Jenny snapped. She was sickened by her brother's hypocritical Christian zeal. 'And as I said, let's not waste time talking about Clive.'

'Are your eyes really that green or you using those colour contacts?' Carla asked, leaning forward to take a closer look.

'They're one of the few things about me that are real,' Jenny said with a self-deprecating laugh.

'So where do you get your hair done? I love that urchin look. Would it suit me? You think I should go more blond, or platinum like you? What make do you use?'

Jenny looked at her companion's hair. Apart from the colour, a badly streaked blond, Carla had added to the over-processing by blowdrying her hair to within an inch of its life. 'Well—'

Before she could respond Carla was off once again, rattling off one question after another, as if she were making a mental list of all the accoutrements needed to be a footballer's wife.

Jenny suddenly took pity on Carla. Who was she to be critical? She had more money than Carla could ever dream of and look at the mess her life was in.

'I've been saving for this really special—'

'Carla,' Jenny interrupted, 'I hope you won't take offence but I've got a whole wardrobe of clothes I've barely worn; you wouldn't be insulted if I gave them to you, would you?'

'Oh no, Jenny, that's brill',' Carla gushed. Her face fell. 'I'm a little bit bigger than you.'

'Don't worry, I wasn't always this size. I've got clothes to fit you.' Jenny stopped herself from advising Carla to go to a gym, knowing that her secret was pills and powder rather than hours spent treading a Stairmaster.

The smile on Carla's face said it all and Jenny felt a glimmer of happiness, a feeling she hadn't experienced in a long time. 'So, after Hendon what happened?'

'Oh you know, I sort of drifted. Left home when I was sixteen, went travelling, bar work, that kind of thing . . .'

'Good, good,' Jenny said, absentmindedly. 'Shall I settle the bill?' The effects of the Valium were already wearing off and all the troubles she managed to keep at bay with chemicals threatened to overwhelm her. Especially thoughts about Michael. Where was he now? Or more importantly, who was he with?

She rose abruptly from the table, hoping that by moving she could stop her mind going through an inventory of Michael's past and present conquests. 'I'd better get back. Michael's bound to be waiting for me.'

Jenny drove slowly through a summer rainstorm towards her East Sussex home, the gentle rhythm of the windscreen wipers hypnotising her. In her head, the showreel of her argument with Michael began its second airing of the day.

As usual it had started from nothing. Michael had been parading in his Calvin Klein's, admiring himself in front of the large Louis XVI mirror. 'I'd say I was a ringer for that film star, Sam Henson, wouldn't you?' he said, flexing his well-defined chest muscles.

Despite being only ten a.m., Jenny had already had a quick snifter, which had done nothing to improve her mood. 'Yeah, you are,' she said. And then added, 'If you mean you're a short arse with mad staring blue eyes and a bad haircut.'

In two strides Michael was in her face. 'You what?' Jenny tried to move away but he grabbed her arm, his fingers digging into the soft flesh of her underarm. 'You washed-up, scrawny old bitch – the only time I've seen anyone who looked remotely like you they were in a fucking coffin.' His mocking voice assaulted her more than if he'd struck her.

She veered the car to the left, the tyres screeching as a car horn blasted her. She tried to concentrate, but her thoughts kept returning to her marriage. Perhaps she was the one at fault; after all it was she who had been married three times, not Michael.

Three years of Clive as her guardian had sent her hurtling into the arms of the first Lothario who'd asked her out. Pete Trimble. It was a close call on who was the bigger bastard – him or Michael. He hadn't even tried to hide that he was a gold digger. She had been so naïve at seventeen, signing papers he put in front of her and only learning from her diminishing bank balance what he was up to.

And then there was sweet Stephen. Too sweet for his own good – and Jenny's. Formative years with the Dorning family plus the financial union with Trimble had caused a hardness in Jenny that couldn't be overcome by a man like Stephen. She had taken an eye for an eye, a tooth for a tooth, making him pay for all the abuse she had suffered in the past. The last she heard he'd been arrested for being drunk and disorderly. That had been her legacy to him.

And now there was Michael. Jenny knew she wasn't staying with him out of choice. She wasn't getting any younger, as he was so fond of pointing out.

As she drove on to the M25, she made herself a promise, she wouldn't give up just yet. Michael was her last chance and she'd take it. Who else would take on a forty-year-old alcoholic who'd already had enough nips and tucks to have left her belly button just under her chin? She would just have to try harder.

'You'd better not have skanked me this time,' Michael grunted, snatching half a dozen wraps out of the dealer's hand and opening one. 'And there better be more coke than talcum powder. Where do you get off giving me shit like that?'

'Hey! Listen, man, it was the supplier. I lost out as well. We all lost out.'

Michael dipped a tiny silver spoon into the coke, lifted it to his nose and snorted. Wetting his forefinger, he wiped the spoon clean and rubbed the coke into his gums. After a few minutes he allowed himself a smile. 'Not bad,' he muttered, propelling the dealer out the front door. 'I'll call you next week.'

He ran up the stairs to the bedroom, where he threw the wraps with a mirror and a blade on to the bed. 'Help yourself.'

The naked woman moaned as some coke spilled on the bed. Clouds of cigarette smoke hung suspended above them in the airless bedroom.

'Like the charlie, doll?'

'Mmm. Come here,' she said, grabbing his arm.

Michael lay on the bed next to her. He watched passively as her tongue flicked lazily around each of his nipples but as it followed the line of hair from his chest to his navel and beyond he felt aggression rising with his erection. She stopped, her large red lips hovering just above his crotch. 'Don't tease,' he snapped as he seized her hair and drove her mouth down on to his cock.

'Don't think you're going to shut me up that easily,' she laughed, lifting up her head. 'Come on, when are you going to get rid of the old bag?'

Michael sighed. 'Not now. *Please.*'

Jumping up suddenly, she pinned down his shoulders with her hands and straddled his thighs. 'You know I could make you happy,' she whispered, as she lowered herself down and drew him into her. 'Very happy.'

Michael thrust upwards. 'I know. Soon, real soon. Now put me out of my misery.'

But even as she moved up and down on top of him he couldn't shake the thought that he was stuck with the misery of his marriage. No fuck in the world, however good, could compensate for the money he'd be giving up if he left Jenny. There was no way he could pay off his gambling debts *and* support his habit without her.

'Oh yeah, baby,' he shouted as he came, his nails digging into her young, firm thighs. 'I'm all yours.'

It had taken Jenny nearly two hours to get home and it was at times like these that she regretted buying somewhere quite so far from London. The only reason she had done so was to try to stop her husband's philandering: she had thought if he was out of London he would be out of temptation's way. Well that certainly hadn't worked.

As she turned her Mercedes into the driveway, she hit the brakes and the car skidded to a halt on the gravel. Only inches in front of her loomed a pink Suzuki Vitara.

Jenny jumped out of the car, and walked as quietly as she could up to the house. The door was unlocked and as she opened it she listened for any sound of movement. The house was silent. In the living room, she saw that the closed-circuit TV was off. So it wasn't a burglar, then, who drove such a loud and vulgar car? Not that she ever really thought it was, but she would have preferred to confront a burglar rather than one of Michael's slags.

No longer trying to be quiet Jenny ran up the sweeping staircase into the bedroom she once shared with Michael. The bed, although empty, told her everything she needed to know. The sheets were all over the place, a pillow lay in the middle and a line of coke lay abandoned on a mirror. And there was no denying the salty smell of sex that permeated every corner of the room. Jenny swallowed as the bile rose in her throat, her imagination replaying exactly what had gone on in her bed.

Michael appeared in the doorway, naked.

'You bastard, you fucking bastard. And why my room?' She lunged at him, feeling one of her false nails snap as she scratched the side of his face.

Michael retaliated with his fist, causing her head

to snap back. Jenny lost her footing and fell to the floor, where she lay perfectly still. Biting her lip, she managed to stifle her sobs until Michael had left the room. Then, using the bed, she levered herself up until she could see her face in the mirror. Already a livid red mark glowed angrily on her left cheek. She tasted blood on her lips.

She stopped looking at herself as she heard the Suzuki's wheels spin on the gravel before driving off. Then the front door slammed and Jenny heard Michael gun the BMW.

Her whole body shook and the whisky she was attempting to pour into a glass slopped over the sides and on to the floor. When she'd managed to get enough of the liquid in, she drank it in one go, wincing as it washed over the cut on her lip.

'What's the point?' she sobbed to herself. She sat on the bed and tried to pull herself together but for several minutes her body was racked by uncontrollable sobs. Finally, when all that was left was a dry heaving in her chest, she managed to lift her head. As she did so she saw that someone, no doubt Michael's mistress, had been looking through her wardrobe. The insults piled on to the injury.

As the rails of clothes came into focus she thought of Carla and her promise to give the girl her cast-offs. Carla was a fighter, that was clear. Where had Jenny's fight gone? Had it been knocked out of her all those years ago? She looked down at her glass, as if surprised to see it in her hand, and it dawned on her that if she were to stand any chance of getting her dignity back, if not Michael, then she was going to have to quit the booze and the drugs.

'Screw Michael and screw Clive. I'll show the bastards,' she shouted at the tear-streaked face in the mirror. Throwing her drink into a plant pot, Jenny picked up the telephone and dialled her doctor's number.

Chapter Five

'Tea's on the house, girl,' the café owner said, refusing to take Tanya's money.

'You're a diamond, you know that?' Tanya cuddled him. 'I'll have that picture for you, Monday.' The café walls boasted several framed photographs of local celebrities – boxers, models, actresses – and the owner had been asking for one of Tanya for weeks. It was something of an East End hall of fame and she was well chuffed to be asked to join it.

'Blinding. Oh yeah, your Keeley was in this morning. Said to give her a bell.' He held the door open for her to leave.

'Shame I missed her,' Tanya said, noticing the bald man who'd been leering at her earlier was still lurking in the street. Concern flashed across her face, a look that didn't go unnoticed by Joey Taylor, a flyweight boxer from Stepney.

'Is that him, Tan?' he asked, stroking his nose. 'Want me to have a word?'

'No, leave it, Joey. I'd have him for breakfast if he started something.'

The boxer shrugged, then bawled over to the bald man. 'Oi, you, why don't you do yourself a favour and fuck off!'

'Joey!' Tanya blushed furiously and walked away along the market, waving to the stall holders who greeted her warmly as she passed. As much as she hated any kind of violence, it gave her a warm feeling to know so many people were looking out for her. She couldn't imagine any other part of the world feeling like home in the way Bethnal Green did.

Turning off the main road she came to her street, a narrow road lined on both sides by Victorian mansion blocks. David was already there and his face lit up as he caught sight of her. When she reached his side he stooped his six-foot-plus frame and kissed her.

Once inside her flat, Tanya walked into the kitchen and switched on the kettle.

David came up behind her and took her in his arms. 'I've been looking forward to this all day.'

'Mmm, me too,' she said. 'By the way, Mum called. She asked if we fancied a picnic this Sunday for a change. But she said to tell you that she was happy to cook if you preferred a proper dinner.'

A Sunday roast with all the family was something of a ritual in the Barry household. At first David, an only child, had been intimidated by the closeness of Tanya's family and had been wary of being drawn in. Eileen and Terry Barry were fiercely protective of their children and viewed all prospective partners with suspicion. But once David had proved himself, he quickly became, in Eileen's words, 'like one of our own', and it had got to the stage where he was disappointed if a Sunday fixture kept him away.

'A picnic's fine,' he said. 'But I don't really fancy a cup of tea at the moment.'

Tanya turned to face him. 'And what do you fancy then?'

David kissed her on the forehead. 'Not what, who.'

She felt herself melt. 'I love you, do you know that?'

'I know,' he replied, taking hold of her hand and leading her into the bedroom.

It was in this room that an unknown facet of Tanya had first been revealed to David. Though he, like millions of other people, had followed her career in the newspapers as she smiled out from Page Three over breakfast, nothing could have prepared him for her secret passion.

The bedroom walls were filled with framed drawings painted by Tanya. Neither representational nor completely abstract, the strange shapes were suggestive of something animal and undeniably sexual. They were quite disturbing and, if the truth were known, David would have preferred if she'd settled for a few framed prints of herself.

'Those things still give me the creeps,' he said, unbuttoning his shirt.

Tanya didn't reply. Although she was sure that David loved her unconditionally, she knew what people expected of her. She was a Page Three girl. Big heart, big hair, big smile, big boobs. A sporty little MG outside, a footballer boyfriend in bed and festoon blinds on every window. The script was practically written in stone.

Barring the blinds, she had them all, and she played the part to perfection. She loved her job, but sometimes she wished people would look at the woman behind the 36DD cups. Why was it so odd that she liked to draw when she came home from work? She wasn't pretending she was any great artist; drawing helped her relax and made her happy. She could do 'glamour model' only so many hours of the day.

Tanya scrutinised her latest drawing, aware that David was watching her undress. Although she took off her clothes every day for different men, it was only undressing for David that meant anything to her. Her body was his and his alone.

'You're beautiful,' he said, climbing into her bed.

'Oh shut up.' She smiled, then picked up a cushion from the bed and threw it at him. 'Anyway you don't think I'm beautiful, you think *they're* beautiful,' she said, undoing the clasp of her bra and sliding in next to him.

David cupped her large, tanned breasts in his hands. 'You've got me there.' In turn, he kissed each breast, licking the aureole before taking the nipple into his mouth. 'Beautiful,' he said again, 'and worth every penny.'

A couple of years earlier, aware that interest in Page Three girls was flagging since their heyday in the mid-eighties, a newspaper had insured Tanya's chest as a publicity stunt. It was now worth a cool million pounds.

'It was just a gimmick,' Tanya said. 'And they're starting to droop. They're not really worth anything.' Tanya knew the shelf-life of a glamour model was short, and she'd been at the top of her profession now for two years. Unless she could make the transition into showbusiness, like Linda Lusardi or Melinda Messenger, soon she'd be out of work. Still, she'd had a good run and she had no complaints. 'I'm thinking about having a reduction.'

David looked horrified. 'You what?'

'Joke, joke,' she said, kissing him. 'If you promise you'll still love me when they're hanging round my knees, I won't touch them.'

'I promise,' he replied pulling her down beside him. 'Tanya, you know I'll never stop loving you.'

'Shhh,' she said, pressing her finger against his lips. 'Don't talk. Just make love to me.'

David acquiesced, showering Tanya's face with kisses as he entered her. Slowly, rhythmically, he drove deep into her body, all the while his eyes fixed on hers. She clawed his back, urging him ever deeper, her breath now coming in short, startled gasps. David bared his teeth and bucked his hips, a sign that he was ready to come. As always this tipped Tanya over the edge and her body exploded in a thousand pinpricks of pleasure.

As their pleasure subsided and their breathing slowly returned to normal, they lay in each other's arms. This was Tanya's favourite part of lovemaking. It was at these times that David was most unguarded, and usually after they made love they would talk long into the night.

Tonight was no exception, and Tanya listened, dreamily content, as David confided in her about the problems facing him for the new season.

'You know what it's like at the beginning of the season,' he said, stroking her hair. 'We're not a team; we're just eleven men out on the pitch who happen to be wearing the same shirt. It takes a while before we start thinking as one, and I don't know how to make that happen quicker. With the UEFA Cup this year, time's a luxury we haven't got.'

'It'll be all right. You're always wound up at this time of year. You know what good form the team's on.'

'I think we should perhaps socialise together more. It might help forge a proper team spirit.'

Tanya looked at him drowsily and pinched his nipple. 'What? You see them two or three nights a week as it is.'

'Yeah, but I mean with wives and girlfriends as well.' David's finger probed her belly button. 'Make it more family oriented.'

'That'd be nice,' she said yawning. Nice wasn't exactly what she was thinking, but if David thought it would help, she was willing to go along with it. So far all her attempts at befriending the other Notting Hill women had been rebuffed. She knew it was her profession that bothered them. They all seemed so insecure, each waiting for the other to steal her man and therefore always on the attack.

Loulou was the worst. Tanya admired the TV presenter's style, beauty and the way she handled the media, and would have loved to have befriended her, but Loulou totally froze her out. Undeniably Andy was a gorgeous man, but couldn't Loulou see that she had nothing to fear from Tanya? Didn't her love for David just radiate out from her?

'It's a great idea,' she mumbled, drifting off into a dream about that love.

It was worse than a primary school PE lesson, and David longed to be back in bed, where he'd left Tanya sleeping two hours earlier. He couldn't get his mind off the fantastic sex they'd had last night.

Those tits, he thought, shaking his head. He was one lucky so-and-so.

'Who's this remind you of, Dave?' Robbie said, running past him with two footballs stuck up his top. 'Any bird you know?'

David stiffened. 'You're out of line, Robbie.'

The look on David's face let Robbie know the joke hadn't gone down well, and reluctantly he let the two balls fall to the ground. 'Just a joke, Dave.'

The session had begun with a few laps of the training fields. Michael had been noticeably sluggish and David had heard Andy make more than one remark about 'nose candy'.

'It's all catching up with you, mate,' Andy said, slapping Michael hard on the back as he lapped him. He turned back to face his colleague and sniffed dramatically.

Michael put his head down and ran at the tall blond footballer, but Andy stepped deftly out of the way and, unsteady on his feet, Michael hit the dirt. Within seconds David was in between them. 'Pack it in, girls,' he ordered.

Before the fight could resume, they were distracted by Robbie's voice.

'*Sieg Heil*,' he shouted, saluting as he made a Hitler moustache with his fingers.

Stefan Lohmann, who had just arrived on the field, looked at Robbie with a mixture of bewilderment and disgust, a look shared by the vexed captain. In less than two weeks, David despaired, this shower would be playing in the first round of the UEFA cup.

Chapter Six

Carla wedged her bare shoulder against the window frame and gave it a hefty push. The rotten wood groaned and began to splinter in places but, thick with many layers of paint, the window held firmly closed. For a moment, Carla pressed her cheek against the dirty glass, grateful for the coolness, while her eyes scoured the room searching for another way of relieving the bed-sit of its unbearable smell.

On the shelf above the chipped hand-basin was a body spray. Giving her armpits a quick squirt, she sprayed the rest of the contents into the frowsy air, then sniffed.

'Smells like a tart's boudoir,' she said aloud, laughing at the accuracy of the statement.

On the unmade single bed lay a bag filled with Jenny's cast-offs. Carla tipped them out and gasped, unable to believe the riches that lay within. Each item of clothing had a name on it she'd previously seen only on perfume bottles. She picked up a dress and held it against her naked body, realising that this single piece of flimsy fabric was worth more than the entire contents of the threadbare room. One day soon, she was sure, she would be able to buy dresses like this for herself.

A car horn sounded outside and she ran to the window thinking it might be Stu, but it was just an impatient driver hurrying a pedestrian across the busy Earl's Court street. If he didn't get there soon, he'd find her in total darkness. The meter hadn't been fed for days and she was certain it was going to run out any second. She doubted Jenny ever had to stand in a supermarket queue waiting to put five pounds on her electricity key. Life was so unfair.

Suddenly overcome with anger, she was gripped by the urge to tear the dress to pieces. But common sense got the better of her, and she opened the door of the rickety fibreboard wardrobe and hung it on a wire hanger.

Quickly she put away the rest of Jenny's dresses, then set about looking for something to wear for Stu. As she'd found out, clothes were *very* important to him. Selecting a black bra and pantie set from the wardrobe shelf, she closed the door and sat down on the bed to think through her game-plan for the evening.

Carla knew that Stu had been avoiding her. Since the Tenerife holiday, she'd left several messages on his answering machine but he'd ignored them all until she'd issued an ultimatum – either he saw her or she was going to let the cat out of the bag. Predictably he had gone into a state of total shock.

Stu hadn't realised that she'd known all along. From the first moment she'd spotted him in the Notting Hill bar she'd suspected there was something odd about him, and on the night he'd taken her back to his place, a quick rummage through his bedroom while he was in the shower had proved her right. What she found had made her feel sick but Carla knew it was her key out of the mess she'd made of her life.

Tonight she was going to give him what he wanted, confident that his need would be far greater than the anger he felt towards her. There weren't many women out there prepared to put up with the likes of Stu Williams. If she could show him that she was comfortable with it, even approved of it, then she was home and dry.

'What a freak!' she laughed, hooking the bra straps over her shoulders. Then she stood up and looked at herself in the mirror as she eased her breasts into the cups, pulling her large dark nipples through the peepholes. Fastening it was something of a struggle and as she pulled the matching panties over her fleshy white thighs, she was forced to admit to herself that she'd put on a little bit of weight. Still, men liked something to get hold of, she reasoned, sucking in her stomach, the nylon frills around the split crotch of her panties bulging obscenely.

'Carla!' a voice shouted from the street.

Carla rearranged the waistband of the knickers so that the roll of fat hanging over them was slightly less pronounced, then ran back to the window and waved down at the footballer.

'Come down and open the bloody door!' he yelled, his face full of fire.

Slipping into her dressing gown, she opened the door, then stopped and went back to the mirror to check her make-up. It was a little faded but it would do. There was no point in wasting expensive lipstick if in a few minutes it was going to be smeared all over her face. Her hair, however, needed a little bit of work.

'Carla!' Stu sounded apoplectic.

She picked up a brush and began to backcomb furiously, lifting the brittle blond hairs high above her head to reveal the dark roots. Suddenly the electricity went out and she was plunged into darkness.

'Jesus!' she hissed, feeling her way in the dark to the chair where she'd left her handbag. Eventually she found the electricity key, then edged back towards the door, hit the light switch in the passage and raced downstairs, her dressing gown flapping open to reveal her in all her lurid glory.

'Stu!' she purred, as she unlocked the street door. 'You couldn't be a darling, could you, and run across to the garage with this.' She proffered him the key. 'A tenner should do it.'

'You're taking the piss,' he said, snatching the key from her, his face barely registering the exotic apparition before him. 'Leave the door on the latch.'

Carla walked back up to her flat, feeling apprehensive. So much was riding on this evening. She was fed up with the crappy hand that life had dealt her. To the men at Notting Hill she was little more than a dirty joke, to their partners, no better than dogshit. She tried comforting herself with the thought that the men laughed at her because they all wanted her so badly. After all, on more than one occasion, when the bar had closed for the evening, she had found herself being bent over a table by one of Notting Hill's finest.

Of course, the other women suspected that she'd been having sex with their men but that wasn't the reason they despised her. No, they hated her because she reminded them so much of themselves. Which one of the Trophy Wives hadn't had to do what she was doing to land her man? The only difference between them was that Carla was prepared to admit she was a tart.

In the dark, she threw off her dressing gown and sat down on the bed, her legs slightly open, waiting for Stu's return. She wanted to be sure that when the lights went on he wouldn't be able to take his eyes off her.

Stu's silhouette appeared in the doorway. 'That's the last bloody time I'm doing that,' he said, throwing the key at her. 'What do you do with your money?'

What did she do with it? After the rent, the pittance Notting Hill paid her barely kept her in cigarettes. If she didn't have her hand in the till, she would have been out on the streets ages ago. Carla quashed the desire to say something smart to him and instead reached above the bed for the meter. 'Don't be like that,' she said, as the light came back on.

'I'm not staying,' Stu said, still standing by the opening door. Then for the first time he noticed her outfit. 'What on earth are you wearing?'

Carla lay back on the bed and opened her legs lasciviously. 'Do you like it?'

Stu's face reddened. 'I said I'm not staying,' he replied, but his eyes said otherwise.

'Be a good boy and shut the door,' she said, letting her fingertips brush against her thighs. 'I don't want everybody to see this.'

The footballer closed the door. 'I think you and me have reached the end of the road,' he said, unable to avert his gaze. 'You knew it was never going to be serious.'

'Who wants to get serious?' she asked, beckoning him over to the bed. 'All I want is a little bit of fun. No strings.'

The bed sagged badly as Stu sat down, pushing them together. Carla hoped that her outfit would prove distracting enough for Stuart not to notice that she had forgotten to shave her legs.

'That's better,' she said, her fingers with their badly chipped nail polish reaching for his crotch.

'You said you wanted to talk to me.'

'We can talk later,' Carla whispered, her fingers now busy with his fly. 'Afterwards . . .'

Suddenly, Stu knocked away her hand and stood up. 'I can't do this. It was a mistake to come here.'

Carla leaped off the bed and threw her arms around him. 'Don't go, Stu, there's something I want to show you. A surprise.'

'Leave it out!' he said, shrugging her off. 'I'm not interested.'

'Oh, but you will be, Stuie.' Her fingers found his crotch again and she reached up to kiss him. Feeling his hardness stirring, she knew she was home and dry. There weren't many men who could resist her once she got started. She was a true pro.

The following morning Stu awoke feeling sick to his stomach. Beside him in the cramped bed Carla lay snoring, her eyes sooty with mascara, a thin line of dribble oozing from the corner of her smudged lips. He felt repulsed, by her and by what he'd allowed himself to do in front of her. Without waking her, he slid from between the dirty sheets and walked over to the sink. There, he scrubbed his face raw to remove every trace of her make-up, hoping that somehow it would remove every trace of her.

When he'd finished, he scrabbled around on the floor looking for his clothes amidst the detritus of the night before. Finding his trousers, he pulled out his wallet and took out a hundred pounds. That would keep her quiet for the moment, he decided, throwing the money on the bedside table. He was under no illusion that she was in it for anything other than the money. How could he have been so stupid to have become entangled with such a hard-faced slag as Carla Ryman?

He didn't linger once he had dressed and within minutes he was driving back through Earl's Court towards Notting Hill, barely able to keep the wheel under control. She was going to ruin him, he was sure of it. Sooner or later, when the bitch was able to draw maximum benefit from it, she was going to tell all. As a wave of panic surged up inside him, he slammed his foot on the brake and made it out of his car only just in time, as the contents of his stomach surged from his throat.

Chapter Seven

As David walked through the changing room the tension was palpable. He could smell it – like the air just before a thunderstorm, heady and heavy. He would have liked to think the edginess was due to the game they were about to play against Schalke, their first match in the UEFA cup. But something told him that the mood was due to other factors. And for the life of him he couldn't work out what, or who, it was. He just hoped it didn't affect the game.

Although it wasn't his job, David usually gave a small pep-talk before the game. He took a deep breath. 'I just want to say that we all know the importance of today's game and how we need to win – and we're going to win. I think Graham wants to start with the usual 4 – 4 – 2 but depending on Schalke's formation, this might change. We'll have a re-think at half-time. Any questions?'

David looked expectantly around the room at the semi-clad bodies but each one of them had resumed getting dressed. 'OK, let's just remember we're a team and this is a team effort.'

A snigger came from the right side of the room. Turning, David saw, as expected, that it had come from Michael. Ignoring the player, he turned back to the rest of the team and told them to be ready in five.

As he ran down the pitch, Stefan tried to concentrate on the game, but even as he watched and shouted for the ball he was aware he was functioning on autopilot. Nothing could take his mind off his unhappiness. That the opposition was German, some of the players friends of his, only accentuated his depression.

Although he had tried to fit in with the other players at Notting Hill, he was shocked at their behaviour. Only two nights ago most of them had gone on a drinking spree, which seemed unbelievable to him considering the importance of this match. None of the players had any discipline and all seem to begrudge his presence.

The ball flashed past Stefan's eyes and he ran after it, the pain of forcing his body pushing all thoughts other than getting the ball and scoring out of his mind.

He could see that Schalke's defence was all over the place and that if he kept up the pace a goal was within sight. As he entered the penalty area, two defenders close on his heels, he kicked the ball hard and low. He watched the ball, as if in slow motion, as it hit the goalpost and went in at an angle that left the goalkeeper helpless to stop it. Stefan had scored Notting Hill's first goal. The crowd went crazy, the noise of their cheering and chanting deafening.

As the other players congratulated him he felt a glimmer of happiness, but once the hugs and back slapping had stopped, he looked up to see Andy McKay staring at him with barely disguised hatred.

When play resumed, Andy soon won possession of the ball. He flew down the pitch, tearing the defence to ribbons and clearly oblivious of anyone else. His foot hovered for a split second above the ball before giving it a powerful kick that sent it flying through the air. It was too high and sailed a safe six feet over the crossbar.

Schalke's defence having woken up, blocked all further attempts by Notting Hill. At half-time the score remained one-nil.

Once back in the changing rooms, Michael wasted no time baiting Andy. 'How much did they pay for you again? I'd say a million for every foot over the post that ball went.'

'Just fuck off, you useless piece of shit,' Andy spat. 'If it wasn't for your tart of a wife you'd have been out on your arse years ago.'

Michael pushed past Robbie and Stefan, and stood threateningly in front of Andy. As he moved closer, shoving Andy with his chest, he felt a restraining hand on his arm.

'There's more at stake here than just you two,' David hissed.

Michael opened his mouth to say something then thought better of it. He shrugged his shoulders and walked away. Andy appeared to be beyond words, his rage almost tangible.

As the second half began, with Notting Hill once again surging towards Schalke's goal, Robbie's long ball caught Andy in two minds and his header fell short of his intended target. He cursed and spat. When he looked across the pitch he saw Michael waving a clenched hand up and down, telling him he was a wanker. Silently Andy vowed to get his revenge. Big time. Something that once and for all would establish his superiority over the other players.

When Tony 'Magic' Anderson passed Andy the ball, he finally showed why the club had paid so much for him. He flicked the ball over a Schalke mid-fielder with his right foot and beat a defender with his left. Then he looped through the middle of the defence, making the goalkeeper come out to meet him. But it was too late to intercept Andy.

'Two-nil, two-nil,' the fans chanted.

For the rest of the game Stefan couldn't get near the ball, his constant pleas for Andy to pass falling on deaf ears. And despite Notting Hill's eventual victory, Stefan felt defeated.

God had to stop it. He had to. But at this precise moment Clive felt powerless to break with the sins of the flesh. He sank to his knees and prayed for deliverance, gripping his hands so tightly together that the rings on his fingers grated against each other.

Standing once more, he looked into the bedroom. She had been watching him all the time, but he was beyond caring what a woman like that thought of him.

He strode into the bedroom. 'On your knees,' he ordered the petite red-head.

She hesitated for a split second before dropping to her knees in a parody of his earlier praying. 'Clive, I—'

'Shut up,' he ordered. He couldn't bring himself to say Terri; using her name would make it personal.

He fumbled with his zip, his hands trembling with excitement. As she took his penis in her mouth, a small cry escaped his lips. For a few moments he was lost to the pleasure, but he knew it wasn't yet complete . . .

While her mouth worked in an expert if bored fashion, Clive groped around on the table behind him for the Polaroid camera. Once in his hands he placed it in a position he knew would give him maximum exposure.

As the flash erupted, so did Clive. It was all over. He pulled away from the girl. 'You can go now,' he hissed, ignoring the shock on her face. 'Use the backdoor over there.'

'But . . .' The word hung in the air; Clive had already left the bedroom.

In his office, he looked briefly at the picture before throwing it into a video box, which he returned to a shelf where dozens of football videos were stacked.

A small mirror propped up on the same shelf revealed his flushed face. He reddened even more at this evidence of his weakness. But now was not the time to berate himself – he was due to congratulate the team on their win. Taking a couple of deep breaths and straightening his tie, he opened the door of his office ready to meet the world.

Outside in the corridor he bumped into a young woman. Taking a step back, he tried to place her, fearing she might be one of the many women who'd knelt before him in his office.

She in turn stared at him, an expression that was both teasing and sullen on her face. Then it occurred to him who she was – another of the club's cheap-looking barmaids.

'Excuse me,' he said stiffly, making to walk around her.

Carla momentarily stopped him with a brush of her hand, then she gave him a come-hither smile. Before he could respond, she had turned and was walking off down the corridor.

Chapter Eight

The suburban landscape, row after row of neat hedges with even neater houses, flashed past. A blur of lights. As usual Michael was driving as if he owned the road.

'You bloody idiot, look where you're going!' he shouted at a hapless pedestrian trying to negotiate at a zebra crossing.

Jenny took no notice of Michael's outburst or the change in scenery as they left behind the safe suburbs. She had only one thing on her mind – alcohol. Or, to be more precise, the lack of it. To stop her drinking herself to death, her doctor had prescribed 'Antabuse', which would make her extremely sick if she drank alcohol. For the last three days – it felt like three months – Jenny had taken the pills religiously.

Although there was no magic pill to stop her abusing cocaine, she had managed to stay off that as well. The absence of narcotics made her realise just how much she had used them to numb her pain.

What she needed was a distraction. 'Michael?'

'What?'

'Why don't we make love more?' she asked, placing a hand on his knee.

Michael banged his hand on the wheel, his face contorted by a sneering laugh. 'Why?' he spluttered. 'Because you make me feel sick. Does that answer your stupid question?'

Well, she'd asked for that one. Still it had had its desired effect. His hurtful words covered up, if only momentarily, the agony of no alcohol. Using pain to stop pain had been a technique she'd mastered as a teenager. She ran a finger over the scars on her wrists; there were more on her thighs and the upper parts of her arms.

She stared out of the window. Nothing good could come of thinking about those dark years, when some part of Jenny had been lost forever. She focused her thoughts on the night ahead.

She and Michael were on their way to the opening of the Three Lions night club in Billericay. The owner, Bill Harry, was a former Notting Hill player and it went without saying that the whole team was expected to turn up.

Jenny was under no illusions as to why it was she who now sat in Michael's car and not his latest tart. If Michael so much as stood next to a woman other than Jenny at an event like this he'd have every paparazzi in the country on the doorstep.

Jenny wrung her hands, wondering how the hell she was going to get through the evening without a drink. Opening her third packet of cigarettes of the day, she consoled herself that at least she still had her nicotine.

As they drove into the car park, Jenny remarked that the club looked like a fall-out shelter. She didn't rate its chances of success. It would open to a double

page in the *Sun* and then six months later the owner
would be bankrupt. It was that fatal mix of ex-
footballer and on-tap alcohol, topped with a total
lack of business sense.

Out of the corner of her eye she saw a flash of pink.
She turned her head quickly but she was dazzled by
a car's full beam. It had looked incredibly like the
Suzuki jeep. Or was she just imagining pink jeeps
instead of pink elephants? Surely, Michael wouldn't
have been so stupid as to have invited his bit on the
side? It had to be a coincidence. Whatever, she knew
better than to say anything.

Jenny followed Michael into the club. The decor
inside matched the outside. Bill had obviously gone
for the distressed industrial look. Jenny couldn't tell
if this was by accident or by design and the overall
impression was a club that had been only half built.
Had the architects got one over on Bill or had he
totally defeated them with his vision?

The surrounding scaffolding rattled in time to the
deafening beat of the disco music. But even the music
wasn't loud enough to drown out the high-pitched
voices of the wives striving to outdo each other.

'Jenny darling, no drink? And you've been here
five minutes,' Suzy, wife of mid-fielder Jamie Carlton,
taunted.

As if she needed reminding. 'Your dress is lovely.
Looks expensive.'

Suzy looked at Jenny as if she'd gone mad. 'Thanks,'
she muttered.

'So who's he fucking then?'

'You bitch,' Suzy hissed, scuttling away.

Jenny laughed. It was common lore amongst the

women that the wife wearing the most expensive dress was the one whose husband had cheated most that week. However, every woman, including the dear Suzy, thought it was true about everyone but themselves. Only Jenny acknowledged the truth about her husband, and that wasn't because Michael bought her expensive dresses.

Jenny looked around for Michael but he had disappeared the second they walked through the door. Had she really seen his mistress's car? Surely even he wouldn't arrange to meet her here? But where was he now?

The temperature in the club soared as more and more guests arrived. Jenny felt disorientated, almost light-headed from lack of alcohol. Yet there was booze everywhere – glasses were held aloft in front of her, drinks were constantly being poured and glasses clinked, while the bitter-sweet smell wafted under her nose – and it assaulted and tormented her senses. She could even touch alcohol with her shoes as they stuck to the floor. The one sense it didn't assault was taste. She couldn't bloody well drink the stuff.

She walked to the bar. 'Vod . . . orange juice, please.'

'Sorry. Was that vodka and orange?' the barmaid asked.

Yes, yes, she wanted to scream. 'No. Just orange juice.'

The barmaid gave her a puzzled look. Jenny wondered if her face gave the game away and it was obvious to everyone that she had spent the last ten years attached to a bottle.

'Ladies and gentlemen,' Bill shouted into a mike, causing ear-splitting feedback. In response to his bellowing, the music was lowered to an almost respectable level. 'Thanks for coming this evening. And now our very own delightful Page Three kitten Tanya is going to help me officially open the Three Lions.'

The room erupted in a cheer. Rather, Jenny noted, the men erupted – the expression on every woman's face showed exactly what they thought of the 'Page Three kitten'. But then nearly every woman hated the other. Unfortunately, they were often thrown together through junkets like this. Marry a footballer and you married the team. Come what may, and no matter how bad it got, you did the dutiful thing and turned up for these endless nights out.

Shaking the champagne bottle, Tanya sprayed the crowd immediately in front of the stage. Luckily, no Notting Hill wives were nearby. Jenny could imagine the uproar if just one drop had hit a Versace or a Thierry Mugler. And what a surprise, Tanya had managed to get her T-shirt wet to leave no one in doubt why she was paid thousands to pose topless.

Jenny glanced at her watch, aware that, without drink, time passed incredibly slowly. Michael had been missing for forty minutes. She looked out at the dance floor, which was now heaving, but couldn't spot Michael.

Jenny managed to cross to the other side, where she spotted Loulou looking as if there was a bad smell under her nose as she reluctantly signed the cast of a dumpy girl with a broken arm. Jenny thought better of asking her if she knew Michael's whereabouts – there was no way she would open herself up to a put-down from that one.

There just didn't seem to be any point being out

if you weren't sloshed. She thought briefly about eating until she reached the dining area and saw the chicken-in-the-basket that was passed off as food.

'Hi, Jenny, how are you?' an enthusiastic voice asked.

It was Carla and she was sat with, of all people, Rachel. Jenny hid her surprise with a smile. 'How are you both?'

'Fine,' Carla replied. 'Rachel here is just filling me in on the joys of motherhood.'

Rachel gave Jenny a painful smile and then immediately looked down at the Babycham she was nursing.

The only explanation Jenny had for Carla talking to Rachel was that she was hoping some of the older woman's virginal image would rub off on her.

'Have either of you seen Michael?'

Rachel shook her head.

'He was over at the bar,' Carla said. 'Which is where I've got to go now. Although I hate to leave you, Rachel – we'd covered only the first three years of your kids' lives.'

Jenny was stunned by Carla's bitchiness. What had the poor, unobtrusive Rachel done to upset that tramp? 'Bye, Rachel. See you soon,' Jenny said in her friendliest tone.

When she finally made it back to the bar her errant husband was still nowhere to be seen.

'Look,' a familiar voice was saying, 'ignore her. Michael doesn't earn enough to pay for the kind of dress his screwing around would need to buy. But then why should he when the stupid cow buys them herself? Just like she bought him really. Oops. Sorry, Jenny, didn't see you there.'

Jenny shoved Martine, wife of 'Magic' Anderson, aside without comment. She'd spotted Michael on the other side of the club. One day she would tell that bitch Martine exactly how her husband came by the nickname 'Magic'.

'Where the hell have you been?'

'Avoiding you,' Michael slurred.

The men surrounding him tittered. Egged on, Michael said, 'What's this I hear about you and an orange juice? You getting so tight you're sneaking in your own vodka?'

Jenny turned and walked away. Her mind trying to blank out the laughter that followed her.

Rachel couldn't believe she'd been stupid enough to think Carla would be interested in her. All the woman had wanted was money. 'A little loan', as she'd described it to Rachel. How she wished she didn't have to come to these parties. It was always the same: she sat alone while Robbie went off with his mates. She didn't blame him for that – he needed to relax, and tonight the team was celebrating its victory over its arch rival Arsenal.

It was her own fault that the other women didn't bother with her. She was dull and dowdy. And, as Carla had kindly pointed out, by wearing clothes that were bought from the high street, Rachel continued to commit the greatest sin. And if that wasn't bad enough, she had the audacity to give them more than one outing. All the other wives had a new outfit for each occasion.

Suddenly, a pair of hands covered her eyes.

'Guess who?' a deep, sonorous male voice teased.

Rachel tugged at the hands and whirled round. 'Chris!' she exclaimed. 'Whatever are you doing here?'

'It's nice to see you too,' he laughed.

Blushing, Rachel stammered. 'I . . . I'm sorry. I just didn't expect to see you.'

'Rachel. Rachel, I'm only joking,' he said, taking hold of her hands. 'Let me take a look at you. You're looking really well. London must agree with you.'

'Get away with you,' she replied, unable to hide the effect his flattery had on her. It was the first time they'd met in over a year and seeing him again reminded Rachel that Wigan hadn't been all bad.

Chris had been the only black man on the youth team and he'd found it hard to deal with the barrage of racist taunts from both the home and away fans. Robbie, or rather Rachel, had offered him solace and support. He had been a constant guest at their home, spending hours talking to her as if she were someone other than the mother of Robbie's children.

'Didn't Robbie tell you I've just been bought by Chelsea? It's a long way from Wigan.'

'Congratulations. No, I didn't know. Where's Cherry?' she asked, peering behind him.

Chris looked down at his feet. 'Let's just say we're having a trial separation. To be honest, the engagement's off.'

'You were so perfect for each other,' Rachel murmured, placing a hand on his arm. She meant it. Cherry was a model – and everything Rachel wasn't. She was beautiful and always immaculately turned out, and she perfectly matched Chris's aquiline grace. Studying him now, Rachel realised he was like one of her romantic heroes – tall, very dark, extremely hand-some. And he was a gentleman.

Chris placed his hand on top of Rachel's. 'Maybe, maybe not.'

It was Rachel's turn to look at the floor. The touch of his hand produced butterflies in her stomach. 'So what are you doing here?'

'I know Bill from yonks ago.'

'Shall I go and find Robbie? He'd be so annoyed if he missed you,' Rachel said hurriedly, knowing that her reaction to Chris was inappropriate for a happily married woman.

'It's all right. I've got to go now. I'll catch up with him again.' Chris leaned forward, his lips brushing against Rachel's as he kissed her cheek.

Rachel jerked back as if she had received an electric shock. Her cheek burned from where his lips had touched her skin.

'You got to be desperate to shag her,' Andy slurred, wagging a finger towards Carla. 'Listen, Stuie, prac-tically *every* man here has fucked her. And the few who haven't have seen her act. I—'

Stuart shrugged off Andy's arm and marched over to the table where Carla was sitting next to Jenny. 'Get your coat,' he ordered 'We're going.'

'But, Stuie—'

'Now!' he shouted, his voice full of pent-up rage.

Jenny looked away, feeling sorry for Carla as she followed Stuart out of the club. No one deserved to be humiliated like that.

Still not satisfied with his meddling, Andy now turned his attention to Michael.

'Hey, Schizo, you know what? Even Carla would be too good for you. Good job you've got that alcoholic wife. 'Cos I'll tell you for nothing, any tart would have to be four sheets to the wind to put up with a no-hoper like you.'

'Come on, guys, let's be friends.' Robbie tried to make light of it.

Michael shoved Robbie aside and grabbed the lapels of Andy's jacket. The room fell silent as a dull thud signalled the contact Andy's back made with the bare brick wall.

'You're not quite so fucking big now, are you, tosser?' Michael shouted, his saliva hitting Andy's face.

Andy, his arms flailing, tried to push Michael away. But Michael now had him pinned by his throat. He looked like an animal caught in a trap. The more he struggled, the worse it got. 'I'm warning you,' he managed to utter, breathless from Michael's forearm pressing on his windpipe.

'Hey, Loulou, what's it like having such a macho stud for a boyfriend?' he sneered, forcing Andy to the floor.

Andy, his face puce with rage, jumped up and raised his fist but Robbie caught his hand.

'Keep out it, Robbie, you thick shit,' Michael shouted.

David moved between the two men. 'That's enough.'

'I might have guessed Goody Two Shoes would step in to save his golden boy,' Michael goaded.

Mortified by Michael's outburst, Jenny wished she could just disappear. At another table Loulou stood up and walked out of the club.

'I think it's time we all went now,' Rachel pleaded, her voice squeaky from fear.

'You go. I need a drink,' Robbie replied gruffly. 'It'll be all right.'

Tanya spoke quietly to David and Jenny saw him shake his head, pointing to the other men. He obviously didn't think it wise to leave them to their own devices.

'You want a lift with me and Rachel?' Tanya asked.

'I think I'd better wait for Michael and drive him home.

'But—'

'I'm sober,' Jenny said quickly, second guessing the other woman's thoughts.

Bill Harry emerged from his office, oblivious to what had been going on in his club. 'Look, I've got to go, but you folks are welcome to stay. Sharon will lock up.' He pointed to the lone barmaid.

Jenny waved her goodbyes to the other women and went to the bar. 'An orange juice, please.'

'Wouldn't you like something stronger? I would after a night like yours,' the barmaid said, giving Jenny a sympathetic look. 'Men. Honestly. I'm going to have one.'

Jenny watched as Sharon poured herself a double vodka. Her hands began to sweat and shake. Surely one drink wouldn't hurt? And the girl was right, she'd had a horrible night and she had done really well. One drink as a reward would be OK. And it would just be one. 'I think I will have a small one.'

'He can get in a real temper, that one,' Sharon commented when she returned.

'What would you know?' Jenny snapped.

'Nothing. Sorry I was speaking out of turn.'

Jenny looked around for Michael. She guessed he was in the toilet and on about his tenth line of coke. She knocked back the drink in one satisfying gulp. 'I'll just have one . . .'

Sharon had read Jenny's mind. Another vodka, larger than the first, was already in front of her. The relief as the alcohol hit the back of Jenny's throat was immense. For the first time that night she felt normal.

But as she drained the last drop, the room started to spin and waves of nausea threatened to overwhelm her. Falling forward, Jenny knocked the glass to the floor where it shattered into dozens of tiny little pieces. A door banged shut, the noise amplified in Jenny's ears. She heard raised voices, distorted as though she were submerged under water. Were Andy and Michael fighting again?

As she tried to get off the stool, she had the weirdest sensation that she was falling, in slow motion, towards the floor.

Chapter Nine

Gradually regaining consciousness, Jenny slowly realised that, although she was lying down, she wasn't in bed. The smell of stale smoke and spilled drink assaulted her nostrils, and as she tentatively opened her eyes, she recognised from the scaffolding above that she was on the floor of the Three Lions nightclub.

The place was dark and dank, and was now very quiet. Sitting up, she rested her back against a box, aware that her whole body was quivering. As she glanced around and got her bearings, she realised that she was behind the DJ's box. Yet as far as she could recall she had been over at the bar, on the other side of the room, having a drink. How had she got here?

Finally, she felt strong enough to stand. To break the room's eerie silence she tried to speak but her voice failed her and only a croaked whisper came out.

The taste of vodka was still on her lips. Why was she so stupid? The doctor had warned her, repeatedly, about what would happen if she drank while taking the pills. But boy, if she ever needed a drink it was now. She wondered, briefly, how many people had witnessed her humiliation.

A trickle of sweat ran down the small of her back and her heart thumped painfully against her chest, each beat louder than the last. She was beginning to panic and her breath came out in short, wheezy gasps. Hesitantly, she pieced together her last minutes of consciousness. She remembered the fight between Michael and Andy, refusing Tanya's offer of a lift, and raised voices. It seemed as if after that it was all a blank, except somewhere at the edges of her mind there was something else, some other thought struggling to be heard.

To calm her erratic breathing, she placed her hand on her chest. It was then that she noticed her clothes. Her blouse was ripped from the collar to just above her breast, revealing a large welt across her chest. Her skirt was half tucked into the waistband of her now-shredded tights. How had she ended up in this state?

Think. Damn it. She recalled feeling the cold concrete floor against the bare skin of her back. She remembered Robbie standing over her. He had looked behind him at Andy. What had he been saying to her? Her throat contracted, she felt so sick. Jenny sat down again, her head in her hands. And David? Yes, she remembered him saying something to her. God, Michael was going to kill her for showing him up like this.

'I think it's time you were going, *Mrs* Waite.' It was Sharon.

Deep in thought, Jenny hadn't heard the other woman approaching. She looked up, her face pleading. 'Sharon, do . . .' Her words faded into nothing. The barmaid's eyes mocked her, and the grim set of her lips forbade any questions.

'The door's over there,' Sharon said dismissively, turning swiftly on her high heels.

Standing once more, Jenny took a few unsteady steps towards the exit. As she made uncertain progress across the dance floor, she became increasingly aware of a warm stickiness between her thighs. Gingerly, she placed her hand on the inside of her leg, and her fingers confirmed what she already knew. She retched, and with not one shred of dignity left, Jenny vomited where she stood.

She was having trouble controlling her body. The trembling had become more uncontrollable, her breathing erratic, as nightmare images rushed through her mind like speeding, crashing cars. Men's faces, men's voices, a man's body. It just couldn't be what she was thinking.

Nearly at the exit she heard a sound to her left. A door banged shut and her husband stumbled towards her. So it was him. He did it to her.

Chapter Ten

Carla picked up the misshapen lipstick and tried to coat her lips but the blunted edge made it almost impossible to apply properly.

'You look like Coco the Clown,' she said to her reflection.

Smoothing the lip line as best she could with a used tissue, she then outlined her lips with a darker pencil. The result was just about passable. Damn him for ruining all her best make-up.

It was over with Stu now. The thought of him fucking her again like *that* made her skin crawl. Even if sex was the only weapon left in her arsenal, she had to draw the line somewhere, and looking at the mass of dirty clothes on the floor she knew exactly where that line was.

She reached into the pocket of her dressing gown and retrieved Stu's folded-up cheque. The five hundred pounds was hush money, plain and simple. Which was fair enough but cash would have kept her a lot quieter. As soon as the cheque went into the bank it would be eaten up by her overdraft.

Untying the cord of the dressing gown, she saw the necklace of love bites around her chest. She hated it when men did that. It was like a tom cat spraying its territory and Carla's body belonged to no man. Not any more. The most anyone could do was rent it for a while. Her first boyfriend had owned her. And he'd hit her. And then he'd sold her to a stream of men who took pleasure from her pain. All the love had been beaten out of her body. The bruised shell that was left was now available only on an hourly basis, and it was she who was collecting the rent.

Applying some concealer to the bites she looked around for something to wear. Practically everything Jenny had given her lay crumpled and stained on the dirty carpet. She picked up a plunge-fronted yellow dress, licked her fingers and tried to rub off the white, crusty marks. Not perfect but it would have to do.

Once dressed, she retrieved her address book from her clutchbag and found Terri's number. The day Carla had bumped into Clive was the last day the other barmaid had been to work. Carla was positive Terri had been in Clive's office and she was sure he'd given her more than her cards.

Picking up the phone she dialled the number. 'Hi, Terri,' she said as soon as the phone was picked up. 'It's Carla. I was wondering if you wanted to meet me for lunch. There's something I need to talk to you about.'

Stu ordered a second pint, and seeing the flicker of recognition on the barman's face, decided to make it his last; this was no place to be spotted. As if things hadn't become dangerous enough with Carla. The relief he'd felt as he'd given her the cheque had evaporated as soon as he'd left her flat. The bitch would be back for more as soon as that ran out, he was certain of it.

A man in a tight T-shirt with tattooed arms and a pierced eyebrow sat down at his table and nodded at him. 'All right?' he asked, shouting over the nosebleed techno.

'Fuck off,' Stu snarled, feeling his fists clenching automatically.

The man shrugged his shoulders and moved away. Stu closed his eyes and told himself to calm down. The guy was probably just after his autograph – it happened all the time. Then again, if he wanted his autograph, that meant he knew who Stu was. The knot in Stu's stomach tightened.

It had been silly to come here. The bar had floor-to-ceiling windows looking straight on to the street. The whole of Soho could see him. To make matters worse, just around the corner, in Wardour Street, there was an after-hours club where he drank occasionally with some of the other guys from Notting Hill. What if Michael or Andy were to walk by and clock him in a . . . he couldn't even bring himself to say the words.

Stu looked around. Although the bar was airy and brightly painted in citrus colours, to him it seemed the darkest, dankest place in the world. The mostly male clientele was young and fit-looking but he knew about their diseases. They disgusted him. How stupid he was to think he might find someone like himself here. And even if there was another one, what would he say to him?

He'd managed to keep a lid on his secret for most of his adult life, only indulging it when the urge became too much to bear. There were clubs and support groups for people like him – he'd seen it on the television – but contacting them would mean giving a name to the thing he feared most in himself. The second he picked up a phone and dialled a help-line he would be branded with that name for ever.

Carla had treated it as a joke and he'd been happy to go along with it, telling himself that it was all just a bit of fun and something probably loads of guys did once in a while. But when she looked him in the eyes afterwards, he could see her disgust and pity. How low had he sunk that a piece of trash like her was able to look down on him?

Stu finished his pint and although his bladder was full to bursting, there was no way he was going to risk the toilets. He stood up and took a deep breath. The night before with Carla was the end of it. The end with her and with this thing. He could control it; he could make it go away.

Pushing through the crowd, flinching every time he came into contact with another body, he made his way to the exit. Standing in front of the door, barring the way, were two heavily muscled men. And they were kissing.

'Excuse me,' Stu mumbled, elbowing his way past. No, the men in this bar were not like him at all.

Carla waved goodbye to Terri and staked her last pound on a bus ride into the West End. She'd had to pay for the other barmaid's lunch to get her to talk, but the money had been well spent. Terri's revelations had spurred Carla to phone Clive Dorning straightaway, but she got his secretary, who told her that Dorning was lunching at the Palace Hotel. Carla couldn't think of a nicer location to put her plan into action.

In the heavy traffic along Piccadilly the bus sat

immobile, leaving her feeling slightly anxious. She didn't want to miss him – at the very least she had to find a way of getting her bus fare home. Looking across at the trees in Green Park, she daydreamed about a life where lunches at the Palace Hotel were commonplace.

Suddenly the bus lurched forward. In the distance Carla spotted the white bulbs spelling out the famous name of the hotel, and she rang the bell.

Paying no heed to the traffic, she crossed the road and walked up to the hotel, not quite sure how to make her entrance. The only hotels she'd ever been into were places that charged for the room by the hour. Self-consciously, she smoothed down Jenny's dress and approached the uniformed doorman.

'Can I help you, miss?'

'You could open the door,' she said flintily.

The doorman looked her up and down suspiciously. 'Have you made a reservation?'

'No, but I'm . . .' Carla stopped as the doorman nodded at a well-dressed couple and ushered them past her into the hotel. She made to follow them but the doorman, ever so discreetly, prevented her from entering.

'You were saying?' he said, his face growing more disdainful by the second.

'Why didn't you ask them if they'd made a reservation?' she asked, beginning to lose her cool.

'As I understand, we're fully booked for lunch,' he replied, not answering her question. 'Perhaps you'd find something more suitable elsewhere. May I suggest Soho?'

'Go fuck yourself sideways,' Carla snarled, and she barged past him into the hotel.

Immediately, another uniformed flunkey was at her side. 'Can I help you, miss?'

'Not unless you've got a fifty and a spare twenty minutes.' She stuck out her chest defiantly and realised immediately that it had been a dumb thing to say. Suddenly her bravado evaporated and she added in a small voice, 'I'm here to meet Clive Dorning – he's expecting me. Could someone tell him Carla Ryman has arrived. Oh yes, and that Terri sent me.'

'Certainly, miss. If you'd just like to wait here.'

Carla watched as the man walked over to a colleague and whispered in his ear. Both men stared at her, the expressions on their faces impenetrable, and one of them disappeared behind a door. She felt massively out of her depth.

In a matter of minutes, the second man returned and walked up to her. 'Mr Dorning says that he has never heard of you.'

'There must be some mistake,' Carla squeaked, her cheeks burning.

'There's no mistake. I'm afraid I'm going to have to ask you to leave.'

Even though the man's voice was reduced to a whisper, she was sure that everybody in the lobby had heard him. She wanted the ground to open up. The sensible thing would have been to leave, but Carla chose to defend her corner. 'I'd like to speak to the manager.'

'You *are* speaking to him,' the man said impassively. 'Would you please leave.'

Carla put her hands on her hips. 'Mr Dorning is

my employer and I don't believe you informed him that I am here. In my time I have visited some of the finest hotels in the world and never have I been treated like this.'

Even as the words flew out of her mouth she knew how ludicrous she sounded, standing there in her dirty hand-me-down dress, looking for all the world like the tart they'd taken her for.

'I assure you, I spoke to Mr Dorning myself. He was quite taken aback to be told that there was someone waiting for him and he was most adamant about wanting to dine alone. Perhaps you should talk to his secretary. Maybe there has been a mix up in his diary.'

His manner was polite but unyielding and Carla knew she would heap only further humiliation upon herself if she continued to argue. 'Y . . . yes, I'll do that,' she said, turning on her heels.

As she left the hotel she deliberately ground her heel into the doorman's foot, but her show of defiance was shortlived as she ran around the corner and burst into tears. She pulled a tissue from her cuff and blew her nose, trying to decide what to do next. Throwing herself under a bus seemed the only available option. She certainly couldn't afford to get on it.

Leaning against a wall, she spotted her reflection in the window of the building opposite. She looked completely dishevelled. Her cheap mascara was running down her face in black spidery lines, and as she wiped her cheeks, she noticed splashes of mascara on the front of her dress. Why on earth had she believed she could pull this off? What had possessed her?

With nowhere to go and no means to get there, she

remained where she was, watching as one well-heeled matron after another passed by her on their way into the hotel. How many of them had once been like her? She bet at least half of them had bitten, clawed and fucked their way into their minks. And she would do the same. Suddenly she felt a fresh surge of defiance.

This new-found boldness carried her for over an hour as she stood waiting for her quarry to appear. Finally he emerged and, predictably, tried to walk right past her.

'Mr Dorning!' she shouted after him.

The chairman didn't turn round; instead he walked into the road, looking up and down for a cab.

Carla sidled up to him, immediately going into tramp overdrive. 'Clive, you naughty thing,' she purred, putting her arm around his waist, thrusting her breast under his nose.

'Do I know you?' the chairman asked, clearly recognising her.

'Of course you do. I work in the bar at Notting Hill.'

'If this is a work matter,' he said, addressing her cleavage, 'you should take it up with your supervisor. Now if you'll excuse me.'

Carla licked her lips and pulled herself tighter against him, feeling the stirring in his crotch. God, men were easy. 'I met Terri today. You remember – she was a barmaid at the club, too? She sends her love.'

The blood drained from the chairman's face. 'You little whore,' he whispered.

'Too right, baby,' she replied, thrusting her breasts against his chest to let him know she wasn't wearing a bra. Passers-by were staring at them, but this was

Carla's last chance and she knew it was no time to play hard to get. 'When can I see you? Couldn't we go some place now? I don't live too far from here.'

Dorning looked as if he were seriously considering her offer, but then he collected himself and pulled away from her. 'If you ever pull a stunt like this again, you're fired. Do you understand?' There was real threat in his voice.

Carla grabbed his hand. 'Don't be like that.'

He dug his fingernails into her palm. 'Let go of me. Now, I don't ever want to be seen with you in public again. Do you understand?'

The pressure of his fingers grew stronger, his creepy religious rings grazing her skin. Carla snatched away her hand, nodding.

'Good. When I want to see you, I'll contact you.' He hailed a cab and, without looking back, climbed in.

Carla allowed herself a brief victory smile, then began the long trudge back to Earl's Court.

Chapter Eleven

Loulou's blue eyes were glazing over and she was struggling to read the autocue. 'And coming up after these messages—'

'Oi, Loulou! Tits out for the lads,' a leery voice shouted from the audience.

The sound-man looked around furiously and the director called cut. 'Do it again, Loulou.'

Lazily Loulou read the link and then slipped off the dayglo psychedelic set for a break. The crowd was particularly noisy tonight and there'd been constant interruptions to the taping. It was the last *Sorted!* of the season and the warm-up man had whipped up the audience a little too much in an attempt to inject a party atmosphere.

One face missing from the audience was Andy's. There was an after-show party and Loulou had originally invited him, but after that cheap little scene at the Three Lions she'd changed her mind. Fighting in public – what on earth had Andy been thinking of? It wasn't even as if they were fighting over her; that she could have accepted – after all, look what it had done for Caroline Aherne.

Kicking off her shoes, she padded into the green room and checked through the running order in her programme notes. All that was left was a dull taped piece by Chrissy Boy, her irksome Mancunian New Lad co-presenter, on an SM restaurant in Hamburg, which had been ripped off from *Eurotrash*, and then her interview with Meret Lee.

By any show's standards, the interview was something of a coup, but for *Sorted!* Loulou had pulled off a near miracle. Meret Lee was the wife of Camel Eskapa, the lead singer with Neurofister, perhaps the biggest band in the world. Or at least they were the biggest band until the day a couple of months earlier when Camel had stuck a shotgun in his mouth and blew his brains out in a motel room in Palm Springs.

Meret hadn't spoken in public since being mobbed at the funeral. Everybody wanted a piece of her but it was Loulou who had hit pay-dirt. Possibly it was her own past as a rock chick that had helped seal the deal. Whatever, it was a world exclusive and the producers of *Sorted!* had milked the publicity for all it was worth, selling the interview the planet over.

'Five minutes,' the floor manager called, putting her head round the door.

'Is she here yet, Mona?' Loulou asked anxiously.

'Judging from the roar outside, I'd say she was on her way.'

Earlier, Loulou had had to fight her way through hundreds of grieving Neurofister fans to get into the building. With their candles, posters and messages of support for Meret, Loulou could see that this was shaping up to be a death cult that would give Monroe and Dean a run for their money.

'Will you let me know the minute she gets here?'

The floor manager nodded and left. Loulou went through her questions feeling a slight attack of nerves. She was much better interviewing men. It was a chemistry thing. A little bit of flirting, a soft blink of the eye and most men, even the gay ones, were eating out of her hand. Women were a much harder proposition and from what she knew of Meret Lee, this one was harder than most.

Engrossed in her notes, she didn't notice Chrissy Boy coming in to the room until he goosed her. She slapped his hand away. 'Don't tell me. Yes you know it's a sexual assault, but as you're a post-Modernist, it was done in inverted commas.'

Chrissy Boy grinned and waggled his dark-framed glasses like Eric Morecambe. 'You read me like a book.'

'Just piss off. Copping a feel is copping a feel. At least the Old Lads were honest about it.'

She could see Chrissy Boy's mind was working overtime to come up with a lame retort, but she was spared the pointless badinage by the arrival of the interviewee. Loulou had been expecting a large entourage but Meret Lee appeared at the door alone.

Dressed in what appeared to be a black cowl, she was wearing dark glasses and seemed to be holding the doorframe for support. She was tiny, perhaps no more than five foot. 'Loulou?' she asked, her voice cracked, barely there.

'Meret, lovely to meet you.' Loulou was unsure whether to offer the woman her condolences. With half the teenagers in London outside screaming theirs, it seemed a little redundant. She went to embrace the woman but Chrissy Boy got in her way.

'Who the fuck are you?' the widow snarled. 'Get this man out of my face.'

Loulou suppressed a smile. 'Would you give us a moment?'

Chrissy Boy scowled and left the room.

'I wanted to be here earlier – so we could talk this thing through. But y'know how things are. We were kinda . . .' Her voice trailed away into nothing.

Loulou realised that the woman was stoned out of her mind. 'Can I get you something? The coffee's pretty dreadful here but I could send someone out.'

Meret took off her glasses and stared at Loulou, emitting a low throaty laugh. 'Coffee?' Her eyes were ringed with black and the pupils were like pinpricks, scarring what was otherwise a pale but beautiful face.

'Are you sure you're up to this? We could always cancel.' Like hell we could, she thought. This was one of the biggest moments of Loulou's career and she'd drag the woman on in an iron lung if necessary.

Meret reached out and stroked Loulou's hair, her sleeve falling back to reveal the bracelet she'd had tattooed on her arm when she'd married the rock star. 'You have a lovely aura, y'know that?'

Loulou didn't know what to say. Normally she'd brush off a remark like that as hippy shit but Meret spoke with obvious sincerity. She'd expected a brash, show business widow – a Mrs Norman Maine – milking the sympathy for all it was worth now that her meal ticket was dead, but it was clear that Meret was in a lot of pain.

'I loved him, y'know,' the other woman said, as if reading her thoughts. 'But it hurt so bad at times. Almost as much as this. It was so hard keeping him alive. I just got tired. That was the first week I'd left him alone in three years. Dumb bastard.'

Loulou embraced her, picturing Andy putting a shotgun in his mouth. Would his death reduce her to this? Bitterly honest with herself, she knew that it wouldn't. Oh, she'd care all right. Care all the way to signing the *Hello* exclusive. And Andy would feel exactly the same about her. That's show business.

Meret produced a hip flask. 'Want some?'

She didn't really but she took a swig for girlie bonding. The alcohol seared the back of her throat, making her gag. 'My God. What is it?'

'Moonshine,' laughed Meret. 'It was a recipe from Camel's daddy. Want some more?'

Loulou went for it and the effect was immediate. When the floor manager reappeared a few minutes later to tell them that they were ready to do the interview, she found the two women slumped on a sofa laughing hysterically.

'Give me quarter of an hour,' Loulou said. 'We need to go over some stuff.'

'The audience is getting bored.'

'Then we'll do it without them. Mona, you know I wanted a closed set anyway. Go and get Chrissy Boy to put a condom over his head again. That's always a crowd pleaser.'

As the floor manager left, the two women resumed their conversation, and when Loulou finally sent out a message saying they were ready over an hour had passed.

Standing in the wings, the two women heard the angry chants of the audience. The warm-up guy sounded close to breakdown as he shouted above them.

'I'm scared,' Meret said, holding Loulou's hand.

'Don't worry. We'll be fine.'

As a gesture of support Loulou kissed the other woman on the lips. But what began as a brief peck continued and grew. Meret's tongue sought out hers and she found herself eagerly responding. They held each other, hungrily exploring each other's mouth, now oblivious to the catcalls from the restless audience.

It was Loulou who broke away first. 'I don't know why I did that,' she said, flushed and confused. 'I'm really sorry.'

'No, you're not.' Meret smiled.

Andy let himself into Loulou's house and called up the stairs. 'Loulou, are you back?' There was no reply. She must still be out with Meret Lee. He'd spoken to her on the phone after the interview and she'd sounded on a real high, saying that she might take Meret on to a club in the Portobello Road after the party. Apparently things had gone swimmingly. It was good to know that one of their careers was on the right track.

Training that day had been pretty disastrous. Michael had continuously riled him about their showdown at the Three Lions, and although Andy had tried to blank the whole evening from his mind, he was unable to stop himself rising to the bait. Michael wouldn't let it drop, and it had taken all of David's diplomacy to avoid a rematch. Andy knew he couldn't beat his team mate physically but there was more than one way to bring a man to his knees.

To make matters worse, the Kraut looked like he was shaping up to be a dynamite player. All of the crap that was going on at Notting Hill seemed to go straight over Lohmann's head, and he remained totally focused on football.

There was room on the team for only one golden boy – and that was him. If he couldn't stop Michael from rattling him, the Kraut was going to steal his thunder.

The other big headache was the chairman. Dorning's demands were getting too much. He'd heard that that slag Carla had set her cap at him, but he knew she wouldn't satisfy the chairman's demands for long. Clive used Andy's past against him but Andy had only ever given women what they had asked for. There was no comparison. The man was an animal and his appetite endless. Andy knew he had signed a pact with the devil.

Eventually somebody would talk. And he had no doubt that the finger would be left pointing at him. He wished Loulou were home. Right now she was the best thing in his life – and it wasn't often he felt that way about her.

He fixed himself a drink and started to climb the stairs, pulling at his clothes on the way. He'd run himself a bath and then sink into bed. It had been ages since he'd had a proper night's sleep.

By the time he reached the bathroom door, he was naked and his glass empty. Intending to run back down and fetch the bottle he turned but then stopped as he heard voices coming from the bathroom. One was Loulou's, the other – American and female – he didn't recognise.

He turned the handle slowly and opened the door. The L-shaped room was heavy with steam and the scent of bergamot. He thought he heard splashing coming from the tub, which was concealed at the bottom of the L, and the American's voice was now loud, impassioned.

'Loulou?'

She didn't reply. Andy crept along to the end of the room and turned the corner, dismayed by the sight that met his eyes.

'Loulou! I can't believe you'd be so stupid.'

Loulou sat up in the Japanese wooden tub and rubbed her eyes. 'What? Oh, Andy. I was asleep.'

Andy switched off the TV, which was perched on a shelf on the wall. 'You could drown doing that.'

'Don't be so melodramatic. Hey, I was watching that. It's a tape of the interview. By now I should have been syndicated from New York to LA.' She splashed him. 'God I'm fabulous.'

'You're drunk as well.'

'Pappy Eskapa's Moonshine, would you believe?' Loulou reached out and stroked Andy's stomach. 'Mmm, looking good.' Andy went to climb in but she stopped him. 'Uh-uh, shower first – you know the rules.'

As its makers intended, Loulou would allow nothing in the bath but water and clean bodies. Bubble bath and scum were not allowed to ruin its pure Japanese aesthetic.

'Well, forget it. You can be really cold, you know that?'

'Meret Lee doesn't think so,' Loulou said, standing

up and signalling for Andy to hand her a towel. 'She liked my aura.'

'Is she still on heroin?' Andy threw the towel at her and turned on the shower.

'I can't hear you,' Loulou shouted as she walked into the bedroom.

As Andy stepped into the shower, hot jets of water assaulted him from all angles and he moaned with relief. After it had worked its magic, he followed Loulou's steps. 'I said is she still a smack head?'

'No,' Loulou said, and Andy noted a certain defensiveness in her voice. 'She's . . . she's really special.'

'Don't tell me she managed to suck you in? She's only here to promote Neurofister's greatest hits. It's her pension plan.'

'I haven't seen you for days,' Loulou said, curled up in her towel on the bed, 'and when you do finally turn up, all you can do is snipe. Why are you being so negative?'

'When's your flight?' he asked, not wanting to be drawn in to discussing his problems.

'It's not until late afternoon. I'm surprised you even remembered I was going to LA. Oh, I've just realised why you're cranky – you're going to miss me, aren't you?'

'Maybe.' He was happy to let her think that. In any case, it was in part true.

Loulou softened suddenly. 'It's only for a few weeks – I'll be back before you know it. I've got such a good feeling about this film.'

Andy sat beside her. 'You're going to be great.'

She knelt up and began massaging his shoulders. 'Wow, you're really knotted. Are you sure you couldn't get away for a few days? Come over and see me. I'll be stuck on my own most of the time.'

'I can't do that,' he groaned, his body responding to her touch. 'That's so good.'

Loulou slipped her hand into his lap, feeling his hardness. 'I can tell,' she whispered in his ear. 'And I know what would really make it better.' With that she slipped off the bed, turned on all the video cameras, dropped her towel and shouted, 'Roll 'em.'

Chapter Twelve

The bedroom was shrouded in darkness, the bedside clock the only sign that it was daytime. For Jenny days blended into nights, punctuated only by Michael leaving and returning.

Jenny raised the bottle of vodka to her lips and drank directly from it. Since the night at the Three Lions she had given up on the Antabuse and just gone for abuse instead. There seemed no point in trying to stop. It wouldn't make Michael love or respect her – the other night was proof of that – and it certainly wouldn't nullify the past. And of course, she consoled herself as she took another hit, there was some fun to it.

Her thoughts turned briefly to Clive. She cursed him for blighting her life – and now he acted as though she were the one at fault, an embarrassment to be barely tolerated.

Families. She despised them – and yet it was a family she wanted more than anything else. Or rather a child she could love and who would love her back. Unconditionally. If she had someone to love she could give up the drink and the drugs. There would be a point to living. She even believed that she could right the wrongs of the past.

'Ha,' she said, her voice exploding into the darkness. What kind of mother did she really think she'd make? In her mind's eye she saw herself tottering down the road in high heels, barely dressed in Versace, hanging on to a bottle of vodka and pushing a pram. Who was she kidding?

Another line of coke was what she needed. As the razor clicked against the mirror she couldn't help but remember an earlier self. An innocent little girl anxious to please. Jenny had spent her childhood striving for her father's attention, to no avail.

Even Clive had joined her in jumping through hoops for the tiniest hint of affection. In the end she had felt like a performing bear who was still whipped despite its best performance. Their father had seemed incapable of any emotion. Business was his only love, his family a necessity. Their mother had slowly wilted under his harshness, and by the time she died she had become an empty shell, merely going through the motions of living. Like Jenny herself really.

This insight was one she could do without. She snorted two lines of coke in quick succession. The inside of her nose protested briefly before she felt the powder burn the back of her throat. Then a warm, comforting and all-too-familiar sensation coursed through her brain.

But uncomfortable thoughts of her childhood still stalked her mind. It was a lost childhood – there were no slumber parties where she whispered through the night with girlfriends about who fancied which Osmond or whether David Cassidy was really better than all five of them. There had been no music in her house. What did it matter that she had been given everything a child could possibly want materially? What use were the expensive toys, the foreign holidays, the fast cars, the big boats when there was no love?

And what, she wanted to scream, was different now? Even in the darkness she could see the riches she had fed herself – jewellery, clothes, ornaments – in an attempt to fill up the void.

A movement outside the door made her look up. She squinted as light from the hallway flooded the room. Leaning against the doorframe, Michael glanced at his wife and then at the coke. Slamming the door, he strode over to the bed and snatched the mirror from her hand.

As the drug took effect, Michael's frown slowly dissolved. 'Hi,' he said.

'How's it going?' Jenny murmured, moving closer to him.

'Fine.'

Jenny placed her hand on his. To her surprise he left it there. Seeing her chance, she lifted her hand and began to undo the buttons of his shirt, gaining more confidence as she moved down his body. He offered no resistance as she unzipped his trousers. Naked, he lay back on the bed.

Jenny kept on her silk robe, grateful for the darkness, which hid the ravages of the last few days. Fearing Michael's impatience she quickly dabbed her finger in the coke and rubbed it gently around the head of his penis. He grunted with pleasure and the more she touched him the harder he became.

For a fleeting moment his face wore the expression of a younger, gentler Michael. But Jenny knew her eyes were deceiving her. What he had put her through at the Three Lions was unforgivable. Yet she wanted to forgive him. To start again. Or perhaps she just wanted sex. It was easy to confuse it with love.

And like the alcohol and the coke and the shopping, Jenny used sex as an analgesic. With sex she gave herself up to the moment – thoughts fell away, the scathing internal voice stopped; there was no future to worry about and definitely no past.

But today, even as she placed Michael's hand between her thighs, thoughts about the night at the club refused to be banished. Something nagged at the fringes of her mind but refused to give itself up. Like a word she knew but couldn't recall.

As Michael's fingers slid into her she tried to picture the same happening at the club. She knew his body so well, the weight of it, every muscular curve, yet she had no recollection of him that night. Either the drink and the pills had really knocked her out or, for once, her mind had been considerate and left her no memories.

Michael's fingers became more insistent and Jenny finally felt the coke and the sex taking over as each sensation became more intense than the last.

They grappled with each other, rolling across the bed. Her damp, hot skin chafing against his. She bit his neck, tasting cK One and the saltiness of his sweat. He was bearing down on top of her, making it hard for her to move her body. Fighting or fucking – sometimes it was hard to tell the difference. She wanted him inside her. 'Now,' she begged.

Michael shifted his body until he was behind her. Both gasped as his penis drove into her. The harder

Michael thrust the more Jenny felt alive. Finally, their orgasms erupted as violently as they were conceived, leaving both breathless and dazed.

Michael flopped back on to the bed and Jenny lay down by his side, her breathing laboured. It always amazed her how, at times, sex with Michael could still blow her mind. Of course, it always had coke as a fuse.

Before the moment could be destroyed Jenny began to speak. 'Michael, I . . . you . . .' she began haltingly and then took a deep breath. 'I really think if we had a baby it would make things right. Something for us to share, to care—'

Nothing could have prepared her for his reaction.

'Have a baby with *you*?' he screamed in her face. 'I wouldn't have a baby with you if you were the last cunt on earth.'

Chapter Thirteen

'How's Robbie Jnr getting on with his alphabet?' The woman's voice was raised so she could be heard above the cacophony of twenty paint-splattered under-fives.

Rachel delayed answering. After going to her local playgroup three times a week for six months, she knew better than to treat it as an innocent question.

Nearly every mother she had encountered thought their child was the most intelligent, the best looking and the greatest son or daughter a parent could have. And none hid their little lights under bushels. Each meeting entailed a catalogue of their latest achievements and an inquisition into the defects of the competition. Their rivalry almost superseded that of the Notting Hill women.

Rachel just couldn't match the one-upmanship. And the way her little Robbie behaved when he was there wasn't much to boast about anyway. She turned to the woman who had asked the question. 'Not too bad,' was all she could manage.

On the other side of the room, one of the woman's over-dressed daughters let out an ear-piercing scream. Rachel's joy at the distraction soon turned to dismay when she saw Robbie Jnr using his teeth to take a chunk out of the little girl's leg. It was time to go home.

Dragging his heels along the newly built roads with their pristine, modern houses, Robbie Jnr whined and cried to be picked up. In the end, as always, Rachel gave in to his demands. Like father, like son, she mused, breaking into a sweat.

Once home, her son wandered off into the garden to inflict death on anything that moved. With Demi at a school friend's for tea, the house was unusually quiet, and Rachel grabbed the opportunity to finish her latest Danielle Steele.

She knew she should try to give up her romantic novels, aware that sometimes she used them in the same way Jenny Waite used drink – to escape life. Although her 'vice' didn't cause her to behave badly. Or did it? Rachel had tried to forget Chris Leonard, but whenever she was reading her books the hero took on Chris's face, his mannerisms, his voice.

Why couldn't she just be happy? Especially now Robbie was calming down. In fact, he seemed a bit subdued, he hadn't even wanted his tea last night. Perhaps he was more upset than he let on about the fight between Michael and Andy. It still made her shudder to think about it.

Or perhaps, she thought, putting down her book, he was worried about this season. His form hadn't been great in the last two matches. The tune of 'You'll Never Walk Alone' disturbed her thoughts. She hated the doorbell but it was the one thing Robbie had added to the house.

'I don't want anything,' she practised out loud as she walked to the front door. Rachel was hopeless when it came to turning away hawkers, whether they were selling double glazing, dishcloths or God.

'I don't . . .' she said as she opened the door and then stopped. 'Chris!'

'R . . . Rachel is . . . is Robbie in?' he asked and then added hurriedly. 'He isn't at the club.'

'No, he's not. Sorry you've had a wasted journey,' she replied formally.

Chris responded with a quizzical look.

Rachel didn't know what to say. It seemed ridiculous not to invite him in; after all, they had been close friends in Wigan, but a nagging voice told her it wasn't the old times she wanted.

In the ensuing silence Rachel looked at Chris as if she had never seen him before. She saw how dark and smooth his skin was, his white T-shirt emphasising not only his colour but his muscular body.

As he shifted nervously from foot to foot all Rachel could think about was how it would feel to have his powerful arms around her, to kiss his sensual lips. 'Come in,' she murmured.

Chris followed her through to the kitchen where she fussed with the kettle, the teapot and the teabags, all the while painfully aware of his proximity.

Rachel kept her back to him, knowing she looked a sight. Her fine fair hair had lost any semblance of its style, while her floral dress looked like an old rag. If only she had known he was coming.

'Nice place,' he said, looking around the country pine kitchen. 'God! Is that Robbie Jnr? I wouldn't have recognised him.'

The mention of her son brought Rachel back to earth. Whatever had she been thinking of? This man wouldn't be interested in her, and she definitely shouldn't be interested in him.

'That's him all right. The little tyke. Do you still take two sugars?'

'Good memory.' His tone was intimate, as if there was more significance to what she had asked.

As Rachel passed him his cup, their hands touched, an innocent gesture that filled Rachel with a longing she had never before felt.

They both began to talk at once. 'You first,' Rachel said, noting that Chris was once again shifting from foot to foot.

But it was Robbie Jnr who spoke next – or rather wailed through the kitchen window. 'Mummy, I've been bit. Mummy!'

'OK, OK, I'm coming. Excuse me a minute,' she said to Chris, running out the door.

In the garden she kissed and consoled her son, aware all the time that it wasn't him she was thinking about.

It occurred to her that her attraction to Chris might just be a bout of silly rebelliousness against her parents. Her father, a tax inspector, and her mother, a happy housewife for thirty years, had had only one ambition for their children – ordinariness. When Rachel had married Robbie, their reaction had been one of horror. How could she marry a man who didn't wear a suit or go to an office every day?

Despite this glitch, Rachel had gone on to become as ordinary as was possible. Yet there had always been a part of her that craved something more, something dangerous. She imagined her parents meeting Chris, a black footballer, and laughed.

'What's funny, Mummy?' Robbie Jnr asked, jumping off her lap.

'Nothing. Go and play on the swing and leave the insects alone.' She stood up and walked slowly back to the house. Seeing Chris watching her through the window, she realised her parents had nothing to do with her feelings.

'I hadn't just called around to see Robbie. I wanted to see you,' Chris said as soon as she walked through the door.

Rachel's heart began to pound. 'I don't—'

'We had great times in Wigan, didn't we?' he said, interrupting her. 'I'd really like it if we could pick up where we left off. Be friends, good friends. You're one of the few genuine people I've met,' he finished.

She tried to hide her disappointment. No claims of undying love then. Or how he had come to London only to be near her. Just friendship. Good old boring Rachel. She was dismayed at her feelings, being a romance junkie was definitely damaging to her health. And then she noticed his dark brooding eyes, the colour of bark, gazing intently at her.

The moment was broken by the bell and its awful tune.

Rachel hurried to the door. Such was her frustration, she had no doubt she could quickly see off whoever was there. But she was in for her second shock of the day. Standing in front of her, red faced and panting, was Robbie's mother. By her feet lay two ominous battered suitcases.

'Ma, what are you doing here?'

'No hello, then, or come in you must have had a terrible journey,' Mary snapped, attempting to get round the side of Rachel. 'Out the way for heaven's sake.'

Rachel moved. 'Ma, why are you here?'

'Which room is mine?' Mary asked, ignoring the question. 'Don't tell me you forgot I was moving in. Robbie arranged it weeks ago. Even you can't be that featherbrained.'

'He never told me,' Rachel exclaimed, panic in her voice.

'I'm sure he did. Still, don't matter, does it? I'm here now.'

'Is anything wrong, Rachel?' Chris asked, walking into the hallway.

Mary stopped at the bottom of the stairs. 'And who's this when he's at home?' she said, not even attempting to hide her disapproval.

Rachel blushed. 'It's Chris Leonard. You must remember him from Wigan? He's a friend of Robbie's.'

Mary looked suspiciously from Rachel to Chris. 'Can't say I do. Anyway Robbie's not here is he? So we won't be keeping you, young man. Rachel and I have some unpacking to do.'

'It's all right, Rachel. I'll see myself out,' he said, smiling and giving her hand a hidden squeeze.

'I'll have another,' Robbie said, handing his glass to the barman. While he waited for his drink he looked around the room. Bojangles was the latest wine bar to open on the Isle of Dogs. It had been an old-fashioned pub in its previous life, but having had everything ripped out, it now had pretensions towards modernism.

The bar had become Robbie's regular watering hole

and a few of the other regulars nodded at him as he passed. They all knew who he was and treated him accordingly. It still gave him a thrill that he was a recognisable face and he liked all the little bonuses that fame brought him.

He studied his fellow drinkers. Most were city types, dressed in formal suits with the ubiquitous mobile phone stuck to their ears. Robbie was glad he didn't have to wear a suit; he was quite happy wearing tracksuit bottoms and a T-shirt whatever the occasion.

Glancing at himself in the enormous gilt mirror behind the bar he wondered if his shoulder-length hair needed cutting. Perhaps a shorter cut would make him appear older than his twenty-six years. But then it suited his purposes to look young.

'Thanks. A bit empty today,' he said as the barman returned.

'It was busy lunchtime. The usual suspects,' the barman replied, smiling.

Robbie smirked in reply. The sign over the door of Bojangles said 'Over 21s Only', which made it all the more attractive to underage teenagers and therefore more attractive to Robbie. At lunchtimes the bar filled up with giggling schoolgirls hiding their uniforms under overcoats and macks.

'Must have sold a lot of orange juice then.'

The barman laughed. 'How do you think you'll do on Saturday?'

Robbie filled him in on the latest news from Notting Hill. He was always striking up conversations and he knew people thought of him as a good sort and down to earth. The truth was he couldn't stand being on his own.

Being on your own wasn't good, he'd decided, and he was glad Rachel would have company now his mother was staying. He hoped his mother had arrived safely; he'd offered to pick her up from the station but she'd insisted on getting a taxi. That's what he loved about his mum – she never wanted to put anyone out.

Rachel had been a bit strange lately. Perhaps with another woman to talk to she would get back to her old self. Robbie thought about the last week and how she had taken to reading out long extracts from her damned romances. He always took it as a slight about his illiteracy when she insisted on reading to him.

Then the other night she had read out a whole article on female orgasms. Robbie was at a loss as to why she had felt the need. There were no complaints in the bed area as far as he could see. Most times she said she was too tired anyway.

But then he had given up trying to work out what women wanted. Take Jenny, she always seemed up for it, especially the other night at the Three Lions. But who knew? He didn't like to think about Jenny. The whole business had left a nasty taste in his mouth. Robbie liked women to be uncomplicated.

Just then the door of the bar opened and Robbie grinned at the familiar face.

Chapter Fourteen

'Did I tell you I sent Loulou a card?' Tanya said, as David's E Type Jag navigated the rutted lane that led to their favourite picnicking spot. 'Let her know that people back here are rooting for her.'

David braked and squeezed her knee. 'That was really nice of you.'

'Well, I know what it's like when you're away from home on a shoot.' She tried picturing herself in Loulou's shoes. There was a big difference between Hollywood and the draughty little photographic studios she worked in. And she bet Loulou never opened her eyes on the set to find the cameraman masturbating. Sometimes she wondered where the glamour in glamour modelling actually was.

'Are you sure you don't mind coming here again?' David asked, getting out of the car.

'Of course not.'

They came here to Epping whenever they got the chance, which this season hadn't been often. David was a creature of habit, and she liked that dependability. Some women might find it boring but not her. Neither of them worked in the most stable career and the sense of order he established was one of the things she loved most about him. David was never going to shock her, she was sure of it.

Knowing how much he valued their time together, she'd dropped her plans to throw a big surprise party for his birthday in a few days' time. As much as she would have loved organising it, she knew he would hate a fuss. Perhaps they could just celebrate it in bed.

Tanya took a bag, containing her sketch pad and some charcoals, from the back seat of the car while David picked up the rug and the hamper. 'I love it here,' she said.

'We could have just gone for a meal somewhere and then gone clubbing tonight – if you'd wanted.'

She kissed him.

'What was that for?' he asked.

'For being the most perfect man in the world.'

Unlike most of the other players from Notting Hill, David didn't want to spend his days off in places like the Three Lions, always being the footballer, on show and one of the lads. That was just the way she wanted it too. Going out in public could be a nightmare. Men, especially when they were drunk, could turn nasty. Hers was such a familiar face (and body) that they often seemed to think they owned a part of her. Worst of all were the ones who thought that because she undressed for a living she was easy.

As they walked through the woods, she looked across at David. He still had the faraway look in his eyes she'd noticed earlier. Almost glazed over.

She stroked his cheek. 'You're grinding your teeth again.'

David forced a smile. 'Better?'

'A little.' His forehead was as furrowed as ever, but the smiles were so rare at the moment, she was grateful for small mercies. 'What about here?' she asked as they came to a clearing. To one side was a stream, reduced to just a trickle in the heat, and beyond that an area covered in waist-high ferns, where they'd made passionate, abandoned love.

'Fine,' David said. 'Whatever you want.'

He laid out the rug and Tanya unpacked the hamper. As always they'd stopped first at the Marks and Spencer in Mare Street to buy the food and wine. They bought practically the same thing every time. David liked it that way. No surprises.

They ate in silence, content in each other's company. Throughout they would, quite unconsciously, reach out and touch one another, a hand on the arm, a foot rubbing against a foot. Bliss, Tanya thought.

David trudged through the bracken, swiping at the branches in front of him. He needed to get as far away from Tanya as possible. Not because he didn't want to be with her – he ached to be with her every second of the day – but because he feared he might let it all spill out. He could barely stop himself from telling her. And then what? It would all be over.

The look on Jenny's face that night in the Three Lions. The smell of alcohol and vomit. The confusion, the struggle, the cries for help. Everything went round and round in his head. It was the first thing that came to him in the morning, his last conscious thought at night.

He had to stop this. He had to think of Notting Hill. The team, the Cup, his job – they were more important. If the team fell to pieces because he couldn't handle this crisis, then they'd lose the Cup and his job would be on the line. And then he could never marry Tanya. But how could he marry her now in light of what had happened?

David sat down on an upended tree and put his head in his hands. He tugged at his hair, as if he could pull every bad thought out of his head. Jenny's torn stockings, her skirt up round her waist. A handful of hair came away in his fingers and he howled.

'Tanya, I'm sorry,' he shouted up into the trees.

Tanya put down her charcoal and listened. It had sounded like David calling her but now all she could hear was birdsong. Her fingers were covered in charcoal and there were smudges on her T-shirt and, she thought, no doubt on her face. It was nice, she reflected, not to have to worry about her appearance for a change.

She looked at what she'd drawn. Although she was working from life, by the time the image passed through her retina, mixed with her imagination and emerged through her fingers it had the same haunting, unreal quality as her more abstract designs. Nothing about the 'real life' Tanya was represented in her pictures.

She worked on, unaware that the sun had moved and she was now sitting directly in the light, until the whiteness of the paper began to burn her eyes. Putting the pad to one side, she poured herself the last of the wine and looked around to see if she could see any sign of David.

On these days out, he would often go off alone. He liked the solace of the woods – it was a good place to plan for the team. Though she was concerned that sometimes he cared too much, she had to admit that it pleased her that work was so important to him. She'd grown up around hard grafters – her dad, her brothers – and they had shaped her image of the way men should be.

Tanya spotted David coming through the trees. He was holding something in his hand, and as he drew closer she realised it was a bunch of daisies, dirt still clinging to the roots.

'You darling,' she said, as he handed them to her. 'What are these for?'

'For being the most perfect girl in the world,' David said, his jaw as rigid as when he'd left.

'I'm a woman,' she said, smiling.

'You'll always be my girl.' David swallowed nervously, and then, out of the blue, blurted out, 'Tanya, will you marry me?'

'Not until you've made your first million,' she laughed, and then she caught the earnest look on his face. 'You silly bugger, you mean it, don't you?'

'I want you to be my wife.'

From the days of Stephen Butler, her first boyfriend at school, when she'd cover her roughbook with her signature, Mrs Tanya Butler, she'd dreamed of the moment a man would say those words to her. And she wanted David more than anybody else to ask her. She wanted to be David's wife, longed for it, and yet she couldn't say that simple word.

'David, this . . . it's knocked me for six. I don't know what to say.'

David's features were now so tense she wondered if his face might break. 'Say yes. Please, Tanya.'

'This is so out of the blue. Of course I've thought

about it. I think you're the man I want to marry, no, I *know* you are, but I thought this would all come one day in the future. You know, when we're sure, really, really sure.'

David knelt down on one knee. 'I've never been more certain about anything. I love you and I want to marry you.'

She looked into his eyes, searching for any flicker of doubt. If there was any she couldn't see it, her own eyes clouded as they were with happiness. 'Then the answer's yes.'

'You mean it?' David looked at her in disbelief.

'Yes, you soppy sod, I mean it. I want to be Mrs Tanya Ashby.'

David picked her up in his arms and spun round. 'Tan, you've made me the happiest man in the world.'

She was spinning so fast she couldn't see that the expression on his face said otherwise. 'Mrs Tanya Ashby,' she shouted at the top of her voice. 'Or then again,' she added, 'what about Mr David Barry?'

David stopped spinning and put her down. 'If that's what you want . . .'

'Don't be stupid. Anyway it sounds horrible.'

David sat down on the rug. 'Wait till I tell the boys.'

'You mustn't,' she said quickly.

'What's up? Having second thoughts already?'

'Not at all. But I just want us to enjoy it at the moment. As soon as it gets out it won't be ours any more. It'll be all over the papers. We'll be running from photographers for days. I want us to go out and choose a ring in private, I don't want the *Sun* breathing down our necks as we're doing it.'

David appeared mollified. 'Like I said, whatever you want.'

He kissed her and they lay down on the rug. David began to lift her T-shirt over her head.

'Not here,' she whispered. 'What if someone sees us?'

'I don't care,' David declared, massaging her breasts in his big hands.

'Then neither do I,' she said, resting back on her elbows.

He nestled his head in her cleavage and she felt his tongue, slightly dry and sand-papery, against her sternum. Like a cat, she thought. 'I bet you wouldn't marry me if I didn't have these.'

'You got me there. To have and to hold – that's what it says.'

She lifted her hips so that he could pull off her jeans, and he threw them into the ferns, followed soon by her knickers. Then his own clothes, and they rolled naked around the clearing, their bodies locked together in all-consuming love.

Well, I was wrong, Tanya thought, her legs wrapped around his buttocks, forcing him deeper into her, he did surprise me.

Chapter Fifteen

Loulou stepped out of soundstage number seven and into the airless LA morning. The fierce sunlight dazzled her eyes and she thought about going back for her sunglasses but instead, wearing a wrap over her costume – a grey silk teddy – she wandered the lot looking for some shade. She could already feel the sun burning her face and Parker Gooch, the director, had been quite specific about her creamy English rose complexion. Spotting a row of palms lining the edge of the car park, she lit a cigarette and ran to take cover.

She'd been told to be in make-up at six, and now, three and a half hours later, not a single person, aside from the hairdresser, had spoken to her and not a single frame of film had been shot.

She yawned – a mixture of boredom and nerves – and took her script out of her bag. Hers was a bedroom scene and although most of her lines were limited to orgasmic grunts, she did have a speech at the beginning that covered two pages. Normally a single glance at her lines was enough to commit them to memory but for some reason these just wouldn't stick.

Reading through the scene a couple of times, and still none the wiser, she threw down the script and retrieved some mail from her bag. There was a letter from her agent asking her to reconsider her decision about *Sorted!*, a couple of telegrams from friends and the usual fan mail.

She picked up an envelope with a London postcode. Inside there was a good luck card, with a fluffy bunny holding a horseshoe and a four-leaf clover. Nobody she knew would dream of exhibiting such bad taste and it came as no surprise to see that it was from Tanya Barry. Laughing at the terrible handwriting, with its circles dotting the 'i's, and little smiley face in the 'y' of the signature, Loulou tore it in half.

'Lou, Mr Gooch wants you on the set – like five minutes ago,' a breathless runner called from the other side of the car park.

'My name's Loulou!' she shouted to the back of his head. A quick look at the Hollywood sign looming above her in the hills reminded her what was at stake and she ran after him.

Parker Gooch looked up as Loulou entered the sound stage. Although he had to be in his fifties, Gooch was every inch the Californian surf god and health freak. Toned, tanned, blond hair tied back in a ponytail, he had started the day, as always, with a T'ai Chi lesson.

Loulou ignored the director's disapproving look. 'Is Ethan here yet?' she asked.

Ethan Mead was the star of the movie. Only just twenty-three, he was already amongst the top ten Hollywood earners. His last film, *Hard Justice*, had made over two hundred million dollars at the box office and Loulou was hoping some of his stardom would rub off on her.

'No, this is just a walk-though with his stand-in. Paul, could you show Lou her mark?'

After another half-hour of waiting, as Gooch and the lighting director discussed angles, the director was finally ready to press ahead with Loulou's big speech.

Seated at a vanity unit, she had a long monologue about the failure of her relationship with Booker, the character Ethan Mead was playing. By the end of the scene the couple would be back in bed together.

'Who am I meant to interact with?' she asked.

'Lou, it doesn't matter, the camera's on you,' Gooch, seated on a camera crane, said.

'Loulou!' she corrected under her breath.

The lights were turned on, a clapperboard snapped in front of her face and Gooch shouted, 'Action!'

Loulou began to make up her face, which was difficult given the thick layer of foundation she was already wearing. She tried to think of her lines but her mind was a total blank. She could feel the anticipation growing as the crew waited for her to start speaking and she tried desperately to visualise the script. If only she could remember the opening sequence.

'And cut! Is there a problem, Lou?'

'I'm sorry. I'm sorry.' Loulou could feel herself turning crimson.

'OK, let's go again.'

The camera started a slow pan around her and she picked up an eye pencil. But still the lines wouldn't come to her. How did it bloody start?

'Cut! Lou, do you need to look at a script, baby?'

Loulou squinted into the dazzling lights. 'No, I'm fine – just a bit of first-night nerves.'

'Let's go straight into it again.'

Loulou took a deep breath. '"Booker, it isn't about love, it never was. I'm . . ."' Her tongue felt like a piece of carpet in her mouth. Snatches of the script came to her but she couldn't make any sense of them.

'Cut!' Gooch jumped down off the crane. 'Would somebody get her a script?'

A script was thrust into Loulou's hand but the words on the page might as well have been hiero-glyphics. She made a show of studying them for a couple of minutes, but as soon as the cameras started rolling she was once again mute.

After take seventeen, Gooch called for a break. Loulou stumbled off the set to her dressing room, expecting the director to follow and offer words of comfort. But he didn't, and the lack of communication served only to freeze her more.

After twenty minutes alone, panic began to set in. She was blowing it before it even began.

A sharp knock at the door startled her. The runner flew in. 'Lou?'

'Are we starting again? I think I'm OK now.'

'Mr Gooch is calling it a day. Same time tomorrow.' The door banged shut.

Feeling totally humiliated, Loulou threw on her clothes and raced out of the building, not even bother-ing to take off her make-up. She just wanted to get away from the studio as quickly as possible.

As she paced up and down the car park, waiting for her driver, a wardrobe girl passed with a rail of clothes, did a double-take and stopped.

'I love you!' she declared. 'You're one of my favour-ites.'

'Thanks,' Loulou said, surprised that the woman had ever seen *Sorted!* 'You're the first friendly voice I've heard all day.'

'And that husband of yours – I love his music!' She started to sing. '*'Cos after all, you're my Wonderwall . . .*'

By the second week of filming, things were beginning to look dire. Although Loulou finally learned her lines, rumours were flying that the producers were extremely unhappy with the dailies. Gooch said little aside from giving her basic directions and Ethan Mead spent all of his time off camera with his Stanislavsky coach. Loulou felt totally isolated.

Matters went from bad to worse on the Thursday when an unexpected visitor arrived on the set. Loulou had just finished a scene set on a New York rooftop when she spotted a handsome middle-aged woman with long, brown, centre-parted hair and dressed in a paisley smock and ethnic jewellery smothering the director in kisses.

'Mother!' she called. 'What a pleasant surprise!' The sarcasm in her tone was unmistakable.

'I didn't know this was your mother,' Gooch said, amazed. 'Laura and I go back a long way. But we haven't seen each other in years.'

'Altamont – that was the last time,' Laura recalled. 'Wasn't it just awful?'

'It felt like the world was ending,' Gooch agreed.

Good grief, Loulou thought. 'So, Laura, what brings you here? Surely you're not laying *another* wreath on Jerry Garcia's grave?' From the day Loulou had married Oran O'Keefe, the two women had barely exchanged a civil word.

Laura pursed her lipstick-free lips and narrowed her eyes. 'I'm on my way to San Francisco. I thought you'd be pleased.'

'That you're on your way to San Francisco? I am. But if you are going – be sure to wear some flowers in your hair.' She turned to leave. 'If you'll excuse me I need to change. I'm sure you two have lots to catch up on.'

As Loulou walked away, her mother shouted after her, 'Your brother's here.'

Loulou spun round. 'Dexter? Why didn't you tell me? Where is he?'

'He's waiting outside – I came in first to check it was OK to bring him in. We're . . .'

Loulou didn't hear the rest of the sentence as she raced outside. There, leaning against a wall was the ten-year-old boy who meant more to her than anyone, or anything, in the world. Sweeping him up in her arms, she smothered him with kisses.

'Dexter! I can't believe you're here,' she said, crushing him in her arms. 'I'm so happy to see you.'

'Mummy says we're not staying long,' the boy said, struggling to breathe. 'We've got a plane to catch.'

'Let her go on alone,' Loulou said, releasing him. 'Stay with me for a few days.'

'She said you'd say that – I can't. She's singing somewhere and she wants me with her.'

Loulou ran her fingers through the boy's blond bowl-cut hair. He looked just as she had at the same age and it tore her apart to think how much of his life she was missing. She took hold of his hand and together they walked through the lot.

'Daddy sends his love,' the boy said. 'He said you

should come over for the summer. I wish you would as well.'

Loulou noted a slight Spanish lilt to his otherwise cut-glass accent. 'I promise I'll try.' She knew that she wouldn't last a day under the same roof as her mother. 'You can always come to stay with me in London. I mean that – if ever it gets too much for you there.'

'Mummy's not been around much this year,' he said, catching her drift. 'And you know Daddy, he spends all of his time in the studio. I get to do what I want really.'

Loulou pictured him wandering on the beach by himself. They were neglecting him – just as they had neglected her. Nothing was more important to them, she thought angrily, than their insatiable need for celebrity, the irony of her thoughts totally escaping her.

'So how do you like being on a film set?' she asked.

'It's all right. Is Arnold Schwarzenegger here?'

'I'm not sure – we could go and look on the other stages.'

'No, I hate him. Jim Carey's my favourite.' Dexter did an impression of Ace Ventura, Pet Detective and doubled up with laughter. 'He's brilliant.'

Loulou laughed too – her first moment of happiness since she'd arrived in LA. But the laughter was tinged with sadness. Stopping by like this, in between flights, was unbearably cruel of her mother. Loulou guessed this was exactly as she'd intended.

'Would you like some ice cream?'

Dexter looked torn. 'Mummy said we'd be only a few minutes – I can't really go off.'

'Next time, then,' Loulou said, feeling the sadness envelop her fully.

They walked back to the soundstage, where Gooch and her mother were still reminiscing.

'If you can remember the sixties, you weren't really there, eh?' Loulou interjected sarcastically.

'Your mother is one of the most amazing women I have ever met,' the director declared.

'Astounding,' Loulou said.

'Totally,' Gooch said.

Typically American, Loulou thought. Total irony by-pass. 'Dexter says you've got to go soon.'

Laura looked at her watch. 'Goodness yes. But, Loulou, I did want a word with you. In private.'

Loulou led her mother to her dressing room. Dexter tagged along behind but Laura made him wait outside the door.

'How much do you want?' Loulou asked without preamble. It had to be about money. Just like everybody else, her mother had bought into all the lies in the media about the huge settlement she'd supposedly received from Oran.

Laura opened her battered old carpet bag and took out some papers. 'I see there's no point in going round the houses. I'd like you to look over these business plans. I'm thinking of going into antiques.'

Loulou had been through this many times before. 'It'll go belly up just like all your other schemes. I'm not interested.'

Laura adopted a mask of sincerity. 'Loulou, I'll be honest with you. Daddy isn't selling as well as he was and the record company's not sure if it will renew my contract. I'm not so worried about us – you know

Daddy and I, we can live like peasants – I just don't want Dexter to miss out on the things we were able to give you. We'd like him to go away to school next year and—'

Loulou stood up. 'Mother, just stop it! I'm sick of you using Dexter to get at me. I knew there had to be a reason why you had him with you.'

'What do you mean?' Laura asked, agitated. 'I wanted him to experience Monterey at sunset. Feed the seals in Carmel. You loved Big Sur, remember?'

'Oh, cut the crap. You'll spend all your time in San Francisco shacked up with one of those awful groupies of yours and Dexter is going to be a massive inconvenience. He's here as emotional leverage, pure and simple.'

'That's not true,' Laura said, looking as if she'd been slapped.

'You have all the maternal instinct of a bluebottle.'

Finally, her mother's hippy cool evaporated completely. 'Well that's rich coming from you,' she hissed. 'You of all people. How you have the nerve! There's nothing I wouldn't do for that boy.'

'Keep your voice down,' Loulou ordered. 'I don't want him to hear this.'

'I bet you don't, Missy. I'm sure there's a lot you don't want him to hear.'

Loulou grabbed at a hairbrush and hurled it at her mother. 'You bitch. You hateful, hateful bitch.'

The door burst open and Dexter rushed in with his hands over his ears. 'Stop it, you two. Please stop it.'

'Dexter, I'm sorry,' Loulou said, dropping to her knees and putting her arms around him.

'Come on, darling.' Laura grabbed his hand. 'We're not wanted here.'

Loulou held on to the bewildered boy. 'You know I'll always want you,' she cried.

'Come on!' Laura pulled harder and Loulou had no choice but to let him go.

As the child was dragged away, Loulou sat back on the dressing-room floor and sobbed.

'Cut!' Parker Gooch screamed. 'What's wrong with you *now*?'

Loulou tried to rub the dust out of her eyes. They were filming along an empty stretch of highway not far from Joshua Tree in the Mojave Desert. The wind, at first a welcome relief from the suffocating heat, was now whipping up the sand and it hurt like hell as it rained against her skin. She couldn't see where she was walking and several times she'd brushed painfully against the Cholla cacti dotting the landscape.

'I've got something in my foot,' she said, spitting sand from her mouth. 'Can't I do this scene with shoes on?'

'Have you read the fuckin' script?' Gooch bellowed. 'You threw them out of the car two hundred miles back.'

'Mr Gooch,' she said, picking a cactus spine from her sole, 'with your God-given Oscar-winning talents, I'm sure it's not beyond you to frame me above the knee.'

Ethan Mead lay back on the bonnet of the red convertible and hooted. Loulou glared at him and turned back to face the director. Ever since the day her mother had turned up, Gooch had been increasingly intolerant of her, picking holes in her performance at every opportunity. It dawned on her that Gooch had probably been one of her mother's many lovers and was still very much in her thrall.

A hush descended on the crew as they waited to see what Gooch would do next.

'Loulou,' he said, taking off his sunglasses and staring her in the eye, 'I've been in this business for thirty-five years. I'll thank you to not tell me where I should put my camera. I can hide your feet – no problem. It's your crummy performance I'm having difficulty covering up.'

His words stung Loulou more than the sand. She looked around, trying to search out one friendly face who would come to her defence. Nobody said a word. 'That's so unfair,' she said quietly, knowing better than to bawl out the director. She needed this part too badly to blow it with a display of temperament.

Gooch wasn't even listening. 'OK, people, that's it. We've lost the light anyway.'

As the crew began to dismantle the equipment, Loulou walked off to her trailer and changed, feeling isolated and alone. It was the weekend and she had no plans. But perhaps by Monday, she consoled herself, this little scene would be forgotten.

She was eager to get back to LA and the comforts of her suite, but when she emerged from her trailer, her driver was nowhere to be seen. She watched as one by one the cast and crew drove off. Ethan was one of the last to leave and he waved as he climbed into his limousine. Bastard, she thought.

To her surprise the car stopped twenty yards down

the road and Ethan's head popped out of the window. 'Do you need a lift?' he called.

'Thank God,' Loulou said, running along the road. She threw her bags into the car and jumped in. 'I had visions of being there all night.'

They sped away and soon the desert scenery became a blur beyond the tinted windows of the limousine.

'Any plans for the weekend?' Loulou asked, easing into the soft leather seats and rejoicing in the air conditioning.

'Please – I'd rather you didn't speak,' the actor said. 'I'm meditating.'

Loulou stifled a laugh and watched him as he sat cross-legged on the seat, his eyes closed.

Like this he was nothing special, she decided. His sandy hair had been shorn to an army brush-cut for this part and it did him no favours. Admittedly his bones were good, finely etched on his tanned face, but his nose was undefined and his mouth a little thin. But when those shockingly blue eyes were open the whole face made sense and she could see why he didn't bother to get out of bed for less than twenty million and a couple of points on the gross.

With nothing to distract her, pretty soon she was asleep. She awoke just as they were pulling up in front of her hotel, and to her horror her head was resting on Ethan's shoulder.

'Sorry,' she said, jumping upright.

'Hey, no problem,' Ethan said. 'Parker was kinda shitty with you today, wasn't he?'

Loulou was unsure how to respond. The star seemed pretty close to the director and she suspected that anything she said would go straight back to Gooch. 'It was the end of the day – we were all tired.'

'No, it was unprofessional of him – I woulda socked the guy if he'd pulled that on me.'

'Look, do you fancy coming up for a drink?' Loulou asked, surprised at the words coming out of her mouth. 'I don't really want to be on my own this evening.'

His reply surprised her just as much. 'Sure.'

As she walked into the lobby of the Château Marmont, she got her first taste of what it was really like to be a Hollywood star. All the time she'd been there, she could have been a chambermaid for all the notice that was taken of her, but now, on Ethan Mead's arm, she was suddenly up there with Julia Roberts.

She giggled as they waited for the lift, a thousand pairs of eyes trained on them. 'Can't wait for the *Enquirer* next week,' she said.

'Don't even go there,' the star said.

There was little preamble as they entered her suite. Loulou knew what was expected of her. There was no point in pretending she'd invited him back for anything other than sex. If screwing Ethan helped her stay in the picture then she'd give him the fuck of his life.

'Would you like a drink?' she asked, pulling her dress over her head.

'Just a Coke,' Ethan said, undoing his belt. 'I'm in recovery.'

She slipped out of her knickers and took a Coke from the fridge. 'Here,' she said, throwing the can at him.

Loulou climbed on to the massive bed, drew back

the covers and lay on the white linen sheets, watching him undress. Not bad, she thought, as he pulled his jeans over his well-developed thighs. Not bad at all.

Ethan lay down beside her and she began kissing his chest, sliding her hand beneath the waistband of his white jockey shorts. In response he pulled her face up to meet his and kissed her hard on the mouth. His fingers found the inside of her thighs and she moaned, squeezing him tight.

She pushed him back on the bed, preparing to straddle him. Just then the phone rang.

'Leave it,' Ethan said, but she had already picked it up.

She motioned for him to be quiet. 'Hello? Andy!' Since being in LA she had barely given the footballer a second thought. 'It's so nice to hear your voice.'

'And you. God, I've been missing you. How's it going?'

The tone of his voice surprised her. 'Fine,' she lied. 'The director's a bit of a prick but I can handle him.'

'What about that Ethan Mead? Fucked him yet?'

'Not yet,' she said, truthfully, a smile touching her lips.

She watched as the actor extricated himself from beneath her and began licking her stomach, working his way down. Andy was talking about the team but all Loulou was aware of was the sound of blood rushing through her ears as Ethan began working magic between her legs.

'What was that?' she gasped.

'I said I love you,' Andy said. 'I wish you'd never gone away.'

'So do I,' she said pressing her hips into Ethan's

face. 'Andy, we're eating out tonight. Can I call you later?'

'Make sure you do. It's so good to talk to you.'

'Love you,' she said, putting down the phone, experiencing the strange sensation that she'd just heard Andy being totally sincere for the first time in their relationship. He'd meant every word. Perhaps he really does love me, she thought.

'Oh yes! Harder!' she sighed bearing down on the actor. God, she hoped the *Enquirer* had got wind of it.

Chapter Sixteen

'Carla, two beers, when you're ready,' Graham Leary, Notting Hill's manager said. 'Will you bring them over?'

'Anything for you, gorgeous,' the barmaid said with a wink.

'What a right old slapper,' Leary said under his breath as he sat down. 'She's dog rough that one.'

'I feel a bit sorry for her,' David declared, thinking about the way the other players were still taking the piss out of Stu for dating her.

Leary stroked his moustache and looked at the player quizzically. 'To be honest with you, David, I wonder about your judgement at times.' Leary let the words sink in and then added, 'Which is why I wanted this quiet word with you.'

'My judgement? What are you talking about?'

Carla put down the beer on the table slowly, maximising the time the two men would have to study her cleavage. 'There you go, boys. Can I get you anything else?'

'How about some penicillin?' Leary asked.

'Cheeky sod!' The barmaid forced a brittle laugh, and returned to the bar.

'I'm talking about politics,' Leary said, supping his pint.

'I'm still not with you,' David said, aware of the tension at the back of his neck. Last night had been one of the better nights this week and he'd still had barely more than four hours sleep. His mind wasn't really sharp enough to deal with anybody being cryptic.

'Clive has spent a lot of time studying the way we can get a better family atmosphere going – bring in a lot more women and kids. That means changing how the players are perceived. Those players who have their sex lives splashed across the tabloids might be good for publicity but are they pulling in the right sort of people to watch the game?'

'Don't you think I'm the wrong person to be telling this?' David said, the blood draining from his face. His mind swam. Who had been talking? Could anybody have been stupid enough to let this one out? 'There's never been even the barest hint of scandal surrounding me.' He took a mouthful of beer and smiled weakly. 'Actually I wouldn't mind a bit,' he joked, the smile dying on his lips.

'I'm not saying there is. I know you're pukka, mate, but Clive's got exacting standards. We're not just living by the FA's rules – with him we're up against God. I'll level with you. I think the old bastard is barking, but he's the one paying the bills and he wants Notting Hill whiter than white.'

David slowly exhaled, relief flooding in. Leary was obviously talking about people like Michael. He knew nothing. 'Some of the lads have been a bit extreme in the past, I'll admit, but they're beginning to shape up – I think they've realised we're in with a real chance of winning one or more of the cups. It's kind of spurred them on.'

'David, mate, you're still missing the point. I don't give a monkey's what the boys are sticking up their noses this week. But I do care about you. You've got potential – don't fuck up on it. Don't let your dick get the better of your head.'

'That's never been my scene,' David said, easing up. 'Look, if you can keep a secret, I've got something to tell you that should set your mind at rest. I've asked Tanya to marry me.'

'Christ!' Leary said, emptying his glass. 'You haven't understood a word I've been saying. Tanya's the bloody problem.'

'Watch it, mate.' David jumped to his feet. 'You're on dodgy ground there.'

'Sit down, you schmuck, and keep your voice down,' Leary hissed. 'For all I know Tanya's a lovely girl, but straight up with you, she's not the sort Clive wants associated with the team.'

David couldn't believe his ears. 'You're having me on.'

'Calm down, mate – don't shoot the messenger. I'm probably moving on at the end of the season and I'm telling you if you're serious about the job you need to have a little think about the company you keep. Now look at Andy – that's a smashing bird he's got.'

'You can't be serious. Loulou Lamb?'

'A tart I'll grant you, but the secret is she's an upmarket one. You don't see her flashing the gash in the papers.'

David was reduced to a seething silence. He wanted to smash the man's face in. Tanya was worth a thousand Loulou Lambs.

'Carla, get the man another pint,' Leary shouted,

getting up to leave. 'I'll let you think about what I said. The sooner she's out of the picture the sooner you get the key to the executive shit-house.'

When Leary left, David stared out of the window, down on to the empty pitch. He loved Tanya, more than he'd ever loved any other woman. But more than a chance of a job in management? And with Notting Hill, a team he had almost grown up with?

And he had to consider that despite all the rumours there had been no other job offers. After all, there were only so many top spots to be had and undoubtedly Notting Hill was one of the best clubs. If Clive valued him that highly he could be taking on the role of player-manager where he was and that was what he really wanted.

Tanya sat down in the cramped dressing room wearing only a white lacy G-string and the obligatory stilettos, a polystyrene cup filled with ice cubes waiting for her. Normally the room temperature was sufficient but today she had the unusual luxury of a heated studio; with a sigh she fished out one of the ice cubes and began rubbing it over her breasts.

Cup size wasn't enough in this game. You also had to have nipples that stuck out like coat hooks. 'What are men like?' she laughed to herself. But, professionally at least, she was glad they were like it.

All morning she'd been filming an advert for the *News*' new lottery game. For that it had been bra on, though the paper had also wanted some topless shots for their centre pages, which was fine other than the large number of 'technicians' who'd suddenly materialised out of the woodwork.

Satisfied she'd reached an adequate pertness, Tanya was just about to return to the set when she heard a knock on the door.

'Come in,' she called, clutching a towel to her breasts.

Jack, the director, a gangly fifty-something with a sparse thatch of ginger hair and a leery smile that revealed a set of suspiciously uniform teeth, walked in. 'You were great out there.'

'Thanks. Could you hand me that dressing gown? There, on the back of the door.'

Jack passed the dressing gown but held on to it a moment too long, and showed no signs of averting his gaze as Tanya struggled to put it on without flashing him.

'Yeah, really great,' he said, eyeing her up and down. 'A real natural.'

'Is Mike ready yet?' she asked, feeling uncomfortable. Mike was the paper's glamour photographer, who she'd worked with countless times and who was a true gentleman. Unlike this one.

'A couple of minutes,' Jack said, sitting on the edge of the dressing table and lighting a small cigar. 'But I wanted to talk to you first. I've a little business proposition for you.'

'You should really talk to my agent,' Tanya said, suspecting what was about to come.

'I won't beat about the bush, if you'll pardon the expression,' the director sniggered. 'I do a lot of work in adult entertainment – the classy stuff – and I reckon you'd go down a bomb. Have you ever thought about acting?'

Acting? Was this man serious? What did acting have

to do with what he was talking about? 'Sorry, I'm not interested,' she said firmly.

'Now, don't just dismiss it out of hand. Hear me out—'

'I said I'm not interested.' Her tone said she wasn't to be messed with. She waved away a cloud of cigar smoke and held open the door. 'Do you mind smoking that somewhere else?'

'If you change your mind,' Jack persisted, completely unabashed, 'give me a call.' He handed her his card and left.

As soon as he'd left, Tanya binned the card and picked out another ice cube. Although her hackles were raised at the man's audacity, she didn't let this sort of request get to her. It was part and parcel of glamour modelling. She was constantly being asked to do full nude work, but that was only one step away from the 'open leg' stuff. Her family would never forgive her. Nor would David. But, most importantly, she'd never forgive herself.

David loved her unconditionally, she was sure of that, and, probably, if nude work was something she really wanted to do, he'd come round and be supportive. He said he'd always stick by her, whatever, and she believed him. She'd asked him countless times if he minded the glamour modelling and he'd always insisted that it made him proud. Other men could see her in the papers but only he could touch her in the flesh.

Nevertheless, she was planning to surprise him. As soon as they were married she was going to give it all up. To her, there was something not quite right about a married woman showing herself off to all and sundry.

It wouldn't be that much of a sacrifice anyway. She couldn't stay at the top much longer and it would be good to go out on a high.

Immersed in thought, she didn't notice the ice cube melting in her hand until she felt the trickle of water on her thigh. The coldness brought her sharply back to the present, and she hurried back to the set.

Chapter Seventeen

Carla ran a cloth over the last of the optics. It had been a slow afternoon. She liked it when all the players were in the bar – time passed much quicker – but today there'd been practically nobody other than David Ashby and Graham Leary. And they were a couple of miserable sods. They'd barely said two words to her. She hadn't been able to hear their conversation but she'd guessed from the look on David's face that he'd been given a bollocking.

She cashed up, annoyed that there wasn't even enough to take her normal cut. Payday was nearly two weeks away, but her salary, like Stu's cheque, had been swallowed up by her overdraft. Worrying about money was driving her crazy. If it wasn't for the food she had stolen from the bar, she wouldn't have eaten for the past week. This was no way to live.

She wondered about tapping Jenny for some money, then decided against it. It was much easier to get money from men and she felt less obligated to pay it back. Stu then? Not if she had to do *that* again. No, it was time to go to the top. It was time to take up that appointment with Clive Dorning, even if he hadn't summoned her.

In the ladies' she fluffed up her hair, put on some

more lipstick and undid a few buttons. Fortunately her uniform – white blouse and short black skirt – was fairly sexy. Thank goodness she didn't have to dress like the cooks in the staff restaurant.

She locked up the bar and walked across to the main office building. Most of the staff had gone for the day but, annoyingly, Clive's secretary Margaret was still at her desk.

She eyed Carla with suspicion, barely concealing her contempt. 'Can I help you?'

'I'm Carla Ryman. I work in the players' bar. Is Mr Dorning in?'

'Yes.' Margaret continued typing.

'Well, can I see him?'

'What for?'

Nosey old cow. She was probably just bitter that the chairman had never asked her to come up and see him sometime. 'He asked me to report back on the bar, if that's all right with you.'

'If you'd like to take a seat, I'll see whether he's available. There's nothing in the appointment book.'

I bet, the barmaid thought. She sat down and leafed through the Notting Hill annual report; the sums mentioned in the booklet made her head spin. No wonder the club had such a turnover when they paid her a pittance.

Margaret put down the phone, her surprise clear on her face. 'He said to go on in.'

Carla smiled smugly before knocking on the chairman's door.

'Come in,' Clive called, gruffly.

Carla entered the office, feeling slightly nervous. Terri had told her what to expect but she wasn't

sure if she should take the initiative or wait for Clive
to do so.

'Close the door,' he ordered.

She did so, noticing the large simple cross adorning
the far wall. Religion, when practised with ardour,
gave her the creeps. Carla believed that piety, as had
been proved so many times with all those American
tele-evangelists, was often a cover for the deeply
perverted. And if Terri was telling the truth, Clive
was about to prove her right once again.

'What do you want?' the chairman asked, fiddling
with the rings on his left hand. He didn't look her in
the eye.

'The other week you told me to come and see you
at the office.' She sashayed across the room and sat
opposite him, her legs slightly apart, her skirt riding
up on her thighs. 'Well, I'm here.'

Clive's face reddened. 'I said I'd call you. You're a
dirty slut, aren't you?'

'I can be – with the right encouragement.' She
ran her hand along her inner thigh and leaned forward in her chair. 'I hear you can be a very dirty
boy, too.'

'Whore!' the chairman whispered.

Sucking in her stomach, Carla undid the last of the
buttons on her blouse.

'Not here!' Clive seethed. 'Get in there, you trollop.' He pointed to his private rooms.

Thinking of her unpaid rent, Carla entered his living
room and took off her blouse. Clive followed her in
and locked the door.

'Who told you to undress?' he hissed, his whole
body shaking. 'I don't want to look at your disgusting

flesh. On your knees, woman, and beg God to forgive you your sins.'

Suddenly Carla felt alarmed. Compared to the chairman, Stu now seemed practically normal. Was this the lot of all women? she wondered, dropping to her knees in front of the leather sofa. She thought about the other women. Loulou Lamb and Tanya Barry had successfully managed to exploit the pathetic needs of men for their own gain – why was she so crap at it? What did they have that she didn't? Tits like bean bags or an accent that made the Queen sound like Danny Baker, she decided, and the thought made her giggle. Clive momentarily stopped reciting from the Bible and glared at her. She could see that he had now worked himself into a right Old Testament state. Fire and brimstone would be raining down on her, but all she could think of was a Sunday school teacher who'd asked to see her knickers in the vestry.

Finally the sermon came to an end and, as Terri had predicted, Clive unzipped his fly. 'Suck it!' he boomed.

Carla licked her lips and complied. As she performed on him, there was a sudden flash of light. She didn't bother to look up. No doubt Clive would want her to think it had been God firing a warning shot, but she knew it was the chairman's Polaroid.

Thankfully it was all over very quickly, though Carla faced her usual dilemma – should she spit or swallow? Manners got the better of her and she swallowed, trying not to think too much about its provenance.

Clive zipped it away and threw her blouse at her. 'Cover yourself up, you Jezebel!'

Carla could feel another fit of the giggles threatening, so she dressed quickly, eager to escape.

Clive thrust some notes into her hand. 'Get out,' he ordered.

Carla ran back through the office, ignoring Clive's demand that she leave through the back door. Margaret was still outside, staring daggers. Carla stopped in front of her and made a show of counting the money. 'Well, that's the rent paid this week,' she said breezily to the open-mouthed secretary.

After the little slut had left, Clive locked the door. Picking up the photograph, he retrieved several video cases from the shelf. Returning to his bedroom, he emptied the contents of the first on to the bed. Then he opened another. And another.

On the patchwork counterpane in front of him lay around a hundred almost identical photographs – only the hair colour changed from picture to picture. Clive added the latest to the pile and spread them out. The desire they provoked within him made him sick to the stomach. When he could stand looking at them no longer, he took off his polyester shirt, oblivious of the powerful odour of sweat that billowed up around him, and pulled his vest over his head. Then he reached into his bedside drawer and took out a thin leather tawse.

'God forgive me,' he cried, beating himself across the shoulders.

The tawse bit into his skin, small flecks of blood appeared on his back. Again and again he brought the instrument down, whipping himself in a frenzy of self-loathing as he called on his Maker to strike

him dead. This was a ritual of cleansing and purifi-
cation he performed every time he slipped from the
righteous path.

Finally spent, he lay on the bed, surrounded by the
evidence of his transgressions. He thought about his
wife and children, and his betrayal of them. But if the
truth be told, there was only ever one person in his
life who was worth anything, someone he loved with
a purity and a passion that had no equal. And he'd told
her time after time. She had loved him back, too, for a
while, but then she'd tried to make him feel dirty. As
if there was something improper, even evil, about the
feelings he had for her.

For a long time he tried to banish her from his
mind, but she remained in his life, staying just out
of his reach, tormenting him, flaunting herself and
her rejection of him. She'd married another man, and
every time he saw that gold band on her finger he
had to stop himself from flying into a murderous
rage. Thou shalt not covet thy neighbour's wife, said
the ninth Commandment. But the seventh said, Thou
shalt not steal, and *he* had stolen her from him.

He collected the photographs and put them back
in the box. Each photograph took him one step away
from being reunited with her, and yet he couldn't stop
himself. Why was God making him suffer like this?

Chapter Eighteen

Rachel fussed and fretted until each sausage roll was in perfect alignment. Making a silent inventory of the food laid out on the dining-room table, she was finally satisfied there was nothing more to be done.

'Haven't you finished yet?' Mary asked querulously.

Rachel jumped, her hand knocking a couple of vol-au-vents on to the floor. 'Why do you always do that?' she asked shrilly, her nervousness about the party getting the better of her.

'What?'

'Sneak up on me like that.'

Mary had developed the habit of appearing silently behind her and hovering like an all-too-real ghost.

'You're a bag of nerves. What's the matter with you, girl?'

Rachel was so tempted to tell Mary the truth, but she held back. She needed her mother-in-law on her side if she was going to get through this ordeal.

It was her own fault. She was the one who had suggested a birthday party for David, knowing Tanya would be too busy with her 'career' to arrange anything. She had ulterior motives, of course, believing it would do no harm to keep Robbie in favour with the captain, and, who knew, maybe she could melt the ice with some of the other wives.

Then there was the other reason.

'So is this it, then?' Mary's piercing voice broke into her thoughts.

'Do you think there's enough?'

'I s'pose so, if your guests don't mind standing around picking at bits and pieces. What have you done to your hair?'

Rachel's hand flew to her head in defensiveness. 'I had it cut and a few highlights put in.'

'Whatever for? You look like those other women. Cheap.'

'I've got to get ready,' Rachel called over her shoulder as she hurried from the room.

The kids had for once gone to bed when told to, and this was the first time in months Rachel had time to spend on herself. With a satisfying click, she locked the bathroom door; she wanted no interruptions. Turning on the radio, she fiddled with the tuner until she hit a station playing back-to-back romantic ballads. As with her novels, Rachel wanted to listen to songs that had no connection with reality – or her reality anyway.

The kids' toys were still floating in the now-cold bath water. Why could Robbie never finish a job? She cleared them away and, while waiting for the bath to fill again, she gingerly smeared a fluorescent green face-pack on her face. By the time her bath was ready, her face was firmly fixed in a grimace. She tried to relax into the scented water, assuring herself it was all going to be fine.

But it wasn't just the party that was causing her to

feel on edge. Christopher was coming. Ever since she'd asked him, she'd spent hours wondering if they would get a chance to talk – and worrying, like a love-sick teenager, about what to wear.

The bath, despite pouring in gallons of lavender oil, did nothing to soothe her. After she washed away the mask, Rachel wiped the steam off the mirror and took a long, critical look at herself. It didn't seem like the face-pack had had any effect either. What did she expect – a miracle?

Nothing would get rid of her narrow chin, which gave her face a pinched appearance, or the fine lines around her small eyes, the scars from being married to Robbie and having two kids.

She contented herself that her body was still firm and, despite Mary's criticisms, her new cut and colour gave her face the lift it needed.

In the bedroom, on her dressing table, lay the make-up she'd bought earlier that day. Usually, Rachel wore only mascara and a hint of pink lipstick, about all she could manage to put on with two children around her feet. The lipstick she now picked up called itself *Vrai Rouge*. Slowly, she outlined her lips and then filled in the colour – as the woman on the beauty counter had shown her – making her lips appear fuller and more sensuous.

Next came the autumn green eye-shadow. The effect was quite startling: her eyes appeared larger and the blue of the irises striking in contrast to the green. Rachel couldn't help but smile at her reflection – who was this woman?

Having taken Carla's catty comments to heart, she had forced herself to go shopping in Bond Street. It had been an ordeal and one she wasn't eager to repeat in a hurry, whatever the incentive. In nearly all the shops, the painfully thin assistants watched her every move as if she were a shoplifter. Rachel had bought the first dress that had fitted her and, such was her hurry to leave the shop, she couldn't have said whether it suited her or not.

Luckily, the dress, a simple black wool affair, complemented her new look perfectly. Twirling in front of a long mirror, Rachel blushed, surprised at the woman dancing back at her. Surely Robbie would notice the difference and be suspicious.

She needn't have worried about Robbie. All he was interested in was how many pints of beer he could sink before the arrival of the guests. Sprawled out on the settee, dressed as usual in T-shirt and tracksuit bottoms, Robbie's eyes rested momentarily on his wife and then returned to the TV. 'Get me a drink, there's a love.'

'Robbie, don't you think you should slow down? You know how Clive feels about alcohol.'

'What about Clive? What he doesn't know can't hurt him.'

'He's coming.'

'He's what? Don't tell me you invited him.'

'Well of course,' she said, her voice sounding doubtful. 'I'm doing this for you. For your career.'

'You're so stupid. That's great. Jesse Yates breathing down our necks. Thanks, Rach,' he said, getting up and walking out of the room.

Busying herself with the plates and serviettes, Rachel ignored the truth – that this party was as much for her own benefit as for Robbie's. But whereas Robbie wouldn't have noticed if she'd danced around the room naked, his mother saw and heard everything.

'Haven't you gone a bit overboard on the make-up?' Mary said, carrying in another plate of meat paste sandwiches, which she had insisted on making. 'My Robbie doesn't like that kind of thing, especially in a wife.'

Rachel was saved by the doorbell. As she walked down the hallway, she knew she'd have to keep the door open, as no one would be able to stand that racket going off every few minutes.

'I'm glad you could make it,' she said to Clive Dorning.

'Thank you for inviting me,' Clive replied stiffly.

'Come in. No one else has arrived yet.'

'Well, you did say eight pm.'

'Yes. Can I get you a drink?'

'An orange juice would be fine.'

'How's your family?'

'Fine.'

'You must miss them.'

'Yes.'

Rachel was at a loss what to say next. Even a conversation with Mary would have been welcome at this moment. Where was her husband when she needed him? 'I'll just get Robbie,' she said, not waiting for Clive's monosyllabic reply.

Robbie was upstairs in his den watching Notting Hill's last match on video.

'Clive's downstairs,' Rachel hissed. 'Go and talk to him.' She could tell from his bloodshot eyes that he was already on the wrong side of drunk. What on earth would he and Clive talk about? Even she had to admit that Robbie wasn't the most diplomatic person in the world, especially after a few drinks.

Luckily, by the time they came back downstairs a few more guests had arrived, including the guest of honour, David. Rachel hovered around, refilling half-full glasses and beseeching everyone to start eating.

The stilted conversation died as Michael and Jenny lurched into the room. Jenny and Clive stared at each other, then turned away at the same time. Michael, seeing an unopened bottle of whisky, abandoned Jenny immediately, and Rachel was left floundering.

'Hi, Rachel, thanks for inviting us.' There was no hiding the slur in Jenny's voice.

'Would you like something to eat?'

'No thanks. Got to think about my figure.'

Rachel could see just how much Jenny looked after her figure. There wasn't much hidden by her extremely short black moleskin skirt and frilly, translucent white blouse. Both would have looked daring on a woman half Jenny's age. She needed, as Mary would say, fattening up. Noticing the arrival of Stefan, Rachel made her excuses and left Jenny standing on her own.

'Hello, it's Stefan, isn't it? Welcome to England. Can I get you a drink?'

'Thanks. A white wine please.'

'Go over and see Robbie, he's talking to Andy,' Rachel said.

Stefan walked over to Robbie and Rachel could see that he wasn't exactly welcomed into the conversation. As he stood on the fringes of the group she handed him his drink.

Soon the living room was heaving with players

and their odd assortment of women, and Rachel moved through her guests perfecting her hostess act. So much for melting the ice, Rachel thought, as she handed Martine another salmon sandwich to the briefest acknowledgement of her existence.

A cluster of people parted as a woman, uttering oaths, elbowed and stumbled her way through the crowd. It was Carla, wearing an orange dress with a neckline that plunged to her waist and a hem line that came up to meet it. Unfortunately, the only thing the fluorescent orange complemented was the orange trying to hide beneath the yellow of Carla's hair. She looked like a demented parrot.

Open-mouthed, Rachel stared at her uninvited guest. Perhaps Robbie had invited her. 'Carla, I didn't know you were coming. Are you with Stuart?'

'No. Thankfully. We're history. Excuse me, I need a drink,' she said, pushing past Rachel and leaving a cloud of cheap perfume in her wake.

Following her movements, Rachel watched as Carla poured red wine into a half-pint glass and then made a beeline for Clive, who was standing on his own. Carla whispered something in his ear. Thinking she should save the chairman, Rachel wound her way through the crowd until she was standing by his side.

Clive had turned to face Carla. 'Miss Ryman, I should warn you I don't appreciate employees being over-familiar with me.'

For anyone else such a knock back would have sent them scuttling in the opposite direction. But Carla simply laughed and shrugged her shoulders before strutting away.

'Would you like another orange juice?'

The doorbell rang before Clive could reply. That bloody tune, Rachel thought. She hoped it wasn't a neighbour complaining about the noise. Someone had taken off her Whitney Houston record, put on a band she'd never even heard of and pushed up the volume.

On the doorstep was a rather young WPC. Her long copper hair was swept up under her hat and Rachel considered she had on much more make-up than was appropriate.

'I'm here to see a David Ashby.'

'What on earth for? We're having a party.'

'Not at liberty to disclose that, ma'am. Now could you show me where he is, please.'

As Rachel led the policewoman through the throng of people, she noticed how the conversations dropped off. David's back was towards Rachel and she tapped him on the shoulder.

'David,' she said in little more than a whisper, 'there's a policewoman to see you.'

David whirled round, his face ashen. 'Wha . . .'

Before he had time to say any more the WPC had thrown off her cap, shaken loose her hair and begun to undo the buttons on her jacket.

The room erupted into shouts of 'Get 'em off!', with Robbie leading the cheering. Rachel walked away in disgust, annoyed with herself for being so gullible, but then judging by the look on David's face, he had believed she was the real article as well. What could he have done to make him look that guilty? she mused. Unpaid parking tickets?

The woman twirled her blouse above her head and threw it into the crowd, where it landed on Jamie

Carlton's head, much to Suzy's annoyance. Next came
the skirt, which fell to the floor, revealing that all the
woman had on underneath was a garish red and black
basque, matching knickers and sheer black stockings.

The glint from Clive's rings caught Rachel's eye
and she shuddered at what he must be thinking. He
was staring at the stripper, the veins in his forehead
pulsating, while the muscles in his cheeks gave invol-
untarily twitches. Clive Dorning slammed down his
glass and made for the door. Rachel ran after him.

'Clive, I'm so sorry. I had no idea.'

'I'm sorry as well. It's not the type of thing I expect
in a family home. Good night.'

Reluctantly returning to the room, Rachel saw that
Mary was in the doorway, her expression slipping
between disgust and disbelief. But even Mary wouldn't
be able to blame her daughter-in-law for this. Perhaps
it was time she saw her innocent little baby for what
he was.

The stripper wiggled her hips and jiggled her breasts
as the men gave a tuneless rendition of 'The Stripper'.
David's face had gone from white to cerise. Holding
out his hands he tried to prevent the woman getting
any closer to him, but taking his reluctance as a
challenge, she flung her arms around him. There was
the tinkle of breaking china as her arm caught one of
Rachel's capo di monte figurines. With tears welling
up, Rachel fled the room.

A hand touched her arm. She looked up to see
Chris standing before her, his eyes filled with concern. The sight of him was too much for Rachel
and her tears spilled over and ran freely down her
cheeks.

'Come here,' he said gently, guiding her into the small cloakroom off the hallway.

'I hate him. Why does he have to ruin everything? He's . . . he's got a stripper in there and it's obvious David's mortified by the whole thing. And what if Demi or Robbie Jnr wakes up? I wish I'd never suggested this damn party.'

Chris held her close to him until her tears slowed down. 'David's a big boy, he knows what they're like. Don't worry about it.'

Rachel pressed closer to him as if his powerful body could protect her. From what she didn't want to answer. His heart beat against hers and she could smell the citrus scent of his soap.

In the distance she could hear the stripper singing 'Happy Birthday' in a breathless parody of Marilyn Monroe followed by more clapping and cheering. Rachel hoped they heralded the end of the distasteful and embarrassing affair.

Rachel pulled away from Chris. The last thing she needed was any of that lot, especially Mary, seeing her like this. 'Thanks for that,' she said, looking up at his face.

He gently wiped away a stray tear. 'Any time. God, you really look lovely tonight.'

'Th . . . thanks. I'm sure I'm all puffy and red-faced now.'

Placing his hands on her cheeks, he said, 'You look lovely. Now let's party.'

When they returned to the living room the WPC was dressed and ready to go. The men, already bored, had turned away and returned to their conversations. The only people watching her now were the women.

Rachel walked towards David and Tanya to apologise, but the expression on David's face stopped her.
It wasn't that he looked so much embarrassed as
depressed. She could see that Tanya was trying to
make light of the situation, even laughing about it,
but the more Tanya cajoled and humoured him, the
more dejected he became.

'I bet you could give her one, Andy.' Robbie's voice
rose above all the others. 'In fact, I bet you have,' he
said, doing a crude imitation of a man having sex with
a woman.

Why couldn't he just shut up for once, Rachel
thought, glad that Loulou wasn't there to unleash her
tongue on how naff the whole thing was, including
Rachel's idea of a party. No doubt Loulou Lamb was
used to only the best in parties and even Rachel knew
this fell below most people's standards.

Before she had the chance to tell Robbie to shut up,
Mary was at her side, tight-lipped, telling her it was
time to pass around more vol-au-vents. Unbelievable
as it was, it was clear to Rachel that Mary held her
responsible for the strippergram.

The party was becoming more raucous by the minute. Robbie was shouting at the top of his voice and
throwing sausage rolls at those nearest to him. Rachel
leaned against the wall wishing everyone would go
home. Well, not quite everyone. She looked over
at Chris, who was in the corner talking to Tony
Anderson.

Next to Chris was Carla, her hand resting on
Stefan's arm.

'Hi, Stefan, I'm Carla.'

'Hi.' Stefan gave her a friendly smile. Apart from Rachel, Carla was the only person who'd spoken to him all evening. 'Which player are you with?' he asked, hoping to be introduced to her partner, which might allow him at least to get a foot in the unwelcoming door of Notting Hill.

'None. I'm freelance.'

'Sorry?' He wished he had bothered to learn more English, maybe then he would have been able to get on better with the other players.

'Tell me about yourself. Where are you from in Germany?'

'Berlin. But I was in Bayern before the transfer.'

'I spent some time in Berlin. Nice place.'

'Doing what?'

'This and that. So you got a girlfriend or wife? I didn't see you with anyone.'

'My fiancée's in Germany. I have yet to persuade her to come to England.'

Carla moved a little closer. That was the best news she'd had all evening, especially after the brush-off from Dorning.

'You should let me show you the sights some time.'

Stefan could feel her breasts lying heavily on his arm. His body began to respond and he looked away, embarrassed. He made himself think about Paula and how she would never have worn something so sexually obvious. But then it was this and Carla's manner that were exciting.

Carla knew what he was thinking; men were so predictable. She had them taped. She edged a little closer, her breath fanning his neck.

'Carla, I—'

'Who the . . .' Carla whirled around to see Robbie sniggering behind her, having just lifted her dress to waist level.

'Oh, Robbie, it's you, you prat. Good job I had my new knickers on. Want a better look?' She lifted up the front of her dress. Out of the corner of her eye she could see Rachel, her face stern and her thin lips pinched together. Uptight cow.

Robbie giggled and Carla turned to resume her conversation with Stefan, but he was walking away. 'Stefan,' she called, 'wait for me.'

'I've got to go now. I'm sorry.'

Carla was a pro and she knew better than to push it. She'd blown it for now but she wasn't going to let Stefan out of her sights in future. 'OK, see you again soon.'

He gave a brief nod in reply.

Enough was enough. Rachel strode towards Robbie, but before she could reach him, she was shoved out of the way by Michael, his eyes flashing with anger as he closed in on his target. Andy.

'Why don't you go and check on your wife?' Andy jeered across the room. 'If Robbie's got a wine cellar she'll probably be there.' Andy easily dodged Michael's flailing fist. 'That's right, you inarticulate bastard, use violence. That's the only language you know.'

Michael, so drunk he had no co-ordination, fell forward on his second attempt at a punch. Putting one hand out to steady himself he clutched on to the corner of the dining table, pulling plates and left-over food crashing to the floor.

Rachel was speechless. Well, the whole lot of them could rot in hell. She left the room and walked wearily up the stairs. She'd check on the children and then hide in her bedroom until the disaster downstairs was a distant memory.

'Rachel! Wait.' Chris caught up with her on the landing. 'Rachel, I've got to go now. Look, don't worry. Everything'll sort itself out. You'll see.'

'What do you mean?'

He looked at her, his gentle eyes reassuring. 'I'll give you a call.'

Watching his retreating back and trying to figure out what he had meant, she wished Chris could have stayed . . . Before her thoughts strayed any further down a forbidden path, she crossed the landing and peeped into Demi's room. Her daughter's bed was empty.

She hurried to Robbie Jnr's room and stopped suddenly in the doorway.

'"And Winnie the Pooh said think, think, think."' Both children were sitting up in bed, listening intently as Jenny Waite read them a story.

Rachel's first thought was to get the inebriated woman away from them but as she moved closer she could see that the children and Jenny were enjoying themselves. Jenny was perched on the side of the bed and the children were leaning towards her, their young faces alight with anticipation and eagerness.

'Jenny.'

'Oh, Rachel. I hope you don't mind. I heard them when I came up to the loo. I thought I'd entertain them.'

'Thank you. I'll finish the story,' Rachel replied,

still feeling it would be best if Demi and Robbie Jnr weren't breathing in alcohol fumes.

'OK.' Jenny rose unsteadily to her feet. At the doorway she turned and said, 'You don't know how lucky you are, Rachel.'

Downstairs there were about half a dozen people left, and only two still standing – David and Tanya.

'You're joking?'

'Tanya, I'm sorry. It's not up to me.'

'Then who is it up to, David? Is my role in life meant to be just standing two steps behind you? This has never been a problem before.' Tanya's voice rose with her growing indignation.

'It will be if I'm manager. Clive doesn't think Page Three modelling is a suitable profession.'

'And you just go along with him.'

David placed a tentative hand on her shoulder but she shrugged him off. Generally even-tempered, Tanya was now shaking with rage. She just couldn't believe what she was hearing, or that David had chosen a party of all places to have this conversation. And after the behaviour displayed that night, the hypocrisy of what he was saying was almost too much to take in.

'I'm not going to be dictated to,' she said loud enough to cause the few people left to turn around.

'Ssh. Look—'

'Don't ssh me. You chose to bring it up now and I want it solved now.' What made her blood boil even more was that she had decided only a few days ago to give up glamour modelling once she and David were married. It would be her chance to do something else. She'd already had several media offers but she wanted to do something out of the limelight.

'I can't believe you enjoy it,' David said, with an intonation she hadn't heard before. Disapproval.

If there was one thing Tanya shared with the rest of her family it was stubbornness, sometimes to the point of ridiculousness. No she didn't always enjoy the modelling, but she'd be damned if she'd admit to it now.

'I love it, that's why I do it, and I'm not going to stop because some crackpot religious fanatic tells me to.' As she grew more and more angry, her East End accent became increasingly pronounced.

They stared at each other in a silent stand-off. It was David who spoke first.

'I don't want to say this but you're leaving me no choice. It's me or the modelling.'

Tanya's mouth dropped open.

The second the words had left David's mouth he wanted to take them back. But it was too late.

'It'll be the bloody job every time,' Tanya shouted, before storming out of the room.

Chapter Nineteen

Sunlight filtered through the stained-glass windows. The small shards highlighted the agonising deaths of the martyrs but their touch did not reach the depths of the church. Inside it was so cold that it was hard to believe that summer was waiting just outside.

Jenny crossed herself and walked up the central aisle. It sounded as if an army was advancing as the clattering of her high heels on the stone floor reverberated high above her. She lit a candle and sat down in the nearest pew.

With her head bowed, she wondered what God, if he existed, made of her. Of all the prayers he should listen to, she didn't think ones from a wealthy drunk who swallowed a pharmacy a day to keep away the pain and demons rated that highly.

A feverish whispering made her realise she wasn't alone. She looked behind, across the seemingly endless pews, to the furthest corner of the church. Someone was praying.

Jenny only occasionally came to St Mary's, a sixteenth-century church that was an oasis of calm in bustling west London. When she did visit she stayed clear of the confessional, knowing she had committed so many sins that she and the priest would be holed up together for at least a week. And then another week would be needed to get through her penance.

On the other hand, Jenny was still influenced enough by Catholicism to believe that if she met death not having confessed, all that would be waiting for her was hell or at least a few thousand years in purgatory. She wondered if it could be much worse than the hell on earth she had managed to create for herself.

The church's heavy oak doors banged shut. Turning, Jenny saw an old woman struggling with a large bouquet of flowers, the weight threatening to overwhelm her five-foot frame. After crossing herself, the woman limped to the altar and began replacing the drooping flowers from the previous Sunday.

Jenny studied the woman, noticing that her face was disfigured by deep lines. Jenny guessed that the vivid signs of ageing were due to a hard life rather than the number of years lived. Yet as the woman moved about her business, wearing a serene expression, she looked at peace with herself, whatever bad cards life had dealt her. Jenny couldn't imagine ever being that content, even if she did manage to get to a ripe old age.

Closing her eyes, Jenny shut out thoughts of the old woman and reflected on why she had come here. That morning she had awoken screaming and bathed in a cold sweat. It had taken her several minutes to realise she was in her own bedroom. Slowly it had all come back to her. The nightmare always began the same way – the feeling of suffocation, the face of her brother looming over her, twisted into a mask of hate, the warning that she was about to enter hell.

But this time, as she drowned in the flames, the face hadn't been Clive's.

Awake, the identity of her tormentor eluded her.

Even now, hours later, she was on edge. But it wasn't just the dream – everything unsettled her. Her mood swings were more pronounced than ever and the simplest things could send her into either floods of tears or paroxysms of anger.

Jenny rested her head on the pew in front of her, a cloak of tiredness enveloping her. She felt that if she closed her eyes she would sleep for ever. A tear ran down her cheek. What was wrong with her? Perhaps she was losing it. Finally.

Despite the numbing effects of the drugs and alcohol, Jenny was still unable to forget her humiliating experience at the Three Lions. How little respect she must have for herself if she would stay with a man who did that to her. 'God,' she whispered, further words eluding her. Why was she here? She wanted peace.

But the quietness of the church had the opposite effect on Jenny. It was an oppressive silence, only broken now and again by the murmuring of the woman praying. The condemning voice in Jenny's head grew louder and louder until she rose from her pew and ran out of the church.

Outside she was momentarily dazzled by the searing bright light. Once her eyes had adjusted, she decided she would fill the rest of her day with shopping. Where God had failed maybe Mammon would succeed.

But today even shopping wasn't the answer to her prayers. A grey silk shift dress by Agnes B did nothing to improve her mood. Through the sheer fabric Jenny could see that she had put on weight. There was a definite paunch around her usually flat stomach. That was all she needed. It wasn't like she was eating anything; she could hardly remember the last time she'd had a proper meal.

She couldn't face being fat again. Most of her teenage years had been spent soaring up and down the scales and sticking her fingers down her throat.

'Everything OK?' the shop assistant asked.

'No,' Jenny snapped, almost tearing the dress in her hurry to get it off and out of there.

She ran out of the shop faster than a thief. If she put on weight Michael would definitely leave her. Then where would she be? Even sadder and more pathetic. If the slimming pills weren't working she might have to start going back to the gym. Hours and hours on the Stairmaster, each punishing mile some sort of expiation for a wasted life.

Jenny decided there was no time like the present – and no excuse as Browning's gym was staring at her from across the road.

The reception area, all Kentia palms, flattering lighting and mirrors that Jenny suspected were designed to knock off the pounds, was buzzing with women like her, who had nothing better to do than worry about the latest ounce revealed on the scales. Many were the wives of Notting Hill players – a life-time membership to one of the best gyms and health spas in London was one of the perks of being a player's wife.

'Hi, Mrs Waite, long time no see,' came the singsong voice of Browning's best advert, Julie the receptionist. Perfect sleek body, beautiful skin and luxurious hair. And she was only twenty.

Jenny nodded her reply, in no mood for anodyne chatter, and went straight into the gym's shop to buy what she needed for a work-out.

Everything on display was designed to make the purchaser look thinner and sexier. The black leotard she chose had a shocking pink stripe to accentuate the breasts and was cut so high on the leg it was bordering on the obscene. But Jenny knew what was required – God forbid one should wear something as practical as baggy tracksuit bottoms and an old T-shirt. Even sweating one had to look ready to strut down the catwalk.

It was a women-only session and the gym was bursting with females in every shape and size running, cycling, weight lifting and performing other tortures that would help get rid of the fat, change the shape of the body, hold back the advancing years. But the place smelled more like a perfume counter in a department store than a gym – nothing as vulgar as the smell of sweat was tolerated. The clashing, overpowering scents made Jenny nauseous.

Jenny moved towards the bank of exercise bikes but stopped. In front of her sat Martine and Suzy, dressed in identical red lycra shorts with matching tops cut off at the midriff. They looked up in mid-gossip, smirked at each other and then studiously ignored her.

Moving around the two women she got on the Stairmaster. As she got into the rhythm, her mind slowed down as her heartbeat increased. She watched, satisfied, as the machine told her the number of calories she was burning off. Perhaps this would be her salvation.

Panting, covered in a layer of sweat and with a stitch

so severe she could hardly breathe, Jenny knew she
had to stop. After six miles of climbing she felt as
though she was going to have a heart attack. It was
at moments like these she worried that the years of
abuse would finally take their revenge and her poor
maltreated heart would rebel. It would be just typical
to die looking a sweaty mess with Martine and Suzy
looking on.

The Stairmaster should have been enough but,
having finally caught her breath, Jenny moved on
to the Olympic-size swimming pool. She welcomed
the pungent smell of the chlorine after the heady aroma
of the gym.

The pool was empty and Jenny dived into the cobalt
blue water. The shock of the cold soon subsided as she
pushed away the water in a confident breast stroke.

Classical music played in the background and with
each length the tension fell away, the water soothing
her screaming muscles. After fifty laps she emerged
from the pool.

In the shower, Jenny relaxed under the pulsating
hot water. For the first time in days she felt hopeful.

'Have you met Michael's latest one?' came the
shrieking voice of Martine.

Jenny froze, turning off the shower so she could
hear more.

'Nah. Why, have you?'

'She came to the match last week, she's really nice.
In fact we got on like a house on fire.'

'Do you think the old bag knows?'

Jenny flinched at Suzy's spiteful words.

'Probably, but then she's got no dignity. She knows
he'll leave her if she makes a fuss. Mind you, I don't

know why he stays with her – or rather I think we all do,' Martine said, cackling. 'Money certainly can buy you things.'

Shivering, Jenny listened intently. She wanted a name. It must be the bitch with the pink jeep. But Martine and Suzy were walking away from the shower area and Jenny could no longer make out what they were saying.

Jenny followed the women into the changing area, grabbing her bag and entering a cubicle. How many more times could she take being humiliated like this? Her head felt like it was going to explode. How could she be so stupid? Why did she let Michael continue to treat her like this?

She hurriedly searched through her bag for a wrap of coke, craving the instant relief it promised. She pulled out everything, tissues, old make-up, half a dozen credit cards. Where was the damn stuff? She tipped the rest of the bag's contents on to the seat. A box of tampons fell to the floor. Jenny stopped suddenly. Her period was over two weeks late.

Chapter Twenty

As the half-time whistle blew, the score one-nil to the home team, the predominantly Italian crowd emitted a thunderous yowl, which seemed to shake the enormous red steel rafters criss-crossing the four corner towers of San Siro. The place was packed to capacity and to David, as he led his players back to the changing room, it seemed that every one of those eighty-seven thousand faces were screaming for AC Milan.

Listening to the players' puerile banter, David saw his future crumbling before his eyes. This shower was what he'd sacrificed Tanya for. Every effort of his to pull them together as a team had been wasted; they were going out of the UEFA Cup in the second round, and after this Clive Dorning wouldn't even give him a job sweeping the terraces. It was over.

The players grew louder, their taunts more vicious. It was the same old crap he'd listened to season after season and he couldn't take it a second longer.

'Why don't you arseholes shut up? For once in your pathetic lives shut the fuck up!' he bellowed, bringing the room to an immediate stunned silence. Nobody had ever seen David lose his cool before. 'I'm sick to death of it. The whole shitty lot of it.'

A beat passed and then Andy shouted, 'Where do you get off talking to anyone like that? Who let in the fucking goal?' He let the remark sink in and then turned to Michael. 'Mind you, with the defence we've got . . . Wea was walking all over you.'

Michael spat on the tiled floor. 'Fuck you, I was shadowing Ba. Blame that arsebandit over there.' He hurled a cup of water at Stu. 'For a footballer you make a fucking great ice-skater.'

The cup hit Stu in the back, soaking his top. For one awful moment he thought Michael was on to him and, slowly, he closed his locker, not turning round. Then he rationalised that if Michael did know, there was no way he would have left it this long to say something. Michael was just mouthing off.

'This is just what I mean,' David said, disgusted. 'Not one of you sad bastards can stop it – even for ninety minutes.' He kicked the door of his locker, breaking its hinges, and stormed out.

Robbie ran after him. 'Dave! Hold on!' The captain ignored him but Robbie raced ahead to cut him off. 'What's the matter, mate? I don't know why everyone's acting like this. I thought things were going well. Your birthday the other night was a real laugh.'

'And what about that night at the Three Lions?' David asked, through clenched teeth. 'Was that a real laugh too?'

Knocked sideways with jetlag, Loulou had slept through the match, but from the despondent look on the waiter's face when she asked him the score, Notting Hill had obviously won. To celebrate she ordered an Amaretto di Savonno to accompany her espresso.

Hopefully the win might make Andy more amenable to her unexpected appearance in Milan.

Her worst nightmare had happened. Production on the film had been shut down and she knew the blame was resting firmly on her shoulders. Sleeping with Ethan had done nothing to secure her position. In fact, she had the sneaking suspicion it had only made it worse. After the night at the hotel he had gone back to hiding behind his acting coach, leaving her to fend for herself against an increasingly hostile Parker Gooch.

Then the money men stepped in to suspend filming until further notice and Loulou packed her bags for the first flight out of LA. Already the troubled film had occupied several columns in *Variety* and it was just a matter of time before the British press ran with the story. It was all too hideous to think about.

She knocked back the Amaretto and followed it with a swig of coffee, the sweet and the bitter mixing pleasantly in her mouth. Andy would be here any minute. What was he going to say?

As usual, the players' wives were banned from trips abroad. Officially this was so that the team would be focused on the game, but Loulou suspected it was more likely so that the men had a free rein with the foreign talent.

She looked around the bar trying to guess which of the female patrons would be Andy's type. The women were super stylish in that effortless Milanese way. Understated, unobstrusive and whispering 'loaded' to only the cognoscenti, they were a million miles away from the flashy, trashy Notting Hill wives.

Her eyes alighted on a tall, thin woman, whose pinched beauty and angular poise were suggestive of the catwalk. Her shiny black hair was pulled back into a ponytail and she was wearing a pair of camel bootleg trousers and a white wide-collared shirt, the simplicity of which rendered her devastating. That's the one, Loulou thought, smiling.

Much to her surprise the woman smiled back. Momentarily flustered, Loulou buried her head in the menu.

'It's so fantastic to see you here.' Andy's voice startled her out of her reverie. He pulled up a chair, and Loulou found herself disappointed that he had obscured the other woman's eyeline.

'Are you sure I'm not cramping your style?' she managed. 'As soon as I got on the plane I regretted it. I should have gone to London.'

'You should have done no such thing,' he insisted.

He drew Loulou towards him, his fingers kneading the back of her neck. Their lips met and there was such passion in his kiss that Loulou believed him.

As Loulou pulled away, Andy squeezed her hand. 'It's great to see you. Hey, we won two-one.'

'I heard. Did you score?'

The warmth in Andy's voice evaporated. 'No. The Kraut took both. Can we get a drink?'

Loulou waved at the waiter, eager to restore Andy's good mood. Any mention of that German player seemed to leave him totally rattled.

Fluent in Italian, she ordered a bottle of wine from the nearby San Combano vineyards. The waiter, as visually impressive as any of the clientele, flirted with her, his raspy Latin voice hitting just the right spot. It had been so long since she'd felt that affirmation and she was sorely tempted to drag Andy straight back to the hotel and seduce him.

'You look stunning,' Andy said, dragging her attention back from the departing waiter.

'I look like a fright,' she replied, knowing she looked nothing of the sort but eager to hear him protest. Her skin had a subtle golden glow and the short, pastel blue cashmere cardigan she was wearing hugged her figure to reveal the benefits she'd drawn from her daily work-outs.

Andy laughed at her. 'You're fishing for compliments. OK then – you look divine, darling. Not since Helen of Troy has any woman—'

'OK, leave it. You look like shit by the way.'

'Liar. You love me best straight off the pitch.'

'Spare me the caveman bit,' she said, kissing him again, tasting the salt on his skin.

The wine arrived and Loulou sipped it, its slightly almondy aftertaste a perfect follow on from the Amaretto. It was so easy to get things right – why couldn't women like Rachel or that dreadful Carla manage it?

'It's been nearly three weeks since I last saw you.' There was a glint in Andy's eye.

'I'm sure you made other arrangements,' Loulou replied.

'I wouldn't do that to you,' Andy insisted, vehemently. 'I just want you to know how much I've missed you.'

He meant it. The fool meant it. Loulou realised that she had misjudged him. She had always assumed he'd viewed their relationship in the same light as she did – mutually convenient until the spotlight faded. But the look in his eyes seemed dangerously like love.

'Me too,' she said with more conviction than she really felt. The idea of being in love with Andy had never occurred to her. He'd told her he loved her on the phone but she had thought that was simply something to say.

Eager to steer them out of sticky waters, she searched for something else to talk about. She glanced over at the woman at the bar, who was still staring at her. She felt unsettled but excited too, and the wine was loosening her up. 'So you ever thought about making out with two beautiful chicks?'

Andy reddened.

'Well? Have you ever done it?' she persisted, pressing against him and longing to feel his bare body against hers.

'Never.'

'You liar. What about those Australian soap opera twins? I read it in the *Sun* so it must be true.'

Andy poured the last of the wine into their glasses and let his hand rest on her thigh. 'I never fucked them together. Within minutes of each other, yes, but never actually in the same bed at the same time.'

'Would you like to?' Loulou asked. 'Tonight, I mean.'

'It's a long way to Melbourne but if it's OK with you . . .'

She tapped him on the chin playfully. 'With me, you twit.' She pointed to the woman at the bar. 'And her.'

'Don't point,' Andy whispered. 'She'll see you.'

'She *has* seen me – she's been watching me since I came in. And you.' The last bit wasn't strictly true; she hadn't looked at Andy at all, but neither had his presence stopped her from eyeing Loulou. 'So, are you game?'

'Of course. What should I say to her?'

'Leave it to me,' Loulou said, standing up and smoothing the creases from her pastel lemon pants.

Andy's bluff had been called. 'Loulou,' he hissed. 'Come back.'

But Loulou didn't listen. Emboldened by the wine she marched straight up to the woman and introduced herself.

'I'm Franca,' the woman replied, her dark burgundy lips parting to reveal a dazzling smile.

'Would you like to join us for a drink?' Strangely, picking up another woman seemed enjoyably easy.

'I'd love to,' Franca said, slipping off her barstool.

She led the woman back to the table, noting the look of barely concealed horror on Andy's face. Momentarily she wondered whether she'd pushed it too far, but it was too late now – they were already involved in the game.

Franca spoke no English, Andy no Italian, so Loulou translated, her interpretations growing lewder and ever further from the truth as her desire to be taken to bed by these two beautiful people grew.

'What do you do for a living?' Loulou asked, waiting for the inevitable reply.

Franca surprised her. 'I'm an architect.'

'What was that?' Andy pressed, growing irritated at being excluded from the conversation.

'I asked her what she liked to do in bed.'

'Loulou, this is going too far,' Andy declared, watching his girlfriend put her arms around the other woman's shoulders. 'Tell her to piss off now.'

Loulou paid no heed. 'Andy says he'd love to watch us together.'

'How presumptuous,' Franca said, but then she planted a kiss on Loulou's neck, leaving a smudge of burgundy. She leaned over to kiss Andy too and he seemed to soften, glad to be the focus of attention once again.

'This is one of my biggest fantasies,' Loulou said in English. In reality it had been only since she'd kissed Meret Lee that she'd ever given the idea of sleeping with another woman a second thought.

'If I said I wanted "Magic" in bed with us, you'd be disgusted,' Andy said, running his fingers down Loulou's spine.

'I'd love it,' Loulou giggled. 'Martine would just keel over and die. She'd want the whole of Harvey Nicholls tied up in a bow for that one.'

'What's he saying now?' Franca asked. 'He doesn't look happy.'

'He says he's not sure that he's man enough for two. What do you think?'

'That's not really the dilemma,' she replied. 'The question is – are you woman enough?'

'Loulou, you're not going to do this.' Andy was torn, both appalled and excited by this turn of events. He wanted it – but he wanted to be in control. He had never liked women taking the upper hand. 'Tell her we're sorry but we're leaving. We're flying back first thing.'

But there was no stopping Loulou. 'Andy wants

to know if you'd like to come back to the hotel with us.'

'I'd really like that,' Franca said, nibbling Andy's earlobe.

Five minutes later, despite Andy's protests, the three of them were walking arm in arm back to the hotel.

Chapter Twenty-One

The doorman moved the red rope to one side and Loulou, an imperious expression on her face, swept past him into the foyer of Supernova. She was in a foul mood and the last thing she needed was a night in a tacky nightclub. In her ten years of being seen around town she had managed to avoid coming here, but Andy had insisted she accompany him tonight to a book launch.

She strode up to the bar and ordered a double gin and tonic. While she waited she studied her image in the mirror behind the bar. Her hair, recently cut, hung down over her shoulders in a perfect straight line, framing her heart-shaped face and perfect cheekbones. And the brown Donna Karan dress she had bought that day was doing exactly what it was designed to, hugging her curves like a second skin. But none of this made her feel better.

The barmaid returned and it was then that Loulou noticed the girl was revealing far more than she was. She turned to Andy to see if he was watching, but surprisingly he was searching absentmindedly through his pocket for money.

Feeling slightly better after downing most of her drink, Loulou glanced around to see who else had arrived. It soon became clear from the gaggle of women in front of her, who were all chirping away in provincial accents, that Supernova was open to members of the public. From the numbers it looked as if they must have arrived by the coach load. 'Christ,' she muttered to herself, the evening was going to be even worse than she had imagined.

It was clear that she hadn't been missing much. Above her, in between the swathes of crimson velvet and ornate chandeliers, were giant cherubs who smiled down on the less-than-cherubic girls flaunting their assets.

It seemed that nearly every female in the club was out to land a rich man and had dressed – or not dressed – accordingly. Half had little more than underwear on, albeit the leather type, and the barmaids now looked overdressed in comparison.

The male clientele, overdressed in suits, were not much better, with their leering, sweaty faces and flabby bodies. Loulou only hoped for the girls' sakes that they had bank balances to match their years.

As more and more of the team arrived it became obvious that more and more of the girls were thinking they had struck lucky. Loulou could see it made no difference that every player had a woman clamped on to his arm. The jostling and the whispering increased as the women surrounded their quarry.

The music was another irritant to Loulou, a bland selection that Radio Two would have been proud of. She moved away from the crowd, the blending of cheap perfumes beginning to smell like a chemical outbreak.

Before she could take another step, a giggling girl

stopped her and asked for her autograph. 'I'd *love* to be like you,' she enthused.

But as Loulou took her pen, the girl moved around to her side and brushed up against Andy. Loulou threw back the pen and grabbed Andy's arm. 'Come on, let's go downstairs.'

She held on to him possessively but when she looked up at his face he seemed oblivious of the acreage of exposed flesh around him. As they walked away, Loulou saw that many of the players were being overrun by girls whose sole intent was to separate them from their partners.

Andy pulled on her arm and manoeuvred her through the enthusiastic crowd until they had reached the stairs, where they made their way down to the book launch.

Loulou nodded to a few media acquaintances but didn't wait to kiss the air with them. She looked around to see what the competition was like. Tara Smythe Jenkinson, old school 'It' girl, appeared in front of Loulou's face.

'Dahling, how's it going?'

'Great, Tara, couldn't be better,' Loulou managed through gritted teeth.

'And this is who?' Tara asked, nodding her precarious hairstyle towards Andy, who was looking off into the distance.

Loulou resisted saying that Tara knew perfectly well who he was; she could play this game with the best of them. 'Andy McKay. But I'm sure you met before. At Brown's, I believe . . .'

'Oh, I forget,' Tara said hurriedly. 'Anyway, see you around.'

'Can you believe that bitch?' Loulou said, turning to Andy.

'Who?'

'Tara can-I-get-into-your-pants-now Smythe Jenkinson.'

Andy shrugged and Loulou realised he hadn't even noticed Tara, despite having told Loulou once how he'd had to fight her off at a similar bash to this. He was in a very strange mood.

Loulou had noticed that Andy had also kept a low profile since they'd walked into the nightclub. What was happening to the media sluts of the nineties? Usually on occasions like this she and Andy didn't see each other all night, which usually suited her fine. Tonight, however, she was relieved they both wanted a quiet life. Briefly she wondered why he was shunning the limelight.

Ever since the night they'd had the threesome in Italy he'd been somewhat withdrawn. She knew that he hadn't liked the way the evening had panned out. Andy didn't like to relinquish control and that night had been strictly about Loulou's desires. His role had been reduced to no more than a bystander and she had the feeling that his offishness was a way of punishing her for stepping out of line.

Hordes of raucous women, trailing after their meal tickets, stomped down the stairs and spread out to perform on the dance floor.

'Come on,' Loulou grabbed Andy's hand, 'we'd better go and see what's-his-name about his book.'

Flashing camera lights exploded around them as they made their way towards a roped-off section in the far corner of the room. Journalists surrounded a table where a pile of hardback books was stacked. Behind them Loulou could just see Harry Cross, former manager of Notting Hill and recently sacked manager of England. And the book – his retribution. *Thinking of England*, stated the press release, was a no-holds-barred, tell-all account of the England team. The people who came off the page unscathed were few and far between.

Although Loulou wanted to be famous more than anything in the world, she didn't want the prying into her past that was fame's natural ally. There was one secret in particular that she never wanted splashed across the tabloid front pages.

Andy squeezed her hand in an unusual show of affection and she hoped she could at least share it with him one day soon. It was such a burden not being able to speak about it.

'Do you mind getting me a drink?' Rachel asked Robbie finally, having stood by his side for ten minutes with barely an acknowledgement that she existed. All he had done since they'd arrived at the club was grunt hello to a few people and stare at his mobile phone. 'I don't know why you've brought that damn thing with you,' she snapped. 'Anyone that would be ringing you is here.'

Robbie looked surprised at the anger in his wife's voice. 'I'm sorry, Rach, I'm just nervous. You know I don't like these things. You're always on show. What do you want to drink?'

Rachel surprised him for a second time by ordering a large vodka and orange; usually she never had more than a small glass of white wine.

With Robbie gone Rachel felt even more self-conscious. If Robbie was nervous, what did he think she was? That she was actually in Supernova, a place she had only ever read about in the gossip pages of magazines, only heightened her fear. Even the music, which was much too loud and modern, strummed at her nerves.

And being surrounded by so many young pretty girls was a nasty reminder of why she was so angry with Robbie. He was completely oblivious to the care she had taken over her appearance. Her dress was more revealing than usual, showing her neck and the top of her pale shoulders. And Robbie still hadn't noticed her hair.

Rachel saw Robbie coming towards her, struggling to talk into his mobile and carry their two drinks. He dumped the vodka and orange in her hand and said, 'I got to take this call outside, can't hear a thing.'

Before Rachel could stop him he'd disappeared into the crowd. What phonecall could be that important that he had to leave her alone?

She searched the faces of the famous and infamous for Chris – something she had promised herself she wouldn't do. She desperately wanted to see him but when Chris had last rung, she had heard the click of the upstairs extension. Her mother-in-law was monitoring her every move. Although the conversation had consisted of no more than general chat about the kids and Chris's last match, immediately afterwards Rachel had gone out and called him from a telephone box. She was brief and to the point: he couldn't contact her again. She had replaced the receiver before he could finish his question. Why?

Rachel was almost relieved that Mary had forced her to take that action. She was getting into dangerous waters with Chris. Even though the phonecalls were innocent now, they were a prelude to something else. Rachel couldn't be unfaithful to Robbie; she knew he wouldn't do that to her and, more importantly, she couldn't do it to the children.

Then she caught sight of Chris. He had his back to her but it was as if he sensed her gaze on him and he turned to face her. Their eyes met and for a moment it was as if there was no one else in the room. Then she looked away.

Carla stood on a chair and looked across the crowded dance floor. Since she had arrived she had first looked for Stefan and then Stu; neither seemed to be present.

Who else was here? After a preliminary glance around she told herself there was no one worth accosting, but in truth there was too much competition. It seemed like every blond bimbo with a half-decent figure was there, and from their suggestive gyrating they looked determined to land themselves a man.

Carla was wearing another of Jenny's dresses. Although Jenny had claimed to have been fatter than she was now there was no way she could ever have been as big as Carla. It puzzled Carla how Jenny could guzzle booze all day and stay like a stick insect, while it seemed if she so much as looked at alcohol another pound piled on.

Before she had a chance to become maudlin she spotted just the right person to get her teeth into – Clive Dorning. She was convinced that his brush-off at

Rachel's party had been for the benefit of other people. All she needed to do was to get him in a corner where no one else could overhear their conversation.

Walking past the table where a drunk Harry Cross was now arguing with anyone who would listen to him, Carla picked up one of the books and made her way towards Clive.

Standing on his own as usual, it was a simple procedure to use her ample body to push him into an empty corner seat. His shock at being manhandled in such a manner quickly turned to anger.

'What do you want?' he spat.

'You, of course, Clive.'

'Look, do you mind letting me out. I don't want to be seen with the likes of you.'

'Oh, I'm good enough to give you a blow job but not good enough to speak to.'

'Keep your voice down.'

Carla flicked through *Thinking of England*. 'Do you think a book on you would be a bestseller? I'm sure there are lots of people out there who'd like to know the *real* Clive Dorning,' she said, giving him a sickly sweet smile.

'You bitch,' he hissed, but his voice sounded more afraid than angry. It was clear from the look on his face that Clive was beginning to realise he'd made one of the biggest mistakes of his life. 'As I said, what do you want?'

'You.'

'Come to my office Friday, ten a.m. We'll talk then. Now please move.'

Carla made a big show of curtseying as he pushed past her.

*   *   *

As she entered Charing Cross Road, Jenny stopped the car and fell out on to the pavement. Despite being surrounded by the dressed-to-the-nines theatre crowd, who were just leaving the surrounding playhouses, she couldn't stop herself vomiting on the pavement. She could hear the tutting and the comments of 'How disgusting'.

She leaned against the car and took deep breaths. A middle-aged American couple were just passing. 'I thought drunks in England weren't allowed to drive,' the woman said in a voice loud enough for the whole street to hear.

Jenny wanted to protest her innocence – for once she wasn't drunk – but another wave of nausea rolled over her.

When she lifted her head she saw a pink Suzuki Vitara parking about fifty yards from her. It couldn't be her. Surely Michael wouldn't have invited her to Supernova – the press was there.

Despite the nausea, Jenny had to know who was driving the Suzuki. She managed to pull herself together sufficiently to walk down the street towards the jeep. A woman got out but in the dark all Jenny could make out was her long, dark hair. Most of the women Jenny knew were from the bottle blond end of the spectrum. Who the hell was this woman?

Ignoring how ill she felt, Jenny began to pick up speed, scared that she might lose sight of the woman. Breaking into a run, she misjudged stepping off the kerb and went sprawling into the road. Her hands saved her from further damage but they were bleeding and badly scratched. She sat down heavily on the pavement, breathing deeply; her black tights were ripped to shreds.

Glancing up, she spotted the mystery woman heading towards Leicester Square. If she made a real effort she might be able to catch up with her. She ran awkwardly on her high heels, managing to keep the dark-haired woman in sight for a few minutes but then she lost her, both of them swamped by rowdy teenagers and bewildered tourists. Jenny ran through Chinatown and then across Shaftesbury Avenue into the glaring lights of Soho. There was still no sign of her.

Stopping to get her breath back, Jenny consoled herself that the woman hadn't gone into Supernova. Where Michael was – or where he *said* he would be. But how did she know? He was probably meeting the woman somewhere else first. That would make sense of why she'd parked her car so far away. It had to be her. Jenny needed a drink.

Rachel looked at her watch for the twentieth time. She couldn't believe that Robbie had been gone for over an hour. Where the hell was he? She couldn't bear walking around the club one more time, getting more and more pitying looks each time she asked the same people if they had seen her errant husband. No doubt Robbie was drunk in a corner somewhere but she was damned if she'd bother to search him out now. It was time to go home. Retrieving her coat from the cloakroom, she felt a hand helping her on with it.

'Going so soon,' Chris said.

'Chris, we have to stop meeting like this,' she said,

trying to make light of the situation but aware that her voice sounded shrill.

'Don't go yet. Come and have a drink with me.'

'I can't. I have to get home. Have you seen Robbie?'

'No.' His expression told her that Robbie was the last person he wanted to talk about.

There was something in Chris's look, the intensity behind his eyes, that took her breath away and made her heart beat faster. But whatever the effect he was having on her, it wasn't right – however badly Robbie had behaved.

Chris moved towards her and took her hand in his. Neither of them said anything and Rachel was hardly aware of the people pushing and shoving to get past them.

'Stay,' he whispered.

Her heart screamed at her to say yes but her mind, which was swamped by images of her children, her mother-in-law and, lastly, Robbie, told her to say no.

'It wouldn't be wise. Not here.' And Rachel knew that with those last two words she had begun something.

Chris smiled and then planted a kiss on her cheek. His mouth moved across her face and for a very brief moment brushed against her lips.

'I've got to go,' Rachel said, pulling away from him and fleeing out the door.

Jenny had gone into the first bar she'd found in Soho that wasn't on full view to the public. It was in Greek Street and looked like the kind of bar none of the Soho trendies – or anyone who would recognise her – would visit.

As she walked through the tatty entrance she caught sight of herself in the mirror. She was a spectacle. With her mascara-streaked face and torn tights she looked like a mad bag-lady. She thought someone might prevent her from entering the bar but no one even bothered to look up from their drinks.

Despite the nausea, which had abated only slightly, she ordered a large vodka and orange. It quelled the sickness so she quickly ordered another one. After a couple more she actually began to feel almost normal, although even through her alcoholic haze it frightened her that the only time she did feel normal nowadays was after a considerable amount to drink.

The one thing she had been avoiding thinking about all day and every day since she'd last been to the gym was whether or not she was pregnant. She just couldn't believe she was; with her lifestyle it would be no surprise that she missed a period.

'Oh Christ,' she muttered suddenly. Maybe she was starting the menopause, that would explain the nausea, the see-sawing emotions and tiredness. And then she would never be able to get pregnant, which would no doubt make Michael happy.

Stumbling slightly she made it to the toilet where she tried to repair the damage to her make-up. As she removed her shredded tights she saw that she had ripped her canary yellow dress, which had cost well over a thousand pounds. Despite all the evidence to the contrary she told herself that she didn't look too bad. One more drink and then she'd be able to face Supernova and Michael – if he was there.

Back in the bar she sat down at an empty table and looked around at the other customers. When she had walked in she hadn't noticed that most of them looked as though they weren't old enough to drive let alone drink.

Martine was right: she was an old hag, and she didn't need these fresh, unlined faces to remind her that everything about her was decrepit and decaying. With these thoughts she went reeling back to the bar, where she demanded a triple vodka.

Then she spotted a face not quite so young. It was that of Robbie Black – and he wasn't on his own. He had his arm draped around a girl, who appeared to be no more than fourteen or fifteen.

Jenny turned away so that he wouldn't see her. She couldn't believe it. She had always thought that Robbie, dumb as he was, was totally committed to the nice but dull Rachel. Well that settled it, every man was the same, every last one of them a bastard.

Finding it ever more difficult to control her body, Jenny slipped off her barstool. The noise made Robbie lift his head and even through bleary eyes and a smoke-filled room, Jenny saw the look of horror on his face when he recognised her.

Chapter Twenty-Two

The week in Ibiza should have been one of the high points of Tanya's professional career. The Rivisco calendar, though not quite in the Pirelli league, was respected in the industry and was starting to become a collector's item. Plus she was working with some name photographers, and the other models, Keisha Colebrook and Lindi Beene, were girls she knew from way back when.

It should have been perfect. Instead it was one of the worst weeks of her life. She couldn't stop crying and the make-up artist was having to work overtime. Being so far away from home somehow made it worse; she knew she wouldn't have contacted David this week if she'd been in London but being stuck here made the break-up so much more final.

Every night she'd lain awake at the villa unable to sleep, partly from the heat but mostly from the fear that she'd just made the biggest mistake in her life letting a man as wonderful as David slip through her fingers. Why couldn't she have just told him that she was planning to jack it all in anyway?

Pride. And because David had tried to make her feel ashamed about what she did. She would never in a million years have believed he felt that way about her career. How could he have lied to her so much? If he'd always felt so strongly and yet had never said a word, what else had he kept from her? Suddenly he seemed like a complete stranger.

'Are you all right?' Keisha asked, rubbing lemon juice into her near-white hair. 'They're all bastards. Mind you, I thought your one was different. I was always dead jealous.'

'He *was* different, Keesh.' She felt the tears coming on again.

Lindi stepped naked from the villa pool, her large dark brown eyes streaming from the chlorine. 'Ohh, that was lovely. Oh, Tan, don't cry, darling.'

Tanya couldn't stop herself and the two models sat either side of her on the sun lounger and cuddled her. 'Them lesbians have the right idea,' Keisha laughed. 'Kill the lot of 'em.'

'Leave us a couple,' Lindi said. 'You know – for when the batteries run out.'

Soon the other girls had Tanya smiling again. It was good to have female company at times like this – something she had missed when all of her fortunes had been so closely tied up with Notting Hill.

But that was behind her now. If she was anything, she was a survivor, and though at this moment the future seemed empty, she was sure she would pull through and create a new life for herself. It was just that David wouldn't be there to share it.

'What do you fancy doing today?' Lindi asked, tying back her long brown hair into a ponytail. Today they were free to do what they wanted. 'I thought I might go into town and do a bit of shopping.'

'I'm staying here,' Keisha said. 'Catch up on a bit of sunbathing.'

Even though it was late October, the weather in Ibiza was unusually warm.

'She thinks melanoma is something you pick up from melons,' Lindi said. 'Keesh, you couldn't possibly get any browner.'

'Watch me,' Keisha said, applying coconut oil to her arms. 'What about you, Tan?'

'I wouldn't mind driving somewhere to do some sketching.'

'Those drawings of yours – they're like something out of a horror film!' Lindi declared.

'So neither of you mind if I take the motor?' Tanya asked, dabbing at her eyes behind her sunglasses. The two models shook their heads. 'Then I think I'll go now. Before it gets too hot.'

She went back to her bedroom and changed from her bikini into an airy linen dress with long, loose arms. Unlike Keisha, she didn't like too much sun.

Tying a scarf around her neck and putting on a wide-brimmed sun-hat, she set off in the Mini Moke, feeling a momentary burst of optimism. So what if she didn't know what she was going to do with her life?

Tanya tried hard to stay in a positive frame of mind as she drove the car across the arid, unforgiving landscape away from Ibiza town. Dust flew up from the wheels and into her eyes, giving her an excuse for the occasional tear.

She had a map but soon she was hopelessly lost. Not that she minded. She had no particular destination in mind and neither had she intended to do much sketching. She merely wanted to escape and be on her own for a while.

Keisha and Lindi were angels but after a while their sympathy tended to make her even sadder. They'd been through the mill themselves, many times, and their stories of disappointment and deceit only served to make what happened between her and David seem inevitable – as if women were always destined to have their hearts broken by men.

Tanya drove for a couple of hours, passing through small sleepy villages and olive groves, scattering herds of goats and forcing the odd farmer to back up against the dry-stone walls lining the narrow roads as she sped past. This was the quieter side of Ibiza, away from the mega clubs, drugs and glitz.

The sun was now at its highest and the few houses she passed had battened down their shutters for siesta. Fortunately, before the heat became too much, the olive groves gave way to pine forests, and as the road ascended into the hills the air became cooler. Seeing a sign to Portinatx, she realised that she'd almost reached the far side of the island.

Wasn't Harrison Lamb's studio somewhere nearby? She admired his work and had a book featuring his early sculptures. Now where was the place? She pulled over and studied the map, hoping if she saw the name it would jog her memory.

San Juan Bautista – that was it. From a rough estimate it looked as if it was only a couple of miles further on. She put her foot down on the gas, glad to have found a destination at last.

As it turned out the studio was clearly signposted. Lamb was one of Ibiza's most famous residents even

though his best work was now many years behind
him. Following a trail of hand-painted signs, she was
surprised to come upon a rather ramshackle villa
with peeling white paint-work and an orange clay roof
pock-marked by missing slates.

Tanya stopped the car and climbed out. There
didn't seem to be anyone around and she feared that
this place too might be closed for the afternoon. An
arrow pointed through an ivy-clad archway and she
followed it into a shaded courtyard with a fountain
sluggishly trickling at its centre.

Around the courtyard were several pieces of Lamb's
work. Tanya didn't recognise any of them and guessed
they were from his later, less successful period. Nevertheless, their gently undulating, feminine curves were
pleasing to the eye and to the touch.

She crossed the courtyard and followed another
arrow into a building adjoining the main villa. Here
she found more finished pieces by the sculptor plus a
gallery containing his sketches. Ambient music played
gently in the background, a mixture of water sounds
and bells, which Tanya found relaxing after the roar
of the Mini Moke.

There was a bench in the middle of the gallery and
she sat down. It was a treacherous thought, she knew,
but as much as she loved her family she wished she
could have been exposed to a life like this when she
was growing up. How lucky Loulou had been.

Tanya screwed the top off a bottle of mineral water
and took a large swig, letting the music wash over her.
She closed her eyes and tried to unwind but as soon
as she let down her guard thoughts of David began to
intrude.

'Go and ask her if she's paid,' a shrill voice behind her shouted.

Tanya looked around and saw a middle-aged couple standing in the doorway. Though the pictures she'd seen of them were at least twenty years old, she recognised the Lambs immediately.

'You there,' Laura called. 'There's an admission fee.'

Tanya turned scarlet with embarrassment. 'I – I'm sorry. I didn't know. There was nobody here.'

'No problem,' Harrison said, his voice much softer than his wife's. Tanya could see that Loulou had inherited her looks from him rather than from her mother.

Harrison was probably in his early sixties but he was still a fine-looking man, his blond hair only just beginning to whiten with age. He walked with a cane but his agile movements suggested it was more for effect than necessity. As he drew closer Tanya saw that his eyes were the same blue as Loulou's and a close-trimmed beard successfully covered up the signs of ageing on his neck.

'Make sure you do it on your way out,' Laura snapped.

'Why can't you leave it, woman?' Harrison asked.

'We haven't got a pot to piss in,' Laura shrieked. 'Have you paid the maid this week? Or, for that matter, for the last three months?'

The couple were shouting at each other as if Tanya were invisible.

'Things are not that bad, Laura. I can't stand it when you get hysterical about money. It'll work itself out.'

Tanya had listened to too much. If they were strangers she wouldn't have cared, but knowing their daughter made it different. She wondered if perhaps she should introduce herself, but it didn't seem the best time to do so.

Instead, she wandered back into the courtyard where, blinded by the sunlight, for a second she thought she saw Loulou. She looked again and realised that it was a young boy. He was crying.

Tanya walked over to him and sat down. 'Hey, what's the matter?' she asked gently.

'It's them,' the boy blurted. 'They never stop. I hate them – and they hate me.' Instinctively Tanya put her arm around the boy. In response, he buried his head in her chest.

She stroked his hair and gradually he grew quiet.

'What makes you say that?'

'She told me,' the boy said, tears rolling down his cheeks.

'There,' Tanya said, squeezing him. 'Of course they don't hate you.' She thought for a second. 'You're . . . Dexter, aren't you?'

'How did you know that?' The surprise stopped his tears.

'I'm Tanya. I'm a friend of your sister's,' she said. Friend wasn't the right word but she hoped Loulou would forgive her given the circumstances. 'Our boy-friends play for the same team. Or at least they did . . .'

Dexter brightened. 'You know Loulou? Cool.'

'You know,' Tanya said, 'I remember when my mum and dad used to argue. It used to scare me, too. I thought that I'd done something to make them angry but I hadn't. Grown-ups just get ratty with each other sometimes.'

'I broke a vase with my football today and Laura told me that if I didn't start behaving myself, she'd get my real mother to come and take me away.'

What a horrible thing to say, Tanya thought. She looked at the boy – he was definitely a Lamb, and, like Loulou, took after his father more than after his mother. She reassessed her thoughts in the gallery: whatever their shortcomings, the Barrys had never left her in any doubt about how much she was loved.

'People say things they don't mean,' she said unconvincingly. From what she'd heard from Laura she could quite believe that the woman meant every word.

'Will you be seeing Loulou soon?' Dexter asked.

'Probably. I bump into her all the time.'

'I did a picture for her. I was going to post it but perhaps you could give it to her – if you don't mind.'

''Course not,' Tanya smiled. 'I'd love to.' With that she had just given herself a link with Notting Hill, if just for a little while longer.

'There's a call for you, Tan.'

Tanya sat up in bed and yawned. 'What? Who is it?'

'It's that love-rat ex of yours,' Keisha said. 'Do you want me to tell him to piss off?'

'Don't you dare!' Tanya shouted, diving out of bed. She ran for the phone. 'Hello?'

The line crackled. 'Tanya? Tanya, is that you? Look, I'm so sorry. You've got to forgive me.'

Tanya remained silent, the tears threatening at the sound of David's voice.

'Tanya? Please speak to me.'

'You shouldn't have phoned, David. You have no idea how much you've hurt me.'

'Don't hang up,' he begged. 'I had no right to say what I did. None at all.'

'How could you have lied to me like that, David? Pretending all this time that you were so proud of me?'

'I didn't lie. I was – I mean I *am* proud of you. Tanya, I feel so mixed up. I don't know why I said the things I did, but I'd do anything to be able to take them back. You're the best thing that's ever happened to me, and the day you said you'd marry me . . .' His voice faded away.

'David?' She could hear the pain in his voice and her resolve just melted away. She loved him unconditionally and that meant she could forgive him anything. Absolutely anything.

'Tan, when you come back – we can sort this out. Can't we?'

She wanted to blurt out that she loved him but she held back, wanting him to understand how much he'd hurt her. 'We'll talk. Sure. Look, I've got to go. Take care of yourself.' She put down the phone and felt her heart soar.

The others were out by the pool when she appeared a few minutes later.

'You've said you'll forgive him,' Keisha said. 'Haven't you?'

'I didn't say anything,' Tanya replied, but the smile beaming across her face told the full story. 'I just said we'd talk.'

'You traitor,' Lindi laughed. 'I thought us single

girls were going to stick together.' Lindi ran at her and grabbed her arm. 'Right, for that you're going in the pool.'

'No!' Tanya screamed but Lindi had already sent her hurtling through the air. Water filled her nose and mouth as she disappeared beneath the surface and for a moment she lost her bearings as she struggled to right herself.

Coughing and spluttering, she emerged from the water. Keisha and Lindi were laughing hysterically. Tanya joined in and suddenly her life seemed filled with hope again. She pulled off the sodden T-shirt and stood by the pool naked.

'That's it, exude, exude,' Keisha laughed, pretending to hold a camera.

Tanya struck a pose, mouth open and tongue lolling from her mouth.

Keisha got on her knees to change angle. 'Gimme them boobies. Yeah, that's it. Lovely.'

Tanya bent forward – the udder shot – and gave her breasts a squeeze. 'Howzat?' she asked.

Keisha shrieked but the smile was suddenly wiped clean from Tanya's face. As she cupped her breasts in her hands, her fingers found what was, unmistakably, a lump.

Chapter Twenty-Three

'Congrat . . .' The doctor looked up from her desk and the word died on her lips, as she saw the look of horror on the woman's face. Congratulations were not in order.

Despite the warmth of the small room Jenny shivered. For several minutes the room was filled with silence while Jenny stared unseeing at a wall-chart in front of her. 'It can't be,' she whispered eventually. 'It just can't be.'

'I'm sorry, Mrs Waite, there is no mistake. You are definitely pregnant.' The doctor picked up the small test that had huge ramifications. The two vivid blue lines stood out accusingly. 'When was your last period?'

Jenny tried to pull herself together. She could hardly think, let alone remember a detail like that. The last couple of months had passed in a haze, aided and abetted by copious quantities of drugs and alcohol. Simultaneously. Oh God, what the hell had she done to the baby? The thought concentrated her mind.

'Um, I think it was about two months ago but I'm not sure. I'm really worr—'

'That would make you eight weeks pregnant. First things first. Are you going to keep it?' A harshness had crept into the doctor's voice.

'I . . . I don't know. My husband doesn't want a baby but it's more I'm afra . . . afraid I've damaged it.'

'What do you mean?'

'I've been drinking and . . .' Jenny took a deep breath. 'And taking a lot of cocaine.'

The doctor's look of concern made Jenny want to cry. What had she done to her baby? No doubt the doctor would now advise her to have an abortion.

'In what quantities?'

'A lot. Sometimes a bottle of vodka a day. And maybe a gramme of coke.' The tawdriness of her life was laid out before this stranger.

The doctor frowned. 'And how long has this been going on?'

For ever, Jenny wanted to say. 'All the time I've been pregnant. Have I harmed the baby?' Jenny's voice broke as tears welled up in her eyes. Her shivering had been replaced by sweating; the room felt so stuffy, she could hardly breathe.

'I can't say one way or another. Although we count you as being pregnant from the day of your last period, you wouldn't actually have conceived for another fortnight. It takes a further week for the egg to implant itself in the womb, so we're talking about five weeks. If you stop abusing yourself now, the baby stands a good chance. Of course, we won't know for certain until it's born.'

Jenny nodded, barely able to take in all the information.

'You need to call us as soon as you've made a decision. And, Mrs Waite. The drinking and the drugs

– they have to stop immediately. I have a couple of numbers for rehab clinics and counsellors. I suggest you contact them whatever you choose to do.'

The doctor began to file her notes. The appointment was over.

Clive's face was contorted with disgust, his voice thin. 'You're sacked, and banned from the grounds of Notting Hill. Am I making myself clear?'

Carla stared at him, speechless. This wasn't in her game-plan. First the disaster with Stu and now this. Her mind worked quickly. She couldn't let this happen. She'd be back to where she started, only worse off – she wasn't sixteen any more.

Although it went against the grain, she decided that the only option open to her was to be conciliatory. She moved slightly on his unmade bed until she was in a position to show him all that she was offering. Carla had spent a lot of time getting ready that morning; she was in full make-up and very few clothes. She was determined all her effort wasn't going to go to waste. As she revealed more and more of her flesh she shivered in the unheated room.

Taking his silence as permission to speak, Carla lowered her voice and sounded slightly breathless. She hoped she sounded contrite and pathetic. 'Clive, I'm really sorry if I upset you. I really didn't mean to. I wouldn't do anything to harm you. I was just scared I'd lose you.' Knowing she was on borrowed time, her words stumbled over each other as she tried to speak as quickly as possible.

Clive snorted derisively in reply.

'We can sort this out. You know I can give you

what you want, when you want.' Carla made a move towards him. 'You know you don't mean it.'

Before he could back away from her Carla dropped to her knees and made a grab at his trousers. She heard the crack of his hand just before she felt the stinging smack across her cheek. Her head jerked back and her face burned from the pain but she stayed where she was. It was nothing compared to the physical abuse she'd suffered throughout her life.

Tentatively, she placed her hand on Clive's zip, holding her breath in anticipation of being slapped again. Nothing happened. Taking this as her cue to continue, she slowly unzipped him.

Clive groaned as she performed. She could feel him move slightly and then came the flash of the Polaroid. It was all over in a matter of minutes.

Zipping himself up he walked towards his bedside table and picked up the phone. 'Margaret, get someone up here to escort Miss Ryman from the building. Could you also inform the Head of Security that she is not allowed on the premises again.'

'You bastard!' Carla screamed, chasing after him into his office.

Clive allowed himself a smug smile. 'You're out of your league, Carla. Go back to the gutter where you belong.'

Before she could say anything else she felt a heavy hand on her shoulder. 'Miss Ryman, this way.' It was Fred, a security guard who had given her the eye every time he spotted her and who now looked through her as if she didn't exist.

'Get your hands off me,' Carla spat, twisting away from his hold on her.

Fred placed his hand back on her, this time with a firmer grip. He began to steer her towards the door. Carla turned to give Clive a final mouthful and spotted him with his latest picture of her. Holding her own against Fred, who at fifty was struggling to keep her moving, she managed to stay still long enough to see Clive put the photo in a video box which he then placed on a shelf. That would be her revenge. If it was the last thing she did she would get hold of those photos. Let the bastard answer to the press.

'You made a huge mistake, Dorning. You just wait and see.'

Fred made a final determined effort and after a couple of hard shoves Carla was out the door.

Jenny's hand shook as she poured the last of the vodka down the sink. Luckily, Michael was away with the team in Amsterdam so she had a few days' grace before she had to explain why their usually full drinks cabinet was completely empty.

She paced the kitchen wondering what to do next. Since seeing the doctor she had spent the last four days on her own. Most of the time she had slept, trying to block out her desperate need for a drink.

Now she felt like she was crawling up the wall. One minute she was sweating, the next shivering and all the time with the most terrible shakes. Her stomach kept cramping and she had a rash over most of her body. She had never quit alcohol long enough before to get what she now assumed was the DTs.

Her mind wandered as she looked at some of the equipment surrounding her, wondering what it was used for. As far as she and Michael were concerned the kitchen was there only to chill drinks and keep the ice.

If she didn't talk to someone soon she'd be out buying replacement drink and searching through drawers for any left-over cocaine. But who could she call? The struggle to come up with someone to turn to made Jenny realise just how alone she was. She had no close women friends. No friends at all.

The thought of talking to any of the other wives filled Jenny with horror. The news of her pregnancy would be all over Notting Hill within minutes.

Then she thought of Rachel. She wasn't a friend but she was the nearest thing to a sane person in an insane world. And she had children; she might be able to give Jenny some advice. Although she couldn't imagine that someone like Rachel had ever faced a dilemma such as the one she did now.

She rang the club secretary and got Rachel's number. The phone was answered on the second ring by a voice she didn't recognise. 'Hi, have I got the right number for Rachel?'

'Yes, who is it?' the woman asked, her voice steeped in suspicion.

'Jenny Waite.'

'Oh,' came the reply, and from that one word Jenny could tell exactly what this stranger knew and thought about her.

'Hello.' Rachel spoke into the receiver a few seconds later sounding puzzled. 'Jenny?'

'I hope I'm not disturbing you but I wondered if you and the children would like to come to the zoo.'

'The zoo? When?'

'Now.'

'Um, well . . .'

Jenny could hear the muffled voice of the other woman in the background.

'I'd love to.'

They arranged to meet at the entrance, Jenny aware that Rachel's reluctance to see her was not as great as her need to escape the woman who had answered the phone.

There was an autumn chill in the air and for once Jenny dressed accordingly with a long black trench coat. She also wore very little make-up. Such was the change in her that Rachel nearly walked right past.

'Rachel, it's me,' Jenny laughed, grabbing hold of the younger woman's arm, relieved to at last be with another human being.

'Hi,' Rachel managed, struggling to keep hold of both children. 'Thanks for thinking of us. We all needed to get out of the house.'

'I know what you mean.'

Then the two women fell silent, both at a loss what to say next. Only the children's squabbles and the howling of the nearby monkeys broke the stillness.

After Jenny insisted on paying the entrance fee, the two women began to speak at once. It broke the ice and they both laughed.

'You first,' Jenny insisted.

'Thanks for inviting us. It really is a nice change. I do get a bit cooped up in the house all day.'

'Same here – and thanks for coming.'

Rachel smiled and they hurried to catch up with the children, who were already at the monkey enclosure. As they wandered around, entertaining the children, the women chatted to each other about nothing in particular – the weather, animals, prices – and as they continued to talk an easiness developed between them.

While they drank their fifth coffee of the afternoon, Jenny studied Rachel as she wiped off the globules of ice-cream decorating Robbie Jnr's coat. She also looked different but Jenny couldn't quite put her finger on what it was. Her clothes were new and more stylish than usual but there was something else.

'I have to tell you how awful it was when I went down Bond Street for a new dress,' Rachel laughed, as if she had read Jenny's thoughts.

While she retold the horrors of her shopping spree, Jenny realised that underneath the plain, mousy Rachel there was another woman struggling to get out. Perhaps they could be friends and she could help the real Rachel to break through.

Despite this insight and the fact that Jenny was desperate to tell Rachel about her pregnancy, she still felt odd confiding in someone who she had barely spoken to before today. She was surprised, therefore, when Rachel took the lead and confided in her.

'The woman who answered the phone is Robbie's mum. She's moved in with us and to say she makes my life miserable would be an understatement.'

'I gather she wasn't too impressed on hearing my name.'

Rachel blushed.

'I know what people think of me, Rachel, and I don't blame them. I am sober now though.'

Rachel nodded. 'Don't worry about what Mary thinks. She doesn't like me that much and she certainly doesn't hide it.'

'Why is she there? Does she need looking after?'

'If only it were that simple. She's got more energy than you and me put together and nowhere to put it except into other's people's business. Or more specifically, mine. That house has become a prison.'

'Have you talked to Robbie about how you feel?'

Rachel gave a scathing laugh. 'He's a mummy's boy and just won't listen to me. He even accused me of being paranoid. But I'm not,' she said vehemently. 'Mary definitely opens my post and more than once I've heard her pick up the extension when I've been on the phone.'

'But why?'

Jenny saw Rachel's face cloud over. Whatever secrets Rachel had, today wasn't the day she would reveal them. 'She's mad, I guess.'

'Well, I think Robbie should support you first and foremost.' Jenny sounded angry.

Rachel looked surprised at Jenny's tone and almost instantly reverted to the Rachel everyone knew. 'Oh, you know what Robbie's like, a real softy. I can't complain. He's not a bad husband,' she said as much to herself as to Jenny.

Jenny said nothing. She knew that to tell Rachel about Robbie and the young girl would do nothing for their budding friendship. Nobody likes the messenger.

'Although,' Rachel continued, as if her last remark had been left unsaid, 'sometimes I think I got married too young. We were married at seventeen, you know. It's like I missed out on all the fun of being young and fancy free.'

Me and you both, Jenny thought. A tiny hand tugged at her sleeve; it was Demi. Jenny stood, picked her up and swung her around in the air, causing the little girl to squeal with delight.

'Now what shall we see next? I'd like to go to the elephant house.'

Demi cooed, taking Jenny's hand and pulling her along. Robbie Jnr, not wanting to be outdone, grabbed her other hand and both children giggled as they played at dragging her down the path.

'Not so fast,' Jenny laughed. 'I'm an old lady.'

When Rachel caught up with them, Jenny was telling the children the backgrounds to the two elephants munching on hay in front of them.

'What a smell,' Rachel exclaimed.

'It's their poo,' Demi lisped.

'Out of the mouths of babes,' Jenny laughed, leaving the children to ogle the animals.

'You're really good with them,' Rachel said. 'Anyway, we've only talked about me, how are you?'

Jenny knew it was now or never. 'I'm pregnant.'

Rachel gave her a huge smile. 'Congratulations. That's fantastic. How far gone are you?'

'About two months.'

Rachel picked up immediately on her tone. 'You are glad, aren't you?'

'To tell you the truth it's been such a huge shock I don't know what I think. And I'm really frightened that I've hurt it with my . . . my lifestyle.'

'What did the doctor say?'

'They can't really say. I just have to wait.'

'What does Michael say?'

'He doesn't know and to be honest I'm dreading

telling him. He doesn't want children. Well, not with me anyway.'

'I'm sure he'll feel differently once you've told him.' But Rachel's voice had lost its certainty. 'Perhaps it'll bring you closer together.'

Jenny said nothing.

Chapter Twenty-Four

'Well done, excellent. Bloody excellent,' David shouted, struggling to be heard above the self-congratulatory voices.

Pushing his fingers through his damp, thinning hair, David allowed himself a satisfied smile. If someone had told him two or three weeks ago that they would have thrashed the Amsterdam team on their own turf he would never have believed it. At that time, the team, like his personal life, had been disintegrating in front of his very eyes.

The tension between Andy and Michael had looked ready to explode at any minute, taking the team with it. But today both players had played well, and David wanted to keep it that way.

He accepted the four-nil score as a sign that all would be well. He was sure that Clive would see that he needed David whoever he went out with or now, hopefully, married. He still couldn't believe that Tanya had forgiven him. What a fool he'd been.

He patted Stefan on the back. 'Good game,' he murmured, but at that moment David had only one thought running through his head: nothing was going to stop him getting what he wanted now, especially not the past. It was his duty to protect the team above all else, and some secrets were meant to be kept.

Stefan accepted David's congratulations but knew the captain was simply going through the motions, as Stefan had played appallingly, and worse still he didn't even care. Paula would be arriving tonight and he was as nervous as he'd been on their first date.

Surely when Paula saw how unhappy he was without her she would agree to come to England, job or no job. When he'd spoken to her last night, she'd sounded sad. He sensed she was weakening and that she was missing him as much as he missed her.

He moved off the bench and began to strip. A smile played at the edges of his mouth. Tonight, he was sure, would be the start of him and Paula being together again. His happiness was only momentarily marred by the sight of Andy, strutting past him, wearing nothing but a gloating smirk.

It was hard to make out the shower cubicles; all twenty were hidden behind a wall of menthol-smelling steam. Eventually Andy found a free one and instantly it began to work its magic as the jets of hot water pounded his body and massaged his aching limbs.

It had been a great game and he knew he had played well, a fact that could only have been highlighted by the Kraut's crap game. There would be just one star striker at Notting Hill.

The blond footballer closed his eyes and leaned back against the tiles. His mind drifted. Thoughts and visual images came thick and fast as his mind flitted from one subject to another until it landed and stayed on Loulou.

Poor Loulou. From her constant frown and uncharacteristic rejection of the limelight, it hadn't taken Andy long to figure out that her acting career wasn't quite the success she had led him to believe.

But this new insecure Loulou suited Andy fine; she was much more pliable and needy. All in all things were looking pretty hunky-dory. His mates were on his side. All he had do was get rid of the Kraut and everything would be perfect. Of course, there was still Michael, but after the night at the Three Lions he had done his best to avoid his team-mate.

'Ouch, watch what you're bloody doing, arsehole,' Michael hissed.

'Christ! Michael, stop being such a baby, it's only a calf strain not a broken leg,' John Cartwright, Notting Hill's physio, retorted. He was used to the players' abuse and at times was extremely tempted to make their injuries worse. And never more so than when he was working on Michael Waite, whose injuries were usually self-inflicted by his aggressive playing.

'Just be a bit more careful, that's all I'm saying.'

If John replied, Michael didn't hear him; he had more important things to think about than a leg injury or football. He had one issue on his mind at the moment: how to get rid of Jenny but keep her money. Short of killing her he couldn't see any way of doing it.

It might not have been so bad if she'd kept her looks. She hadn't been bad for an older bird when he'd first met her but she'd let herself go. Not only had she begun to look years older, but now, for Christ's sake,

she'd started to pile on the pounds. Michael had found
the photographs of Jenny when she was in her teens
and as fat as a house. It wasn't a pretty sight.

The thought of Jenny's flabby body immediately
made him think about his mistress's nubile flesh,
which led him back to his original problem – if he
didn't work out how to keep the money, without
Jenny, that firm piece of ass would be walking out
of his life.

'Aagh, fuck, what was that?' Michael shouted,
jumping up. A cold wet towel fell to the floor.

In front of him was Robbie, laughing like a schoolkid.

'Wanker,' Michael said but only half seriously.
Robbie was one of the few people who liked him at
Notting Hill. Even Michael realised he had to have a
few allies.

Robbie gave Michael a wave and wandered off.

'W . . . w . . . where's y . . . your kit, Robbie?'

'O . . . o . . . on the s . . . s . . . seat, Dougie,' Robbie
laughed. 'Try using your eyes if not your head.'

Dougie Styles, the team's kit man slunk off, cursing
under his breath. He hated Robbie Black, not that the
others were much better. It didn't matter if they won
or lost, the outcome for Dougie was always the same –
if they weren't taking the mickey they were assaulting
him with their smelly socks and wet towels. Still, as his
doctor had pointed out, he was lucky to have the job.

'Come on, guys, hurry up, I want to hit the town,'
Robbie shouted, giving himself a brief once over in the
mirror. His mother was right, with his hair longer he
looked young and innocent.

Just being away from Rachel was enough to put Robbie in a good mood. What the hell was wrong with her at the moment? All she did was gripe about him and his mother. No wonder he needed some light relief. It was a shame Jenny had spotted him but with the way she'd behaved at the Three Lions, she was in no position to talk. Thankfully Rachel never spoke to Jenny or for that matter any of the other women. Gossip at Notting Hill spread faster than a dose of clap. For once, Rachel's lack of popularity was a bonus – his secret was safe.

Robbie sat down next to Stu, who was miles away.

'Cheer up, mate, it's all going to happen tonight.'

Stu certainly hoped so. As he sat on the bench, unconsciously tugging at his red bushy hair, he veered between uncontrollable excitement and self-hatred. This would be his last time, he promised himself. One big finale and then he would bow out before he got caught. And there probably wasn't a better place to do it than Amsterdam.

Stefan got swept up by the others as the group lurched down the street. They were like an amoeba in both shape and behaviour.

'In here,' shouted Robbie, who had taken charge of the drunken party. Stefan had lost count of how many beers the others had had. Fortunately, no one had noticed that he'd left his untouched in each bar they visited.

But now they were entering a coffee shop – one that sold hash.

'What would you like, boys – Purple Haze, Skunk

or . . .' Robbie peered through the fog of marijuana smoke.

Stefan thought he was joking until he heard him order the Purple Haze and a packet of papers. No one else seemed to think anything about it. Why should they? From what Stefan had heard, hash was nothing compared to the harder drugs some of them were taking.

Even David seemed to ignore the whole episode. Stefan studied the captain as he ordered a coffee. His earlier buoyancy had disappeared, his smile replaced by a scowl. Stefan wondered if his loss of humour was down to the players. He wouldn't have blamed him.

An arm stretched across Stefan, knocking his wire-framed glasses to one side. It was Michael's and there was no apology as he snatched Robbie's purchase. His dextrous fingers soon produced a six-inch joint. With Robbie, Tony Anderson, Jamie Carlton and a couple of the reserves, Michael added another layer of haze to the already clouded, stuffy room. Stefan was convinced he was getting high from just being in the place.

He looked at his watch: Paula was still an hour away. His life was on hold until he could once again embrace her. In the meantime he had to grin and bear the company of his team-mates.

'I bet you a ton that I shag more birds than you tonight,' Tony slurred to Michael.

'Come on, make it a bit interesting, a grand at least.'

'You're on.'

'What about you, Stefan – you think you're up to

taking on us Brits? I bet you two grand I'll be screwing more women than you.'

'I'm sure you can, Michael.' God, when was he going to be able to leave? He'd only come along because if he didn't it would only make their taunting worse. They already saw him as someone who thought he was above them, which was partly true. Aside from David and a couple of the other players, he thought most of them were a disgrace to the game and their team.

Another joint later and they were ready to hit the streets again. Nearly every player had only one thing on his mind – the Red Light district. They charged down the road, screaming and shouting and threatening each other with a swim in the canal.

The tiny streets, with their subsiding ancient houses, were teeming with life. Lost tourists rubbed shoulders with the pimps and the pushers, oblivious to what was being offered to them. There was a distinctive smell in the air, a potent mix of stale fried food and urine, the latter running freely into the streets and the canals from the many open-air *pissoirs*.

Robbie, still leading the pack, was the first to find a prostitute. The middle-aged woman, who had obviously seen better years, was sitting in a window, dressed only in a red peep-hole bra and crotchless knickers.

'How much, love?' he shouted, thrusting his pelvis towards the glass.

'Give her one, Robbie.'

'And one from me.'

Robbie looked again. The mere thought of touching her saggy flesh made him want to puke. Suddenly they

were all distracted by the retching behind them. Magic
Anderson was bent over double. Another retch and
vomit splashed on the pavement.

'Wayhey,' Robbie shouted. 'I'll have whatever you've
had, Tony.'

With the cheering, the jeering and the vomiting, the
team was indistinguishable from the more rowdy fans
who followed them from town to city, from country
to country. It was time for Stefan to go.

'I'm going,' he said in little more than a whisper.

'You what?' Michael asked, his face threateningly
close to Stefan's.

'I've got to meet someone.'

'You pre-book a whore earlier?' Michael laughed,
turning to share his line with the rest of the team.

Stefan tried to smile in the face of their tittering.
'No. My fiancée.' He turned quickly, not waiting
for any smart reply. As he broke into a run down
Warmoesstraat he tried to shut out the catcalls that
followed him.

Stefan paced up and down, ignoring the stares from
the hotel's other guests. Paula's plane should have
landed two hours ago but there was still no sign of
her. Worried for her safety, he asked the receptionist
to check with the airport.

'Certainly, Mr Lohmann,' the receptionist said,
handing him a fax. 'This came for you earlier.'

Stefan read the brief message several times, unable
to believe what it said.

*I'm sorry. I can't come. It's over. Please don't call
me again.*

How could Paula be so heartless and cruel, telling

him that everything between them was over in a fax?

As David wandered down the street, the conflicting, competing music of a dozen different Europop records assaulted his ears. How quickly things changed. His earlier elation had disappeared and now he had plunged into new depths of despair. Just before coming out he had spoken to Tanya. She had sounded upset but she had refused to tell him why. He was convinced she must have changed her mind.

Who could blame her? What he had said about her career was unforgivable. How dare Leary suggest that Tanya would bring the team into disrepute. No one could bring notoriety to that bunch of sex-mad boozers.

Suddenly he noticed that he had long ago left the others behind. The street had become darker with each footstep, and there were no women in windows or lurid, loud sex shops; just houses and the occasional bar.

Turning, he retraced his footsteps and then stopped. He spotted Michael and the others disappearing into a club that boasted 'REAL FUCKING LIVE SHOW' in a rainbow of neon lights.

David realised then that it wasn't simply Tanya that was worrying him. The night at the Three Lions was plaguing him and he knew that sooner or later one of these losers was going to get caught out. And where would David Ashby be then?

Robbie had no idea where the others had gone. He

was hoping to go off with Michael but had ended up with Andy.

'How much?' Andy shouted. And then in response to the woman's reply, 'On your bike, you old slapper.' There was unmistakable aggression in his voice.

This was the fourth tart Andy had turned down and Robbie could see that there was no way his team-mate was going to pay for sex. It was clear that Andy thought they should pay him for the privilege. And having seen him in action, Robbie had no doubt that the lucky bugger could get a woman to pay him.

Robbie hadn't bothered with any of the women although he'd had a good look and a laugh, peering through all the windows as, one by one, the semi-clad women, in every shape, colour, size and age, found a punter and pulled the curtains. But all were too old for his tastes.

'Hey, look at this,' Andy shouted to Robbie. 'The Erotic Discount Centre, that should be right up your street.'

Taking in the window display, Robbie's eyes nearly popped out – who came up with this kind of stuff? he wondered, particularly fascinated by the disembodied plastic vagina lying on a foil pie dish. He went inside the store.

The place held a cornucopia of sexual gadgetry, a library for the sexually deviant – and Robbie loved it. Ignoring all the battery-operated goods he went straight to the magazines, which catered for every taste. But there was only one area Robbie was interested in: he avidly leafed through one mag after another – *Seventeen*, *Lesbian Teenager*, *Sexy Schoolgirl*. The pictures said it all and there were no words to fear. Robbie was in heaven.

'Come on, love, give us a break. I'm not some stupid fucking tourist, you know,' Michael said, his tone becoming increasingly belligerent. Although he had to admit that the young Thai woman, dressed only in a transparent short white dress, was the best he'd seen yet.

'I give you good time. You see,' she said in response.

'I'm sure but cheaper, much cheaper.'

'OK, I do you special deal.'

After a few more minutes of haggling they finally agreed a price.

'Hey, Stu,' Michael shouted, 'I'm in here. See you back at the hotel.'

He saw Stu nod. Michael took in the tart his team mate was chatting to. Not much of a looker.

'Come, lie here,' Rosie said, pulling the curtain on the little room that housed nothing more than a rickety old bed. The room smelled of rubber and semen despite the perfumed candles and the woman's cheap scent.

'Take off your clothes.'

Michael did as he was told. The bartering with pro after pro had been like foreplay and he was ready to go the whole hog. He lay back on the bed, which creaked and groaned precariously, his erection standing up at a right angle to his stomach.

Rosie unwrapped a condom and quickly and expertly covered his cock. 'Now we ready,' she said as she straddled his waist.

It was all over in a couple of minutes and Michael clocked the look of relief on the prostitute's face.

'You got any coke?' he asked.

Stu was relieved to have finally got rid of Michael. There had been no way he could ask for what he wanted while the other player had been in earshot. Now there was no going back. He had now found the ideal candidate.

'I zink you need more rouge,' Stevie said, in a husky broken English.

Stu studied himself in the tarnished gilt mirror, amazed at his image. Stevie's reflection revealed nothing of her true self – she looked every inch the woman she had always wanted to be. And now she was using her magic on Stu.

Stu took the advice and brushed another streak of blusher across his cheeks. This was to be the last time; he had to look his best and savour every minute of his transformation.

'Now the dress,' Stevie said, jumping off the bed and taking a low-cut, off-the-shoulder purple number from a hanger on the door.

Stu stood up and straightened out the padded bra before drawing the dress up over his legs. He had declined Stevie's offer of a shave. There was no way he'd be able to explain that away.

Moving behind Stu, Stevie began to zip him up, but she stopped when she heard a commotion outside.

'Are you in there? Stu?' It was Michael's voice.

'Shit!' Stu exclaimed, tearing at the dress in his haste to get it off.

The outfit was halfway round his knees when the door burst open.

'Caught you . . .'

Michael came to a halt and looked from Stu to Stevie and then back again. His expression quickly went from disbelief to disgust. 'You're a fucking tranny,' he screeched.

'Michael – it's not what it looks like—'

'I don't fucking believe it,' Michael said, laughing hysterically. He backed out of the door. 'You're finished, you perv.'

Stu stayed motionless long after Michael had left, hardly able to take it all in. His secret was out. He was finished.

Chapter Twenty-Five

Half awake, Loulou reached out for Andy and knocked over the ashtray that had been perched on the pillow beside her. It took a few seconds for her to remember that he was still away and she lay motionless until the smell of ash forced her to throw back the sheets and stagger out of bed.

As she stood up, her hangover kicked in with a vengeance and she was sorely tempted to climb back under the sheets, cigarette butts and all. Not normally a heavy drinker, in the past two days she had drunk every last drop of alcohol in the house, mired in self-pity following the curt letter informing her that she had been dropped from the film.

The phone rang but the last forty-eight hours had taught her not to pick it up and the answer machine clicked on. Loulou turned up the sound.

'Loulou? Are you there, darling? No? It's Mira here and I just wanted to tell you that I don't believe a word of it. Not one awful word. Have you got on to a lawyer – I'm sure there must be ample grounds to sue? Of course, *Vita* won't be printing a single sentence until we hear from you. Big kisses, darling, and keep your chin up.'

Loulou could practically hear the smile on Mira's

face. Amongst other things the tabloids had accused her of being unprofessional, a lousy actress and a tart. Apparently she'd seduced every man on the set and funnily enough the only one who had supposedly turned her down was Ethan Mead. Being called a tart she could deal with but the other accusations were more of a problem. Work offers weren't exactly flying thick and fast.

Hearing Anna, the housekeeper, letting herself out the front door, Loulou crept down the stairs, half expecting to be waylaid by a photographer. She'd seen them on their stepladders behind the garden wall and she wouldn't have been surprised if one of them had made it into the house. Peering out of the kitchen window she saw that they had all gone. Relief was mixed with the unpleasant realisation that she wasn't that hot a story.

Several cups of black coffee subdued the alcohol anxiety slightly and Loulou decided she had to act fast to salvage something from the debacle. She showered and dressed, dug out a pair of dark sunglasses, then ordered a taxi.

It was only when she left the house that she spotted the hordes of paparazzi drinking coffee outside the café on the other side of the road.

'Loulou!' they roared in unison, running towards her, but she deftly nipped into the taxi and left them all behind.

Twenty minutes later, the taxi was negotiating the mid-morning traffic along the Westway, with Loulou in the back rehearsing the speech she planned to give to Lawrence Shaw, the producer of *Sorted!* As far as she knew no replacement for her had been found for the next series and despite everything that had happened she was sure he'd jump at the chance to have her back.

A temporary set-back, she told herself, as the taxi approached the production offices in King's Cross. Another series while she rethought her career plans and she'd soon have her star in the ascendant again.

'Put this on the *Sorted!* account,' she told the driver, stepping into the street, and with her head held high, she marched into the building and made straight for Shaw's office, ignoring Chrissy Boy, who stared at her incredulously as she passed him in a corridor.

'Well, well, well,' the producer said, looking up from his desk. He pushed his retro black spectacles back on the bridge of his nose. 'Loulou Lamb. What an unexpected surprise.'

His malicious grin told her that he was anything but surprised and momentarily Loulou faltered. 'Lawrence, I . . .'

'How lovely of you to take time out of your busy schedule to come see us. I take it this is a social call?'

Loulou sat down opposite him and forced a smile. Eating humble pie didn't come easy to her and she could see that Shaw was expecting the full hair shirt. 'Lawrence, I won't beat about the bush – I'm here because I want my job back.' As hard as she tried, she couldn't quite hide the desperation in her voice.

'I bet you do. But after what you did to me, why should I give it to you?'

Resting her elbows on the desk, she said, 'Come on, anybody in my position would have done the same.'

'I thought we were friends.'

'We were – I mean we are.'

'Then why did I have to read about your plans in *Vita*? Why couldn't you have talked to me first?'

'It all happened so fast,' she replied lamely. 'Initially what I intended was to take a sabbatical – I know how good the programme has been for me. But Mira got wind of the story and ran with it and the whole thing gathered a momentum of its own.'

Shaw stared at her and Loulou wondered whether it would be *de trop* to cry. Deciding that the producer knew her too well to buy it, she shrugged her shoulders in what she hoped was an endearing manner.

Shaw took off his glasses and squinted at her thoughtfully. 'If you want me to give you your job there's something you're going to have to do for me.'

Oh God, he wants to fuck me again, Loulou thought. She'd got the job in the first place by pretending his needle dick had given her more satisfaction than one had believed was humanly possible. 'Just say the word,' she said huskily.

There was a pregnant pause as Shaw let her stew for a while before he said, 'I want you to beg.'

Wide-eyed, Loulou sat bolt upright, unable to believe she'd heard him correctly. 'What?'

'You heard me,' Shaw laughed. 'I want you to get on your hands and knees and beg me to give you your job back.'

'Couldn't we just fuck?'

Shaw roared with laughter. 'You're unbelievable. You'd rather offer your snatch than an apology.'

'Lawrence, this is more than an apology . . .'

The producer sat back in his chair and folded his arms. He was clearly enjoying himself. 'Well, that's the deal. You beg or you walk.'

'You're serious, aren't you?'

'As a heart attack.'

Loulou didn't have to fake the tears this time. Burning with shame, she dropped to her knees in front of the desk and said, 'Please, Lawrence, I want my job back.'

'Beg,' the producer said.

'I beg you – let me have my job back.'

Shaw got up from his seat and came round to her side of the desk. Looking down at her he said, shaking his head, 'How anybody could say you are a lousy actress is beyond me. That was truly beautiful. Award-winning even.'

'Did it win me my job?' Loulou asked, feeling that this was lower than she'd ever sunk in her life.

'Well it *would* do,' Shaw replied, 'if Channel Four ever decided to recommission us. They cancelled the series.'

'What?'

'They cancelled the series. Didn't you know?'

'A lady here to talk with you,' Anna said, putting her head around the bedroom door.

'I told you not to answer it,' Loulou said groggily. 'I can't believe you let someone into the house. It could be a journalist.'

'She say she frien',' the housekeeper said, tut-tutting as she surveyed the wreckage of Loulou's room. 'You talk to her – I clean here.'

The stern look on Anna's face showed she would

brook no retorts. Since her meeting with Lawrence Shaw, Loulou had taken to her bed and had let Anna take over the running of her life.

In creased and stained silk pyjamas, Loulou walked downstairs fully expecting to see Mira Ramirez coiled on a sofa waiting to pounce. To her surprise she found Tanya Barry perched nervously on the edge of an armchair.

'Come to gloat, have you?' Loulou asked, throwing herself down in a chair. 'I thought the ladies of Notting Hill had been a bit quiet.'

Tanya spoke softly. 'I've just got back from a shoot – I haven't talked to anyone at Notting Hill. Me and David are going through a difficult time and I didn't want people like Martine knowing all my business.'

'Frankly, Tanya, I'm a bit low on the sympathy front at the moment. You may not have heard but my career has turned to shit. So I'm sorry that you and David are having a lovers' tiff but I'm sure you'll work it out fine without any help from me.'

'I can see I've called at a bad time,' the model said, standing up to leave. 'I only popped in to say I was thinking about you – I'm not gloating, despite what you think. Oh, and I was asked to give you this.' She reached into her handbag and gave Loulou a sheet of carefully rolled paper.

'What is it?' Loulou studied the picture.

'It's from your brother.'

'You've seen Dexter? How? When?'

Tanya told her about the visit to the gallery. 'It's not for me to say how other people should bring up their children and I don't want to seem like I'm slagging off your mum but I don't think she should have said that to him. You know – about not being his real mother. It really upset him.'

Loulou looked at the picture again and could no longer hold back the tears. 'Oh, Tanya, I've made such a mess of my life.'

'Hey, there.' Tanya sat down next to her and put a soothing arm around her. 'No you haven't – well, it's nothing you can't put right.'

'It's not that,' Loulou said, wiping her nose on her sleeve. 'There are some things . . .' She stopped herself, realising that she was just about to tell her darkest secret to a woman she regarded as a complete fluff-head. 'Do you know why my parents were arguing?'

'I shouldn't really have been listening – I feel like I'm telling tales out of school – but it was about money. Your mum seemed really wound up.'

'Poor Dexter,' Loulou said, her face crumpling again.

'Where's your kitchen?' the model asked. 'I think you could do with a nice cup of tea.'

'First on the right,' Loulou said, curling up in a ball. It was somewhat bizarre having Tanya in her house dishing out the tea and sympathy, but aside from Anna, shoulders to cry on had been few and far between. Surprisingly, Loulou found she felt comforted having Tanya there.

Tanya reappeared with two mugs. 'Loulou, your house is beautiful.'

'Thanks. I might have to sell it if things carry on like this.'

'You don't mean that. It can't be that bad. Couldn't you go back to *Sorted!*?'

Loulou laughed bitterly. 'I've already tried that,

but Channel Four isn't commissioning another series,' she said evasively. She felt the tears coming on again. 'Tanya, I really appreciate you coming over. If I'd been in your position I don't think I would have bothered. I've been a real bitch to you at times.'

'Yeah, you have,' Tanya laughed. 'But don't worry about it. Everyone's the same at Notting Hill. That place breeds insecurity. And I reckon the men encourage it. Deep down they'd hate it if we all got on because if we weren't caught up with all this silly back-biting we'd be on to them like a shot. Divide and rule and all that.'

'That's so true.' Loulou realised that she had been completely wrong about Tanya. She was far from being a bimbo. Probably further than Loulou herself. 'Is that what the argument between you and David was over? Andy told me that you'd split up.'

'I don't really know,' Tanya said, clearly troubled by the question.

'I didn't mean to pry – it's none of my business.'

'It's OK. Actually David wants us to get back together. He wants me to marry him.'

'Is that good or bad? You don't seem too pleased.'

Tanya explained the reason for the break up. 'I've never been beholden to any man. As much as I love David, I don't want him to think he can tell me what I can and can't do. I would have given up my job in my own good time – but for me, not because he said so.'

'Still, he's apologised – can't you put it behind you?'

Tanya looked even more troubled. 'I think so. Actually, Loulou, it's not really him that's bothering me at the moment. If I tell you something, will you promise me not to say anything to anyone?'

'Sure.'

Instinctively, Tanya put her hand on her chest. 'I . . . I found a lump in my breast while I was away.'

'What? Have you seen a doctor?'

The model looked down at her feet. 'No.'

'But you must. As soon as possible. Surely David must agree?'

'I haven't told him yet.' Tanya continued to look down, pulling at the bottom of her sweater. 'I don't want him to worry.'

Loulou was shocked. 'You should tell him, and you've *got* to see someone.'

For the first time Tanya looked rattled. 'I'm really scared.'

Loulou stood up. 'Where's that number?' She picked up her address book and flicked through. 'There's someone in Harley Street I see. I'll make you an appointment.'

'You don't have to—.'

'I'll come with you,' Loulou interrupted, feeling relieved to have something other than her own problems to think about. She booked the appointment and put down the phone. 'It's all arranged. Ten o'clock tomorrow.'

'Thanks, that's really good of you. Look, I've got to go – I haven't even unpacked. I just wanted you to get the drawing as soon as possible – I knew it would cheer you up.'

Loulou showed Tanya to the door and, aware that a connection had been made between them, awkwardly kissed her goodbye. 'I'll see you in the morning.'

Watching Tanya drive away, she punched an international number into her phone and waited as the fuzzy line connected to Ibiza. 'Hi, there,' she said. 'No. Surprisingly it's you I wanted to speak to. Do you still want my money? You do? OK I'm prepared to buy into the business. But you've got to promise me you'll keep your mouth shut.'

Chapter Twenty-Six

Stu switched off the engine as he pulled up outside Carla's flat. The image of his team-mates' faces when he'd turned up at Schiphol Airport still burned into his mind. On the plane they'd pelted him with tampons and Michael had run up and down the gangway wearing a pair of false tits. This would be only the beginning.

These men had been his friends but it was never going to be the same again. How could it? They were disgusted by him and he couldn't blame them. A transvestite football player – there were some fucking teams in the country which were still having a hard time accepting blacks on their squads. Blokes in dresses were way down the list.

As bad as things were, he couldn't help thinking about those few minutes with the brass when she'd made him feel like the most normal man in the world. It had felt so good being with someone who understood him. He looked up at the light shining from Carla's window. She didn't understand either but at least she was prepared to put up with it – for a price.

Stu rang the bell and seconds later Carla stuck her head out of the window.

'What do you want?' she shouted.

'Carla, I've had a long day. Let me in.'

'And have all my underwear stretched to buggery?' she cackled. 'I don't think so.'

Stu bit on the insult forming on his lips. 'Does everybody have to know our business?'

'*Your* business, Sonny Jim. Not mine. Why don't you piss off?'

Cold sweat trickled down his neck. He turned and walked back to the car, uncertain where he was going to go now. Everything seemed black. Every road a dead-end. Football was finished, that was for certain. He'd never be able to face any of those men again, and even if he could it wouldn't be long before somebody told the papers. He imagined walking out on to a pitch with fifty thousand fans knowing that he liked to get off wearing a teddy.

Stu leaned on the bonnet of the car and called up to the window again. 'Carla, I've got money.'

A few seconds passed then the window opened and a set of keys landed at his feet.

'I've missed you,' he lied, as he walked into the bed-sit, that familiar dirty smell assaulting his nostrils.

'How much?' Carla was sitting on the bed wearing an old cardigan over some greyish underwear, looking, if possible, more rancid than ever.

'I thought about you while I was in Amsterdam. I was wondering if perhaps we could make a go of it.' He sat on the bed next to her and stroked her bare thigh, fighting the urge to recoil at the feel of her dimply, mottled flesh.

Carla slapped his hand away. 'I mean how much money?'

He took his cash-point card from his wallet and gave it to her. 'Here. Take what you want.'

The barmaid seemed to soften. 'I suppose you want to stay the night?'

'And then see how it goes, eh? Me and you could have had something special going. Maybe we could again.'

'What's happened?' she asked suspiciously, pocketing the card. 'You couldn't wait to get rid of me before.'

He thought about confiding in her, throwing himself at her mercy but rejected the idea instantly. The woman didn't have a good side, and whatever he told her she'd be sure to use to her advantage. 'Like I said, I missed you.' He let his hand slip down her inner thigh. 'I missed it.'

A wan smile appeared on her face and Stu guessed that as much as they both knew he was lying, part of her wanted to believe him. 'Well, we'll see how it goes then – I'm not promising you anything.'

Despite all the trouble over the last few days, he felt the desire rising in him again. This ... thing ... had such a hold. 'I want to fuck you,' he said, kissing her pudgy breasts.

He ran his fingers over the nylon frills of her bra and he hardened, responding more to the fabric than to what lay beneath. Carla pulled his face up to hers, and as their lips locked together, Stu fought the instinct to draw back when he tasted the staleness of her breath. She repelled him, he repelled himself. They were a match made in hell.

'I suppose you want to dress up,' she said disinterestedly.

'No, I don't,' he protested, his voice reduced to a

squeak. 'We don't have to, I mean, we could . . . Do you mind?' His body shook with anticipation.

'Whatever rocks your boat,' Carla said, lying back on the bed and lighting a cigarette. 'You know where the wardrobe is. Take your pick.'

Stu opened the wardrobe door, barely able to contain himself. He took a black evening dress from its hanger and held it to his chest. Transfixed by his image in the mirror, the battle between desire and self disgust raged inside him, and he began to cry. Sobbing like a child, he opened Carla's underwear drawer and selected some panties.

The assistant folded the white silk underwear and wrapped it in tissue paper before putting it into a bag. Vowing that she wouldn't let Stu wear these, Carla opened her purse and handed over more of the money he'd given her that morning. A thousand pounds – Carla could hardly believe her luck. Collecting up all of her shopping bags, she left the store and headed to the bank further along Knightsbridge. There she withdrew another two hundred pounds and hailed a cab.

'Earl's Court please,' she said, noting how much politer the driver had been after he'd clocked all the brand names on her carrier bags.

She knew Stu was lying through his teeth about missing her but she hadn't pushed him on the real reason he'd come back. She didn't want to know. OK, so she'd promised herself that she wouldn't let him sleep with her again dressed as Stephanie, but since being sacked she was in no position to look a gift horse in the mouth.

For the sheer hell of it she gave the driver a ten-pound tip, even though the drive had been no more than fifteen minutes. She let herself into the block, for once hoping she might meet the landlord. She was going to relish tearing up the notice to vacate he had given her. Not that she intended staying in this hole a moment longer than necessary. There was no reason why she couldn't move in to Stu's house immediately.

'I'm back,' she said, kicking open the door of the bed-sit and throwing the bags in before her.

She peered around the door and spotted Stu asleep on the sofa, looking rather fetching in a red and black Ann Summers basque set. Much to her surprise, he didn't look too bad in a Rocky Horror sort of way. God, she was going soft, but then blowing a thousand pounds in a couple of hours could do that to a girl.

'Come on, Stephanie. Wake up. You're taking me out to dinner.'

She shook Stu by the shoulder, noticing immediately how cold he felt.

'Stu! Wake up!'

The footballer didn't respond and Carla was consumed by panic as she noticed that the faded lipstick he was wearing couldn't hide the ominous shade of blue of his lips.

'Stu! You silly bastard. Oh my God!'

She knelt beside him and put her ear to his chest. At first all she could hear was the sound of her own blood pounding in her head but straining she heard the faint rattle of his lungs. She shook him again and then slapped his face hard, her fear showing in the force of the blow.

'You stupid, stupid bastard.'

It was then that she noticed the empty bottle of sleeping tablets on the floor by the sofa. He must have got them from her cabinet; she tried to remember how many had been in there. Enough to kill him?

She looked at his face, his ghastly appearance all the worse for the make-up he was wearing. 'I can't believe you've fucking done this to me,' she screamed at him.

She knew she should call an ambulance – Stu could be dying before her eyes – but she remained rooted to the spot. The police would be called, there would be publicity, the papers – any hope of a better life would go out the window. If it was possible, she'd be even more of a laughing stock than she was already.

The thought of the newspapers cut a swathe through her panic. Maybe it wouldn't be so bad after all. Perhaps she could even sell her story. It might set her up nicely. She began to calm down.

'Carla?' Stu groaned, half opening his eyes.

The sound of his voice spurred her into action and, for once, she dismissed all thoughts of money. Even she wasn't that hard. Struggling with the dead weight of his body, she forced him to sit upright. He spoke again but his words were unintelligible and he seemed to be passing in and out of consciousness.

'Come on, Stu,' she said, trying to drag him to his feet. 'You've got to fight this.' She put his arm around her shoulder and heaved. 'You've got to help me. I can't do it on my own.' The tremor in her voice frightened her and tears filled her eyes. 'Oh, you silly bastard.'

She couldn't lift him and she slumped back on the

sofa. What did people do in films when this happened? Help them walk it off? Put them under a cold shower? Make them throw up? Well, she couldn't lift him so there was no way they would make it to the communal bathroom along the landing.

She slapped him again. 'Stu. Please wake up.'

The footballer moaned. Carla pushed his head down between his legs and then slid her fingers into his mouth hoping that he would gag. At first there was nothing and squeamishly Carla forced her fingers deeper into his throat. His body convulsed and then he retched, a poisonous-smelling bile spilling over her hand.

Fighting down her own nausea, Carla rubbed his back to try to soothe him. 'Come on, Stu, you can do this.'

The footballer's chest heaved again and then he half raised his head. 'Stop,' he gasped.

'You've got to stand up,' she ordered. 'Come on. Lean on me.'

This time she managed to get him to his feet and she dragged him across the room, convinced that her legs would buckle any second. All the time she kept up a stream of encouraging words, trying to keep her voice calm as she walked him around in circles.

Carla didn't know how long she kept him walking. Minutes turned into hours and it grew dark long before she was satisfied that the worst of the crisis was behind them. Eventually though, Stu gathered enough strength to support his own weight and he sat down on the bed, watching in silence as she made them a cup of tea.

'Why did you do it?' Carla asked finally.

'Not now, Carla. I don't want to talk about it.' His voice was cracked and small.

Carla didn't push it. She was exhausted and she really didn't want to know anyway. Now that he was out of danger all she wanted was for him to leave. She couldn't face another episode like this.

'Drink this,' she said, handing him the tea, 'and then I'll drive you home.'

'Can't I stay here?'

'This has all been a bit much for me,' she said. 'I need a few hours to myself. I'll come and see you tomorrow.' She wasn't sure if she meant it or not.

'Please – I don't want to be on my own tonight.'

Carla looked at the puddle of vomit on the floor. 'Stu, I can't handle this. You're asking too much of me.'

'I know and I'm sorry. But there's no one else. You're the only one I can turn to.'

Stu looked so pathetic sitting there, shivering in the basque, she almost gave in. What was wrong with her? It wasn't like her to let *any* man get under her skin, no matter what they said or did. 'Come on. Get dressed,' she said. 'Where are your car keys?'

It took Stu a long time to orient himself when he woke. Expecting to see the drab surrounds of Carla's bed-sit, he was surprised to find that he had fallen asleep on the sofa in his own living room. How had he got there?

Gradually the memory of the night before came back to him. Why had Carla been driving his car? He winced as the reason came to him, the dull throb in his parched throat a reminder of her fingers pressing against his tongue. The pills. He had tried to kill himself.

How long had he slept? Looking at his watch, he noticed the red polish still on his nails. By now the whole world probably knew his secret and, much to his surprise, he found he no longer cared. Nothing mattered any more. Not Michael, not Carla, not his career. A sense of elation filled him as he realised that the cloud had finally lifted. He was free.

'I'm a fucking tranny,' he said out loud and laughed. 'The Premier League's first fucking cross-dressing superstar.' He pictured Stephanie running out on to the pitch at Wembley and roared.

Stu couldn't stop laughing. He laughed all the way out to the garage, chuckled as he attached a hose to the exhaust pipe and threaded it through the driver's window, giggled as he climbed in behind the wheel, and gave one last big shit-eating grin as he turned on the engine.

Chapter Twenty-Seven

Clive re-read the front page of the *Sun*, as if reading it again would alter the scandalous story surrounding Stu Williams' suicide. Clive's top lip curled up with distaste. How could he not have known about the man's perversion? The article confirmed that Stuart had been dead on arrival at hospital but, as Clive knew, his death was a mere detail in the titillating story that would run and run. He threw down the paper.

'We're here, sir,' his driver informed him, pulling up outside the church.

Clive looked through the smoke-grey glass. There were so many journalists huddled together they could easily outnumber the mourners – if that's what the Notting Hill players and the female flotsam surrounding them could be called. With a deep sigh Clive opened the car door. He barely had a foot on the pavement when he was ambushed by the news hounds and the scandal mongers.

'No comment, no comment,' he muttered, breaking into a trot to escape the rumble of questions.

As he entered the church he felt as though every face had turned to watch him. He strode purposefully towards the front, nodding now and again to his

players. All had obeyed his instructions to turn up –
Clive's attempt to restore some dignity to the club.

In the first pew sat Carla. The sight of her made
him shiver – for a fleeting moment it was his name
he saw in lurid headlines across every tabloid in the
country.

She looked up and stared at him through the black
netting covering her face. Clive glared back – noting
that for once Carla was wearing clothes that went from
her neck to her ankles. It was clear she was keen to play
the grieving girlfriend to the hilt. But she looked more
Dallas than Dagenham – where Stu's family lived and
wanted their son buried.

The vicar entered from the vestry and everyone
rose to begin a tuneless rendition of 'The Lord is
my Shepherd'.

Clive mouthed the words, his mind still on Carla.
He promised God, yet again, that he would give up
the women – he really would this time – if God would
rid him of Carla Ryman.

Carla smirked under the net. She knew just what
Clive Dorning was thinking – she'd seen the fearful
expression cross his face when he'd stared at her. The
power she had over him more than compensated for
her dismissal. But she needed to get her hands on some
hard evidence – no one would believe someone like her
without proof.

Thankfully, the hymn had ended and she could sit
back down. Her brand-new six-inch heels were killing
her. With the money she'd had left over from Stu's
twelve hundred she'd been able to kit herself out for
the funeral, and although she felt like a nun at the

moment, both the blouse and the skirt were held together by buttons that could easily be undone.

'We're gathered here today for Stuart Patrick Williams, beloved son, friend and colleague of . . .'

Carla stopped listening to the vicar's droning voice and, for the first time, looked properly at the coffin. Her tired bunch of chrysanthemums looked pathetic against the backdrop of the dozens of white lilies from Stu's parents.

She shuddered, finding it hard to believe that Stu's body was really in there and that in another hour he would be nothing more than ashes.

Her bottom lip began to tremble and tears threatened. Carla screwed up her eyes. She didn't want to think about the part she had played in his last hours. The thought that she could have done more troubled her. But realistically what could she have done? Perhaps if she had let him stay the night . . . She dismissed the notion. In retrospect, from the moment Michael had found Stu out, his suicide had been inevitable.

As hard as she tried, Carla couldn't prevent the tears escaping from her eyes. She was crying not only for Stu but also for herself and the realisation that if she were the one lying in the coffin there would be nobody to grieve for her.

It took several minutes for Carla to regain her composure and she barely realised that the congregation had stood up for another tedious hymn. She got to her feet and gave an apologetic smile to Stu's parents.

Listening to the melancholic tone of the organ, Carla forced herself to snap out of her lament. She couldn't afford to feel sorry for herself. Boring Rachel had organised a gathering at her house – and Carla knew that this could be her last entree into the world of football. She was going to have to work fast if she was going to keep her head above water. Turning ever so slightly, out of the corner of her eye she saw the solution to her problems – Stefan.

Gulping down air, Jenny tried to still the nausea, made worse by the cloying smell of the lilies. But it wasn't just the pregnancy that was turning her stomach – it was her husband also. She didn't know how Michael had the nerve to turn up at the funeral when everyone knew he'd contributed to Stu's death.

Of course, he'd argued that he hadn't gone to the press until *after* the player's suicide, and that Stu must have realised it was only a matter of days before the world knew his secret. But Michael had not just told the story – he'd sold it. No doubt his thirty pieces of silver had already been sunk into his bottomless debts.

Her disgust had been yet another reason not to tell him about the baby. Yesterday she'd had her first scan and she'd been so happy she had almost blurted it out. But one look at her husband had stopped her in her tracks. He was fuming because there was no alcohol in the house, and when she'd explained that she was trying to dry out, his only comment was that it wouldn't be long before an old soak like her hit the bottle again.

Jenny was just about managing to stay off the booze and the coke, but her cigarette consumption had almost doubled. However, now she'd seen the pictures of her baby, which were already dog-eared, she was determined to quit smoking too. She was full of wonder at the little life growing inside her and although no damage had been detected, she wouldn't know for certain until the baby was born.

Exhausted, she hoped the funeral would be short. It had been days since she'd slept properly. Her abstinence meant that her recurring nightmares were no longer numbed and they now dominated her nights; but now there was a new, terrifying one, where several men bore down on her, threatening her with the fires of hell.

She looked up. In front of her was a statue of the crucified Christ and the words 'suffer the little children' came to mind. Jenny prayed with all her heart that her baby would be fine. Stu's death emphasised the importance of life, especially her baby's.

Tanya, her eyes clouded by unchecked tears, stumbled as she followed the other mourners out of the church. David's hand reached out and steadied her, making her want to weep even more.

'Tanya! Are you all right, darling? Come here,' he murmured, pulling her towards him.

She leaned against him, wishing that his strong arms could take away her fears. Would it be her funeral next?

She was seeing Loulou's doctor the next day for the results of the biopsy and she was convinced that it was bad news. And David was insisting they go out and choose the engagement ring tomorrow, of all days. Nothing could be further from her mind but she knew that if she put it off David would want to know why, and she just couldn't face telling him.

He seemed to have so many problems of his own – which he'd chosen not to share with her either.

Loulou looked down the side aisle and saw a door she guessed led to a back exit. There was no way she was running the gauntlet again with the so-called journalists outside the front of the church. For a moment they had lost interest in Stu and his secret and gunned for Loulou. And the same question was on every hack's lips. 'What went wrong in Hollywood?'

At least the Stu scandal had forced her off the headlines. Although, when she had rushed to her local newsagent at the ungodly hour of seven that morning, she had spotted a picture of herself and several paragraphs reporting her on-going decline a few pages on. She tried to cheer herself up with the thought that most people got bored after reading the first page or two.

'You go on,' she said to Andy, who was steering her into the aisle.

'What?'

'I need a few moments alone.' She couldn't face admitting her fears to him. Lately, it had seemed that Andy was feeding off her failure, his confidence gaining as hers plummeted. But perhaps she was just becoming paranoid; it wouldn't surprise her considering the pressure she was under.

Andy shrugged and gave her a look that said he didn't believe her for one second.

Once more Rachel found herself playing hostess – and once again it was for the same reason. She had managed to convince Mary that it was the least she could do for poor Stuart, but she was all too aware that her motives weren't pure. She ignored the little detail that she'd never even said hello to the dead man, and that Chris had only met Stu on a couple of occasions; it was enough, as far as Rachel was concerned, to justify inviting him.

Rachel wondered what she was feeling for Chris. Was it love or simply lust? It was certainly something powerful to make her put herself through the ordeal of another party. At least this time, Rachel thought, as she hurried around the living room hiding Demi's decapitated Barbie dolls and Robbie Jnr's victorious Power Rangers, it would be a respectable staid affair. There would be no naked woman.

The house seemed unnaturally quiet with both the kids and her mother-in-law out for the day, Mary having decided that a wake, and especially one for such a sick and disgusting man, was no place for children. Their absence liberated Rachel.

The cars began to pull up outside the house and Rachel peeped out from behind the net curtain, her eyes roving up and down the line searching for one face in particular. Since that one kiss in Supernova, Rachel had been awash with feelings of shame mixed with excitement – the type of emotions she imagined the heroines of her novels felt just before they abandoned themselves to their desires.

There was Chris walking up the path. Rachel's chest constricted, making it difficult to breathe, while her heart beat so loudly it pounded in her ears.

She ran to the door and threw it open. Chris's face broke into a huge smile and then crinkled as he gave her a wink. 'How are you?'

'Fine. All the better for seeing you,' she said, her

voice little above a whisper. Rachel was surprised by her forwardness, but then she was finding it hard to believe that she could feel this strongly about someone. It was almost too much to have Chris this close; she could hardly bear not being able to touch him, but with everyone else now arriving, she had no choice.

'Come in, come in,' she said, sweeping them all in with her hand.

In no time the house was filled with the so-called mourners. The only absentees were Clive and Stu's parents.

Rachel ran around making sure everyone had a drink, but her mind was elsewhere. At every opportunity she would glance across at Chris, who was standing on his own, watching her every move. God, she wanted him but having been up until now an honest and faithful wife she had no idea how to engineer a meeting. The ringing of the phone broke into her thoughts.

'I want to speak to Robbie.' The caller was female and she sounded very young.

Another fan, Rachel thought. One had phoned a couple of nights earlier. How did they got hold of the number? 'I'm sorry but he's busy right now,' she said, trying to sound polite but firm.

'Get him for me *now*!'

Rachel realised that it was the same girl and there was a real threat in her voice. 'Excuse me, but who are you?'

'I know you know who I am and I know you're trying to keep Robbie from me.'

Rachel was stunned. 'What are you talking about?'

'He doesn't love you, you ugly old bag. He wants me and if you don't get him for me there's going to be big trouble.' The girl then launched into a stream of expletives.

Chilled, Rachel dropped the phone and ran to find Robbie, determined to know what was going on. Was her husband just like all the others? In the space of a few seconds, she felt her whole world falling apart.

As always Robbie was playing the fool, dancing around the kitchen with a lampshade on his head.

'What's the matter with you?' he asked, seeing the horror-struck look on her face.

Rachel was shaking so much she could barely get her words out. 'That girl's on the phone again. She says I'm keeping you from her. What the hell is she on about?'

'Calm down. What girl?'

'You said she was just a fan.'

'What . . . that one? She's just some silly kid. Why are you taking any notice of her? Christ, Rachel, get a grip on yourself.'

Robbie didn't seem in the least concerned and Rachel realised that she had let herself get carried away. It must be the stress of the funeral. And maybe her guilty conscience about Chris. 'Well, can you deal with her?' she asked sheepishly.

'Oh, babe, just take the phone off the hook.' Robbie had turned his back to her and was dancing again.

Carla was furious. How dare they be so heartless? Since she'd arrived at Rachel's she'd had little more than a nod of recognition from anyone other than Jenny. The older woman had squeezed her hand and said how sorry she was but she didn't look at all well, and Carla guessed she was pissed.

Perhaps she should have taken up the offer from Mr
and Mrs Williams and gone back to their house. She
could at least have tapped them for some money. She
was just wondering whether it was too late to go over
there when Stefan walked into the room. Her knight
in shining armour. Or so he would be by the time
she'd finished with him.

'Stefan, how nice of you to come,' she said as if the
wake were her idea.

It was clear from Stefan's expression that he hadn't
forgotten their last meeting but that didn't put Carla
off.

'Let me get you a drink. Orange juice, isn't it?' she
asked, playing the gracious hostess.

He nodded mutely.

'Wait here.'

Once Carla had located the orange juice she mixed
a liberal amount of vodka with it. By hook or by
crook.

'There you go,' she said, returning to his side, glad
he was still alone. It looked as if Stefan Lohmann was
as popular as she was. Well good, she'd take it as an
omen that they were meant for each other, but first
she needed to find out if there was any competition.

'How's your fiancée? Is she coming over soon?'

Stefan grimaced. For a second Carla worried that he
could taste the vodka until she realised his expression
was in response to her question. His pain was unmistakable.

'I'm afraid it is over. Finished,' he murmured, drinking the rest of the laced juice.

'Oh, I am sorry to hear that,' she said, battling to
keep a straight face. 'Here, let me get you another.'

Feeling emboldened, this time Carla mixed even more vodka with the juice, convinced that Stefan was much too steeped in misery to think about what he was drinking.

After a few more of Carla's orange juices Stefan was slurring and Carla decided it was now or never. With each drink their bodies had been getting closer and closer and now was the moment to put the next part of her plan into action – skin against skin.

She took Stefan's hand. 'Come with me,' she whispered in his ear.

Rachel's frustration at not being able to have even a conversation with Chris, let alone anything else, was threatening to overwhelm her. It was manifesting itself physically – she had sweaty palms, a thumping headache and a cramping stomach. When would they ever get to be alone?

'We'd better be going,' Tanya said, looking as miserable as Rachel felt. 'Where are our coats?'

'I'll get them,' Rachel replied, relieved that she had something to do.

She hurried upstairs and pushed open the door leading into Robbie Jnr's room. She switched on the light and was puzzled to see all the coats lying on the floor. She was sure . . . Then she let out an ear-piercing scream. In that instant the two naked bodies writhing around on her son's bed stopped and two surprised faces turned towards her. Carla and Stefan looked up at her.

'Get dressed now and get out!' she screamed hysterically.

Picking up their crumpled clothes, Rachel threw

them over the couple. Even in her fury it was clear to Rachel that if Stefan could choose death at that moment he would, but Carla was as brazen as ever, flaunting her body as she dressed slowly and deliberately.

'And you, Carla Ryman, how could you? Stu's hardly cold.'

When Carla finally spoke her voice was calm and steely. 'And you, Rachel Black, you're just a frustrated old cow who can't stand anyone else enjoying themselves.'

'Just get out of my house!' Rachel shouted, frightened that any minute now she'd do something she'd never even contemplated before – slap another woman. She left the room. Outside she concentrated on controlling her breathing and tried to stem the tears. Where was that useless husband of hers when she needed him? She yelled for him as she ran down the stairs.

'What the hell's wrong now?' Robbie asked when she finally located him slumped in the kitchen.

'Carla and Stu have been having sex on our son's bed and . . .'

Robbie began to snigger.

'And . . . and she called me a frustrated old cow.'

Robbie burst out laughing. 'Well, she's not wrong there,' he said, making a lunge at her.

Rachel jumped back and Robbie fell to the floor in a drunken heap.

She felt a hand placed on her shoulder and turned quickly, hoping to see Chris but it was Jenny.

'Come on, ignore him, he's drunk. He doesn't know what he's saying. And *I* should know,' she added, trying to make light of the situation.

'I just can't believe people can be so disrespectful.

I mean someone *did* die. Surely Carla must have felt something for Stu?'

Even as she spoke Rachel knew that her upset had nothing to do with the memory of Stu. She glanced round the room for Chris, thinking that she was little better than Carla. All Stu Williams' death had been to Rachel was a smoke-screen; a means to see a man she wasn't married to.

A cackle came from behind them. Jenny and Rachel spun round to face Martine.

Nudging Suzy, Martine said, 'For God's sake, you silly cows, if the last man you'd screwed had worn sling-backs, wouldn't you want the first man who preferred trousers to your dresses?'

Suzy shrieked with laughter.

'You two are disgusting. Do you know that?' Jenny and Rachel were surprised to hear Tanya's voice.

'Listen to you,' Martine snapped. 'If anyone knows what disgusting is it's you, what with getting your tired old tits out all the time. Still,' she paused, 'I suppose that's all you've got going for you.'

Tanya couldn't stop the tears, the result of many days of tension.

LouLou angrily joined in. 'Listen, you stupid cheap cow—'

'Oh my God, it's Meryl Streep,' Martine laughed, cutting her short. 'Don't think we haven't all seen the stories. Not quite the big "I am" now, are we? You'll be lucky to get work as a Teletubby.'

'You think you're so clever, don't you, Martine.' Jenny's voice was low but menacing. 'Yet you don't even know about your own husband. Why do you think he's called "Magic"?'

'Look, you drunken tart, don't you start—'

'I've never been more sober or more keen to tell someone the truth in my life.' Jenny was enjoying herself now. How she'd waited for this moment. 'The reason it's Tony "Magic" Anderson, *Martine*, has nothing to do with his footballing prowess, as you have so trustingly believed. No, it's referring to his magic fingers with the girls. And let me assure you, many, many of them have had the opportunity to feel his famous wand.'

'You're just saying that. You think I wouldn't know something like that?'

'Ask your good friend Suzy. I'm sure she could tell you all about it.'

Martine turned to her friend, the look of horror on Suzy's face telling her all she needed to know.

'Tony!' she screeched, bolting from the room.

'You bitches,' Suzy hissed, before running after Martine.

The four women – Jenny, Rachel, Loulou and Tanya – looked at each other and burst out laughing.

Chapter Twenty-Eight

'Can I take it off yet?' Loulou asked, tugging at the blindfold.

'Not just yet,' Andy replied, squeezing her hand. He leaned forward and spoke to the cab driver. 'Here will do fine.'

The cold air hit Loulou's face as she stepped out of the cab. 'If we're at the club, I'm going to slap you so hard,' she declared. The scenes at yesterday's funeral had just about finished her off.

'Look, there's Martine!' Andy called from behind her.

'You bastard!' Loulou yelled, ripping off the blindfold. Instead of Notting Hill, before her stood Waterloo Station. 'What are we doing here?'

Andy was paying the cab driver, two suitcases at his feet. 'Trainspotting,' he said. 'I thought it was time we found an interest we could share. Aside from the obvious, that is,' he added with a grin as he picked up the bags. 'Come on, we're going to be late.'

'For what?' she asked, wrapping her fake fur coat tightly around her against the chill of the wind.

Andy smiled mysteriously. 'You'll see.'

He raced into the station, Loulou struggling to keep

up with his pace, all the while keeping her head down so as not to be recognised.

She'd been on the front of the newspapers again that morning; this time it was photographs from the funeral. Coupled with that, Oran had given an 'exclusive' to the *Sun*. It was all the same old 'she bled me dry' crap he'd been peddling for years but it was doing her no end of damage. For once, Loulou believed that staying out of the news might just do her some good.

'Hold up,' she gasped. 'It may have escaped your attention but I'm wearing five-inch heels.'

'Loulou, when you're wearing those heels it never escapes my attention,' Andy called over his shoulder. 'This way.'

As soon as she'd seen the station, Loulou had half an idea where they might be heading, and gratifyingly, as she suspected, Andy came to a halt at the Eurostar terminus.

'How does Paris grab you?' he asked.

'I haven't got my passport. More importantly I haven't got my make-up. I wish you'd given me some warning,' she protested. Secretly, she was delighted.

'Relax,' he replied. 'I've packed everything.'

She threw her arms around him. 'Thank you.' Paris was exactly what she needed.

When the tickets had been sorted out, they were shown to a first-class compartment, and if their uniformed escort recognised them he was discreet enough not to mention it.

They sat at a table, a bottle of champagne already on ice, but as the train pulled out of the station and passed through the grim surrounds of south London,

Loulou felt her spirits sinking again. As wonderful as Paris would be, it was just a momentary break from all of her problems.

'You're very quiet,' Andy said, stroking her cheek. 'You did want to go, didn't you?'

'Of course. Andy, it was darling of you to surprise me like this. Honestly, I'm fine.'

A businessman walked by, a newspaper folded under his arm. It showed a photo of Loulou with Oran in front of the church on their wedding day. She looked incredibly young and naive. Andy saw her wince as she spotted it.

'This isn't like you,' he said, putting his arm around her shoulders. 'You've had bad publicity before and you've always come out fighting.'

'I'm not sure I'll be able to wing it this time,' she admitted. 'I've seen this happen to people before. It's a feeding frenzy. They're going to tear me to shreds until there's nothing left.'

'I'll take care of you. It'll be all right.'

'That's not the point. I—' Loulou stopped herself, trying to put a check on her vulnerability. She didn't let Andy see her like this very often; it wasn't attractive. A moment's silence passed. 'Why are you being so nice to me? I don't trust you when you're like this.'

Andy looked deep into her eyes. 'Why is it so difficult to believe I love you?'

Love was an act of selflessness, something Loulou didn't think Andy was capable of. With Andy there was always an angle. But then again, this wasn't the first time he'd said this to her. Perhaps it was more than just talk. Maybe he did love her. The idea confused Loulou. Did she love him? If love was the same as need then she guessed she did. Never had she needed a man on her side as much as she did at this moment.

There was a time not too long ago when they would taunt each other mercilessly about any negative story in the media. Both were so obsessed with chasing their own celebrity that they almost resented any good notice given to the other. What had happened to change Andy so much?

Loulou realised that Andy was waiting for some response to his comment. She could tell that he wanted her to say the 'L' word back but she just couldn't. It required a total re-evaluation of their relationship and she wasn't sure she was ready to do that.

Finally she spoke. 'If you know me so well, tell me what I'm thinking now.'

'How lucky you are to have a man like me so hopelessly devoted to you?' Andy guessed, half seriously.

'As if,' she laughed. 'Actually I was thinking about trains and tunnels. You know, all that Freudian stuff.'

'And?'

'And I was wondering if you wanted to join the mile-deep club?'

Andy roared with laughter. 'Loulou, it's ages until we get to the tunnel.'

'Then perhaps this time I'll actually get some foreplay,' Loulou said, giggling. She grabbed the bottle of champagne and, taking Andy's hand, headed off to the toilets.

When Stefan opened his eyes again he could still see two lampshades hanging from the ceiling and it was several seconds before they fused into one. Finally convinced that the ceiling wasn't moving, he eased himself up on his elbows and looked around the hotel room, his brain rattling inside his skull with every movement.

It was a hangover to end all hangovers yet he couldn't remember drinking anything other than orange juice. He realised he was naked under the sheets and wondered how he had managed to get undressed the night before in such a state. More to the point, how had he even got back to the hotel?

Keeping dead still, the crashing in his head abated long enough for him to notice that his bladder was full to bursting. Tentatively he swung one leg out of the bed, then followed it with the other and, unsteadily, got to his feet. The movement sent a fresh wave of pain surging across his forehead. What had made him get so out of control?

The answer was lying in the bath up to her neck in bubbles.

'Good morning,' Carla said, blowing him a kiss. 'Or should that be *Guten Morgen*?'

Stefan groaned as suddenly everything came back to him. Carla must have spiked his drink. At a funeral, for God's sake! How disrespectful could you get?

'Get in,' Carla said. 'It's still hot. And the water's not too cold either.'

Lifting the toilet seat, Stefan turned his back to her and peed. He didn't really understand what she'd just said but he could guess the meaning from her dirty laugh. How had he ended up with such a vulgar woman?

Flushing, he turned to her and said weakly, 'My head hurts.'

Carla's hand reached out from under the bubbles and stroked his crotch. 'I know just the cure.'

'I don't think we . . .' As Carla knelt up in the bath and began to kiss his stomach, Stefan found himself unable to finish his sentence.

At the Gard du Nord a limousine was waiting for Loulou and Andy. They had emerged from the tunnel in a blizzard, which had died down by the time they had reached Paris but the Boulevard de Magenta was still covered in a thick blanket of snow.

'Your carriage awaits,' Andy said, opening the door for her.

Loulou slid on to the back seat of the sedan, glad of the warmth inside. Andy jumped in beside her, rubbing his hands. 'God, it's cold,' he said.

'But beautiful,' Loulou replied, looking out the tinted windows. 'I thought Paris was meant to be at its best in the spring but this is lovely.'

The car drove slowly through the icy streets and Loulou cuddled Andy, still dreamy after their frantic lovemaking on the train. Even if she wasn't sure whether or not she loved him, she was glad to have a man who paid so much attention to detail. Everything so far had been perfect.

'Where are we going?' she asked, resting her head on his chest.

'The Rue St Honoré,' Andy replied, closing his eyes.

'The Royal? Of course.' Perfect, just perfect. Andy had taken her there when they first met. A little bit more of this treatment and she might very well fall in love with him. Loulou wondered if it would be as painful to be in love with Andy as it had been with Oran. She couldn't bear feeling that out of control again.

The investment in love was too high, the returns too small. For Oran she'd made a sacrifice greater than any woman should ever have to make and she did it in the belief that his love for her would be eternal. But of course it wasn't and she lived with the guilt of what she'd surrendered every day of her life.

The only way she could cope with that knowledge was to believe in the Loulou Lamb she had created for the media – hard-faced, hard-headed and definitely hard of heart.

Loulou leaned forward and spoke to the driver in French. 'Could you go via the Rue de Rivoli?' Then she turned to Andy. 'I want to see the Tuileries in the snow.'

'I thought you might be keen to check-in first. The suite I've ordered has a magnificent bedroom.'

'Wonderful – I could sleep for days.'

Playfully Andy nudged her in the ribs. 'We're only here for a night – you can sleep when we get back to London.'

The gardens of the Tuileries were deserted, the snow virginal.

'Stop the car!' she shouted, and she threw open the door and ran out along the avenue of bare white-decked trees.

Andy ran after her towards the Louvre. 'What are you doing?' he asked, catching up with her by a frozen fountain.

'It's so lovely. I just wanted to capture the moment,' she replied, her breath steaming in the air.

Andy put his arms around her and kissed her passionately, almost lifting her off her feet. 'Loulou, I was going to wait until dinner tonight but this seems the right moment . . .'

It wasn't the sub-zero temperature that froze Loulou to the spot. Please don't spoil this, she thought, knowing what was coming next. It could be so good between them. Why did he want to make it more than it was?

Andy reached into the pocket of his jacket and produced a small box with the word Tiffany emblazoned in gold. 'I love you,' he said, handing it to her.

Her fingers numb, she had trouble freeing the clasp. Finally she opened it and the large diamond solitaire confirmed her worst suspicions. 'It's lovely,' she said, quietly.

'I want you to marry me,' Andy said, sliding the ring on to her frozen finger. 'I've never wanted something so much in all my life.'

Loulou just stared at him.

Chapter Twenty-Nine

'The size of that diamond! It looks like a fake.'

David turned to Tanya and saw that she was staring off along Bond Street. Another wave of Christmas shoppers passed, forcing them closer against the jeweller's window. David grabbed Tanya's hands, fearing she might be swept away by the crowd.

'It's not really what I want,' Tanya said, distractedly. 'It's a bit showy.'

David was eager to buy her an engagement ring, wishing to put behind them all of the unpleasantness of their break-up. But somehow this wasn't the special moment he wanted it to be. Tanya was showing little enthusiasm and, as ever, worries about the team crowded out happier thoughts.

'There's another place further along,' he said, nudging past a woman who was juggling large numbers of bags and an unruly Great Dane.

Tanya petted the dog. 'We should have gone to that jeweller's in Bethnal Green like I said. It's where my dad bought my mum her ring.'

'Well, we can if we don't find anything here.'

It was getting dark and the temperature was dropping. The couple walked along huddled together, neither one of them taking any notice of the shop windows with their extravagant Christmas displays. The sound of a Salvation Army band playing carols on the other side of Oxford Street wafted along behind them, but even the stirring brass rendition of 'God Rest Ye Merry Gentlemen' failed to alleviate their spirits.

'Did you see the *Mirror* this morning?' David asked. 'There was a photograph of Magic with some bird on his arm going into a club.'

'What?' Tanya said, miles away. 'That's such a horrible thing to call a woman. Do you think I'm "some bird"?'

'How many more times do I have to tell him?' David continued to himself. With Stu's death, press attention on the team had reached new heights. They couldn't fart at the moment without it making the front page. David was amazed there wasn't some hack trailing them now. 'It's going to get worse before it gets better. If Magic could just keep it in his trousers until the end of the season.'

Tanya stopped walking and looked at her watch. 'Perhaps we should leave it for today. I've got to get off now anyway.'

'But we're buying your engagement ring. I thought this was important.'

'It is. I've just got a lot of other things to do.'

David looked at her and for the first time that afternoon saw the worry etched on Tanya's face. 'Tanya. What's up? You haven't changed your mind, have you? Please don't tell me that. I thought we were straight.'

'We are. I just don't think you're really into it at the moment. You keep going on about work – maybe we should wait until you're less stressed.'

David was engulfed by guilt. He wanted this to be one of the most romantic moments of Tanya's life and yet he was ruining it going on about Notting Hill. It was unforgivable. 'Tan, I'm so sorry. I don't know what to say. You know I get a bit worked up but, I'll tell you now, whatever happens with the team, nothing is as important as knowing that you're all right. Please – I want to buy you a ring today. This means so much to me.'

Tanya stopped to give some change to a young girl begging in a doorway. 'Forget about it,' she said sharply.

'I can't,' David said, shocked by the coldness in her voice. 'Tan, please!' He tried to cuddle her but she shrugged him off. It was then that he noticed the tears in her eyes. 'What's the matter?'

Tanya crumpled. 'David, I'm not all right.'

'Oh, I know, and it's all my fault—'

'It's not you. It's me. It's this.' She placed her hand on her chest. 'I think I might have breast cancer.'

David stood in the middle of the pavement, open-mouthed.

Tanya shook as her story poured out. Behind her a Santa collecting for charity ho-ho-hoed and rang a bell. 'So Loulou took me to see her doctor and I've got to go back for the results today.'

David felt like the biggest bastard in the world. Yet again he'd put himself and his silly problems first. He hadn't noticed a thing and his darling Tanya had been forced to go to a near stranger for help.

And yet could he help her? Cancer. The image of his emaciated mother lying on her deathbed flashed through his mind. That couldn't happen to Tanya.

'It's going to be all right, Tan. You'll see.' He spoke with absolutely no conviction. 'It's going to be all right.'

'Will you come with me?' she asked, her lip trembling.

'Of course I will,' he said, wishing he could be anywhere else in the world at that moment.

Jenny pulled the sheets from the bed and then, straining, shifted the mattress too. She felt a twinge of pain in her abdomen and realised that it was a stupid thing to have done. Cupping her stomach, she made soothing noises to the child growing inside.

'I'm sorry,' she said to her unborn baby, 'but I'm doing this for you.'

Whatever she was looking for, it wasn't in the bed. How about underneath? She crouched on all fours and squinted, groping in the dark. Nothing there but dust bunnies.

A clue, that was what she was searching for. Anything that would help reveal the identity of the woman in the pink jeep. Michael had fucked her in their bed again, Jenny was sure of it, and although it was a long shot, she hoped the trollop might have left something behind.

Carefully, she eased the mattress back on to the bed and scanned the room. Where else might she look? She sniffed the air to see if there was any trace of the woman's perfume. Nothing.

With sobriety, the need to know the identity of Michael's mistress had gained a new urgency. For her child to be in with a fighting chance of a half-decent life everything that was wrong about her marriage had to be put right. Until that woman was out of the picture, Jenny couldn't tell Michael she was carrying his child.

More than anything Jenny wanted to create a normal family with two loving parents. She believed that as the child was healing her so it could Michael. The pure unconditional love of a child could soothe his anger with the world. Whatever Michael had done in the past could be laid to rest with this new chance they were being given.

Tanya gripped David's hand under the desk. The look on the doctor's face told her all she needed to know.

'Remember we spoke about the histologic grade?' he asked gravely, looking at the results of the biopsy.

Tanya didn't answer. Quite advanced, he'd said. She was going to die.

'We check the tumour cells against normal cells and grade them from one to four according to their abnormality and their growth rate. A four is the most abnormal and fastest growing. It also means the cancer has the highest chance of recurrence. Yours is a three.'

Tanya looked out of the window. It had started to rain and she remembered that she'd left her umbrella at her mum's. A three. How long did she have to live?

'With stage one and two cancers it's been proved that a lumpectomy followed by radiation treatment is as successful as a full mastectomy. However, in your case a modified radical mastectomy, that is to say removal of the entire breast and some of the axillary nodes under your arm, would be the more usual course of action. The chances of then needing further radiation treatment would be minimal.'

She'd have to remember to tell David that she'd hidden his Christmas present at the top of her airing cupboard, along with the rest of the family's. Lucky he hadn't got around to buying her a ring earlier. What a waste of money it would have been.

'Although the need for treatment is urgent I would suggest that you take some time to consider the options. I've given you my opinion and of course you must feel free to seek a second. There are other issues to go over such as reconstruction. It can be done at the same time as the initial surgery, although some women prefer to wait. Others choose not to have it at all.'

Although Tanya was aware that he was still talking, all she could hear was the sound of the rain beating against the window.

Chapter Thirty

David hardly saw the ball as it sailed past him into the net. Thank God it was only a friendly because they would have been in deep shit if it had been a serious game. He knew his mind was on other things but he was at a loss to know what was wrong with the rest of them.

All David could think about was Tanya's breast cancer. The minute the doctor told them the news David had wondered if he could go through with it – the wedding, staying with her, supporting her, looking after her – everything. It wasn't Tanya losing her breast, although that was a shocking thought in itself, it was that he wasn't sure he could go through it all again, watching someone fight cancer. A battle that he of all people knew could very well end in defeat.

He tried to bury the image of his mother just before she died but it was as clear as ever. She had looked like a survivor of Belsen. He couldn't watch his beautiful Tanya fade day by day. He couldn't watch her die.

He swiped angrily at his eyes, his tears blinding him. How much longer did they have to play?

Perhaps Tanya's disease was his punishment. He

knew that what he had done was unforgivable, but surely no God could be that cruel. He heard his name being screamed. Two Schoenberg players were nearly on top of him. They were one kick away from their third goal.

Michael looked on open-mouthed as the Schoenberg striker scored once more. What the fuck was going on?

'Why don't you start bloody defending?' David shouted at Michael.

'You what?'

Before David could reply the ball was back in play. Michael stayed where he was, seething. What an arsehole. But David was the least of his problems.

Jenny was the bane of his life. Over the last month, ever since she'd given up the booze and coke, she'd been like a bitch with a sore head. If she'd nagged him before it was nothing compared to how she was now. If the stupid old cow wasn't trying to make him give up every pleasure he had, she was constantly interrogating him about his affair – Who was she? Where had they met? How long had it been going on? She was obsessed.

The other thing about her that was different was that she kept her distance – especially when they were arguing – always looking as if she were ready to flee should he attack her. So far that hadn't happened. Not because she hadn't asked for it – she had on more than one occasion – but Michael sensed a subtle change and something told him that if he lifted a finger against her that would be the end. And there was no way he was ready to let her –

or rather her money – walk out of the door just like that.

He cheered up a little when he remembered the stash of coke he had in the changing room. A little lift for when he hit the hotspots of Berlin.

'Oi! Schizo,' Andy shouted.

Michael looked up to see the ball flash past him.

'Wanker,' Andy spat, bending over slightly to get his breath back.

Was he the only one playing in this match? Andy cast a brief look at the miserable faces of his team-mates. He would have put it down to the three-nil score, only none of them had appeared much happier before the game had even started.

Which was unfortunate, because Andy McKay was feeling on top of the world. Ever since he'd asked Loulou to marry him he'd felt as though it signified a new beginning. Although she hadn't said yes yet, he was sure she would. In fact, with every new story that was leaked about her Hollywood debacle the more likely their marriage was.

He wanted a big wedding. Marriage would put a full stop on his past. The book would be closed. Not that there was anything to worry about any more. If it was going to come out it would have done so by now.

His thoughts returned to the game. Robbie was half-heartedly tackling a Schoenberg defender. It was strange, even Robbie the clown wasn't his usual cheerful, inane self.

Robbie hoped that any minute the ref was going to

blow the whistle, signalling the end of this dismal game. It was humiliating but he just didn't have the energy to care. Fear had kept him awake nearly all of the night before. He'd never felt so worried – even after that night at the Three Lions. Perhaps this would be the same and the problem would just disappear.

But he doubted that Zoë was simply going to disappear, if her increasing number of phonecalls was anything to go by. Soon even Rachel was bound to become suspicious.

He had tried to explain to her that although he didn't want to end it, he didn't have any choice. At the end of the day, he didn't want to leave Rachel and the children or, more to the point, them to leave him. He was just a red-blooded male who wanted a bit on the side – solely on the side. But Zoë had just laughed and told him there was no way she was being dumped. Zoë's phonecall during the wake had been a really close shave but it seemed as if Rachel had bought his story. Luckily, Carla's antics had eclipsed all else.

Stefan was glad everyone else was playing as badly as he was. Or nearly everyone anyway. No one could criticise the perfect Andy. But at least he had a good excuse this time – some of the Schoenberg team were taunting him for being a traitor. Every time he got the ball he was savagely tackled and he'd even felt a globule of spit running down the back of his neck.

Still, at least Notting Hill were beginning to accept him more. Well, nearly all of them. Andy was still the exception. But the frightening reason behind this new-won acceptance was Carla. Ever since they'd had sex it was like he'd passed an initiation test. Somehow, once you'd slept with Carla you were one of the lads. Stefan tried not to dwell on this, sensing he was not the first player to bed her, or the second or the third or the last.

Even more worrying was that now Carla had him in her sights it was clear she wasn't going to let him go. She had even insisted, much to his chagrin and the others' amusement, on accompanying him to the airport to see him off.

But that wasn't to say he didn't enjoy the screwing. He'd never had sex like it before – dirty, debased, thrilling. Stefan had made love to Paula; with Carla you could only fuck.

She'd given up the grieving girlfriend act but her behaviour put Stefan in mind of the Black Widow and he wasn't sure he was strong enough to stop her consuming him. Carla was an ill-wind that would blow no good in his life.

Stefan lurched out on to the street. One more stein of beer and he'd be either unconscious or extremely sick. The snow that had been threatening to fall all day had now covered the streets in a thick coat of white and Stefan gained a small amount of relief as the ice-cold feathery flakes fell on to his face.

'Come on,' Robbie shouted, smacking him on the back. 'This is your town, show us the sights.'

'We've seen them all,' he said, his accent having become much more guttural, a combination of being back in Germany and the numerous beers.

'Nah, we can't come to Berlin without visiting a strip club.'

'I don't know. It's late.'

'You don't want everyone thinking you're a party-pooper. You'll have a great time.'

Stefan managed to lift his head to see that in front of him was a lane that was just a blur of colourful lights. The rest of the gang were already studying the hoardings outside the various clubs.

Andy had moved on further down the street and was calling to them. 'This is the place,' he shouted. 'I've been here before.'

Magic Anderson glanced up at the neon sign above the entrance and started to laugh. He looked at Stefan, shook his head and then turned to Andy, 'You're such a bastard.'

Stefan didn't understand the interchange between the two men but as the others piled into the club, he reluctantly followed on behind.

Inside, the sudden heat and stale, smoky air threatened to finish him off completely. He took deep breaths and tried to avoid looking at the blood-red carpet and matching velvet curtains. He began mouthing a silent mantra, repeatedly telling himself he couldn't be sick, not in front of this lot, not in front of Andy.

Once they'd made it through the lobby, the large room they fell into did little to make Stefan feel any better, although all the others seemed to cheer up. Whether this was from being in a warm place or from the naked bodies gyrating in front of them, he wasn't quite sure. All he knew was that he felt even worse, if that were possible. His olfactory and auditory senses were becoming completely enmeshed as the smell of hundreds of cigarettes bounced in time to the booming bass of the trashy music.

'Let's get a drink. Beer for you, Stefan?'

Robbie's voice came from a great distance and Stefan knew it would take more energy than he possessed to answer him. He stayed mute and motionless.

The next thing he knew Robbie was shaking his shoulder and proffering the largest glass of drink he'd ever seen.

'Robbie, I can't.'

'Come on, mate, don't let the side down.'

Stefan took a sip of the beer and gagged.

'Maybe you should have a rest. It wouldn't look too good if you brought your boots up in here. We've got our reputations to think of.'

Stefan put down his glass and forced himself to look up at the stage. His team mates were in a semicircle, chanting, stamping their feet and generally yelling abuse at the young woman in front of them. They wanted her clothes off – sooner rather than later.

Managing to ease himself up off the seat, Stefan stumbled into the group.

'Watch it, you arsehole.'

Stefan moved away from Michael only to step on Andy's foot. He almost cringed, waiting for a verbal pasting, but Andy said nothing. When Stefan glanced up at his face he was staring straight ahead. Following Andy's eyes Stefan saw that on the stage the stripper had been joined by another woman who was rubbing herself up against her. They began to kiss.

'Ugh. Bloody disgusting,' Andy spat. 'I didn't pay decent money to see a pair of dykes making out.'

'It's only an act,' Tony said, laughing. 'And a bloody good one at that.'

Andy frowned in reply. 'I can't help it, it turns my stomach. I'm going to the bar.'

He brushed past Stefan as if he were unaware of the other man's presence. Stefan tried to make his eyes align so he could watch the two women, who were now feeling each other's breasts. In the end he realised to get a clearer picture he would have to close one eye.

Suddenly, Andy's voice called out from behind him. 'Oi, Stefan, come here.'

Stefan slowly turned his head. Andy was by the bar smirking and beckoning. What the hell did Andy want with him? It was definitely out of character for Andy to include him in his little laughs with the boys.

Stefan wished his mind would clear so he could figure out exactly what was going on but he knew it was a losing battle and he gave himself up to the moment as he walked with the others towards where Andy was standing.

Behind Andy's head, decorating the back of the bar, was photo after photo of women in a variety of poses and various states of undress. All of them the club's present and past artistes.

Stefan shrugged his shoulders as his eyes, never quite focusing, skirted over each pornographic picture. The photos left nothing to the imagination. And then his eyes stopped moving. There in front of him, legs splayed and naked, apart from some heavy gold chains around her neck and stomach, was Carla.

Stefan vomited.

Chapter Thirty-One

Rachel looked across at her mother-in-law. The sound of Mary masticating both fascinated and repulsed her. How did she manage to make such a racket? she wondered, as she studied the old woman's mouth moving up and down while her tongue lolled from side to side. The final straw was her false teeth, which worked completely independently to the rest of Mary's mouth.

The phone rang, making Rachel jump and Mary's teeth clack shut.

'I hope it's Robbie,' his mother said.

Hopefully not, Rachel thought. She had been quite happy not to have heard from him since he'd left for Berlin. Although in the past Rachel had been quick to forgive, at that moment she couldn't find it in herself to think anything nice about her husband. He had totally humiliated her at the wake, and if it hadn't been for Jenny, Tanya and Loulou she didn't know what she would have done.

Life was strange. She would never have believed there would come a day when she would feel grateful to those three women. Although she and Jenny were slowly developing a friendship, she didn't expect things to go any further with either Loulou or Tanya

– they were much too glamorous for the likes of her. The funeral had probably made them slightly more sentimental than usual. Still, it had been nice while it lasted.

'Aren't you going to answer the phone?'

Rachel knew she was stalling because she feared it was Robbie. But then again it could be Chris. He'd also been away with Chelsea and he'd promised to ring her as soon as he got back. She jumped up off the sofa.

'Hello,' she said hesitantly, fearing the worst and hoping for the best.

'Is Robbie there?' came a familiar young voice.

Rachel slammed down the phone, the noise waking Robbie Jnr from his morning nap. 'Is that Daddy? I want to speak to Daddy.'

'Me do as well,' Demi whined.

'It's not him,' Rachel shouted.

The phone rang again. 'I need to speak to Robbie.'

'Well, you can't. Why don't you leave us alone!'

'You tell him either he rings Zoë or he'll regret it. Big time.'

'I don't—' The phone had gone dead.

'Who was it?' Mary asked. Obviously she had been listening on the other side of the door.

Perturbed, Rachel didn't answer. Who was this Zoë? Was she merely a fan or was Robbie hiding something from her? He hadn't seemed the least bit concerned by her last call – but when did Robbie show concern about anything?

'Who was it?' Mary demanded again.

'It's a girl. Robbie claims she's just a fan. Does the name Zoë mean anything to you?'

Mary shook her head. 'And I'm sure it doesn't mean anything to my Robbie either. If he says it's a fan, then it's a fan. I'm surprised at you questioning his word. And while we're on the subject of you and Robbie, what's wrong between the two of you? You hardly said two words to him before he left for Berlin. It's not good for the kids, you know.'

Rachel could hear a distant female voice and then realised she was being told to replace the receiver. As she did so, the phone rang again immediately. She didn't care who it was, at least they were saving her from Mary's interrogation.

'Hello,' she began once more. 'Oh, Mrs Jones, it's you. How are you?'

Mary tutted and walked back into the living room.

Rachel smiled. 'Chris,' she whispered. 'Sorry about that, you know who's here.'

'Thank God for that,' he replied, his voice sounding full of laughter. 'I thought she'd finally sent you round the bend.'

'Almost,' said Rachel, who laughed then fell silent. What could she say?

He was silent in return.

'Say something,' Rachel urged.

'Perhaps the silence says it all. There's too much to say and none of it suitable for a phone conversation. Can we meet up? Today?'

'Today,' Rachel exclaimed, and then quietly, 'Where could we meet?'

'I know a pub where no one will recognise us. Jump in a cab and I'll meet you there in an hour. Say yes, Rachel, please.'

Rachel looked to see if Mary was listening but she

was busy making herself one of the thirty cups of tea she managed to drink a day.

'OK. Hopefully I'll be able to persuade Mary to look after the kids.'

He gave her the pub's name and address. 'See you in an hour.'

Rachel put down the phone, and went to talk to Mary. 'Ma, that was Mrs Jones—'

'So?'

'Well, she's not very well and she wondered if I could help look after her children. Could you have Robbie Jnr and Demi while I pop out for a couple of hours? I'd take them but I think the noise of four children might be too much for poor Mrs Jones,' she gabbled.

'What's wrong with her?'

'Wrong? Well, um, well she's got a fever, aches and pains, that sort of thing.'

'Don't you catch anything. Your two are much too boisterous for me to look after for more than a couple of hours.'

'Perhaps you could take them to see Santa and the Christmas lights.'

'I was planning to watch *Vanessa*.'

'Sorry.'

'All right I'll take them,' Mary said, begrudgingly.

'Thanks, Ma, you're a gem,' Rachel gushed.

Mary gave Rachel a quizzical look.

Rachel jumped into the taxi and attempted to calm her ragged breathing and trembling hands. She felt as if she'd just suffered the most excruciating twenty

minutes of her life. First of all she had had to leave
the house as if she were truly going to Mrs Jones's,
then she had to find a phone box to order a cab,
and then she had to look as inconspicuous as possible while she waited on the street corner for fifteen
minutes.

As the driver sped off Rachel searched through her
bag for her make-up. She couldn't put it on at home
as it would have only aroused Mary's suspicions, but
from the way she was being jolted about it didn't look
as if she'd be able to put it on in the car either. 'Damn,'
she muttered to herself, as her mascara wand poked
her in the eye.

'Sorry, missus.'

'It's OK, I was just trying to put my make-up on
but it's a little too bumpy,' Rachel giggled nervously,
feeling like a complete fool.

'Aw, you women. You're as bad as me old lady.
Why you can't do it at home, I don't know. Look,
I'll pull in here then you'll get it done in a jiffy.'

'Oh, I don't know if you should—'

'We don't want you meeting him not looking your
best, do we?'

How did he know she was meeting a man? Was she
that obvious? As she studied herself in her compact
mirror she guessed her flushed cheeks and sparkling,
excited eyes gave it away. She finished putting lash-
ings of mascara on her eyes and quickly covered
her lips with a dark pink lipstick. A quick brush
of her hair and she felt like a completely different woman. One who was definitely in need of a
new man.

'I'm ready. Thank you.'

'No trouble, doll, and if you don't mind me saying, you look gorgeous.'

'Th...thanks,' Rachel stammered, blushing furiously.

For the rest of the journey all Rachel could think about was seeing Chris. Her stomach was churning in anticipation.

'I think the Greyhound is down here,' the driver said eventually, turning left into a narrow lane. 'Funny place to meet.'

'Why's that?'

But the tiny dilapidated pub in front of them answered her question.

'You sure he said this pub?'

'Yes,' Rachel said doubtfully, wondering if, in her excitement, she had completely misheard Chris.

'Do you want me to wait?'

'No, I'm sure it must be right, I couldn't have made it up.'

'S'ppose not. That'll be a nice round tenner.'

She returned the driver's wave and walked into the pub. Inside it was so dark she could hardly make out anything. She waited until her eyes had adjusted and then looked quickly around the room. Chris was walking towards her.

'Hi,' he said, taking hold of her hands. 'I'm so glad you're here. I was worried the old witch would discover our secret and put a wicked spell on you.'

'I'm sure she would if she could,' Rachel said giggling. 'I thought I had the wrong place, it seemed so old and ruined.'

Chris chuckled and Rachel's stomach lurched. He was so beautiful when he laughed.

'And it's nearly always empty at this time, which

is exactly why I chose it. Let me get you a drink – white wine?'

Rachel nodded.

After they had been sitting for a while and Rachel had drunk most of her wine she began to feel more relaxed.

'I've been thinking about you all the time,' Chris said, moving closer to her.

'I've been thinking about you,' Rachel replied, allowing herself to lean against his powerful body.

'I mean *all* the time, from nearly the first minute we met.'

'No,' Rachel said, shocked and sitting upright. 'Surely not.'

'I remember the day Robbie first brought me round and you made me feel so welcome, and you looked so innocent and—'

'What about Cherry?'

'Cherry and I were totally different people. I think she was really only with me for the high life and that's not want I want. I never loved Cherry like I love you.'

'Oh, Chris, I don't . . .' Rachel stopped talking. She felt like she was going to burst and she didn't know whether it was from happiness or sadness. Happiness that here was a man who had loved her for years or sadness that here was a man who loved her and could never be hers. 'Why tell me now?' she asked suddenly.

'Because I'm in London. No, that's not really it. I wouldn't have said anything, I know how you feel about marriage and you want the best for your children, but I just can't stand seeing how Robbie treats you. Every time I've been around he's been the same – he's a prat and you deserve better.'

'Oh, Chris, please don't. He's not that bad,' Rachel said, forcing herself to defend her husband. She blanked out the memory of Zoë's insistent demands. 'He's just a bit immature; there's nothing malicious about him. He wouldn't do anything to hurt me and the kids.'

Chris just grunted.

It was Rachel's turn to take his hands. 'I feel the same way about you, but it just can't be.'

'I don't believe that,' Chris whispered, stroking her hair. 'Otherwise you wouldn't be here.'

His breath tickled her cheek and she felt herself being drawn closer and closer towards him. Their lips met and any misgivings Rachel had about them kissing were smothered. As Chris's tongue searched out hers Rachel realised that she had never been kissed like this before. The warm sensation radiated all the way down to her pelvis, making her simultaneously shiver and blush. It was all she could do to stop herself from ripping off her dress and making love to him there and then.

Eventually they pulled away from each other. Breathless, Rachel looked round the room. But Chris had been right – there was nobody there.

'Come back to mine,' Chris whispered.

Rachel slowly shook her head. 'I can't. It wouldn't be right,' she pleaded.

'What's wrong about two people feeling the way we do?'

'I'm married. That's what's wrong. Take me home, Chris. Now, please.'

'OK, OK. I'm sorry if I've pushed too hard,' he said, standing and leading her out of the pub.

'Don't be, and you can never feel as sorry as I do. God I want you, Chris, and perhaps you'll never know how much.'

'Don't say that,' he murmured, opening the car door for her.

The journey back was silent. Rachel knew that if she opened her mouth she'd beg him to take her back to his place. Instead, she busied herself taking off her make-up. The last thing she needed was an inquisition from Mary.

As they neared her house, Rachel finally spoke. 'You'd better drop me off here. I'd hate to be hung for a lamb.'

Chris smiled. 'That would be ironic.' He switched off the engine and turned to face Rachel. 'I'm really sorry if I've upset or embarrassed you, or put pressure on you. I just—'

Rachel silenced him with her lips. Once again she lost herself in the kiss despite one part of her mind telling her that it must never go further than this.

Chris's arms enveloped her. If only this moment could last forever. She felt so happy.

Suddenly there was a thumping on the window. Rachel and Chris flew apart. Rachel turned, terrified. Pressed up against the glass was the distorted, furious face of her mother-in-law.

Chapter Thirty-Two

Rachel walked back into the house, ready for the inevitable explosion. Mary was waiting in the kitchen, drumming her fingers on the work surface.

'The children want fishfingers for their tea,' her mother-in-law said, injecting more venom into that innocuous statement than Rachel thought possible.

'R-right then,' she said, opening the freezer. She threw some fishfingers under the grill and opened a tin of beans, aware of Mary's eyes drilling into her back. Any second now, Rachel thought. Her shoulders hunched in anticipation of the opening tirade.

'Aren't you going to do chips? They want chips,' Mary barked.

'Of course. I don't know what I was thinking of.' She turned off the grill and lit the oven.

'I'm sure you didn't,' Mary commented, the noise of her fingers sounding like thunder to Rachel.

Robbie Jnr ran into the kitchen waving a plastic sword.

'Where did you get that?' Rachel asked, bending down to kiss him.

'Tell your mother about Father Christmas,' Mary ordered.

'Father Christmas gave me this,' Robbie Jnr said.

'Lovely,' Rachel said. 'Wasn't that nice of Nanna to take you?'

'It got me out of the house,' Mary commented. 'Conveniently.'

'Go and tell Demi your tea's nearly ready,' Rachel said, shooing him away.

Alone with Mary, she tried not to catch the woman's eye as she finished making the tea. Half the oven chips went on the floor, her hands were shaking so much, and the fishfingers were practically chargrilled.

Throughout the meal Mary restricted herself to the odd waspish comment, and although Rachel was glad she refrained from saying too much in front of the children, it made the anticipation of the inevitable barrage all the more unbearable.

Later, when Rachel kissed the children goodnight and closed their bedroom door, she stood at the top of the stairs and contemplated going to bed herself. But she knew she couldn't put off Mary for ever.

The older woman was drying the last of the washing-up when Rachel walked back into the kitchen. She banged down a plate on the draining board, making Rachel jump.

'I always said my Robbie was too good for the likes of you,' Mary said, squaring up to her and speaking inches away from Rachel's face.

'Mary, I can explain,' she said lamely. But she couldn't.

'Carrying on in the street like a common prostitute. You didn't even have the decency to do it behind closed doors. Don't you care what people think? What about your children? Thank God they were still in the sweet shop. It would have broken their little hearts.'

Rachel couldn't speak. She backed away from her mother-in-law and found herself pressed up against the fridge.

'Dirty! Filthy! Immoral! And if it wasn't bad enough that you were doing it you had to go and pick a black one.'

'That's a disgusting thing to say,' Rachel said softly. She couldn't defend herself but she wouldn't let Mary get away with talk like that.

'I wish my Robbie had seen it with his own eyes. Wait till I tell him what a good-for-nothing little scrubber you really are.'

'Please don't tell him,' Rachel begged. 'Please. For the sake of the children.'

'For the children's sake?' Mary shouted, building up to a full head of steam. 'You weren't thinking about them when you were cavorting with your fancy man in that car. If there was one ounce of love in you for those poor little beggars you could never have done it.'

'Those kids are my life,' Rachel protested.

'Wait till I tell my Robbie,' Mary replied, ignoring her. 'He'll have you out on your arse before you know what's hit you. And I'll back him in every court in the land to make sure you don't get custody. You're not a fit mother.'

'Please. I made a mistake. I'll never see him again.' Rachel could feel the tears pricking her eyes. Appealing to Mary's better side was a mistake. There was no better side and the more she begged the more vituperative her mother-in-law was growing.

'You're a tart, that's what you are, and I don't want

my grandchildren being brought up by a slut like you. My Robbie's out there every day working hard to give you and his family everything. And this is how you repay him. You wanted for nothing, lady. But you were greedy.'

Greedy? Rachel thought. Greedy for what? For someone to show her a little bit of love and affection. This was the first time in nine years she'd put herself before anybody else. The first time she wasn't Robbie's stupid, dull, dutiful wife, the first time she wasn't the children's stupid, dull, dutiful mother. For just a couple of hours she had been Rachel, her own woman.

'And don't you even try going after his money. We'll see to it that you don't get a penny. Still, from what I saw today, you'll probably still be able to earn yourself pin money.'

Rachel put her hands over her ears and closed her eyes to blot out the stinging words. Mary's attack kept coming, each sentence more spiteful than the last. None of what Mary was saying was true. She knew she was a good person, good to everyone until it had drained her of all her spirit.

Finally she could take no more and a voice she didn't recognise screamed, 'Shut up! Shut up, you bitter, evil old woman!'

'What?' Mary yelped, sounding as if she'd been slapped.

Rachel opened her eyes. 'I said shut up.'

Mary pursed her lips.

'Thank you,' Rachel said, instilled with a new confidence. 'I want you out of my house now.'

'Pardon?'

'Pack your things and get out now.' It didn't all go, Rachel thought. I still have some of my spirit.

'Don't you go thinking my Robbie will stand for this. He won't see me out on the streets with the likes of you sitting pretty.'

'If I have to drag you by the scruff of the neck I will. I never wanted you in my home but I suffered you for Robbie's sake. It was a mistake. And now I'm rectifying it.' Rachel was amazed at how easy it was. She'd had this power all along – all she had to do was open her mouth.

Mary seemed to shrink to half her size but she wasn't quite done. 'Even if you do throw me out, you can't stop me telling him.'

Rachel laughed. 'He won't believe you. Who would think that dull and dutiful Rachel would have the gumption to go out and have herself an affair? No one. No matter what you tell Robbie, he'll think you've gone mad.'

Mary grasped the table for support. 'Please. I'm an old woman. You can't put me out on the streets at this time of night. Where would I go?'

Rachel considered the question. As triumphant as she felt at this moment, she wouldn't see Mary homeless. 'I'm prepared to strike a deal,' she said, sounding like one of those confident businesswomen she watched all the time on the soaps. This wasn't her at all. Where was it all coming from? 'I will finish with Chris. In return you will say nothing to Robbie. And I'll agree to you staying here. This offer isn't up for negotiation. Take it or leave it.'

'Whatever you say,' Mary said weakly.

Chapter Thirty-Three

Bad weather delayed the departure of the Lufthansa flight bringing the Notting Hill boys back from Berlin, and when Rachel arrived at Heathrow she found she was facing a long wait. Normally she would have fretted, worrying that something would happen to the plane but today she was grateful to have as much extra time as possible to try to get her thoughts in order.

Jenny was already there, as usual sitting apart from the other wives. She waved as Rachel approached. 'I didn't think you were coming,' she called.

Rachel sat down beside her. 'The traffic was terrible.'

'I thought perhaps Chris had whisked you off somewhere,' Jenny whispered mischievously.

'Don't even joke about it. Jenny, what am I going to tell Robbie?'

'There's nothing to tell. If I was you . . .' Something caught Jenny's eye and her voice trailed away.

'Who are you staring at?'

'I thought it was her. The other woman. Honestly I'm obsessed – I think I see her everywhere.'

'It's completely understandable,' Rachel said, the guilt welling up inside her. This was what affairs did to people. The pain Michael was causing Jenny would be the same as the hurt Rachel would do to Robbie unless she cut Chris out of her life forever.

'I'm dying for a drink,' Jenny declared.

Rachel stared at her. 'You wouldn't. I know what Michael is doing is terrible but you'd only be hurting yourself even more.'

'By ordering a pot of tea?'

'I'm sorry. I thought . . .'

Jenny smiled. 'I know what you thought but it isn't going to happen. This baby means too much to me.'

The older woman went off to fetch the tea and Rachel thought back to the last time they'd all been at the airport together. She remembered how drunk Jenny had been and how much she'd disapproved. But today Jenny was a completely different woman and Rachel admired the way she had managed to turn her life around for the sake of her unborn child. If only Rachel had been able to put her own children first.

That thought had kept her awake ever since her confrontation with Mary, and the euphoria she had felt at finally silencing her mother-in-law soon dissolved into a welter of self-recrimination and regret. No matter how much Robbie neglected their marriage, her children should not be made to suffer.

A voice interrupted her thoughts.

'Have you seen Loulou?'

It was Tanya, and she looked absolutely dreadful. Her normally buoyant platinum curls lay dark and limp and her face was pale and drawn, a fact she hadn't bothered to hide behind make-up. Rachel shook her head not wanting to speak, knowing her voice would betray her surprise.

Tanya began to walk away. 'If you do see her, tell her I'm looking for her,' she mumbled.

'Tanya, wait! Is something wrong?'

The model turned round, tears streaming down her face.

Jenny queued at the cashier's desk, staring into the bar. Of course she still wanted alcohol, she craved it constantly. There probably wasn't a worse time to give up all one's vices than when pregnant. The stress of Michael's likely reaction to the news, combined with her fears about her ability to be a fit mother, made her want to turn to the familiar crutches all the more.

Catching sight of her reflection in the bar window brought Jenny up short. If she didn't hold herself just so, the lump showed. How could Michael fail to notice? She forced herself to set a date to tell him and chose New Year's Day. Out with the old and in with the new. She hoped.

As she walked back to their table she saw that Rachel had been joined by Tanya and something was amiss. Tanya looked awful.

'What's up?' Jenny mouthed to Rachel.

Rachel shrugged her shoulders.

Jenny sat down next to Tanya and put her arm around the younger woman. 'Hey, what's up?' she asked. 'Would it help to talk about it?'

Jenny looked up to see that Tanya's state had drawn the attention of Martine and Suzy. She narrowed her eyes, sending them a warning signal to back off. 'Come on,' she urged, 'it can't be that bad.'

Taking a deep breath, Tanya said, 'I've got breast cancer.'

Immediately, Jenny wished she could have eaten her words. She was just about to apologise when the first camera flash went off.

Loulou flew out of the taxi and raced into the terminal. She'd spent hours sitting in a traffic jam. The plane would have landed long ago and Andy was probably already on his way back to Notting Hill. She'd wanted to be there for him because she had come to a decision. And that decision was basically to wait and see. She would agree to a long engagement with no fixed date for a wedding in the hope that in time she would be able to make up her mind about him one way or the other.

It was the best she could offer him, and to show goodwill she was now wearing the engagement ring even though it was bound to draw the attention of the press.

Loulou read the flight details on the arrivals board and was relieved to find out that the plane hadn't landed. The other reason she'd wanted to get there early was to see Tanya. The model still hadn't returned any of her calls.

It wasn't hard to find her. Half the airport seemed to be watching the altercation involving Rachel, Jenny and Tanya and a group of reporters.

'Leave her alone!' Rachel shouted, stepping in between Tanya and a cameraman.

'I swear, sooner or later, I'm going to swing for one of you bastards,' Jenny warned, grabbing the lens of another.

Loulou's first instinct was to flee. She really didn't need to be caught up in another bad scene, but the wish to protect Tanya forced her into the fray. What on earth was happening?

'This way,' she said, grabbing Tanya's hand and making a run for it. Jenny and Rachel followed up the rear and Loulou led them into the ladies'. The three women bundled Tanya inside and Loulou locked the door behind them.

'What's happened?' Loulou asked, breathlessly.

Jenny was bent over double clutching her sides. 'Ow, I don't think the baby liked all that excitement.'

'You're pregnant!' Tanya said, wiping her eyes with her hand. 'Oh, Jenny, you shouldn't have done that.'

'Look, it's fine,' the older woman replied. 'I shouldn't have said anything. Michael doesn't know yet.'

Loulou looked to Rachel for an explanation of what was happening. 'Tanya was upset and all of a sudden that lot were trying to take pictures of her.'

A chill ran through Loulou and she put her arms around the model. 'I guess it was bad news.'

Tanya was shaking. 'I've got to have a radical mastectomy.'

'Tanya, I don't know what to say. I was so sure that it was going to be nothing.' Loulou kept hold of the model but surreptitiously removed her engagement ring. It seemed completely inappropriate. 'Women beat this all the time. You *will* get through it.'

Rachel handed Tanya some tissues. 'Of course you will.'

Jenny had regained her composure. 'I don't know you very well, Tanya, but one thing I do know about you is that, girl, you're a fighter.'

'I thought I'd come to terms with it. The other day

I was fine but this morning I told my parents and they just went to pieces. It's devastated them. I've never seen my dad cry before.' A fresh wave of tears engulfed her.

As someone banged on the locked door, the four women held on to each other, Tanya's tears causing the floodgates to open for all of them.

'I thought you should know – the plane's landed,' a voice shouted.

Loulou pulled away and opened the door to reveal Carla standing there.

'They're here,' the barmaid said excitedly.

'We're not interested.' Loulou banged the door in her face.

Stupid stuck-up cow, Carla thought, racing back to the arrivals gate, I was only trying to do her a favour.

One by one the players came through and Carla waved at Stefan. She ran to help him with his bags but he pushed her away.

'Hello, sexy,' she said, trying to kiss him. '*Wie gehst du?*'

'I'm fine,' Stefan replied coldly.

'Are you ready for the best *Weihnachtsferien* of your life?'

'It will be very quiet, I feel.'

Carla could hear the hostility in his voice. What was wrong now? 'Shall I get a cab? I take it you'd rather we spent Christmas at your hotel. My flat's a bit cold.'

The footballer tried to walk away from her. 'Carla, it's not right to have Christmas with you.'

That familiar sinking sensation lurched up from the

pit of her stomach. 'Don't be silly,' she said, running after him. 'You can't spend the holiday on your own. I don't mind – I hadn't planned anything special. I'd really enjoy it.'

'No. I would not like it.'

Her panic grew. 'Stefan, what's the matter?'

'You made me look very stupid.'

'How? What did I do? I didn't tell anybody about us.'

'You have taken photographs with your legs open. I saw these pictures in a bar. It was very embarrassing for me with the others.'

Carla's mouth fell open. She knew immediately what had happened. They could have walked into any one of a dozen strip bars in Berlin but those pigs had taken him there. Why did the players hate her so much? 'Stefan, please! That was years ago.'

'I don't think I like you very well. Now, I am going home. Alone.'

'Stefan . . . Stefan!'

The footballer didn't turn round and, heavy hearted, Carla set off to the Tube, racking her brains to come up with a way to win him back.

Chapter Thirty-Four

It was New Year's Day at the Three Lions but few of the Trophy Wives looked like they had anything to celebrate. Martine and Suzy were miffed that they had turned up wearing the same dress and their foul tempers reflected the general mood pervading the cavernous club. Even the Christmas trimmings, drooping from the scaffolding, looked miserable.

Yet again Robbie had left Rachel to fend for herself, but for once she was glad as it gave her an opportunity to find Chris. Despite Jenny's advice that she should follow her heart, she was going to tell him that they wouldn't be meeting again. Mary had kept her mouth shut and now she had to keep her side of the bargain.

This Christmas had been the most stressful Rachel had ever known. In the past week she and Robbie had argued more than they had throughout their entire marriage. Zoë had been calling again and, after a particularly nasty exchange on Christmas Day when the girl had threatened to turn up on the doorstep, Rachel realised that she no longer believed her husband's protestations of innocence.

However, the ensuing arguments were more to vent her own frustrations than to find out the truth. Rachel didn't care what Robbie was up to. She was trapped in a loveless marriage and had accepted that, for the sake of the children, this was her lot.

It was strange walking around the club and receiving admiring looks from men who'd looked straight through her a million times before. The other wives had noticed how good she was looking, their pity replaced by suspicious stares. Feeling she was about to wither under their collective glare, Rachel was glad to spot Jenny, sitting alone at a table by the stage.

'Happy New Year,' she said morosely.

'I know how you feel,' Jenny replied, kissing her on the cheek. 'I hate this place.'

'I spoke to Tanya earlier. She told me to say thanks again for what happened at the airport.'

'That poor girl. I take it she isn't coming this evening. I saw David talking to Andy just now. You'd have thought he would have been at home with her at a time like this.'

'She said that she and Loulou are going to have a quiet night in together.'

'I must be honest,' Jenny said, staring into the crowd distractedly, 'Loulou's taken me by surprise. I wouldn't have suspected that she had a genuine bone in her body but she seems very concerned about Tanya.'

'It is awful,' Rachel said, feeling her spirits plunging even more as she thought about what Tanya was about to undergo.

Both women fell silent and after a while Rachel realised that Jenny, like she, was scanning the crowd, looking for someone.

'Do you think she might be here?' Rachel asked finally.

'I'm sure of it,' Jenny replied. 'But whether I find her or not, tonight's the night I'm going to tell Michael.'

Rachel squeezed her friend's shoulder. 'Even if he's a bit shocked, he'll come round to the idea. Just you wait, in a year from now he'll be signing his son up for a Notting Hill apprenticeship and telling everybody it was his idea that you started a family.'

'Rachel!' somebody from behind her called.

Rachel jerked her head. 'Chris,' she whispered. She looked back at Jenny, her eyes revealing her confusion.

'Go on, go to him,' Jenny urged. 'Then at least one of us can salvage something from this evening.'

Rachel stood up and allowed the footballer to lead her by the elbow to a dimly lit area far away from the stage. It was all Rachel could do to stop herself from throwing her arms around him. Telling Chris it was over wasn't going to be easy.

'I can't stand this any more,' he began without any preamble. 'I can't bear to see you and not be able to touch you. I'm sorry, Rachel, but if you won't leave Robbie, this will be the last time we see each other. It's just too painful.'

Even though this was exactly what Rachel had planned to say to him, it grieved her to hear Chris speaking with such finality. She was a fool. She'd opened Pandora's box – how did she think she would be able to return to being the Rachel who was content to live her life through slushy novels? The answer was that she couldn't, and yet her happiness could not be put above that of her children. Her life with Robbie was the bed she'd made and she was going to have to lie on it.

'You can't mean it, Chris,' she said, despite herself. 'I don't know what I'd do if I never saw you again.'

'I'm sorry, Rach, I really am. I have to think about my own sanity,' he said quietly, and then, angrily, 'For God's sake, Rachel, leave him.'

'I can't,' she cried. 'It's not fair on the children.'

Chris stepped back from her. 'And you think being with a man you no longer love is fair on them?'

Rachel simply shook her head. She was beyond words.

'I've got to go,' he said, trying to extricate his arm from her hands. 'If you ever change your mind . . .'

Through a mist of tears, Rachel watched on helplessly as he walked out of her life.

'Are you sure you wouldn't rather have gone with Andy?' Tanya asked, handing Loulou a glass of champagne.

'If you hadn't invited me over I would have been in bed by now,' Loulou said truthfully. 'There isn't anyone at the Three Lions I particularly wanted to see the new year in with.'

'Rachel and Jenny were going. Rachel called me earlier to see how I was. I really appreciated what she did at the airport.'

'I was amazed when I saw her taking on that photographer. It wasn't like her at all. But then she does seem to have changed a lot recently. Have you noticed the way she's dressing?'

Tanya nodded. 'A lot less mumsy. I wonder what's brought it on?'

'Perhaps she's having an affair.'

Both women laughed and said in unison, '*Not Rachel!*'

A picture on the wall caught Loulou's eye. 'Hey, where did you get that? It's really unusual.'

She walked over to study the drawing and saw that there were several more in the room. Although Tanya's flat wasn't quite as 'Page Three' as she had expected, the artwork still seemed completely out of place.

'I did it,' Tanya admitted timidly. 'They're all mine.'

'Are you serious?' Loulou was unable to hide her surprise. '*You* did these?'

'I know what you're thinking and you're not the first.'

'I'm sorry. That was incredibly rude of me. It just seems so at odds with the . . .'

'Go on, say it. The job. I know that. I know what a glamour model is and isn't supposed to be. I was always good at art. Well, I always liked it, at least. But even at school no one took notice of anything other than my boobs.'

'But you're incredibly talented,' Loulou declared.

'I don't know about that. I do know I was a very good glamour model. I'm proud of what I did.'

Loulou bit her tongue to stop herself apologising yet again. Tanya confounded her. It was true that, at one time, she'd written the other woman off as a bimbo and yet there was so much going on beneath the surface. She was truly a remarkable person. 'Tanya, I'm no expert but I think your work is very special.

Would you mind terribly if I took a few of the
drawings to show people? I know a few dealers who
might be interested.'

'Oh, I don't know. It's really just something I do
for myself.'

'Please? If you want, I won't say they're yours.'

'If you like, but nothing will come of it.'

Loulou framed a section of one of the drawings
with her hands. 'This would really work well as a
necklace.' She looked around the room. 'In fact, a
lot of your drawings look like jewellery designs. You
really should give it some thought.' She shook her
head in amazement. 'Are there any other secret talents
you've got hidden up your sleeve?'

'Only a talent for messing things up. Did you
know that David and I were meant to be buying an
engagement ring? But I let this thing get in the way.'

Loulou noticed Tanya clutching her chest protec-
tively. She'd resolved not to talk about the cancer this
evening but it was hard to ignore how pale Tanya
was. 'How can you say that you messed things up?
David understands, I'm sure. Your health is far more
important. Don't be so hard on yourself.'

'If I was tougher on myself I wouldn't have got into
such a state at the airport.'

'Look at the mess *I've* made of things. What's my
excuse? Incidentally, you're not the only one who's
supposed to be getting engaged. Andy asked me to
marry him in Paris.'

'Oh, Loulou, that's fantastic!' Tanya said, reaching
for the champagne bottle and refilling their glasses.

'Well, it isn't really. I haven't quite accepted. At
this moment Andy's probably the only thing in my

life that's right but I couldn't bring myself to say yes.'

'Why not?'

'Because, like you, I've got a talent for messing things up.'

Tanya laughed. 'We're a right pair, aren't we?'

Jenny was obsessed. She paced up and down, her eyes constantly on the move. She scanned the usual suspects for the woman who was Michael's mistress. Ignoring all the blondes, she concentrated on those with dark hair, whatever the hue. At least it cut down the odds. But most of the women she could see, she knew, and for one reason or another dismissed them as not the one she was searching for.

The Three Lions was the last place she wanted to be. Jenny hadn't forgotten her humiliating night here, but her need to find Michael's mistress was of greater importance than a few hours of agony.

And she knew she had been right to come. As soon as she and Michael had parked, she'd seen the vehicle of her nightmares. But how to match the car with the woman?

'Jenny. Good to see you,' Bill Harry said, oblivious as ever to the goings-on in his club.

'Hi,' Jenny mumbled, about to dismiss him, but then it occurred to her that he might be of some use after all.

'I'm glad I bumped into you, Bill,' she said, forcing herself to smile. 'I did a silly thing in the car park, I managed to hit a pink jeep, a Suzuki Vitara. It's only a scratch but I'd just like to confess to the owner. You wouldn't have any idea who it belongs to?'

'Oh, that's easy, it's our Sharon's. She works behind

the bar,' he said, pointing to a woman busy with a cocktail shaker.

Jenny looked across at the barmaid. Sharon was the bitch who had thrown her out after her ordeal, the cow who had almost force-fed her vodka. Now it all began to make sense.

'Although,' Bill continued, unaware of the look of horror on Jenny's face, 'I don't know whether I'd recommend you tell her, that's her pride and joy.'

Jenny felt like saying that she was quite prepared to demolish the tart's pride and joy; instead she managed to thank Bill.

She shoved and elbowed her way through the crowd like a heat-seeking missile.

'Sharon!' Jenny barked. 'I want to speak to you.'

There was no mistaking the expression on Sharon's face – fear. The game was up.

'I'm busy,' she hissed, trying to brazen it out.

'Not any more you're not,' Jenny snapped, darting behind the bar and catching the barmaid by her long raven hair. With a determined pull, Jenny managed to drag Sharon to the end of the bar.

'I'm going to tell you this only once. Stay away from my fucking husband. If I so much as catch you looking at him, I'll—'

Jenny was grabbed from behind.

'Let go of her, you stupid bitch,' Michael spat.

Jenny twisted and turned but was no match for Michael's grip. Worried that he might hit her, she let go of Sharon. He pushed her roughly to one side.

Edging her way back from him, all the while thinking about how exposed her baby was to his fists, she tried to figure out what to do next.

Luckily, a commotion on the stage distracted Michael. A woman, who could barely stand, let alone speak, had picked up the karaoke mike and was trying to talk into it.

'I shus wanna shing a song for Tony.'

The DJ clearly thought the woman much more entertaining than his repertoire of records and turned off the music.

'I'm gonna sing,' she laughed, stumbling across the stage, '"Get Down On It" for my man Tony, who says,' she paused, 'I give the best blow jobs.'

Jenny saw a humiliated Martine flee the room but was unable to feel any sympathy for the other woman.

The tune began but before the woman even had the chance to open her mouth four players, including Michael and Sandy Ruther's husband, Ian, were up on the stage dragging her off.

'I can guess why they're so eager to get her off the stage,' Sandy, who had just noticed Jenny, commented. 'God knows what she could say about the rest of them.'

Michael had not said one word to Jenny since pulling her off Sharon. Jenny hadn't spoken either, but now, as they neared their home, she decided it was now or never.

'I'm pregnant,' she said, her voice barely above a whisper.

'What?'

'I'm pregnant,' she said, loud enough for him to hear.

'That old trick. I don't think so.'

'What do you mean? I'm telling you something bloody serious here,' she shouted.

'You'd better not be,' he snarled, leaning so close to her that she swerved the car.

'Get away from me. I'm keeping it and that's that. If you don't want to be a father then good riddance to you.' She stopped the car.

'Father! Me? I can't be. You bloody whore! Who have you been screwing?'

'What are you talking about?' Jenny began to feel extremely frightened, as if she knew the answer to a question that hadn't yet been asked.

'I *can't* be a fucking father. I'm infertile. IT'S NOT FUCKING MINE,' he screamed.

'Well, it must be a miracle,' she said, grasping at straws.

'No, you're a slut – and a fucking hypocritical one at that.'

'But I swear I haven't—'

Michael began to pummel her with his fists. 'Lying bitch,' he shouted over and over again.

Fearing for her life, and the life of the baby inside her, Jenny opened the car door and fell out. Picking herself up she ran into some bushes, her whole body aching from the beating and the sub-zero temperature. As she heard the sound of the car pulling away, she tried to piece together the implications of what her husband had said. There was only one question to be answered – who *was* the father?

Chapter Thirty-Five

One hundred and sixty-eight hours. That's how long it had taken Jenny to come to her decision. Every painful hour had simultaneously stretched a life-time and disappeared in the blink of an eye. As far as Jenny could see, she had no other option – the baby had to be aborted.

The private clinic she had booked herself into looked much the same as the hotel where she had stayed hidden for the last two weeks. Her room had identical beige, nondescript furniture and similar inoffensive prints. But this wasn't a hotel; this was the place where they were going to kill her baby. All in the best taste, of course.

In a further attempt to hide the true purpose of the place, there was an overabundance of potpourri. But Jenny could still smell death in the disinfectant and other chemical odours that the sickly perfume failed to mask.

Jenny looked down at her bulge. At just over eighteen weeks she was definitely showing. How could something she had wanted so much have been brought to her through such terrible means? She could barely believe that she had had sex with another man, drunk to the point of unconsciousness. And, furthermore, she didn't even know who he was. From her limited memory of the Three Lions night, she knew that the father of her baby could be one of three men – Andy, David or Robbie – and the thought of it being any one of them was almost too much to bear.

Just as she had started to make friends with Rachel, Tanya and Loulou, she had to go and fuck one of their partners. Jenny buried her head in her hands, doubling up as her torment manifested itself in physical pain. But this pain would be nothing compared to the induced labour that the abortion would entail. She felt like a trapped animal. Whichever way she turned, whatever solution she sought, there was no escape.

There was a gentle knock on the door.

'Come in.'

'Hi, Jenny, my name's Sue and I'm the clinic's counsellor. I wonder if you'd mind having a chat,' an unprepossessing woman, who was as beige as the room, said.

Jenny shrugged her shoulders. 'I've made up my mind.'

'I'm not here to change it. I just want to make sure that you understand all the implications of your decision.' She sat down on the corner of the bed. 'First of all, if you don't mind, could you tell me why you've decided to have a termination?'

A shrill laughed escaped from Jenny's lips. 'How long have you got? My life's a complete mess. My husband tells me he can't be the father of my baby – he's infertile – and I have no idea who is. The only night it could have happened was when I mixed alcohol with anti-alcohol pills at a club. I woke up on the floor. Three of my husband's team-mates had been there, so I guess I must have had sex with one of them. I'd always thought it was Michael and . . .' Her voice trailed off.

'And,' Jenny began again, her voice faint, 'and on top of everything else, the baby's probably damaged anyway by my drinking and drug taking. I can't live with myself. I'm the one who deserves to die. I wanted a baby so much.'

By the time Jenny had finished her monologue she was completely hysterical. It was a while before she realised Sue was hugging her.

'OK, OK,' Sue murmured. 'Ssh, it'll be OK.'

'But it won't, will it? I'll never get over this.'

'Let's start from the beginning. Go back to those lost hours. What, if anything, can you remember?'

Jenny took deep breaths to calm herself. At first her mind refused to focus and it was several minutes before she could concentrate on the night she had conceived. 'We went to an opening of a night club. All I can remember was drinking large vodkas and falling off my stool. I vaguely remember that the three men had been stood around me at one stage. Then I woke up on the other side of the club with my clothes ripped.'

'Your clothes were ripped?'

'Yeah, I must have got carried away with one of them. I guess it all got a bit rough. God knows how I was behaving.'

'Don't you think it's rather strange that your clothes were ripped if it was consensual sex?'

Aghast, Jenny didn't respond.

'Please, Jenny, think. Is it possible you were raped?'

'Raped?' Jenny whispered. She'd been over that

night so many times, especially in the last week, yet any new information refused to yield itself.

But as she allowed herself the comfort of being wrapped in Sue's embrace, new images began to emerge. While Andy and Rob had been standing over her, David had been behind them – what was the expression on his face? Fear, horror, guilt? But it couldn't possibly have been David.

'I don't know what happened,' she cried.

'Let's take it one step at a time.'

Jenny jumped up off the bed and paced around the room. As her mind reluctantly retraced the night at the Three Lions it was as if she were back there. She remembered the nausea, felt the coldness of the stone floor; she heard men's voices arguing. Then she began to feel a hand – a man's – tearing at her flesh, her clothes ripping. The pain as a man entered her. The man who, until recently, she had believed was Michael.

But which man was it? Jenny felt movement in her stomach. 'Oh my God,' she howled, collapsing on to the bed. 'The baby just moved. How could a baby, an innocent baby, be conceived through such a violent act?' She looked up at Sue, tears streaming down her face. 'How?' she pleaded, as if the counsellor could provide all the answers.

'I don't know, Jenny. I'm so sorry. Do you want me to contact the police?'

'No!'

'OK, fine. Just let me go and get something to calm you down.'

Jenny sobbed. 'Don't leave me, please. I think I always knew what happened. I just couldn't face the truth. Who could?' she asked bitterly. 'I'm sure that's why I'd decided on an abortion despite it going against everything I believe in.'

Sue sat back down, looking on helplessly at the distraught woman.

Jenny slowly calmed down. 'It just seems so unfair. This baby dies because of some bastard.'

'It doesn't have to.'

'It doesn't?'

'There could be something really good coming out of something really terrible.'

'I don't know . . . How could I . . .'

'Isn't it possible that despite the way the baby was conceived you could love it?'

'What about the father and I? Oh, you don't understand.' Jenny began to weep again. 'Their wives are friends of mine. They'd all hate me.'

'Jenny, it wasn't your fault. You have to remember that. I realise all of this is extremely difficult but you said you wanted a baby so much. And you have to think about the future – how you'd feel having had an termination.'

Jenny felt as if her brain was about to explode. How could anyone expect her to make any rational decisions? Her whole life had been turned upside down. She felt the baby kick again as if it was fighting for its life.

'I don't know,' was all she managed.

'Why don't you sleep on it?'

'Sleep. Now that would be a novel idea.'

Jenny turned from side to side as the man in black threatened her and her bastard child with hell. Clive's face loomed above her. She sat upright in bed, panting, a cold sweat coating her entire body. She switched on the bedside lamp, hoping the light would dispel her demons, but they refused to go away. It had always happened in the depths of the night. He'd come to her then. She felt her chest tighten as she remembered the dread and fear, how it had been repeated over and over again.

Why had it happened to her? And not just once. It must be her fault. There was no way she deserved a baby. She had to go ahead with the abortion. Jenny accepted God would never forgive her – and she'd never forgive herself.

Hesitantly, Loulou put her head around the door. 'Tanya?'

'Loulou! Come in.'

Loulou didn't know what she expected – drips, tubes, a dying Tanya – but Tanya looked relatively well. Considering. However, as she got nearer to the bed she saw that not only was the model even paler than when she'd last seen her on New Year's Day but, with just a faded hospital gown on, it was clear she had lost a lot of weight. And both arms were painted in bruises.

Loulou felt vain in comparison. Only that morning she had visited the hairdresser, had a facial, and bought a new dress that she didn't need and was now wearing. She looked great but felt awful.

Loulou nodded at David, who appeared to be very morose.

'Hi, Loulou,' he mumbled, not meeting her eyes.

Loulou felt a jolt of anger. This was about Tanya,

not David. He should be doing everything he could
to make her feel better. The sight of his long face
could be of no benefit to her friend. Thinking of
Tanya as a friend made her smile inwardly. She hadn't
had a friend since she was twelve! After that her
life had been a rollercoaster of one-upmanship and
secrets.

Loulou just hoped they would have the time to
develop that friendship. Selfishly, she thought what
a relief it would be to unburden those secrets that had
made her life such a solitary one. It was only since
she'd got to know Tanya that Loulou had realised
just how unhappy and alone she'd been. No wonder
she had turned into such a bitch.

'Sit down.' Tanya motioned to a red plastic chair.
'You just missed Rachel.'

'How is she?'

'Distracted. I don't know what's going on but
something is definitely up.'

'You shouldn't concern yourself about anyone else,'
David said sharply. 'I've got to go, I'm afraid.' He
stood up too quickly and knocked a pile of magazines
from the bed.

'But, David—'

'I'm really sorry, Tanya, but . . . I have . . . look, I'll
see you this evening.'

Tanya looked hurt and defenceless. Bloody men,
Loulou thought bitterly, they were neither use nor
ornament, as her mother was fond of telling her father.
Loulou had always found that a bit rich coming from
a woman who had a degree in using men and treating
them like accessories.

As soon as David left, Tanya explained, 'His mother

died of cancer. I think it's all too painful and frightening for him.'

'Well, I'm sure it's pretty frightening for you,' Loulou replied tartly, wondering why so many women apologised for men. She would never do that for Andy; he could sink or swim on his own lack of merit.

Tanya dismissed the subject. 'How's Andy?'

'To be honest he's been acting very peculiar lately.'

'What do you mean?'

'Oh, I don't know. I'm sure in other relationships it's perfectly normal behaviour – you know, lovey dovey, wanting to be with me all the time. In other words, not like a footballer. And most definitely not like Andy.'

'David's like that.' Tanya paused. 'Well, he was.'

'I know I should be happy but I feel a bit hemmed in, that's all,' Loulou added hurriedly, wanting to steer clear of David and his treatment of Tanya. 'When's the operation?'

'Monday morning. Bright and early.' Tanya's voice faltered.

'Oh, Tanya, I'm—'

'Look, I want to be distracted. How's Dexter?'

How Loulou wanted to talk about Dexter, but now was neither the time nor the place. There would be other times, she told herself. There had to be. She couldn't lose Tanya now.

'He's fine. I think my parents are behaving a little more reasonably. By their standards anyway.'

The door was thrown open. 'Miss Barry, I'm Mr Anderson, the senior surgeon,' a man in a shabby suit and ill-fitting glasses declared. 'I've got a spare minute so I thought I'd go through the procedure with you now. We find it puts our patients more at ease if they know exactly what will happen.'

'I doubt that,' Tanya said, trying to smile.

'I'd better be going,' Loulou said, rising.

'Don't,' Tanya cried, grabbing her hand. 'Please.'

Loulou sat back down again and Tanya tightened her grip.

The surgeon went into far too much detail for Loulou's liking and she could see that, if anything, his pre-op talk was terrifying Tanya.

Finally Mr Anderson finished. 'Any questions?'

'I think you've covered everything I didn't want to know. So there goes half a million quid.'

'Pardon?'

'Oh, just a joke. My breasts were insured for a million pounds as a publicity stunt.'

'You'd better start filling in your claim then,' the surgeon replied, trying to be humorous.

Loulou found his remark completely inappropriate.

'It wasn't for real,' Tanya added quietly.

'Right then, I'll be off. See you tomorrow,' the surgeon said breezily.

For a few seconds after he'd swept out of the room, the women just stared at each other, speechless from the worst bedside manner since Dr Crippen. Then they began to snigger, which turned into giggles and the next thing they were laughing hysterically, tears running down their faces.

'That's a man for you. Always knows the right thing to say at the right time,' Loulou managed finally.

'Thanks for coming,' Tanya said, her laughter disappearing as quickly as it had arrived. 'I'd better have a rest now. It's exhausting just lying here being prodded and poked by all and sundry. You'll come tomorrow?'

'Try stopping me.'

Jenny looked out the window as a weak sun struggled to be seen through heavy hanging clouds. She hadn't slept at all. How could she when she was up against such a horrific deadline? But after ten hours she was no nearer a decision. An hour earlier she had convinced herself that she had no choice but to terminate. Now it was all up in the air again.

The same list of questions haunted her. Could she ever forget that the baby's father was a rapist? And what about the damage she had possibly caused? She wouldn't know until the baby was born, and then it would be too late. But if she went ahead with the abortion, then she'd never know what could have been. She doubted there would ever be another chance for her to conceive.

For the hundredth time she relived the rape but she was still no nearer knowing who her assailant had been. Thoughts of that rape led straight to Clive. Her brother. Her guardian. A loud harsh laugh escaped her lips.

She lay down, exhausted. Moving her hand over her stomach, she began to talk to the baby.

'I'm so sorry,' she began. 'I love you. I know it wasn't your fault.'

Her eyes closed and she awaited the return of the nightmare.

'Jenny, wake up.' A nurse stood by Jenny's bed with

both hands held out in front of her – one holding a small cup, the other a pill. 'It's time to take your pre-med.'

'What . . . where . . .' Jenny looked at the woman as if she had no idea what she was talking about. 'Pre-med?' she mumbled, sinking back into the pillows.

'You'll be going down to theatre soon. Come on, there's a good girl.'

'No. I can't do it,' Jenny cried, jumping up in bed. The enormity of it was just too great. 'Leave me alone.' She knocked the paper cup from the nurse's hand.

'All right. Calm down. Let me get Sue.'

Jenny wasn't listening. She was frantically pulling on her clothes, the only thought in her mind to get out of the clinic and save her baby's life.

Sue appeared moments later. 'Jenny. Are you all right?' she asked, breathless from running.

'I can't kill it. I just can't.' Without realising it, she had the counsellor by the arm and was shaking her violently.

'That's fine. But just sit down a minute and calm down. Is there anyone we can call for you?'

'Rachel, Rachel Black,' Jenny replied immediately, rummaging through her bag until she located her address book. 'There's her number.'

Sue handed the book to the nurse. 'What made you change your mind?'

'I'm not quite sure. I know I would never have been able to forgive myself. But it's more than that. Just before I finally fell asleep I was talking to the baby and then in my dreams it was like it was talking back. Telling me everything was going to be all right. Does that sound mad?'

'Not at all,' Sue said, squeezing Jenny's hand.

'There are other reasons. I spent a lot of the time reliving my past, until I came to the conclusion that there are many things I haven't been responsible for,' Jenny said, quietly and calmly. 'Although, up until now, I've always blamed myself – and punished myself accordingly.'

'What do you mean?'

'It's a long and painful story but the end result of all this heart searching is that I don't think my baby deserves to die for something that wasn't either its fault or its mother's. And maybe it was meant to be. I could never have had a child with Michael yet that's all I ever really wanted. But more than anything I realise that my love for this baby is greater than my hate for the rapist.' And for myself, she thought.

The nurse came back in. 'Mrs Black will be here in about fifteen minutes.'

'We'd better get you all packed.'

When Rachel arrived she looked worried, her eyes moving from Jenny, to Sue, to the nurse and back again.

Jenny guessed she must look quite a fright. Her hair was growing out at the roots and out of the crop. She hadn't slept for what felt like weeks and her crumpled, baggy clothes were more Primark than Prada.

She patted Rachel on the back as if that were enough. Jenny could see that, although still wearing her new look, Rachel had lost her new-found vitality; her eyes were sad and despondent despite the now expertly applied make-up.

'I don't understand,' Rachel began.

'I'll explain in the car,' Jenny said, bundling her out the door. She turned to Sue. 'Thank you. You've been a great help – more than you'll ever know.'

'It's you who's done all the hard work. Feel free to call me any time. Good luck.'

'I'm going to need it.'

On the stairs Rachel began again. 'Jenny, I don't understand, this is an abortion clinic. I thought you said the first scan looked fine.'

'That wasn't the reason.' Jenny now realised what she'd done. She hadn't been thinking straight when she'd given the nurse Rachel's number; she had simply wanted to see a friendly, reassuring face. If she explained the situation to Rachel, she was going to have to reveal that Robbie was there. How the hell would Rachel react to the possibility that her beloved Robbie was a rapist?

'But I thought you wanted it.' Rachel's voice had become high pitched.

'Obviously I do. It's not Michael's.'

'You've been—'

'No,' Jenny snapped, precluding any more conversation until they were safely in the car.

'Jenny,' Rachel persevered once they were seated, 'tell me. Who's the father?'

'I don't know. And before you say anything it isn't because I slept with a load of men. I didn't voluntarily have sex with anyone other than Michael.'

'What do you mean "voluntarily"?'

'I was raped.' Jenny said it calmly and dry eyed. She'd done all her crying the night before.

'Raped! But why didn't you tell me before? Have you contacted the police?'

'I can't. I don't know who it was.'

'Where did it happen?'

'The Three Lions. Remember the night Andy and Michael had a fight? It was after you'd left. I'd started drinking vodka which, with the anti-alcohol pills I was on, made me pass out. But . . .'

'Go on,' Rachel urged.

'You're not going to like this and I'm not saying it was him—'

'Robbie,' Rachel said faintly.

'I don't think it was him but he was there and so were Andy and David.'

'Surely there were other men there? What about, what's his name, Bill?'

'No, he left at the same time as you. I can remember all three of them standing above me.'

'Why didn't you tell me this earlier?'

'I tried to block it out. Quite successfully,' she said and then more quietly, 'I'm good at that.' Jenny turned to face her friend. 'But I couldn't stop the truth coming out after Michael told me he was infertile.'

'I don't know what to say. What if it's Robbie? You've got to go to the police. I can't stand not knowing. Why was he there? Oh God, what am I going to do?' Rachel asked, banging the steering wheel.

'I'm sorry. I shouldn't have told you.'

'Yes you should have,' Rachel said vehemently, 'and you should tell the police. No one should be allowed to get away with that.'

'I need time to think. The last week's been a nightmare. Now I've decided to keep the baby I need to work out what to do next. Please, Rachel, promise me you won't say anything to anyone. Not even Robbie.'

'Jenny, I can't promise that. You know I can't. I'm going to have to consider what to do next as well.'

Chapter Thirty-Six

'Jenny,' the counsellor said gently, 'I know this is all very painful for you but believe me it's better out in the open.'

Jenny stared at the floor. It was easy for him to say but until a week ago she had kept every nasty secret safely locked away. Now the barriers she had erected to protect herself from the painful truth of her past were being torn down and she wasn't sure whether she could take much more of the hurt.

'Don't you think . . . I must have . . .' She stopped speaking. This was old ground she was covering yet again. She blamed herself for both Clive and the rape and it seemed impossible to get round this. 'I got the results of the HIV test,' she said, changing the subject. 'It was negative.'

The counsellor smiled at her kindly. 'Great. One less thing to worry about.'

Jenny laughed. 'Now for the hundred others.'

'What I'd like to do is take you back to your childhood but you have to be both the child and the adult. You have to feel what it was like when you were young and all those awful things were happening to you. And as the adult you have to protect that child and love her. Think of your teenage self as another girl. I'm sure you won't be blaming her for what happened.'

As the afternoon progressed, Jenny gave up the last vestiges of embarrassment and started on the path to loving herself in a way she had never done before. As the role play unfolded she moved on from her brother to the night of the Three Lions. Her love for the baby and the need to protect it were much stronger than her hate for the man who had defiled her. At last, she felt a glimmer of hope.

Rachel looked around the players' lounge thinking it was the last place she wanted to be. And the party atmosphere – Notting Hill had just beaten Newcastle – seemed a personal affront. From where she was standing she could see Robbie, Andy and David. The sight of them made her sick to her stomach. Why was she here? To keep up appearances? No one else seemed to give a damn about the way they looked or what they did.

She stared at David, wondering what on earth he was doing here when his girlfriend was undergoing major surgery. Since her conversation with Jenny, Rachel had been unable to visit Tanya again. The need to unburden herself was too great and Tanya was in no state to hear such devastating news.

But why would David care about a little thing like breast cancer? After all he was sitting there, smiling and drinking, like he didn't have a care in the world, when all the time there was Jenny going through hell over . . .

Rachel couldn't bear to think about it, and yet she could think of nothing else. She had barely slept a second over the past few days. Sharing the same bed as Robbie had been a nightmare and her flesh crawled any time even a hand strayed near her body. So much so that now she had taken to sleeping on their sofa.

Robbie spotted her and walked over.

'Don't,' she snapped, flinching as he tried to put his arm around her.

'Don't what?'

'Crowd me,' she said, rubbing her bare arms, feeling soiled.

'What the hell are you talking about, woman?' Robbie asked. 'Lighten up a bit. You've had a face on you all week.'

Andy and David came over to talk to Robbie and the men chatted as if everything was completely normal. How could they put it out of their minds even for a second? She couldn't.

Rachel looked at each of them in turn, trying to see if she could divine something about them from their eyes. One of them was hiding something. Maybe all three. Every innocent gesture, every wink of the eye or toss of the hand suddenly became demonic to her and she felt relieved when the three men finally wandered away.

'Hi, Rachel.'

'Loulou, um, hi,' Rachel said, desperate to share Jenny's secret but knowing it was hers to carry alone. 'How's Tanya?'

Loulou grimaced. 'Bearing up in the circumstances. Where's Jenny? I haven't seen her around.'

'Fine. Busy,' Rachel replied. Before she could think of anything to say that would distract Loulou from the subject of Jenny, Carla Ryman barged through the doors and Rachel spotted Stefan trying to shrink into the corner.

Carla, still crimson from outrunning the security guard, shouted for silence and was surprised to see that the players and their women obeyed her. Stefan, who she hadn't seen since the airport, had his head in his hands, but she had something to say that she hoped would put the smile back on his face.

Bold as brass, Carla, dressed in the last of Jenny's outfits, walked over to his table, swiped his pint, drank it and said to the now gob-struck room, 'I have an announcement to make.' Carla took a deep breath. 'Stefan Lohmann and I are going to have a baby.'

'*Was?*' Stefan asked, his German cutting through the mass of muttering English voices. '*Was sagst du?*'

Carla waited for the noise to die down, wanting the next part of her announcement to stick. 'And I know he's too shy to say anything but I wanted to tell you that he's asked me to marry him and I've said yes. I'm so happy I'm fit to burst.'

There was a scattering of polite applause, which did nothing to drown out the roar of laughter from the Notting Hill crew. She dragged the bewildered German to his feet and kissed him, choosing to interpret the stunned look on his face as one of love.

Another day, another hangover. Stefan thought this was probably what it was like to be English. Maybe he was acclimatising at last. He looked over at Carla sleeping next to him. There were some things that he would never get used to.

He couldn't breathe. The hotel room was heavy with the smell of their sex. Trying not to wake Carla, he slid out of bed and opened a window, gulping in the fresh air, feeling like a prisoner.

'Good morning, *liebchen*,' a voice behind him said.

He turned round slowly, wanting to delay the start of another day with this awful woman. 'Good morning,' he said formally. Maybe he could pretend that his hangover had made it too difficult for him to speak in English.

He watched as Carla sat up in bed and lit a cigarette, yet one more thing that repulsed him about her.

'I know you're not happy about me being pregnant but . . .' Carla began.

Stefan perked up slightly. Maybe they could have an honest conversation after all. 'I was very surprised,' he said, cautiously.

He was even more surprised when the next thing Carla did was to burst into tears. 'We can call the whole thing off, if you want. Say the word and I'll get rid of the baby,' she sobbed, snot hanging from her nose.

Awkwardly Stefan put his arm around her, feeling like a complete shit-heel. 'Please don't cry,' he said, knowing he was on the verge of saying something he would regret. He was just about to be set free. If he stayed quiet perhaps this woman would talk herself out of the whole deal.

He maintained his silence as Carla reeled off a long and involved story about the many, many men who had mistreated her in her life.

'I was only sixteen and all alone in Berlin,' she cried. 'He had stolen all of my savings and left me with all his debts. Men he owed money to were knocking on the door all hours of the day and night threatening me.

If I had had the plane fare I would have come home. But they told me they were watching me and not to even think about doing a runner.'

I'm a total bastard, Stefan thought, feeling his resolve weaken. 'That must have been very bad for you.'

She lit another cigarette. 'That's why I took the job in the strip bar. What else could I do? I can't type. I couldn't speak German very well.'

Stefan's chest was wet with her tears. What an awful life she'd had and now he was about to add to her misery. 'I understand,' he said. 'You don't have to explain any more.'

'I'll never feel clean again,' Carla bawled, a fresh wave of tears flooding down her cheeks. She continued with her stories, each more degrading than the last. Wiping her eyes, she concluded, 'I know it's wrong but I just don't trust men any more. You're all the same.'

'We're not all the same,' Stefan said, biting the bullet. 'I'm not going to desert you. We will get married. We will have a happy family.'

Carla brightened immediately and threw back the sheets. 'Come here, you lovely man.' And for once in her life Carla was telling the truth. Of course she was desperate for money and security but underneath all her hardness she knew that Stefan was a good man, no doubt too good for her. And how many more chances would she have at finding such a decent man?

Morosely, Stefan lay down beside her, the feeling of suffocation returning.

*   *   *

'Tanya?' David was certain he'd seen her eyes flicker. 'Are you awake, hon'?'

Maybe he'd just imagined it. It was three days since the operation but she still seemed to sleep most of the day. It was only eight in the morning and he wanted to see her before going to the club.

In the hot hospital room, the flowers from Loulou were beginning to wilt and David had to force himself not to think about things rotting. That was the trouble with hospitals, the strong antiseptic smell did nothing to disguise the underlying odour of decay.

Tanya opened her eyes. 'Hello,' she said, her voice croaky and weak.

'Hi, there,' David said, forcing himself to sound bright and sparky.

She half raised her hand but it got caught in the drainage tube emanating from beneath her bandaged torso. David tried not to think about what it might look like underneath.

'I'm so tired,' Tanya said, and her eyes closed again.

Am I strong enough to do this? David asked himself. The doctors had said that the operation had gone well and there was no evidence that the cancer had spread. But they'd told him the same thing about his mother and eighteen months later her whole body was riddled.

It was never over with cancer, he knew that. Tanya might go into remission but it would be hanging over them always. And he knew that, just at the moment when he let his guard down, thinking she was safe, that's when it would strike and he would lose her.

He couldn't do it again, couldn't stand by and watch

as someone he loved went through that much pain. He was a coward. Tanya deserved better. She needed him to be a man, just as his mother had needed him to be when he was still a boy. He had failed his mum then, hadn't been able to protect her, and he would do the same again with Tanya.

Nobody had protected Jenny either. When she had been lying there on the wet floor ... He stopped himself, feeling he might explode. Kissing Tanya on the forehead, he left the room.

'Is she awake?' a nurse asked.

David didn't respond. Instead, he put his head down and ran. He just had to get away from that smell, that pain, those expectations he just couldn't meet.

'Where's the fire?' the man on the newsstand joked as David flew by.

He stopped short to see who was addressing him but the man had already returned to sorting through his papers. Newspapers that were carrying a large photograph of Robbie on the front. David picked up a copy and the accompanying story made him feel dizzy. It wasn't going to be long before the game was up.

Chapter Thirty-Seven

The living room was a shambles. Broken toys lay where they had been dropped, a layer of dust covered every surface, and even the mother-in-law's tongue had finally given in to the drought.

Rachel propped herself up on the sofa, looked round at the debris and then flopped back down again. Who cared? She turned slightly to alleviate the pain in her back from too many nights sleeping on the sofa. Either her head or her feet had to be up on an arm; whichever she chose, it still made for a painful and restless night. But anything was better than sleeping in the same bed as her husband.

Last night he'd been so drunk he hadn't even noticed she'd gone straight back downstairs. She'd told him she'd been having problems sleeping; he'd believed her, or perhaps he simply didn't care enough to delve further. Or, as Rachel suspected more and more, Robbie had a guilty conscience.

It was only six a.m. but Rachel knew that there was no chance of any more sleep. She might just as well get up. She looked a mess. Her face was smeared with old make-up, a red and black abstract pattern decorating her cheeks. She had gone to bed in her clothes, which now looked no better than the rags she kept for cleaning.

Groaning slightly, she made her way to the kitchen to make a cup of tea. The sink was piled so high with dirty dishes she had trouble filling the kettle. Mary had bemoaned that she was far too old to chase around clearing up after Rachel. Rachel hadn't bothered to defend herself.

The tea made, she went to fetch the morning paper, but there was nothing at the door. Typical, Rachel thought, just when she could do with something to distract her.

She crept up the stairs so as not to wake the children, Mary or Robbie. She couldn't face any of them. She was desperate to wash and change into some new clothes. Perhaps then she would feel some normalcy.

Peeping around her bedroom door she found the bed empty. Where was Robbie? He couldn't be in the bathroom. She looked in the children's rooms but there was no sign of him. And she knew that, however unhealthy she considered his relationship with his mother, he definitely wouldn't be in her room. He had clearly gone out, taking the paper with him. His absence went only further in confirming his guilt.

After another cup of tea, the silence of the house was so oppressive Rachel was tempted to get the children up. But she knew what she really wanted to do was phone Chris, although no doubt six forty-five was a bit early. And what would she say?

'Mummy, Mummy,' Robbie Jnr was crying from the top of the stairs.

'Hi there, precious. Come down and I'll put the TV on for you.'

Once she'd settled him down on the settee, she went into the kitchen to make some toast. Mary entered shortly afterwards, a scowl on her face.

The phone began to ring. 'I'd better get—'

'Mummy, Mummy, come look! Daddy's on telly.'

'I've seen him lots of times, darling.'

'And on the papers. He's famous,' Robbie Jnr said proudly.

What on earth was her son on about? Rachel walked back into the living room and was greeted by a sight that made her blood, as her bodice rippers described it, run cold. Robbie was front-page news on every tabloid in the land.

All the papers had the same story, which the presenter was discussing in vivid detail. Robbie stood accused of having had a two-year affair with an underage girl named Zoë.

'Turn it off,' Mary shouted. 'Those children shouldn't hear lies about their father.' But Rachel didn't move and the revelations kept coming. Zoë had certainly kissed and told.

'The police,' the presenter announced, 'wish to talk to the footballer in connection with these allegations.'

Eventually Rachel moved, the tears pouring down her face as she switched off the set. For the sake of the children she had to think quickly; the press would be on their doorstep any second.

'Mary, get the children ready and take them to Mrs Jones's.'

For once Mary was speechless and meekly did as she was told. The kids protested but soon realised from their mother's face that this was no time to play up.

Rachel looked out the front door. The estate was empty apart from a few early risers going to work. She beckoned to Mary and the kids. 'Don't talk to anyone. I'll ring you later.'

Mary nodded obediently. She looked like a helpless old woman.

Once they were gone Rachel ran round the house drawing all the curtains and closing all the blinds. Then she sat in the darkened, eerily silent living room to consider what to do next.

But all she could think about was what a fool she had been. *Two years* it had been going on. Surely if he'd managed to keep that hidden from her, he could quite as easily hide other things – including rape? For God's sake, having sex with a fourteen-year-old was tantamount to rape.

Rachel jumped up and ran to their bedroom. Frantically opening every drawer, she dragged out all of Robbie's clothes. She could find nothing unusual but then she didn't really know what she was looking for. Ransacking the desk, she threw pieces of paper all over the floor. However, everything was above board – football contracts, the house deeds, insurance details.

But now she'd started she couldn't stop. She threw open the doors of the wardrobe and riffled through the clothes, searching every pocket. Nothing. On shelves above the clothes were two suitcases. In that instant Rachel decided to get out of the house and far away. She pulled down a case but the weight of it took her by surprise and nearly knocked her over as it fell to the ground.

Puzzled, she opened it, but as soon as she'd done so she wished she hadn't. The case was overflowing with pornographic magazines, but it wasn't the lewd photographs that made her want to be sick; it was the titles – *Seventeen*, *Lesbian Teenager*, *Pervert Teenager*, *Sexy Schoolgirl* – that almost unhinged her.

Nothing had prepared her for this moment. Her whole marriage had been a sham – she was married to a pervert.

Tipping out the disgusting stash she began to throw her clothes into the case, grabbing at anything that came to hand. Breathless, she sat down and told herself to think straight. Where could she go? There was only one answer and she picked up the phone.

'Have you heard?'

'Yes,' Chris said quietly.

'Come and get me.'

By the time Chris arrived so had half of Wapping. Rachel watched through the window as he fought his way past the gang of reporters to the front door. Chris ran into the house, bellowed questions following him. Rachel slammed the door in reply.

Chris took her in his arms and held her. 'It'll be all right. I'm here now. I'll look after you,' he said, repeating the words until the beat of her heart and her breathing had returned to something resembling normal.

'I'm so sorry to drag you into this.'

'Don't you dare be sorry. There's only one person in the wrong here. Have you heard from him?'

'No, and I don't want to. How could he do this to the children? What shall I do about them?'

'Where are they?'

'At a neighbour's with Mary.'

'Leave them there. Let's just get you out of here first. Are you packed and ready?'

Rachel nodded. 'What about them?'

'We're just going to have to fight our way to the car. Whatever you do don't stop.'

Chris took hold of her hand. 'Ready?'

Rachel took a deep breath and opened the door.

Bulbs flashed, blinding her.

'Rachel, where's Robbie?'

'Mrs Black, over here. Are you going to be seeing your husband?'

'How are your children bearing up?'

The strident, jarring voices chased them all the way to the car, where Chris had to physically push the baying crowd back so that he could open the door for Rachel. 'Leave her alone,' he shouted.

'Chris, are you and Rachel having an affair?'

He raised his fist but Rachel grabbed his arm. 'Leave them, they're not worth it.'

Chris lowered his hand but shoved the reporter to the floor. The others, not wanting to be pushed, moved back slightly as he walked round to the driver's side, although the questions kept coming thick and fast.

Gunning the engine, Chris pulled away with a screech of tyres. Rachel saw that most of her neighbours had left their homes to watch the spectacle. She thought she would die of shame.

Neither spoke until they were safely on the A13.

'Where shall we go?'

'I know somewhere in Southend. It's as good a place as any.'

'Fine.'

Rachel's thoughts were all over the place. Half-formed ideas about Zoë and Jenny poured out of her and she hoped somehow that Chris would be able to piece the whole story together. But even if he couldn't, just being sat next to him was a great comfort.

The hotel, an eighteenth-century house in acres of ground, was just on the outskirts of the town. It looked exclusive and peaceful.

'We'd like two rooms,' Chris said to the receptionist.

Rachel rested her hand on his arm. 'One will be fine.'

'Are you sure?'

'Yes.'

The room was beautiful and Rachel wished she was here under better circumstances. Although she had suggested one room, she now felt unsure. Was she just compounding the situation? Was she sleeping with Chris simply to block out Robbie? Or was it retaliation? As Chris walked into the room she knew for sure that it was none of these. She'd never wanted something so much in all her life.

'Rachel, I—'

Rachel laid a finger on his lips. 'Ssh,' she whispered. 'I need a bath. Will you join me?'

She filled the tub with bubble bath, so that the room smelled of roses and bubbles rose alarmingly until they floated through the air and on to the floor. Then she began to undress, her shyness and fear that Chris wouldn't like her body making it almost too painful to continue. But she couldn't stop now.

Sensing her discomfort, Chris busied himself and

allowed her to step into the bath first, the bubbles giving her some protection against her vulnerability. He joined her quickly and, blushing, Rachel averted her eyes as he stepped into the tub.

As they sat opposite each other, Rachel could feel her tensed muscles responding to the warm water and her body responding to the gentle touch of Chris's hands.

Bit by bit, Chris soaped her, his fingers savouring every detail of her body. First her shoulder blades, then gently down her arms and across to her breasts.

She groaned with pleasure as the tips of his fingers delicately traced around her nipples.

'You're beautiful,' he murmured. 'I can't believe this moment is finally happening.' While he spoke his hands moved to the softness of her stomach, down to her thighs. Then he paused.

'Don't stop,' she begged.

As she felt his fingers explore her she thought she was going to faint with pleasure, her whole body reacting to every caress, however slight. But it still wasn't enough; she wanted all of him.

'Let's go to bed,' she murmured, her breath ragged with excitement and need.

They stood up as one and embraced, their bodies pressed hard against each other.

'I want you so much,' Rachel said, pulling Chris out of the bath.

They fell on to the bed, their wet bodies slipping and sliding against each other. Chris moved on top of her and her legs parted in response; slowly he entered her, and she groaned with pleasure as she welcomed him inside her. It was a moment Rachel knew she would never forget. Soon their bodies were moving in unison and Rachel gradually gave herself up to a sensation she had never before experienced. It grew more and more intense, almost unbearable, and then, refusing to be restrained any longer, exploded. At last she'd had an orgasm – and it was fantastic.

Chapter Thirty-Eight

Tanya waved goodbye to Loulou and Andy and waited in front of the hospital for David to drive the car round from the car park. Although the day was overcast and cold, it felt great to finally be out in the fresh air. All the staff had been caring and considerate but she hoped that she'd never have to stay in hospital again. She just wanted to go back to her flat and get on with living as normal a life as possible.

The consultant had talked to her about breast reconstruction but she couldn't even begin to think about it at the moment. She was still in a great deal of pain and the idea of voluntarily putting herself through more was just too much. Gingerly, she placed her hand on her chest, feeling the absence for the millionth time. A one-breasted Page Three girl; what on earth was she going to do with her life?

Don't go down that road, she berated herself. No self-pity. She had made the decision to give up modelling prior to the diagnosis. Nothing had changed, except that her hand had now been forced. Tanya vowed that the mastectomy would only make her work all the harder to succeed with her new life.

David beeped his horn and Tanya shuffled over to the car. Just climbing into the back seat sent waves of pain through her body but she smiled at David, not wanting him to see her agony. The poor guy had been a rock but she knew he'd been worried out of his mind. Although he hadn't said anything, her condition must have brought back a lot of terrible memories for him.

As they drove off, she eased herself into a position where, without too much discomfort, she could stroke his neck.

'Where do you want to go? To your mum's?' David asked.

'No, she said she'd be over later with Keeley. I just want to go home and have a cup of tea in my own flat. I've been fantasising about it. Oh, we'll have to stop and get some milk.'

'Don't worry about it. I've done all your shopping.'

'You're a diamond. Thanks, I know you've been really busy. How did the match go on Monday? Wasn't it the first one for the FA Cup?'

Since she'd been in hospital, David had kept the whole world at bay. The team, the papers, everything. He didn't want her thinking about anything other than herself and getting better.

'We won. Just. But with Robbie on the run . . .' David stopped.

'What do you mean, on the run?'

David didn't reply.

'Come on, tell me – what's he been up to?'

David sighed. 'I didn't want you worrying about all this. Robbie has been having an affair with some underage girl. She went to the papers with her story and Robbie did a bunk. The police are still looking for him.'

'That's awful,' Tanya said, shocked. Poor Rachel. She lived for her family. 'How long had it been going on? And just how young was she?'

'All I know is what I read in the papers. Robbie certainly never let on. Maybe it isn't even true.'

'I hope for his wife's sake it isn't. But do you think a girl would really put herself through all that if it was a lie?'

'She wouldn't be the first.'

Tanya was a little surprised. Another of the many things she loved about David was the respect he had for women. He didn't toe his mates' line that all women were conniving cows who lived only to screw over men. 'And he wouldn't be the first man to play around, would he?' she said sharply.

'Like I said – we haven't heard his side of the story.'

Tanya felt the knotting in David's neck. She could tell that the incident had upset him. 'I know he's a good friend of yours, but with little girls?'

'That little girl has really dropped us in it.'

'David!' Tanya exclaimed. 'You're beginning to sound like all the others.'

'I'm sorry, Tan. It's just that Clive's on the warpath. He says one more story like this and he'll sell the club. He means it.'

'And are there any more stories like that?' Tanya tried to picture herself in Rachel's shoes but couldn't. It was impossible that David could ever do something so disgusting.

'This is why I didn't tell you anything,' David sighed. 'I knew you'd start worrying. The most important thing at the moment is for you to get better. What happens at the club is irrelevant. Let's just drop it.'

Tanya sat back, regretting the conversation. Poor David. With all this happening on top of her operation, he was probably near breaking point.

'All right we'll live together first and see how it goes,' Loulou said, hoping that this would put an end to the marriage discussion.

'Great!' Andy smiled and patted her knee.

Loulou was barely aware of his answer. All she could think about was Tanya. 'I hope she's going to be all right,' she murmured.

'Who?' Andy asked, drumming his fingers on the steering wheel.

'Who do you think?' Loulou replied sharply. 'Although it isn't just Tanya. There's poor Rachel as well.'

'Since when have you cared about that wet blanket?'

'There's a lot you don't know about me.' Loulou picked up the paper that had Robbie's picture on the front page.

Andy glanced over at it. 'Trust Robbie to get caught.'

'Is that all you've got to say?' Loulou asked. 'She was underage. It's terrible.'

'She's some little tart from a council estate who made a wise career move choosing to shag a footballer rather than some unemployed brickie from round the corner. She's made a few bob out of it. I haven't got any sympathy for her.'

Loulou looked at him in amazement. 'Don't you think it's abuse? She's far too young to be able to deal with it.'

'She looks like she's dealing with it fine. You're

naïve if you think these girls don't know exactly what they're doing.'

'I didn't,' Loulou said, hurt that Andy seemed to show no understanding of what she had been through herself with Oran O'Keefe.

There had been nobody to look out for her, to tell her that what she was doing was wrong. Her mother may have been furious that Loulou was seeing her former lover but she treated her like the other woman rather than her daughter who was in need of love and some parental guidance.

Loulou thought of Dexter, worrying that he was going to go the same way. Childhood was something precious which needed protecting and she didn't think Laura Lamb was fit for the job.

Andy ignored her remark, probably because any talk about her first husband made him jealous. 'Look, Robbie's a little bit out of control at the moment, I'll give you that. His judgement's been off on a couple of occasions.'

'Oh? What else has he been up to?'

Andy changed the subject. 'Where do you want to eat tonight?'

Loulou wasn't really interested in what other sordid little escapades Robbie was involved in so she let the matter drop. 'You choose.'

There was a mountain of mail waiting for Tanya. Most of it more cards from well-wishers. At the hospital she'd been inundated with flowers and get-well messages and she was incredibly touched by how concerned complete strangers had been.

As David put her bags away and made her a cup of

tea, Tanya eased herself into an armchair and opened a few of the envelopes. Some of the messages brought her close to tears.

The most moving were from women writing that Tanya's bravery had convinced them to see their own doctors for screening. If there was any point at all to what had happened, it was this. If she helped just one woman avoid the trauma she had gone through herself . . . But Tanya couldn't honestly say that it would all have been worthwhile. That was something people said without thinking. Nothing could make it worthwhile.

Feeling a rare moment of self-pity about to engulf her, Tanya shuffled through her mail, looking for something to take her mind off the operation.

'There you go,' David said, putting a cup down beside her. 'In the car – I'm sorry I was a bit short with you.'

'Forget it. We're both a bit tense at the moment,' Tanya replied. 'What Robbie does is nothing to do with you. I don't know why it bothered me so much.'

She came across a letter from the *News* and thought about putting it to one side. Work was the last thing she wanted to think about. But she did feel obliged to give them an interview at some point. After all, they'd insisted on paying all her hospital bills.

Tanya opened the letter and read it in astonished silence, tears welling up in her eyes.

'Tan, what's wrong?' David tried to snatch the letter out of her hands. 'If those bastards are billing you for the hospital, I'll break that fucking editor's neck.'

Tanya looked up at him, speechless, then re-read

the letter. Finally she spoke, 'I can't believe this is happening. That insurance policy . . .'

'What insurance policy?'

'My breasts. It was for real. The insurance company are going to pay out.' Tanya handed him the letter. 'They are going to give me a million pounds.'

As David read the letter from the *News*' solicitor, Tanya sat there dazed. A million pounds. If she didn't go too mad, she need never work again. Not that she wanted that but the pressure she was feeling about the direction her life was going to take evaporated instantly.

'That's great,' David said quietly.

'Maybe we could invest in a little business. Perhaps a sportswear shop – you know, with you endorsing a line of products. It doesn't have to be anything to do with Notting Hill. You can just stick your two fingers up at them at the end of the season. If we give it a while until I get the all-clear then we can—'

'Tan, stop it!' David snapped. He let the letter drop to the floor. 'It isn't going to happen.'

'Why not? You read it yourself. They say the money'll be in the bank in the next couple of months. I just have to sign the paperwork when I feel up to it.'

'Please, Tan, you're not listening. It isn't going to happen. You and me, I mean.'

Tanya grabbed his hand, the sudden movement sending shockwaves of pain ripping through her sternum. 'I know Clive didn't want you to marry me but that doesn't matter any more. Nothing does. Just you and me.'

'I can't do it,' he said, recoiling from her touch. 'I can't pretend that it's going to be all right when I know it isn't. When my mum was in that hospital and I sat by her, holding her hand as she died, as hard as it was, do you know what I felt? I felt relieved, knowing that I'd never have to go through it again.'

'But, David, I'm not going to die,' Tanya sobbed. 'I'm not going to die.'

'I'm not strong enough. I love you more than anything in the world but I'm just not strong enough to see you through this.'

'We'll do it together,' Tanya cried. 'Between the two of us, we can get through it.'

'I can't take the risk that I'll let you down when the going gets tough. It's better for you to know that now. It'd be wrong of me to lead you on. You deserve better.'

'There isn't anyone better than you.' Tanya was fighting back the hysteria. Not caring about how much it hurt, she dropped to her knees and grasped his legs. 'Please don't say this. Not now. You're not thinking straight. You've been under a lot of pressure but it'll be all right.'

'No it won't. Not tomorrow. Not ever. We'll always have it hanging over us. I'm a coward, Tanya.'

'You're not. You're the strongest, bravest man I know. Please don't leave me.'

Tanya's conviction that she would never beg a man for anything disappeared. At that moment she knew she would say or do anything to keep David.

'If I did die, the money would all be yours,' she said, grief sending her to a place beyond physical pain. 'You can have it all now anyway. You can have anything, just say that you'll stay with me.'

David was crying now and trying to stand up as

she clutched his legs tighter. 'Look what I'm doing to you.' He tried to free himself from her grip. 'I love you, Tanya. But it won't work. I don't expect you ever to forgive me but one day you'll understand that you were better off without me.'

Tanya lay on the floor totally shattered. 'I love you,' she screamed as she heard David closing the street door behind him. 'Come back!'

Chapter Thirty-Nine

Rachel threw the *Sun* to one side in disgust. When was the press going to get bored with the story? It had been nearly two weeks since Robbie had disappeared. God knows where he was – she didn't really care, except that she'd like an end to the whole situation. On top of everything else he was a coward. How she despised him.

She picked up the paper again. It was like a scab she couldn't stop picking. The story continued on pages four and five, and also on the centre pages, the latter concentrating on the effect Robbie's crime and disappearance were having on the club. Apparently, all responsibility for the team's poor performance lay with him.

Never mind the effect he'd had on the team, what about her and how she felt. Destroyed was the only way to describe it. Rachel was as angry with herself as she was with Robbie. She was a bigger fool than even the other wives had suspected. And although her budding relationship with Chris was wonderful, it couldn't take away the humiliation. Self-pitying tears stung her eyes and she swiped at them. Rachel made herself a promise that she would never again be a doormat.

Rachel closed the paper, having more important things to do than rake over old news. She had been to see a solicitor to start divorce proceedings and had been instructed to get their financial papers in order.

The house was quiet but not peaceful: Mary had returned to Wigan and Rachel doubted she would see her again; Demi and Robbie Jnr had gone to stay with her parents, who, while not saying it, had had 'I told you so' written all over their faces. Rachel had omitted to tell them she was staying at Chris's.

He was the one bright light in the whole disaster and she was convinced that, without him, she would have been carted off to the funny farm by now. And, it went without saying, she was having the best sex of her life! It seemed improper at a time like this but she couldn't help herself and was surprised at how little guilt she felt.

She had spoken to Jenny several times and both Loulou and Tanya had phoned to offer their support. Her new friends and her new relationship gave her hope for the future. Rachel was certain it wouldn't always feel as dark and desperate as it did now.

Jenny was still adamant she didn't want to tell the police about the rape, but Rachel knew she had to find out whether Robbie was the culprit. All the evidence certainly pointed towards him.

Putting off the task the solicitor had set, she toyed with the idea of confronting David. But he'd obviously seen fit to keep quiet so far, plus she didn't want to alert any of those involved that she knew. That left the barmaid, Sharon. Jenny had said how Michael's mistress had thrown her out of the club; surely she must have seen or heard something.

It was nearly evening and Rachel decided to chance the club being open that early. After twenty minutes of driving around Billericay in circles, she finally located the place. It looked even more tatty than she remembered and half the neon Three Lions sign had blown a fuse.

Hers was the only car in the car park. She'd wait if she had to, she decided, hammering on a large metal door. Getting no response, she banged even harder until she heard keys jangling on the other side.

'Hang on,' a disgruntled female voice called out.

The door was opened by a woman answering Jenny's description of Sharon. 'We're not open yet,' she said, looking Rachel up and down.

'Are you Sharon?'

'Yeah,' she said, uncertainly. 'Who wants to know?'

'I do,' Rachel said, pushing past her.

'Oi. You can't just barge in here.'

'I won't take up much of your time,' Rachel said, knowing she sounded like someone out of a TV police procedural. Her words echoed around the empty dark, damp club. 'I'm a friend of Jenny Waite's and I want—'

'I don't have to answer to you. Get out of here,' Sharon shouted, trying to shove Rachel towards the door.

Rachel managed to stand her ground, wondering where she was finding her nerve. 'I'm not here to talk about your sordid little affair with Michael, if that's what you're worried about. Jenny was badly hurt the night this club opened and I want to find out who was responsible.'

Sharon laughed in her face. 'Is that all? How should I know? I'm sure the old slapper deserved it.'

All the anger Rachel felt towards Robbie swelled up and threatened to consume her. Grabbing Sharon by the throat she pinned the startled woman against the wall. 'You're a disgrace. How could any woman think that another woman deserved to be raped?'

'Rape! Who said anything about rape?' Sharon whimpered, clearly frightened by the mad woman who was possibly going to strangle her. 'I thought she'd gone with them voluntarily.'

'Who are you talking about?' Rachel asked, loosening her grip slightly.

'The three blokes that were here. Andy, David and the one in the papers – Robbie Black?'

Rachel flinched at the mention of her husband's name. 'What – they all raped her?' she asked incredulously.

'Look. I told you, I don't know anything about rape. I was, you know, in the loo with Michael.'

The thought of this woman having sex with Michael while Jenny was being violated just outside churned Rachel's stomach, but she had to remain focused. 'And then what? I know you saw her, because you threw her out.'

'I thought she was drunk.'

'And whose fault was that?' Rachel spat. 'You were almost force feeding her drink so you could go with Michael.'

Sharon's body slumped. 'All I can tell you is that David gave me fifty quid and told me to keep my mouth shut. I just assumed he didn't want me running to the papers saying what a depraved lot they were. It never occurred to me it was anything like you're saying.'

Rachel let go of the girl, exhausted both mentally

and physically. What did all this mean? Was it David who had raped Jenny? Or was it worse and all three had participated? Her mind was reeling. Stumbling past Sharon she opened the door and gulped huge mouthfuls of air.

Chapter Forty

'Where do you want this, love?' the removal man asked, heaving a tea chest through the front door.

'Anywhere you fucking like and don't call me love,' Loulou snapped, still enraged that Andy hadn't put his furniture into storage.

Although Loulou had felt pressurised into agreeing to having Andy move in, she had thought it wouldn't make much difference as he was always at her place anyway. But as another removal man appeared with a trophy case on a wheelbarrow, the thought that his cups and shields were actually going to be on display in her beautiful architect-designed living room made her want to weep.

'Anna!'

The housekeeper came running into the room, holding on to an armful of Andy's clothes. 'Yes, Miss Lamb?'

'I'm going out for a while. Don't let them break anything.'

Loulou picked up her car keys and fled.

The traffic in town was appalling and Loulou's temper flared even more. Everything was going wrong. When she'd called her agent this morning, there hadn't been a single fresh job offer.

If something didn't happen soon she could see she was going to end up just another footballer's wife. In another couple of years she'd be no better than Martine.

Approaching East London, she got lost and her mood blackened. By the time she finally pulled up outside Tanya's flat she was on the verge of screaming.

However, the sight of Tanya, opening the door in her dressing gown, looking frail and vulnerable, made her forget her problems instantly.

'You look well,' she lied, kissing the other woman and following her into the flat.

'It was really nice of you to come.'

'Don't be silly,' Loulou said, feeling immensely guilty. Once she had believed that Tanya's niceness was just an act, but the more she got to know her, the more she realised that Tanya was solid gold through and through.

'How's Notting Hill?'

Loulou pulled a face. 'Same as always. Boring. Although you did miss an excellent display by Carla Ryman.' Loulou plumped some pillows behind the model. 'Did David tell you about it?'

Tanya shook her head.

'Honestly, that boyfriend of yours is useless. The one good bit of gossip. She's only been knocked up by Stefan Lohmann. The poor dupe is facing a shotgun wedding.'

Tanya didn't comment and Loulou thought she might have made a gaffe about David – she knew how loyal Tanya could be.

Tanya burst into tears.

Loulou was horrified. 'Honey, what's the matter?'

She reeled as Tanya told her the news, unable to believe that anyone could do such a thing to someone in Tanya's position. 'I'm so sorry. I know how much you feel for him but, really, he's the lowest of the low. I know it's easy to say now, but you will get through this without him. You're strong enough. And, Tanya, anything you want me to do, I'm there for you.'

'That's really nice to know,' Tanya said, wiping her eyes. 'I'll be all right.'

'I mean it. Money, anything – just say the word.'

'Money is the one thing I don't need. Haven't you heard?' She filled Loulou in on the insurance policy. 'Sure, it's comforting to have that security, but I'd give it all away to have him back.'

'No man is worth it. Isn't that what you told me?'

'The money doesn't mean anything without him.'

'I'm not talking about the money. I'm talking about self-respect.' How dare he do this to her? Loulou thought.

'But don't you feel that way about Andy? Wouldn't you give up everything for him?'

Loulou thought how she didn't even want to give up space in her closet for him. If two lovebirds like Tanya and David couldn't make it work, she and Andy didn't stand a chance.

'I think I've just made a huge mistake agreeing to live with him.'

'Oh, Loulou, you don't mean that! He's a lovely guy. You two go so well together.'

'Do you seriously think that if Andy were in a similar position to David he wouldn't do exactly the same thing? It's the nature of men. They're all cowardly, self-obsessed liars. Look at what Robbie did to Rachel. A fourteen-year-old girl for God's sake.'

'Yeah, that was disgusting,' Tanya agreed. 'Why do you think he did it?'

Thoughts of her first marriage filled Loulou's mind. 'Oh please – they were probably on the same mental level. Do you know one woman who couldn't run rings around the man she's with? Men know it, we know it. And yet we still all end up falling into the same trap. Why? Why do we still allow ourselves to believe we'd be nothing without them? Where's the proof?'

Loulou stopped, realising her voice was raised. 'I'm sorry. It's very patronising of me to be giving you a lecture in elementary feminism. Especially when you've been far more principled around men than I've ever been.'

Tanya smiled. 'So not everything written about you is a lie then?'

'As much as it irritates me about the lies the papers make up, I've always been grateful for the truths they've decided not to print.'

'Such as?'

Loulou didn't reply.

Tanya was quiet for a moment. 'Would you do me a huge favour?'

'Anything.'

'Would you ask Andy to speak to David? I know everything you've said is true but I can't help it. I still love him.'

Loulou agreed, thinking someone as unique as

Tanya deserved so much better than a spineless wonder like David Ashby.

When Loulou arrived back at her house, the removal men had finished. Andy's things were everywhere. It made her feel as if her life was no longer her own, and to an extent it was true. Why, oh why, had she let him move in?

Visiting Tanya had been a humbling experience. Knowing that anything could easily go wrong at any time like it had for Tanya – and knowing that she would be foolish to expect Andy to be more of a man than David – convinced her that she would have to do something drastic about her situation.

Firstly, she was going to put a bit of the fun back into her life. She thought of the old Loulou, the wild child. What would she do? The immediacy with which the answer came surprised her.

There was a message on the answer machine from Andy saying that he was going out, which was perfect. She could put her plan into action right away.

Feeling light-headed with excitement, she bathed, then dressed in one of her sheerest outfits, applied her reddest lipstick, slipped on her highest heels and left the house.

Her destination, Bar(x2)Ella, was only a few streets away, and though the night air was cold and she was barely dressed, her excitement kept her warm.

Loulou walked up to the entrance of the bar but the female bouncer, recognising her, barred her way.

'You do know this is a lesbian bar?'

Loulou nodded. One could hardly not know. Bar(x2)Ella was the most fashionable women-only

bar in London and the subject of numerous piece:
on the unstoppable rise of the lipstick lesbian in th
style magazines.

The bouncer stood out of the way and Loulou
walked in.

As she ordered a drink at the bar, Loulou fel
slightly disappointed that nobody was taking notice
that the infamous Loulou Lamb was in their midst
What was the point of doing something shocking i
nobody noticed?

She downed her drink, finally admitting that he
reason for being there had nothing to do with shockin;
anyone. She was there to scratch an itch and th
realisation unnerved her.

Leaning against the bar, Loulou looked around. Th
ultraviolet lighting cast an otherworldly glow over th
place and faces were hard to distinguish. She had n
idea where to start. Where men were concerned sh
knew exactly what she was doing, but this was a whol
different ball game.

Boldly, she crossed the small dance-floor and bega
swaying in time to the trance music. Bodies presse
up against hers in the crush and she scanned each fac
hoping for a flicker of something. Nothing.

Loulou was perplexed. Five minutes in a straigh
bar and she would have had several men come on t
her. Here the clientele seemed studiously to ignor
her. Then it clicked. Of course everyone knew wh
she was – and they knew she was heterosexual. The
were just giving her her space.

I'll have to make the first move, she decided, an
then wondered what type of woman she found attract
ive. She'd never given it much thought. Practicall

every woman in the bar was drop-dead gorgeous, that much she knew, but as for actually fancying anyone . . .

As Loulou pondered, she failed to notice the woman approaching her until she was practically face to face with Loulou.

'I thought it was you.'

It took Loulou a few seconds to realise that the woman standing in front of her was Meret Lee. She hadn't seen her since the *Sorted!* interview and the American looked so much better than she had that night. She'd put on a little weight, lost that haunted look and was no longer wearing the widow's weeds. This is *exactly* the type of woman, Loulou decided.

'Meret, you look wonderful!' she said, kissing her.

'You too, babe.' Meret produced her hip flask and handed it to Loulou. 'I see from the papers that you're still with the footballer. How's the straight life treating you?'

Loulou sipped the potent liquid. 'The fact that I'm here should tell you the answer to that one.' She gave the flask back to Meret and then kissed her again, harder this time. 'Oh fuck it. Meret, can we go some place?'

'I'm right behind you, baby.'

Quietly, Loulou let herself into her house, holding her shoes in her hand. Meret had wanted her to stay the night but Loulou knew it would be more trouble than it was worth. She and Andy had been live-in lovers for barely more than two minutes and already she was cheating on him. With a woman.

Loulou was thrilled at the thought that she'd actually made love to another woman. This was the old
Loulou back in action again. She would never end up
as dull as Martine. Never.

Tipsily she climbed the stairs, wondering if she was
a lesbian. As much as she'd enjoyed the experience,
she had told Meret that it was strictly a one off. Was
that true?

Loulou was hoping that Andy would be asleep,
leaving her alone with her thoughts, but when she
entered the bedroom she found him sitting up in bed
watching a replay of Notting Hill's last match on TV.

'Have a good evening?' she asked, pulling her dress
over her head.

'The usual,' he said, his eyes fixed on the TV.

'And what about you? Did you have a nice time
too? How was your day?' Loulou was a little aggra-
vated that he showed absolutely no interest that she
was stumbling in at gone four o'clock in the morning.

'Shh, I'm watching this,' he said, his voice slurred.
He had obviously been drinking, too. Much, much
more than she had.

Loulou went into the bathroom and turned on the
shower, glad at least that his disinterest would give
her the chance to remove every trace of Meret from
her body.

When she'd finished, she returned to the bedroom,
towelling her hair, remembering that she had to do
a favour for someone. 'I saw Tanya today,' she said.
'Did you know David has left her? Because of the
breast cancer. Don't you think that's disgusting?'

Not bothering to hide his annoyance, Andy picked

up the remote and turned off the TV. 'No, I think it's disgusting that a team as good as Notting Hill is falling apart.'

'Is that all that's important to you? Winning a fucking game?' Loulou threw down her towel and glared at him. 'That woman is seriously ill.'

'That woman is a bitch just like the rest. If you all held back with your own fucking problems for five minutes we might be able to concentrate on the football.'

'I can't believe I'm hearing this. So it's Tanya's fault that David is a spineless bastard? And it's Rachel's fault that Robbie is screwing some teenybopper?'

'If that uptight cow was giving it to him properly, he wouldn't have to be looking elsewhere, now would he?'

'You are so disgusting. I suppose . . . I suppose you think Jenny deserves it too every time Michael beats her up?' Loulou shouted.

'Don't talk to me about that cunt. She's the worst of the lot. I tell you if we go out of the Cup, it will be entirely that bitch's fault.'

Loulou was totally sickened. 'Is that really what you think women are? Bitches and cunts? Is that what I am?'

'I didn't say that. But, hey, if the cap fits.'

Loulou lashed out, hitting the bedside lamp, sending it crashing to the floor. Glass lay scattered around her bare feet. 'You rotten bastard,' she yelled and ran from the room.

Downstairs she picked up the phone and dialled a number. 'Meret, when can I see you again?'

Chapter Forty-One

To Jenny, walking up the pathway to her house felt like climbing Everest. Each step was taking her closer and closer to the site of so much pain, distress and violence. It was fear of Michael and what he might do that was making her slow her pace with every step she took.

Over the last few weeks she'd stayed at the alternative therapy retreat. Although she didn't give much credence to the crystals and the feng shui, the hours spent talking to the counsellor had been worth every one of the thousands of pounds she'd paid to stay there. But at the end of the day, as he pointed out, only she could heal herself and that meant confronting the past as well as the present.

So here she was, returning to the home that had been far from happy. The baby, as if sensing her apprehension, began to do somersaults, reminding her that it wasn't just for herself she had to be brave.

After several attempts Jenny managed to get the key in the lock. The door swung open and silence greeted her.

'Michael,' she said in little more than a whisper. Then, a little louder, 'Michael, are you here?'

Nothing. Feeling relief that perhaps after all she

wasn't going to have to confront her husband, she walked through the hallway and into the living room. There was no sign of him and it looked as if he hadn't been around for days – overflowing ashtrays, empty beer bottles and old yellowing newspapers littered the place.

Jenny ran up the stairs just to make sure. In the bedroom the wardrobes and drawers were open; all his clothes were gone. Jenny had realised that there was no future for her with Michael but now relief mixed with regret. This truly was the end. The only thing that puzzled her was that he had gone so quietly. She shuddered. Michael would return sooner or later. Her money meant too much to him.

Back in the living room she sat down and waited. Rachel would be arriving any minute. Poor Rachel, she didn't deserve what Robbie had done to her, and Jenny regretted that she hadn't been able to offer much support in the past month. They had spoken on the phone a few times and it seemed that Rachel was finding solace with Chris. Jenny hoped they would find lasting happiness together.

Jenny got out the photos of her baby taken at the twenty-week scan. They were nearly a month old, but the image of the baby – asleep and sucking its thumb – was the one Jenny held in her head. Even though the result of the amniocentesis was normal, she was still finding it hard to believe that everything was, in all likelihood, going to be all right.

The doorbell rang and Jenny jumped; her mind had drifted far away and she hadn't heard Rachel's car.

Jenny and Rachel took one look at each other and

372 K a r r e n   B r a d y

threw their arms around one another. In seconds tears were coursing down their cheeks.

Jenny was the first to pull away. 'It's so good to see you. Let me look at you,' she said, examining her friend. 'You're looking great. Considering.'

'That's the love of a good man,' Rachel replied in an American twang. 'As the songs say.'

Jenny laughed. 'Good on you. Your hair's different. It's great.'

'You're not looking too bad yourself. Brown hair suits you. You look five years younger.'

'You're my friend for life,' Jenny said, ushering Rachel into the kitchen.

Jenny had to admit that since she'd dyed her hair back to its natural colour and let the severe crop grow out, there had been a vast improvement in how she looked. And without the booze and the drugs, and now even the cigarettes, she positively glowed.

She was even beginning to dress her age which, and the irony was not lost on Jenny, made her appear much younger than her forty years. Much more so than all the times she'd squeezed herself into those tight, gaudy and inappropriate little numbers.

'You're blooming,' Rachel declared.

'Well, now the little tyke isn't making me throw up or want to sleep twenty hours a day, I must say I feel pretty good. Although,' she said, fiddling with the plunger on the cafetiere, 'there is my head to sort out; it needs a complete overhaul! But before we get on to me, which could take all day, what's happening about Robbie? Has he come forward?'

'No, the coward. No one knows where he is. I can't believe he's managed to stay hidden for so long. His damn picture's in every paper,' Rachel paused. 'Clive rang me today.'

Jenny's pulled a face. 'What did *he* want?'

'To tell me that they'd be releasing Robbie from his contract. It's a good job I put money away otherwise I swear the house would be gone by now.'

'He's all heart, Clive. Fucking hypocrite.'

'Why do you say that?' Rachel asked, surprised at the bitterness in her friend's voice.

'Another time. Coffee?'

'Thanks. Anyway I'm going to go back to the house with the kids soon. I really miss them and the sooner things get back to normal the better.'

'Kids are resilient. Look at this one,' she said, patting her stomach. 'It's hung on in there despite its mother.'

'And what about the father? Are you going to do anything?' Rachel felt guilty asking, aware her motives were selfish. The need to know was as much for her benefit as Jenny's.

'The sixty-four-thousand-dollar question. I—'

'Are you annoyed that I went to see Sharon?' Rachel interjected.

Jenny shook her head. 'It was very brave of you. I guess Michael must be staying with her. She's welcome to him.' Jenny noticed that Rachel was still looking concerned. 'Rachel, I know you had to do it and part of me does want to find out who it is. I'm just scared.'

Rachel hugged her friend. 'I'm with you now. Everything will be fine.'

'Do you think it was David? I just wouldn't believe it of him.'

'A couple of weeks ago I wouldn't have believed

it of Robbie. Are you going to talk to Tanya and Loulou?'

'I don't think so. Tanya, especially, has got enough on her plate, don't you think?'

'I suppose so. But I think all four of us have been kept in the dark far too long. Those men were all there. They're guilty of complicity if nothing else.'

Jenny agreed but was still reluctant to tell Tanya and Loulou.

But Rachel had changed. She was no longer prepared to sit back and let life happen. 'I'm going to ring them.'

When Loulou and Tanya finally arrived there were several minutes of greeting and hugs and compliments to both Rachel and Jenny on how well they looked and how pregnancy suited Jenny.

Sadly, Jenny could not say that Tanya was looking well. She was shocked at how thin Tanya was and with no make-up she looked like a vulnerable child. Jenny wanted to hug her rather that tell her about David.

Loulou also seemed different. Jenny couldn't quite put her finger on what it was, but Loulou's face appeared to have lost the haughtiness that had marred her looks. Now softer, her face was truly beautiful. Furthermore, Loulou's concern for Tanya's well-being, reflected in her startlingly blue eyes, was something Jenny could never have predicted.

The women chatted on for another thirty minutes catching up on the more palatable parts of each other's lives. But after a few pointed looks from Rachel Jenny knew that she couldn't put off telling Tanya and Loulou about the rape much longer.

'Um, it's not ... I don't know how ... Michael's not the father of my baby.'

'Who is?' Loulou asked immediately.

'I'm not sure. What I mean is ... I ... they.' Jenny turned to Rachel with a panicked expression. 'Rachel.'

Rachel swallowed. 'Jenny was raped.'

'Oh my God!' Tanya exclaimed. 'By who?'

Nervously, Rachel said, 'We're not sure but it was either Robbie, David or Andy.'

'What are you talking about?' Loulou asked, rising from her seat.

Rachel recounted the events of the night at the Three Lions. 'I'm really sorry,' she said eventually, addressing Tanya, 'but I really thought you both should know. There's a conspiracy of silence, which in my book makes them all as guilty as each other.'

'But rape? Are you sure?' Loulou asked.

'Over the last few weeks I've thought of almost nothing else; I've been having flashbacks – more and more frequently – and I've gradually pieced events together. Believe me,' she pleaded, 'it *was* rape. I just can't fit a face to the man leaning over me.'

'Besides,' Tanya added quietly, 'why would David pay if it wasn't?'

Loulou didn't reply.

Tanya continued. 'He's been behaving very oddly recently and, looking back, it started around that time.'

'You're bound to say that now,' Loulou said. 'And I really think that with all you've got to deal with this is the last thing you should be thinking about.' She looked pointedly at Rachel and Jenny.

'I know, I'm sorry,' Jenny said.

'It's my fault. I persuaded Jenny that I should call you,' Rachel jumped in.

'Loulou, it's all right. I'd rather know. And it's not as if we're together any more.'

'What?' Jenny was incredulous. 'When did that happen?' Both Jenny and Rachel were shocked that Tanya was on her own at a time like this.

Tanya told them how David had abandoned her.

Rachel hugged Tanya. 'God, what a sorry lot we've been caught up with. I shouldn't have insisted that Jenny tell you everything.'

'I would rather know. Honestly,' Tanya sighed, squeezing Rachel's hand. 'How can we find out who did it?'

'Why don't we just ask them? Although I don't think Robbie will be around for questioning.'

'If it's any consolation, Loulou,' Rachel snapped, 'I think Robbie is the most likely candidate.'

Loulou's shoulders visibly slumped. 'I'm sorry, Rachel, I'm out of order. It's just a lot to take in. I mean, for God's sake, I might be living with a rapist, or a man who thinks it's OK, at the very least, to cover up a rape. And, like Tanya, I have to admit Andy hasn't exactly been acting normally. I mean, even the marriage proposal was a bit out of left field. I'll kill the bastard if it's him.'

There was a note of hysteria in all the women's voices as they went over and over who it could have been. Tanya and Loulou looked like their worlds were falling apart, as Jenny's and Rachel's had already done.

The front door slammed shut. All four women

stopped speaking. Rachel glanced at Jenny. Her friend looked terrified.

'What the fuck are you doing back here?' Michael shouted as soon he entered the room. 'And what's with the coven?'

'Michael, I—'

'And *you*,' he spat, standing in front of Rachel. 'If you ever go near Sharon again you'll answer to me. Spreading all that crap about rape. She's a whore and she knows it,' he sneered, pointing at his wife.

'Please, Michael, it's true,' Jenny sobbed.

'You were just pissed as always.'

'I think the words pot and kettle come to mind,' Loulou hissed.

'Keep it shut, you uppity cunt!' He turned his attention back to Jenny. 'Nobody raped you. Why would they have to? You couldn't give it away.'

Rachel walked across the room and slapped Michael across the face as hard as she could. With so much drink in him, he stumbled backwards but recovered sufficiently to lunge at her.

As with Sharon, the anger Rachel harboured towards her husband was unleashed on Michael. The mouse-like Rachel of yore disappeared as her nails clawed at his face.

Michael tried to grab Rachel's hair but before his hand found purchase, Loulou rushed at him, fists flying. This second attack unbalanced him completely and he fell to the floor, crumbling beneath a welter of kicks and punches.

'Now you know what it feels like,' Jenny screamed, standing over him. She ground her heel into his groin. 'You bastard.'

Michael roared like a wounded animal. Scrabbling to his feet, gasping for breath, he fought back, bleeding heavily from a gash on his forehead. Savagely, he punched Loulou in the stomach. As she crumpled, there was a loud crash.

Michael fell to the floor beside Loulou. Tanya stood where he'd been, clearly surprised to see a broken vase in her hand. 'Oh my God, have I killed him?'

'Hopefully,' Loulou said, from the floor. Blood was trickling from her nose and she was finding it hard to catch her breath. Rachel helped her to her feet.

Tanya bent over the player's inert body. 'He's still breathing. Jenny, call the police.'

'But—'

Michael's eyes flicked open. 'Bitches,' he groaned. He inched up onto his elbows and gingerly touched the blood that was already beginning to mat his hair.

'Quickly, before he starts again,' Rachel urged.

'Get out, Michael, just get out!' Jenny screamed. 'This is my house and I'll have you arrested if you ever come anywhere near me again.'

The four women stood shoulder to shoulder waiting for his response.

Michael stood up and walked towards them unsteadily.

'I'm warning you,' Jenny said. 'Leave now while you can still walk.'

Michael spat in her face. 'You're not worth it.'

Loulou's hand flew up ready to strike him but Jenny caught her wrist. 'Leave it, he's going.'

Her husband turned his back on them and staggered towards the door.

Long after he had left, everyone remained shaken and speechless.

It was Tanya who eventually broke the silence. 'Jenny, I really think you should go to the police about the rape. They'll find out who did it.'

'And so would the whole world. I don't want anyone else to know that was how my baby was conceived.'

Chapter Forty-Two

Tanya woke with a start, her heart thudding against her bruised ribcage. Someone was watching her. Waiting.

'Hi. Are you awake?'

Relief flooded through her. It was only Loulou. She was standing in the doorway holding two mugs of tea. 'Just about. I didn't sleep much.'

'Me neither,' Loulou said, sitting at the end of the bed. 'I don't think anyone did.'

'Are Rachel and Jenny awake?'

'They're downstairs in the kitchen. They've not been up long.'

'What time is it?'

'Eight.'

Tanya groaned. 'Two hours' sleep. I don't think I've ever talked so much in my life. It's so strange that something so awful has brought us all together. I wish it was under different circumstances.'

'I know. It's even weirder for me. I never thought there would come a day when I would care about women in the way I do about you guys.'

'I wanted to wake up today and it all be a dream,' Tanya said, getting out of bed and staring through the blinds. 'And it didn't even happen to me. God knows

how Jenny must feel. If it had been me, I don't think
I would have been able to go on.'

'Of course you would,' Loulou said firmly. 'You're
strong. And if we stick together now, we'll all get
through this.'

'Loulou, I want to ask you a question. Promise me
that you'll answer it truthfully.'

'I promise,' Loulou said, staring into her tea.

'Do you think it could have been David?'

'Of course not,' Loulou said, a little too quickly.
'What I mean is that I can't believe any of them did
it.'

'So you think Jenny's lying?'

'No. She's telling the truth. I'm one hundred per
cent sure about that.'

Tanya rested her elbows on the windowsill, her
head in her hands. 'Then one of us has been sleeping
with a rapist.'

Loulou jumped up from the bed and put her arm
around her friend. 'We don't know anything.'

'I've got to speak to him. Jenny can't tell us this and
then expect us to go on like nothing has happened. I've
got to know the truth.'

'Jenny understands. It's OK. I told her we would
see Andy and David today.'

'What about Rachel?'

'Well there's not a lot she can do. She said she'll
stay here for the moment with Jenny. It's all been
settled.'

'I just wish it was all a bad dream,' Tanya repeated.
'The really awful thing is that it doesn't matter who
actually committed the rape because the other two
were involved in some way.'

'I know.'

'I'm frightened.'

'So am I,' Loulou confessed. 'But we'll be together. They'll both be in the bar this afternoon. We can look out for each other.'

When Tanya and Loulou arrived at Notting Hill, Magic was just getting into his car.

'Tony!' Loulou called, winding down her window. 'Have you seen Andy and David?'

'David's just coming,' Tony shouted, looking surprised that Loulou Lamb had even addressed him. 'But Andy left ages ago. I think he said he was going home.'

'Shit!' Loulou said to Tanya. 'What are we going to do?'

'You go off and find him, I'll be all right here.'

'Are you sure? I could wait for you.'

'I'll be fine,' Tanya said uncertainly. 'Just call me as soon as it's possible to let me know what he has to say.'

Tanya's instinct was to add a warning to be careful but she held her tongue, not wanting Loulou to think she thought Andy was guilty. Instead, she simply kissed Loulou goodbye, sensing that her friend had wanted to say the same thing to her.

Magic followed Loulou out of the gates and Tanya was left alone. She hadn't seen David since the day he'd walked out of her flat, three weeks previously, and she didn't know how she would feel seeing him now. The man she'd loved unconditionally could possibly be a monster, and conflicting emotions pulled her every which way.

Minutes went by, her nerves growing more jagged by the second, but when David finally appeared, her first impulse was to run over and throw her arms around him. Despite everything.

'David!' she called.

He looked startled. 'What are you doing here?'

'I'm meeting Loulou,' she lied. 'She's picking me up in a minute.'

He was now only a few feet away and Tanya could see that his startled look had given way to one of deep shame. Immediately she thought that it signified his guilt, then she realised she was being too hasty. The man had a lot to feel ashamed about regardless of Jenny.

'How's it going?' he asked, hovering awkwardly in front of her.

He tried to kiss her but Tanya took a step back. 'Not too bad. My doctor's pleased with the progress I'm making.'

'That's brilliant,' he said, looking more and more uncomfortable by the second.

Tanya wasn't sure what to say next. Until the previous night she had thought she had known and loved every part of this man, but today he was a stranger. Never in a million years would she have believed he was capable of rape but the very fact that he had been capable of keeping the matter a secret proved that she didn't know the first thing about him.

'How's your mum?' he asked.

'She's fine.'

'And Keeley?'

'She's fi . . .' Tanya stopped and took a deep breath.

'David, do you remember the night we went to the opening of the Three Lions?'

David's gaze drifted to his feet. 'What about it?'

'Did something happen that night?'

David seemed to be groping for an answer. 'Nothing that doesn't happen every time the boys go out en masse. The fights, the drinking – you know what it's like.'

'I don't think I do,' Tanya said coldly. He was obviously avoiding the issue. 'Do the boys also attack women every time they go out?'

'What do you mean?'

'What happened to Jenny?'

'She got pissed. Something else that happens every time we go out.'

Tanya kept her voice calm but inside she was near hysterical. She had expected that a confrontation would lead to an immediate confession but it appeared he was still prepared to keep up the lie. He really was a complete stranger. But a rapist too?

'Then what happened?' She wanted to add, *Look at me, you coward*.

'Why are we having this conversation? It was something and nothing and it's all in the past.'

Every utterance served to seal his guilt that little bit more. How could rape ever be something and nothing? What type of man could say such a thing? 'Somebody hurt Jenny very badly that night.'

'Jenny hurt herself.'

'How?' Tanya couldn't believe her ears.

'She was falling all over the place. You saw the way she was drinking. A few words were exchanged, some people lost their temper but it all blew over very quickly.'

A few words were exchanged? Did David really think it was as trivial a matter as that? Maybe he really didn't know what had happened. Tanya was prepared to clutch at a straw then she remembered the pay-off. Of course he knew everything. 'That barmaid Sharon said you—'

'Tan, I can't really talk now, I've got a meeting with Clive.'

'I'll wait in the bar then. We need to sort this thing out.'

'I'm sorry but I just can't deal with anything at the moment. Seeing you – it's too difficult. We'll meet up soon. I promise.'

Tanya watched, stunned, as once again he walked away from her.

As Loulou walked up the stairs she could hear Andy talking on the phone.

'Are you sure she knows . . . well calm down . . . it'll be all right, I'll get it sorted . . . David, if you lose your head over this . . . I'll talk to her . . . it's our word against hers . . .'

Loulou wanted to run but for Jenny's sake she needed to hear what he had to say. 'I'm home,' Loulou shouted, trying to sound as bright and breezy as possible.

Andy slammed down the phone. 'I'm in here.'

She went into their bedroom and found him sitting on their bed, a half-empty bottle of whisky at his side.

'Just getting in?' he said sarcastically. 'It must have been a very, very good night.'

'Not that it's any of your business, but I stayed with a friend.'

'And which "friend" was that?'

Loulou poured herself a large glass of whisky. 'I was with Tanya.'

'Well, she obviously can't bear to be parted from you. She phoned earlier.'

'What did she say?' Loulou asked anxiously.

'She says if you find a tit in your car, it's hers. Apparently she's lost one.'

What an unbelievably heartless, sick bastard, Loulou thought. 'What did she really say?'

'She said she'd call you laa'er when she got 'ome,' he said, aping Tanya's accent.

Resisting the urge to smash him over the head with the bottle, Loulou asked, 'Who were you just on the phone to?'

'None of your bloody business.'

'A bit touchy, aren't we?' Loulou goaded.

'Go to hell.'

'I'm sure you'll get there first,' Loulou muttered, deciding she might just as well come straight out with it. 'What happened to Jenny at the Three Lions?'

Andy's reply shocked and revolted her, and yet filled her with relief at the same time. 'You mean with Robbie?'

'So it's all true?' she said, unable to keep the horror out of her voice.

'I don't know why you're looking so surprised. She's not trying to pretend it didn't happen is she?'

'Far from it,' Loulou said, refilling her glass. As far as she was concerned he had told her all she needed to know. She would phone Tanya and they'd work out a way of breaking the news to Rachel. 'I think I'll have a shower.'

'Don't you want to know the whole story?' Andy asked, following her to the bathroom.

Loulou was faintly surprised at how forthcoming he was but guessed drink, as usual, was helping to loosen his belligerent tongue. She flopped onto a sofa and kicked off her shoes. 'Spare me the full Technicolor details.'

'She's such an old slapper.' Andy laughed. 'She was trying it on with everyone. You know she actually asked me? I told her I wouldn't touch it with a barge pole. And a fucking barge pole would be about the only thing that could fill it.'

Loulou cringed. Just how much did this man hate women? And why hadn't she seen it before? 'How can you talk about her like that? When you know Robbie raped her?'

Andy stared at her, wide-eyed. 'Hold on a minute. Who said anything about rape? I just told you she'd begged every man in the place to give her a portion. Robbie was the only one who was that desperate. He said that Rachel's twat could only make ice cubes.'

Nauseated by his misogyny, Loulou forgot Jenny's request to hold back on all the details. 'If Jenny agreed to have sex with Robbie, then why did David have to pay the barmaid to keep quiet?'

Andy looked at her like she was a complete idiot. 'David was waiting outside for a cab. When I told him what Robbie was up to he was nervous about the effect it could have on morale at the club.'

'He paid her off because of football?' Loulou was scandalised.

'Too right. If Michael had found out from his girlfriend that his wife was fucking his best mate, he would have gone apeshit. I've told you that Jenny Waite was out to destroy the team. It's the only way she can think of winning the grudge match she's got with that psycho husband of hers. But it's not going to happen.'

As much as she hated to admit it, much of what Andy said made sense, and Loulou's conviction about the veracity of Jenny's story faltered. At the time the woman was an out-of-control drunk. Maybe she did have sex with Robbie out of a skewed sense of revenge. Loulou had to admit that she herself would be capable of doing something similar. But would she cry rape afterwards?

Loulou decided she wouldn't but perhaps Jenny truthfully didn't know that she had consented. That wouldn't be beyond the realms of possibility either. There had been several times when Loulou had woken in the morning next to a man she would have sworn she couldn't have willingly agreed to sleep with.

At that moment though, whether Jenny was or wasn't raped seemed like a side issue. That it was a very close call either way and the fact that the three men had hushed it up disgusted her. As did Andy's all-consuming hatred of women.

Reminding herself that Andy's version of the events of that night was refracted through his misogyny, Loulou decided to keep an open mind and her mouth shut about Jenny's pregnancy. What was certain, however, was that she could no longer stay with this man.

'I want you out of this house as soon as possible,' she announced.

Andy laughed. 'Because of this?'

'It would be enough. Maybe Jenny wasn't raped, but you couldn't know for certain. And the fact is that you chose to cover up what happened for the sake of your career.'

'As far as I've heard, I'm not the only one who's prepared to go to desperate measures to keep their job. Who was it who fucked Ethan Mead?'

Loulou was stunned. How did he know? 'All right, I fucked him. I didn't fuck him over.'

'Only because you didn't have the clout. Anyway, that's all in the past, and I'm magnanimous enough to draw a veil over it.'

'That's big of you. But you're still out.'

Andy emptied the last of the whisky into his glass. 'No I'm not,' he said calmly.

Loulou nearly laughed at his arrogance. 'And why?'

'Because it wouldn't do your failing career the slightest bit of good if the papers were to find out you were a lesbian. Still muff-diving with Meret?'

This time Loulou was speechless. How did he know so much about her?

Andy seemed to read her mind. 'It's amazing how cost-effective a private detective can be. I wouldn't trust you as far as I could throw you. Do you really think I was going to walk into this relationship totally blind? I saw what you did to Oran O'Keefe. I just wanted a little insurance policy so you couldn't do the same to me. I never realised the dividends would pay out so early on.'

Loulou was winded but she decided to call his bluff.

'Do what you like. Tell the papers I'm a lesbian. Worse things have been said about me. And maybe I am one. Who knows? Who cares? Besides, lesbian or not, they'll be very interested to hear from me about the way you covered up what happened to Jenny.'

'You can't win this one,' Andy hissed, his face tensing with anger. He walked over to her, unsteady on his feet. 'What if the papers found out you were a lesbian who got pregnant at fourteen by her mother's boyfriend? And then secretly gave the baby to her mother to raise? Then married the father but left the baby to rot. How will you feel when Dexter finds out that his lesbo sister is really his minge-munching mummy?'

Loulou flew at Andy, her fingers aiming at his eyes. 'You bastard. You fucking bastard.'

Andy grabbed her wrists and threw her back on to the sofa. 'I told you I knew everything.'

'You have no idea what I went through,' she said, bursting into tears. 'I was fourteen. Oran said he'd leave me if I kept Dexter. My mother was pressurising me so much to give him up. I could barely look after myself let alone a baby . . .'

'All that shit I've listened to about Laura. That endless bitching about how she's an unfit mother. Perhaps she is – after all she brought you up – but it seems bad mothers run in the family.'

Loulou was sobbing. 'When she agreed to adopt Dexter I thought she was the best mother in the world. It took me a long time to realise that she didn't do it out of love. She did it for revenge. She took my baby from me because I took Oran from her.'

'So tragic,' Andy mocked. 'Spare me your sob

stories. There's been plenty of time since then for you to have put things right. You kept your mouth shut because of your career. And you're going to keep your mouth shut now for mine.'

Loulou knew that what he was saying was true and she wept. If Dexter ever found out she had abandoned him it would destroy him. How could she ever tell him that leaving him at the mercy of Laura was for the best? She knew he was unhappy and yet still she kept quiet. It was unforgivable.

'Have we got a deal?' Andy pressed.

Loulou just sobbed.

'Have we got a deal?'

He was as good as holding a gun to her head. Loulou knew she had no choice but to go along with him. She nodded.

'Smart decision. It suits me at the moment to play happy couples. Understood? Now be a good girl and dry those tears because you've got a phone call to make. I want you to tell Jenny that you've had time to reconsider and you're sorry but you think she made the whole thing up.'

Chapter Forty-Three

Jenny paced the floor longing for her friends to ring. She was almost beside herself waiting to hear their news: wanting and not wanting the rapist's name. One minute she was convinced it was Robbie, the next David. And then her memory would change completely and she believed it to be Andy. The anguish of not knowing was now at fever pitch.

The phone rang and Jenny snatched at the receiver. 'Hello,' she said tentatively.

'Jenny. It's Loulou.'

'Do you know who it is?'

There was silence on the other end.

'Loulou? Are you there?'

'Yes.'

'Are you all right?'

'Yes.'

Jenny could tell that Loulou had been crying. Her heart began to pound. Did this mean it was Andy? 'Loulou, speak to me.'

'I . . . I don't . . . I've had time to think and I'm sorry I don't believe you were raped.'

'What!' Jenny shouted. 'Loulou, what's happened? How can you say this?'

'You were drunk. You just don't remember what happened. I've got to go now.'

'You can't do this to me,' Jenny cried.

'I'm sorry,' Loulou whispered.

The line went dead.

Jenny wandered back to the living room. Loulou's words hurt almost as much as the rape. It was as if all they had been through had meant nothing. Every painful victory she'd gained in therapy was undone in one fell swoop and Jenny was back in her place as a drunken, worthless slut who brought everything on herself.

'Please,' she cried out loud, 'don't let Rachel and Tanya abandon me.'

Carla stretched out her legs, luxuriating in the feel of clean cotton sheets. There was a lot to be said for hotel living but sooner rather than later she and Stefan were going to have to find a home. She wondered whether to ring room service for some breakfast or have a bath. She lit a cigarette instead. Stefan was out so he couldn't moan about her disgusting habit.

He was out jogging in preparation for the match that afternoon. Against all odds Notting Hill had got through to the semi-final of the UEFA Cup. The result for Carla was that Stefan had refused sex the night before, arguing that he needed all his strength. No amount of pestering would get the German to change his mind. Finally, Carla had been forced to give up. He didn't realise that she needed to have as much sex as possible. Losing Stefan wasn't an option. Not only was he a cash cow, he was also a good catch. Surely, this time, she had hit gold.

She heard his footsteps outside the door and quickly stubbed out her cigarette. Her hair, matted in hair lacquer, would allow nothing more than a mere brush of the hand over the rigid, sticky ends.

'Oh, Stefan,' she exclaimed, seeing the dozen red roses in his hand. In the other, he was holding a small blue box that surely held a ring. She sat up in the bed. 'And what's that?'

'Also for you,' he said, throwing the roses on the bed and sitting next to her.

He opened the box and there inside was a perfect solitaire. Carla tried to grab it from him but he pulled back.

'And here's another present for you,' he said, rummaging around in his tracksuit pocket. He handed her another box. It contained a pregnancy test kit.

'What's that?' Carla asked shrilly.

'You know what it is. Here's what I think. You go into the bathroom and try this test. If it says yes, you can have the ring. But if it says no baby, well . . .'

Carla tried to think fast but there wasn't one excuse she could come up with that would get her out of it. 'Don't you trust me?' she said, desperately trying to stall for time.

Stefan merely shrugged.

'I can't believe you're doing this,' she said, knocking the kit out of his hand.

Stefan calmly picked up the box and placed his hand on Carla's arm. 'Now. Please.'

Carla knew she had no choice but to comply. Snatching the box, she stomped into the bathroom and locked the door. What on earth was she going to do? Although she had made sure they had been having sex like rabbits she was certain that, despite all her attempts, she hadn't managed to get herself pregnant, and even if she had it wouldn't show up yet. She guessed she could mess it up but he'd only go out and get another one. She wanted to weep.

Slowly she unwrapped the kit and reluctantly peed on the stick, although why she went even this far with the charade she wasn't quite sure. Some desperate hope perhaps.

Stefan banged on the door. 'Hurry up. I must leave soon.'

Carla opened the door and Stefan took the test.

'No baby, eh?'

'I don't understand it,' she began. 'I'm nearly two months late.'

'Stop your silly acting. Clive told me this was how it would be. You disgust me,' he said, turning away from her.

'Clive? What's he got to do with it?'

'He was protecting me. You are a whore and a liar.'

'How dare you speak to me like that.'

'Oh, Carla,' he said, laughing mirthlessly. 'You get what you deserve. I'm going now and I don't want to see you again.'

'But I care about you – a lot.'

'No you don't, Carla. There's only one person you care about.'

'That's not true. You don't understand,' she pleaded.

'Unfortunately, I think I do. Now please, go.'

'But I've nowhere to go,' she cried.

'You are not my problem any more. Thank God.' Stefan left.

'You can tell that bastard Dorning that he'll rue

the day he fucked up my life,' she shouted at the closed door.

'I just can't believe Loulou would be so heartless,' Rachel said. Both she and Jenny were in Tanya's flat. All three women were despondent.

'I think something's wrong,' Tanya said. 'I've tried to ring her for the last couple of days and all I get is the answerphone.'

'Maybe we were all wrong about her and she hasn't changed a bit,' Rachel continued.

'No. I can't believe she would abandon me like this unless something was really wrong.'

Jenny looked down at the floor. She wanted to believe that something was wrong and that Loulou hadn't meant one word of her cruel pronouncement. 'Perhaps she realised which side her bread is buttered. I'm sure with her career not going that well she needs Andy at the moment.'

Tanya was near to tears. 'I can't believe I'm that bad a judge of character. She was so lovely to me.'

A heavy silence followed until Tanya finally spoke again. 'Why don't we go round and see her? Perhaps face to face we can sort this all out.'

Before either Jenny or Rachel could reply Tanya's phone started to ring.

'Hello ... hello ... who's there?' Tanya asked but at the other end the phone was placed back on the hook.

Andy twisted Loulou's arm until it was behind her back. 'Who were you ringing?'

'Let go of me. You're hurting me.'

'I asked you a question.'

'No one.'

Andy pushed her arm up until it felt like it was breaking.

'Tanya,' she screamed. 'Are you satisfied? You fucking animal!'

He let go of her. 'I don't want you talking to any of those bitches, or I might just have to do some talking of my own – to the press.'

'I don't understand why you're being like this. You can't keep me prisoner forever.'

Andy gave her a smile that frightened her much more than the threat of violence.

'If you're so worried about that old slag I'll do something about it. Then we're even.'

'What do you—'

'Shut up,' he ordered. He picked up the phone and dialled three digits. 'Police, please ... Thank you,' He grinned at Loulou at he was put through 'Is that the police? Yes. I know the whereabouts of Robbie Black ...'

Chapter Forty-Four

Loulou studied her reflection. The nightmare of the last ten days showed clearly in the dark shadows under her eyes. Surely it couldn't get any worse?

She heard the front door close as Andy left for the match. It was the first time he'd let her out of his sight since he'd reported Robbie. Loulou had no words to describe what she thought of him.

Why had he told the police anyway? Was it the last vestiges of his conscience on display? But if Robbie had raped Jenny, wasn't there a chance that he would crack under police pressure and tell? And wouldn't Andy and David then be charged as accomplices? The other alternative was . . . no, the other alternative was too horrible to think about.

As she walked past a full-length mirror she caught sight of a thin, haggard woman. It was a few seconds before she realised it was herself. Oh God, it was all happening again. She tried to remember when she'd last eaten. Days ago. She felt like an out-of-control teenager again, caught up in someone else's madness.

She had to think straight. Andy's behaviour was making her behave as irrationally as him. The most pressing thing on her mind now was how to protect her son. Sooner or later she would put a foot wrong,

and with Andy in his current state of mind, she had
no doubt he would carry out his threat. There was
really only one answer: she would have to tell Dexter
the truth.

Without further thought she rang Ibiza. 'Daddy,
it's Loulou. I want to to tell Dexter the whole story.'

The international line crackled with static.

'Daddy? Are you still there?'

'Yes. Do you think that's wise? I'm not sure he's
up to it.'

'I've been thinking about it for ages. And there are
things that have happened here that make it pressing.'

'Darling, what do you mean?'

'Never mind. I'll tell you when I get there. Hopefully I'll be able to get a flight straight away.'

Sensing a presence, Loulou stopped talking. She
turned round and saw Andy's powerful body framed
in the doorway.

'You're going nowhere.'

'Daddy. I'll have to call you back.' She glared at the
player. 'You can't stop me.'

Andy laughed harshly. 'It's a good job I forgot
my mobile, I might have missed this.' He ripped
the phone from the wall and his voice dropped to
a threatening hiss. 'You're staying here and that's
final. Unless, of course, you don't mind me going
public.'

'Do what you like. I don't care any more,' Loulou
said, sounding much braver than she felt.

'That may well be true. So having had time to
think about this, I thought the papers might also
be interested in a little bit of juicy gossip about
Robbie and Jenny. Yeah, I think they'd really like

to know what kind of woman she is. The type that'll get falling-down drunk and fuck her friend's husband and—'

'Just shut up,' Loulou screamed. 'I can't take any more. You're driving me crazy.'

'Well, you always were a bit unstable,' he sneered.

Loulou ran from the room and locked herself in the bathroom. Realising she was hyperventilating she tried to calm her breathing and get her thoughts in order. But it was all just a jumbled mess. She didn't know what to believe any more. How could she protect her son? And how could she not add to the hurt she'd already caused Jenny?

The answer chilled her. For now she would have to stay with Andy.

Tanya, Rachel and Jenny sipped their tea and stared into space.

'We're going round and round in circles,' Rachel said, eventually. 'And doing nothing.'

'This is driving me into the ground,' Jenny murmured. 'I think we should give up.'

'No,' Rachel said vehemently.

'I still think we should have tried to see Loulou,' Tanya said wearily. She felt as exhausted as she appeared.

'You're too trusting,' Rachel retorted. 'It's just Loulou being Loulou. Watching her own back as always.'

'I don't want to talk about this any more.' Jenny said. 'Turn on the TV. Jerry Springer's on in a minute. When I watch that show, somehow my own life doesn't seem that bad.'

The other two laughed as Jenny's gallows humour finally broke the mood.

Rachel switched on the TV and was startled to see her husband's sheepish face staring out from the screen. The voice of a reporter informed them that Robbie was now being held at West End Central police station for questioning.

'He owes me,' Rachel said. 'Come on, get your coats. We're going to do some interrogating of our own.'

Robbie was blinded by lights. All around him cameras flashed as he attempted to leave the police station. Scared, he looked younger than ever. After several hours of humiliating questions the police had finally let him go. Zoë had refused to press charges. The parting shot of the frustrated officer in charge was that they would be watching him from now on.

'Robbie,' Zoë said, throwing herself at him on the station steps. 'I'm so sorry. My parents made me do it.'

Grateful that Zoë had withdrawn her statement, it didn't occur to Robbie to ask her if it was her parents who had made her sell her story to the press. He was simply pleased to see a friendly and non-judgemental face. The police had sneered at him, making him feel like a pervert, the type that dressed in dirty macs and preyed on little girls.

When he looked up from her embrace they were completely surrounded by reporters and photographers. He just wanted to get home, well not home but a place where he could lie low, away from the prying eyes of the world. When he was caught he'd been hiding in the house of a friend from Wigan but he couldn't go back there now.

And there was no way he could go back to Rachel and the kids. The thought of Demi and Robbie Jnr brought tears to his eyes, self-pitying tears that had been looming ever since the police had bashed down his friend's door.

From what the police had said, they'd definitely been tipped off. Robbie still didn't know who'd ratted on him. Only a few of the team knew of his where-abouts. And why would anyone at Notting Hill do that to him? He was everybody's friend. Or he had been. Clive Dorning had already made it clear through a press release that he was no longer welcome at Notting Hill.

Zoë clung to Robbie's arm. 'I love you, Robbie. I want us to stay together,' she shouted over the clamour of the journalists.

'Let's just get out of here first,' Robbie mumbled, frantically looking for a way to escape his inquisitors. Maybe they should go back into the police station? Robbie wasn't sure which was worse.

Just then a car beeped its horn and nudged its way through the crowd until it was parked in front of them.

It was Rachel. 'Get in,' she ordered.

Without thinking any further, Robbie grabbed Zoë's hand and did as he was told. A look of incompre-hension crossed his face as he realised that Jenny and Tanya were also passengers.

Rachel sped off. A few reporters managed to get to their cars and gave chase. But Rachel's adrenaline was flowing, and she drove as if at Brand's Hatch, the sound and smell of squealing, burning tyres filling the car. Finally she lost their pursuers, and she turned into a quiet road and killed the engine.

Zoë began almost immediately. 'He isn't coming back to you and that's it. So it's no good kidnapping us. He's mine.'

'For God's sake, shut up, little girl,' Rachel snapped. 'You're welcome to him. I wouldn't want him if he was the last man on earth. There's one reason and one reason only that I helped you back there.'

Robbie looked expectantly at his wife.

'Did you rape Jenny?'

Chapter Forty-Five

The final whistle blew.

'Two-nil, two-nil,' the supporters roared.

Only they weren't roaring in English.

Notting Hill were out of the UEFA Cup.

As the team walked dejectedly off the pitch, barely able to acknowledge each other let alone their crashing defeat, David knew that he had to shoulder the greatest responsibility for their failure.

Michael had been substituted in the first few minutes and David should have seen that he was too drugged-up to play. Likewise Andy was too rattled and Stefan just plain worn down. And with Robbie at the police station they barely had a half functioning team. But these were insignificant details to what was hanging over them and was, in all probability, about to blow any minute.

It was all over.

At Andy's insistence, Loulou had gone to the match with him preventing her from making a run for the airport. Now she would have to sit in the bar, the atmosphere like a wake, until he decided they could go home.

'Where the fuck were you?' Andy shouted, sliding from his barstool.

Loulou cringed as everyone in the bar glanced up to see who Andy was yelling at. Under the onslaught of the past few days the hard, shiny shell she'd cultivated over the years to protect herself was now shattered and she felt herself wither under the attention.

'Keep your voice down,' she whispered, catching his arm and directing him back on to his seat. 'I just went to the loo.'

'Good result, eh?' he snarled. 'I bet you're pleased with yourself.'

'What did it have to do with me? You're the footballer.' Loulou began to tremble; she knew that she couldn't take much more of Andy's abuse – for anyone's sake, not even Dexter's.

'You don't think any of the shit you've put me through recently has had an effect?'

Loulou tried to mollify him. 'I'm sorry you lost, really I am. And if I made it worse, I'm sorry for that too.' She would say anything to keep him calm. More to the point, to keep him quiet.

'You insincere bitch.' He tried to put his glass back on the bar but missed and it crashed to the floor. 'Now look what you made me do.'

Martine stared at her disapprovingly, as if it was Loulou's fault for not controlling her boyfriend.

'I'll get you another,' she said, quickly.

'Oi, Martine,' he called. 'My wife fancies you.'

'Please be quiet, Andy.' Loulou handed him another drink, knowing it would only make matters worse but at a loss as to what would appease him.

Andy was not to be put off his stride. 'She does. I reckon she wants to get into your knickers. She likes a bit of fishfinger does Loulou.'

The men in the bar sniggered while their wives tutted in disgust. Loulou reddened, wondering just how far Andy was prepared to go with this.

The answer was all the way. Andy climbed onto his barstool and clapped his hands. 'Ladies and gentlemen, I've got an announcement to make.'

'Andy, leave it,' Loulou pleaded.

'I'm living with a fucking lesbian,' he shouted at the top of his voice. 'From henceforth she wants to be called Loulou Lez.'

Loulou reddened, unable to control the situation. But as the men roared with laughter, rescue came from an unexpected source.

Clive marched over and said, 'Andy, get down off that stool and show Loulou a bit of respect.'

The room watched, waiting for Andy's response, but thankfully he climbed down. Loulou couldn't even bring herself to look at him.

'If I ever see you in this condition again, it will be the end of your career at Notting Hill,' Clive warned. He turned to face the room. 'Is it any wonder we lost? I'm ashamed of the lot of you.'

Letting his words sink in, he walked out. Loulou planned to follow him but Andy grabbed her arm.

'Oh no you don't. You don't get out of it that easy.'

'Why are you doing this to me?' she asked. 'I did everything you wanted me to do.'

'Martine. Get this one. It's even better than the lezzie bit. Did you know that my wife has got a ten-year-old son?'

With every shred of dignity stripped from her, Loulou burst into tears and began to walk away. Just how much of a sadist was Andy?

Before she could get to the door, Andy had grabbed her by the arm. Although she struggled she was no match for his strength.

'You're staying.'

'Leave me alone,' she shouted hysterically.

Nothing could have prepared her for Andy's next move. She was knocked backwards as his fist drove into her face.

'That's enough!' David shouted. 'Leave her alone.'

'You weak pussy-whipped bastard.'

David ignored Andy and helped Loulou to her feet. 'Come on, let's get you out of here.

'I'm really sorry about that,' he said, putting his arm around her.

'I feel so humiliated.'

'Calm down,' he said softly. 'Nobody took any notice of what he was saying. He's just drunk and shooting his mouth off.'

'But it's all true.'

If David was at all surprised he didn't let it register on his face. Instead, he led her to the steps of a fire escape and they sat down.

'Do you want to talk about it?' he asked.

Loulou told him everything. Words just tumbled out – about Dexter, Jenny, Andy's threats.

'I thought it would be all right when Robbie was arrested but he hasn't even been charged,' she said. 'I feel so guilty about letting Jenny down. It was a disgusting thing to do to her.'

She thought telling somebody might make her feel better but as she heard the words coming out of her mouth she realised how awful it all sounded. Each confession was swept out on a new wave of tears, and it took her a while to realise that she wasn't the only one crying.

She looked up at David 'What is it?'

'You've got to get away from Andy. You mustn't spend another minute with him. He swore that night at the Three Lions was just a one-off but I think there's something seriously wrong with him.'

'What are you saying?' she asked, though deep down she already knew the answer. 'Oh God, no.'

'What happened to Jenny – it was Andy.'

Loulou howled. 'Please God, no!'

'I'm sorry. I'm so sorry.'

She was living with a rapist. She lay with him night after night, encouraging all of his sexual fantasies, while all the time that was what he really thought about women. Struggling to her feet, she threw up.

Sick until her stomach ached from retching, Loulou tried to blot out the image of Andy violating Jenny. She felt like an accomplice. What if Jenny wasn't the only one? What if there were others?

She must have known.

The girlfriends are always the last to know.

She knew.

But I honestly didn't know, she thought, I didn't have a clue. Loulou Lamb, dumbest of all the Trophy Wives.

'Are you OK?' David asked.

Loulou shook her head. 'Why are you telling me this now?'

'Because I . . . oh, Loulou, there are so many reasons, as many as the wrong decisions I've made. But seeing him just now scared me. He's not right. And neither am I,' he said quietly. 'I'm never going to forgive myself.'

'I need you to tell me everything.'

David sat down again on the step and sighed. 'You remember the way Andy and Michael were arguing that night. It was the same old thing. Michael came up through the ranks and he's always resented the way Andy started straight out on twenty grand a week. Andy winds him up and in return Michael uses his fists. Andy felt humiliated in front of you.'

Loulou remembered walking out of the club, angry that Andy was showing her up. If she'd stayed none of it might have happened.

'He felt that his manhood had been called into question and he told me he was going to screw Jenny to settle the score.'

'And she turned him down.' Loulou remembered how Andy had bragged about Jenny coming on to him and the vile remarks he had made about her body.

David continued. 'He couldn't believe a drunken old slapper – those were his words – could turn him down.'

'And so he raped her. And you stood by and watched.'

'No! No!' David dropped his head into his hands. 'Robbie found them. Andy was leaning over her body. She was unconscious. I was outside waiting for a cab. Robbie came and got me.'

'Did Robbie know she'd been raped?'

'I don't know what he thought. We knew something wasn't right. And Andy knew we knew. That's why he threatened us.'

'Physically? And you were frightened of him?'

Anger was beginning to surface. How had two grown men stood by and let this happen? How had they managed to keep it a secret?

'Not physically,' David said, his shame sounding in the thinness of his voice. 'He warned Robbie that he would tell Rachel about the young girls.'

'So you did all know about that? Didn't you ever stop to think about Rachel? You're all so pathetic. What secret did he have over you? Who were you screwing behind Tanya's back?'

'I was always faithful,' David said defensively. 'Andy asked me to think of the team. We were in with a chance of being the best – we needed a tight squad. I could never have kept them together if Michael had found out that Andy had had sex with his wife.'

Loulou corrected him. 'That wasn't sex. It was rape.'

'I was under such pressure. I convinced myself that it had just got a little out of hand. That it was basically consensual sex. This was my last season, I needed to convince the powers that be that I could hack it in management. I had to keep the team going. It's pathetic, I know.'

'You're telling me. How can you live with yourself?'

'I had to think of my future. I wanted to have something to offer Tanya.'

'Don't you dare try and put any of this on Tanya's doorstep. She didn't need anything from you other than love. Do any of you know how to love a woman?'

'Sometimes I think we don't. Not me, not Andy, Robbie or Michael.'

'Where was Michael when all this was happening?'

'In the toilets having sex with the barmaid. When she came out and saw us looking at Jenny I knew I had to go one way or the other. So I gave her money to keep quiet. From then on I was involved.'

'You're an accomplice, you know that?'

'I think about it all the time. I wanted to believe Andy but deep down I knew he had done something wrong. I kept my mouth shut and I'm going to have to live with that for the rest of my life.'

'It won't hurt as much as what Jenny has to live with.'

'I'll never be able to forgive myself,' David said, his body shaking.

Loulou started to admonish him and then stopped, realising she was simply transfering her own guilt. Was the way she had denied Jenny really any better?

'Loulou! You fucking bitch! I know you're still here – I can see your car.' Andy's voice boomed across the car park.

Loulou froze. 'David, I'm scared. I don't know what to do.'

'I'll take him back to the bar. You just get out of here.'

Loulou waited until she was sure the coast was clear and then ran for her car. In a daze she started the engine and pulled away, unsure of where she was actually intending to go. Jenny's? The police?

Passing through the main gates, deep in thought, she didn't even notice that she had pulled out in front of another car. She swerved, narrowly avoiding it, and then put her foot on the pedal. The other car sounded its horn angrily.

Loulou sped away but the other car followed h
flashing its lights. If she had to face a confrontatio
with an angry driver she thought she might ju
collapse. She drove faster but still the other car ke
up and finally at a crossing she forced herself to loo
over her shoulder.

A woman stuck her head out of the driver's wi
dow.

'Loulou. Thank God you're all right!'

It was Rachel.

Chapter Forty-Six

As soon as she caught sight of Jenny, Loulou burst into tears again. Tanya opened the back door for her and she climbed in, preparing to throw herself on Jenny's mercy.

'Am I glad to see you,' Tanya said. 'What's happened to your face?'

'Jenny, I'm so sorry,' Loulou wept. 'I don't know how to tell you this . . . it was Andy.'

Tanya held her hand. 'We know. Robbie told us and as soon as he did we came to find you. Did he do this to you?'

Loulou nodded. 'David was there. He told me everything.'

'So David was a part of it,' Tanya wept.

'Does Andy know you know?' Rachel asked, trying to keep everything together.

Loulou shook her head and then explained what had happened since she had last seen them. 'I know it seems like I was trying to protect myself but honestly it was for Dexter. Jenny, it's the most awful thing I've ever done to a person. I'm just so sorry.'

By now the other three women's tears were as strong as her own.

'It doesn't matter,' Jenny said. 'All of us would

have done the same. I'm just glad you got out o
there safely.'

'So are you going to the police now?' Loulou
asked.

'I haven't changed my mind. No.'

'So he just gets away with it? You can't let tha
happen.'

'I think we should kill him,' Loulou said.

Tanya looked at her in astonishment.

'I'm serious.'

'We can't,' Rachel said.

'I think I could,' Tanya replied.

Hysteria was now the common denominator betweer
the women.

'I know where we can get a gun,' Loulou said.

'Haven't we been through enough?' Jenny said
trying to calm the others. 'I don't want anything tha
would come back on us. I'd like to see him dead to
but I can't let any of you do it and I'm not sure
could pull the trigger myself.'

'Then go and see Clive,' Rachel urged. 'He'll knov
what to do.'

'I will not speak to that man and that's final,
Jenny said.

At the mention of the chairman's name, Loulo
suddenly remembered his warning to Andy earlie
that evening. 'It doesn't seem much but I think
know how we could ruin his career. That would b
some compensation, wouldn't it?'

Loulou's hand shook as she put her key in the lock
Before opening the door she looked along the stree
to check that the three women had managed to follov

her from Meret's. Seeing Rachel park the car, she went in.

'A–Andy?' She cleared her throat and called again. 'Andy, are you there?'

There was no reply, but to be sure she quickly ran from room to room to check. The house was empty.

Lighting a cigarette, Loulou returned to the living room, poured herself a drink and sat down to wait, growing more frightened by the minute. What if David had told Andy that she knew? Could she trust David after all the lying he had done? The man had stuck by Andy so far – why wouldn't he go on protecting him? And even if he hadn't told him, the mood Andy was in there was no saying what he might do.

An hour had passed when she finally heard the door open and her heart was in her mouth. Stay calm, she told herself.

'You're back,' she said, as neutrally as she could manage. She didn't want to provoke him in any way. 'Can I get you a drink?'

Andy tripped as he walked over to an armchair and Loulou relaxed a fraction. He was completely drunk. Half of her job was already done.

'Yes,' he said, falling into the chair.

Loulou poured a large measure of whisky into the glass, then walked into the kitchen.

'Where are you going?' he called.

'I'm just getting some ice,' she replied, opening the freezer door. Sure that she couldn't be seen from the living room, she slipped her hand into her pocket and produced a small packet containing the two crushed sleeping tablets Meret had given her.

She added them to the whisky and threw in a few cubes of ice.

'Here you go,' she said, handing him the drink.

She watched as he downed it in one, wondering how long the sleeping tablets would take to work. Meret had said anything up to half an hour.

'Come here,' Andy said, the aggression he'd shown in the bar still there in his voice.

Loulou remained rooted to the spot.

'Please?' he asked, more gently.

Feeling the fear rise again, she took a step towards him. 'Yes?' Too cold. She sat on the arm of the chair and forced herself to put her hand on his shoulder. 'Are you all right?'

'I'm fine.'

Merely touching him made her flesh crawl and she glanced at her watch. No more than a few minutes had passed. It seemed like forever.

'I'm sorry, Loulou. About what I said. I shouldn't have done that in the bar. I was upset.'

'It doesn't matter,' she said, flinching as she felt his lips brush against her hand. 'Forget about it.'

'I can't. You're the best thing that ever happened to me and I want to know how I can make it up to you.'

He reached up and felt her breast. Loulou had to subdue the scream rising in her throat.

'I want to make love to you. Let me show you how much I care about you.'

That was it, she couldn't hold back any more, whatever the consequences. 'Make love? What do you know about love? The only thing you know how to do is abuse people. You raped her, you fucking bastard, lying son of a bitch. You raped her!'

Andy lunged at her, but with the drink and the pills beginning to work she moved out of his way in time.

'You believe that cunt's word over mine?'

'It wasn't Jenny who told me, it was your precious mate,' Loulou spat. 'Do you know what you did to her? Do you have any idea what she's going through? She's carrying your fucking child!'

Momentarily, Andy stopped moving towards her, she could see that he was shocked by her revelation. 'She's lying!'

'Why would she lie about that? Do you think she wanted to carry a rapist's child?'

'She's lying. I'll kill the bitch if she doesn't shut her stinking mouth. And you.'

He grabbed her again. This time she wasn't fast enough and she found herself pressed up against the wall.

'Don't hurt me,' she pleaded, terrified.

'There's not one shred of evidence, not one. It could be anyone's kid. Don't you blame her bastard child on me. I'll see to . . .' His voice began to slow down, until the sentence trailed off into an incomprehensible slur.

'Andy?'

There was no answer. She felt his hand go slack and she guided him to the sofa. With one push, he was out flat.

'Andy?' she whispered.

His mouth dropped open but nothing came out. His eyes were tightly shut.

With no time to lose, she reached for her handbag and withdrew the other things Meret had given her – a syringe and a small bag of brown powder. Loulou went back into the kitchen, turned on the gas and went over Meret's instructions on how to heat the heroin.

Some wild child, she thought. She didn't even know how to prepare a fix. Doubt crept into her mind as she sucked the liquid into the syringe. Was it too much? Not enough?

Too little was the more worrying prospect. He could wake up and catch them. Too much and he would die. No great loss.

She returned to the living room. His breathing was slow and regular. He was deep in sleep. Holding the needle in her hand she dialled Rachel's mobile and whispered, 'He's nearly ready. Five minutes.'

Loulou took a deep breath and walked over to him. One arm hung over the side of the chair and she knelt beside it. Pushing back the sleeve of his T-shirt, she gripped his elbow and, checking once more that all the air was out of the syringe, aimed for his vein.

As the needle pierced his skin, Andy writhed in his sleep, but Loulou held firm as she emptied the drug into his blood.

Luckily, Meret had been able to locate a dealer almost immediately. For good measure Loulou had also bought a selection of other drugs, including amphetamine, Ecstasy and some Special K.

Loulou jumped when she heard the letterbox open and she rushed to the door, the syringe still in her hand.

Rachel was standing on the doorstep looking anxious

'I've done it,' she said, waving the syringe.

'Oh my God!'

'Quickly, I don't know how long we've got.'

'I told Jenny and Tanya to wait in the car. They can't really help.' Rachel followed Loulou back into the house.

'We'll manage fine,' Loulou said, unsure if in fact they could. Andy was a big man and unconscious he was a dead weight.

Loulou wrapped the used syringe in some paper and put it into her handbag, along with the selection of drugs. Then she threw the bag over her shoulder and said, 'Here goes.'

Getting him to his feet was the hardest part. His body was completely limp.

'We'll never do it,' Rachel wailed, as he fell back into the chair for the third time.

'Of course we can.'

Loulou slapped Andy around the face. 'Andy, wake up!'

The footballer half opened his eyes. All that was visible were the whites.

'Now, Rachel, pull!'

'Whhhaa?' Andy said, groaning.

'Pull!'

Holding him by the shoulders, somehow they hoisted him to a standing position. Loulou wedged her shoulder under his arm on one side, then Rachel arranged herself on the other.

They lurched towards the hall but when Andy decided to take a different direction they had no choice but to follow. It took them a good ten minutes to get him to the street door.

Jenny and Tanya were waiting outside. Loulou threw Jenny the keys to Andy's car before navigating the steps in front of the house, and it was another quarter of an hour before they'd finally managed to get him into the passenger seat.

'Do you want me to come with you?' Jenny asked 'If we get stopped, I can tell them I did it.'

Without warning, Jenny balled her fist and punched Andy in the jaw. He moaned incomprehensibly.

'I think it's better if I go alone,' Loulou said. 'Don' worry. I have no intention of getting stopped. I'll meet you at the club.'

Although she was still as nervous as hell, Loulou drove carefully, not wanting to do anything that would attract attention. So far it had all gone swimmingly and she didn't want to lose it this late in the game.

She stopped Andy's car in front of the Notting Hill grounds and waited for Rachel to pull up.

'He should be in the driving seat,' Loulou said.

'I knew you were going to say that,' Rachel sighed

By the time Andy was behind the wheel the two women were breathless.

'I hope this works,' Rachel said, as Loulou threw the drugs and the used syringe onto the dashboard o the car and closed the door.

'It has to,' Loulou said, trying to imagine the consequences for her if they were caught out.

They ran back to the other car.

'Right, did anyone notice a phone box on the way?' Rachel asked, as she started the engine.

'I want to make the call,' Jenny said. 'I owe th bastard that much.'

'I feel completely useless,' Tanya declared.

'I know what you can do,' Loulou said. 'Who do you know on the papers?'

'Of course. Just about everyone.'

'Give it a couple of hours,' Jenny advised, 'then call them. Or it'll look like a set-up. And, for God's sake, don't let them know who you are.'

They stopped a few streets away and Jenny made the call to the police, reporting a man acting suspiciously in a car outside the main entrance to the Notting Hill stadium.

Then they drove back to Rachel's where they sat up waiting for the news to break on TV. Finally, at five a.m., they were rewarded with the sight of a very angry Clive Dorning being interviewed about Andy's arrest outside the club. The charge – possession of Class A drugs. As the chairman promised a press conference for later in the day, the four women cheered.

Chapter Forty-Seven

When Andy eventually emerged from the cell Clive was the only person there to greet him. The chairman had had to pull quite a few strings to get the press off Andy's back and now a group of reporters were on their way *en masse* to a totally unconnected police station.

On his way there, Clive had tried to figure out what had happened to the club. It was one scandal after another, first Stu Williams, then Robbie, and now Andy. They were a bunch of reprobates and Clive didn't want to be tainted by their failures.

The chairman couldn't believe how ill the player looked but then what could you expect from that kind of drug cocktail? It just went to show, you never really did know someone. He would never have placed Andy as a junkie, although it probably explained his dangerous behaviour.

Clive opened the door of the limousine and Andy climbed in behind him. At first the player sat perfectly still and said nothing. Finally, he muttered, 'I was set up. Loulou did it.'

Clive let out a guffaw. 'That's rather far-fetched.'

'I'm telling you the truth, Clive. I know I was tanked-up but I can remember getting home and talking to her. It must be Loulou. I have never taken drugs in my life.'

Clive ignored his protest. 'Are the police pressing charges?'

Andy nodded sullenly.

'They obviously don't believe your cock-and-bull story either.'

Andy sighed. 'Whatever.'

'Anyway, this isn't a social call. I'm simply here to tell you that the club will no longer be requiring your services. This is one scandal too many. I sense that there are still a lot of worms waiting to come out of the woodwork. Like that woman who accused you of rape. I might have paid her off but, sooner or later, those types always resurface. And I won't have any more sex scandals associated with the club.'

Leaning towards the chairman, Andy said, 'She wanted it and you need me.'

Clive smelled the stale alcohol on Andy's breath and could see that the player's pupils were little bigger than pinpricks. Moving back slightly, he sneered, 'I noticed last night you were in excellent form. How many goals did you miss? I lost count. So, as I was saying, like Robbie, you're out. I suggest you go quietly. I think you've had quite enough publicity for one season.'

'What about the publicity you could get, Clive? A fine upstanding Christian and all those girls? It's not just a normal sex scandal, is it? Pretty kinky stuff, I've heard. Fancy yourself as a photographer, do you?'

'You'll never prove it,' Clive hissed. 'Everyone will think it's just sour grapes.'

'Not when they talk to the girls they won't. You see I've covered myself. I've got the name and address

of every girl I've procured for you. And I'm sure with
a little cheque-book journalism they'd be more than
willing to spill the beans. You'll make Robbie look as
innocent as the girls he fucks.'

Clive spluttered in reply. 'You can't do that.'

'I can. As you said to me on more than one occasion,
it's quid pro quo. I go down and you come with me.
The choice is yours.'

'I have to go in.'

'Jenny, please. I'm sure it won't be good for you or
the baby. Just wait here in the car,' Rachel pleaded.

'I want to see it through to the end. I want to see
the bastard get his come-uppance.'

'Look, we'd better get going,' Loulou said, her voice
shaky. 'We don't want to miss it.'

The four women huddled close together, feeling
there was definitely safety in numbers. Inside, Notting
Hill's press room was overflowing with journalists
from every major newspaper. Luckily they were all
too busy talking to each other to notice the women
at the back, looking nervous and out of place.

There was a hushed silence as Clive entered the
room, followed by Andy and an extremely unhappy-
looking David. Then the journalists erupted, all shouting questions at once. Clive held up his hand for
quiet.

Clive's usual composure had disappeared. His forehead shone with a sheen of sweat and he looked old
and defeated. Andy was no better, the dark shadows
under his eyes a stark contrast to his ashen skin. A
nervous twitch played around the corner of one eye.
His usual good looks were no longer in evidence.

David simply had the air of a condemned man.

'I'm going to make a short statement, which will not be followed by any questions,' Clive declared, his voice hoarse. 'I know I don't have to go over why we're all here,' he said, glancing at Andy. His hatred for the footballer clear for all to see. 'As you know, I have very strong views on alcohol and drug abuse and I am extremely upset that the team's star player felt so bad about the team losing the UEFA match that he turned to drugs. But it is my Christian duty to forgive him. I don't condone Andy's behaviour but I will try to understand it. He has given his word it will never happen again and has agreed to be tested on a regular basis. That's it. Thank you for coming.'

There was a cry from the back of the room and every head turned to stare at the four women. Jenny was crying, the other three looked shell-shocked.

Suddenly, there was banging and shouting at the front. Like an audience at a tennis match all heads simultaneously swivelled towards the front, keen to see what was causing the commotion. Clive and David were wrestling over the mike. The chairman was no match for the angry younger man.

'From this moment I've resigned,' David shouted, causing an ear-piercing feedback. He threw the mike at Clive and walked out of the room.

Carla fumbled with the box and it dropped to the floor. She swore and picked it up, only to discover yet another video. Where were the damn photos? Her hands shook as she pulled another box off Clive's shelf. She knew that any minute he might be back in the office, and then having given fat old disgusting

Fred a hand job would have all been for nothing. She'd never be able to get back in once Clive knew what she'd been doing and there was no way she was going to have time to clear up this mess.

She started on the next shelf down, swiping clear all the Dorning family photographs. Carla ground her heel into one she found particularly offensive, showing Clive sporting a smug grin. Soon another half-dozen boxes lay around her. Perhaps he had moved them. She would give herself five more minutes and then she was out of there.

'Bingo,' she whispered. Rifling through the pictures she finally found the ones of herself. She stuffed them into her bag and threw the rest on the desk.

Ready to leave, she heard footsteps and then Clive's voice. Panicking, she ran towards the door but she could hear that he was almost upon her. She tried to think quickly, looking desperately around the room for a hiding place. The only chance she had was his flat. Hopefully, as soon as he saw the photos, he'd go out to find a guard and then she could make a run for it.

Inside the flat, she went straight to the bedroom and hid under the bed. Placing her hand over her mouth, she tried to silence the uncontrollable gasps of fear.

'How could you do this to me?' Jenny shouted.

'I don't know what you're talking about,' Clive said, looking at the opened videos all over his desk. Oh God, the pictures. Someone had got the pictures. He gathered them up quickly, trying to figure out who'd ransacked his office. It couldn't be Andy, he had been with him, and anyway no one knew where he kept them hidden. Or at least that was what he'd thought

Who was it? Clive was sweating profusely. Fear welled up inside him. It was over. Oh God. He couldn't make sense of what his sister was saying. He'd seen that she was pregnant but that made no sense either.

'Are you listening to me? I set Andy up and then you, you fucking hypocrite, let him off.'

'You set him up? Why?' Clive felt that his world was going mad. What did Jenny have to do with Andy?

'Why?' she shouted. 'Because he raped me! Made me pregnant. And I wanted him to be punished.'

'Rape? What are you talking about?' Clive was desperately trying to piece everything together. 'Have you gone to the police?'

'I never want my child to know that its father was a rapist,' she said, her voice barely above a whisper. 'You have to get rid of Andy McKay.'

'I can't.'

'What do you mean you can't? Of course you can.'

'It's my Christian duty to—'

'Stuff your duty. You just don't think he did anything wrong. Do you? How could you when you did the same thing to me? Again and again. I was just a child.'

Why was she saying these terrible things? 'Jenny, stop it. That's not true. I *loved* you,' Clive cried. 'It was something special between us. You make it sound sordid. No one's ever loved you like I have.'

Jenny felt faint, unable to take in Clive's perverted

words. 'You're depraved. Sick. You ruined my life. Look,' she said, holding up her scarred wrists. 'That's what your love did for me. You made me hate myself so much I could only hurt myself. Because I always believed it was my fault; thought I had encouraged it. You and your disgusting needs. Why did you think I was a drunk and a drug addict? Fun? No, it was to stop the nightmares. But now thanks to Andy I know I'm not to blame. With him or with you. I was fourteen, for God's sake,' she cried. 'How could you?'

'I loved you. I still do. There's never been anyone else.' Clive made a grab for Jenny.

Jumping back, Jenny stumbled and fell to the floor. 'Keep away from me.' She felt a wetness between her legs; looking down she saw a damp patch spreading across her dress. What was happening?

Clive's hand touched her shoulder. 'Jenny, are you all right? Speak to me.'

She flinched. 'Get away from me!' she screamed. 'You make me feel sick.' Oh no, please God. Blood was trickling down her legs.

Managing to get to her feet she edged backwards, away from Clive towards the door. Something was terribly wrong. She needed to find help but she felt like she was moving in slow motion. Suddenly, Jenny felt a pain like no other she'd ever experienced. 'The baby! It's coming. Call an ambulance,' she gasped.

She couldn't speak any more. It felt as if a hand had reached into her stomach and was ripping out her entrails.

It was several minutes before Carla realised she was now free to escape. She had heard every unbelievable

word. Her heart, such as it was, went out to Jenny.
Their lives had not been so very different, after all. As
she had listened to Jenny's story, her own memories
had come stampeding back.

Carla could never return to the start of her nightmare. There was no vengeance that she could visit on
her abuser, but she could get Clive for Jenny. She had
been the same age as Jenny, fourteen, when she had
been bought and sold, battered and bruised. Jenny was
right. She also had been only a child, a little girl who
had lost all hope before she had even found any.

Anger boiled to the surface. Unsteadily she made
her way back into the office. Retrieving the video
box, she grabbed dozens of the photos and stuffed
them into a bag until it was overflowing.

Looking out the window, she saw Clive standing
motionless, watching the ambulance, its siren screaming, disappearing through the stadium gates.

Carla wasn't sure what she could do but she knew
that whatever it was there would be no Clive Dorning
or Andy McKay by the time she'd finished.

Chapter Forty-Eight

The paramedics ran alongside the trolley on which Jenny lay screaming and crying. They called out a stream of information to the doctor that made no sense to Rachel or Loulou who were running behind. Tanya was having to walk at a much slower pace, her wound chafing against its bandage.

A doctor stuck out his arms and barred them from following Jenny into the operating theatre. 'I'm sorry you're going to have to wait. We're going to have to perform an emergency caesarean. Do you know how many weeks pregnant she is?'

'I think about twenty-eight, twenty-nine,' Rachel replied. 'It's too early, isn't it? The baby's going to die.'

All of them could hear Jenny moaning for her friends on the other side of the doors.

'I can't say. But we'll do everything we can.'

The doctor left the three women standing in the corridor clutching on to each other, feeling bereft. As if in a trance they waited, silent, grim, full of foreboding, none of them knowing whether minutes or hours had passed them by before they finally heard the heart-wrenching sound of a baby's first cry.

Eventually Jenny's doctor reappeared.

'Mrs Waite has had a little girl. She's obviously very

small and like all babies this premature is having problems breathing. Her lungs are not fully developed, so we're going to have to help her breathe.'

'But she's going to live?' Rachel wasn't sure whether Jenny would be able to survive if she suffered another tragedy.

'We'll have to wait and see if she's a fighter or not. It's too early to say.'

'How's Jenny?' Loulou asked, not wanting the doctor to say any more about the baby's chances.

'Fine. We'll be taking her upstairs to her room soon, you'll be able to see her then.'

Jenny opened her eyes. Where was she? A fluorescent light above forced her to close them again. She tried to swallow but gagged. It was as if her mouth was full of cotton wool. Her baby. What had happened? Tentatively, she opened her eyes once more. Looking around she could see that she was in hospital and attached to a drip. She tried to move, but an agonising pain ripped across her stomach. She cried out for help.

Tanya, Rachel and Loulou rushed into the room.

'What's happened?' Jenny pleaded in a croaky voice.

'You've had a baby girl,' the other three women said in unison.

'I can't have. It's too early.'

'She's doing fine. They've put her in an incubator,' Rachel reassured her, trying to instil as much confidence in her inflection as she could muster.

'A girl,' Jenny cried. 'Oh my God. I have to see her.'

As Tanya left the room to get a nurse, Loulou and Rachel held Jenny's hands, trying to comfort her as she sobbed.

A nurse followed Tanya into the room, and approached Jenny.

'How is she?' Jenny cried, choking back her sobs.

'Jenny. Your little girl is in intensive care. As you know she was very premature and needs help breathing. But so far there have been no other complications.'

'Can I see her?' Jenny was rocking back and forth hypnotically, no longer caring about the physical pain. The anguish of being separated from her daughter was far greater.

'In a little while. The doctors are with her at the moment.'

'She will survive, won't she? Please tell me she's going to make it,' Jenny wailed.

'We're doing the best we can.'

Loulou excused herself and walked down the corridor searching for a telephone. Tears streamed down her face as she thought about Jenny's baby. And her own child, the baby she had been forced to give away. She had to get Dexter back before it was too late.

The money refused to go into the slot and Loulou punched the phone with frustration. Finally, it went in and Loulou heard her mother's voice.

'It's me,' she said, her voice hoarse with emotion. 'I want Dexter back.'

She could hear her mother's voice but she couldn't make out the words; she had no interest in hearing anything her mother had to say.

'You stole my baby from me. You stole my happiness and if I leave Dexter with you any longer you'll find a way of stealing his. You can't help yourself. I want you to put my baby on the first available plane or I'm coming after you.'

She knew she sounded like a crazy woman but she didn't care. Her need for Dexter had opened up an abyss in her heart. Only he could make her whole again.

'I mean it, Laura. Give me back my baby.'

'Jenny, we're going to take you to see your baby,' a portly nurse, who was struggling with an unwieldy wheelchair, said. 'Let me help you up. That's it, slowly does it.'

It was a painful and drawn-out process as Jenny moved off the bed and into the chair. 'Can my friends come with me?'

'They can watch through the window.'

Rachel, Tanya and Loulou were lost in their own thoughts as they followed quietly behind Jenny and the nurse. Even the sound of their footsteps felt inappropriate at such a moment.

In the ICU there were half a dozen incubators. The babies, none weighing more than a bag of sugar and all attached to various machines, looked so small and defenceless. It was a pitiful sight.

'Which one is my daughter?' Jenny asked, her voice full of anguish.

'There she is,' the nurse said gently, pointing to a baby that was more blue than pink and so small Jenny could have held her in one hand.

'Oh my God, she's so tiny. What are all those tubes for?'

'They're helping her to breathe.'

Jenny could not stop the tears.

'Let me take you in.'

Through the glass window the three women watched as Jenny stroked her daughter's hand, the expression on her face changing from grief to wonderment. After just the briefest of precious moments, the nurse was wheeling her out again.

'She can't die,' Jenny sobbed to no one in particular. 'She can't.'

Back in Jenny's room no one spoke. What words could be of comfort at a time like this?

There was a sharp knock on the door and all four women were amazed to see Carla Ryman appear. She looked even more of a mess than usual. Her dark roots, now covering half her head, contrasted with what was left of the peroxide to make her look like a badger. From her unwashed smell and grubby, crumpled clothes, it was obvious that she'd been wearing the same shirt and jeans for several days and nights.

Loulou jumped out of her seat. 'What the hell do you think you're doing here? You're the last thing Jenny needs.'

Jenny motioned for her friend to be quiet. 'What do you want, Carla?'

'Is the baby OK?'

'We don't know,' Rachel interjected, seeing that Jenny was beyond answering.

'Jenny, I need to speak to you in private.'

'This is hardly the time or the place,' Loulou said, ignoring Jenny's earlier request.

'It's all right. Let me have five minutes with Carla.'

'Are you sure? You're—'

Jenny waved the others away and they left begrudgingly.

'What is it, Carla?' Jenny asked wearily.

'I know no one thinks I'm any good and I guess to a certain degree they'd be right. I've done a lot of terrible things in my life that I'm not proud of but perhaps you of all people would understand.'

'What do you mean?'

'Well,' Carla began and then clearly thought better of it. 'Oh nothing, it doesn't matter now. All I wanted to say is I've never forgotten your kindness to me. You didn't look down your nose at me the way everybody else did. So I'm going to sort everything out.'

Jenny thought the anaesthetic must be clouding her mind, she had no idea what the girl was talking about. 'Carla, I don't understand.'

'It's probably better you don't. I'm just going to make everything right. I hope. I've got to go now. Bye. And, Jenny, good luck. I really hope the baby's all right.' Without another puzzling word she left the room.

As Carla walked down the hospital steps, she realised that she recognised the agonised features of the man slumped over the wheel of the car parked in the ambulance bay. She knocked on the window but the man didn't look up.

'Clive?'

She opened the passenger door, momentarily lost for words by the sight of her former employer. He smelled and looked terrible. His skin appeared waxen and his steely blue eyes had a dead, fish-like flatness. The usually immaculate suit was creased as if, like Carla, he had spent the night sleeping in his clothes. Although from his appearance Carla rather doubted he'd slept. Serves the bastard right, she thought. By the time she'd finished with him, she doubted he'd ever get a good night's sleep again.

'For what it's worth, the baby is alive.'

She waited for him to shout and tell her to get out but he was a defeated man.

'What do you want, Carla?' he asked, his voice emotionless.

She wanted to answer 'Blood!' but instead, in as calm a voice as she could manage, she asked for a few minutes of his time. She strengthened the force of her request by throwing one of the Polaroids into his lap. The tawdry picture of her fellating Clive stared up at them accusingly.

Lulled into a false sense of security by Clive's subdued demeanour, she was unprepared for his reaction. He turned and lunged at her throat.

As he squeezed tighter he hissed at her. 'I should have known it was you! I want every one of those pictures back. Now.'

Carla would have laughed if she could have caught her breath. She tried to wriggle away from his grasp. Christ! He was going to kill her.

The same thought must have occurred to Clive and he let go as quickly as he had grabbed her. Slumping back into his seat, he said, in a voice reminiscent of the old Clive, 'Let me guess. You want money?'

Carla rubbed her neck while spluttering, 'You're damn right I do. But it's more than the money, Clive, so much more.'

'Well, you blackmailing little slut, you can take

those pictures and just leave because there's no proof it's me.'

Carla allowed herself a triumphant smile. 'Not quite, Clive. Look,' she said, pointing to the hand in the photograph. 'Those rings are unmistakably yours.'

Clive seemed to slip back into his trance.

'And, of course, there are the other women. Remember Terri? You're a sick man,' she spat, thinking of Jenny's teenage torment.

Images of the dozens of women he had used and photographed crowded his mind, followed by thoughts of his wife and daughters. He knew Carla would go to the papers if he didn't pay up. There was no way he would be able to live with the shame. The brazen whore had won.

'So, Clive, as I was saying—'

'Shut up! How much?'

'You're a very rich man, Clive. I would have thought two hundred grand wouldn't make much of a dent in your finances.'

'You've got to be joking. Get out of this car.'

For a moment Carla wondered if the whole scam was going to collapse. It couldn't, not now she'd got this far. 'I'm sure I'll get more from the papers,' she said.

Clive's game of bluff was nearing its end. There was no point in taking it further. He had lost. 'A hundred and that's my final offer.'

'Cash.'

He gave a brief nod. 'If you've finished, I'd like to be left on my own.'

'But I'm not finished, Clive. There's one more thing to sort out. Andy McKay.'

Clive's face lost what little colour it still had. 'What's McKay got to do with you?'

'Never mind that. I want you to sack him. Call him on the phone now. I want to be there when you do it.'

'Nothing would give me greater pleasure,' Clive said through gritted teeth, 'but I ... he ...' Clive began to sob.

'Cut the tears and the crap, Clive. If you don't, I'll go to the papers whether you pay up or not.'

Clive knew he was trapped in a no-win situation. Andy or Carla – both had the same story to sell. But at that moment he hated McKay more than the wretched girl beside him. Composing himself, he dialled the player's number.

'Andy, this is Clive. I want you to meet me at the club in ten minutes ... You don't have any choice. Just be there.'

Clive started the engine and drove out of the hospital car park. Carla couldn't hold back any longer. 'I know what you did to Jenny, you perverted bastard. You make me want to puke.'

'How do you ... Shut up, you monster. You don't know anything,' he shouted. A wooden crucifix was hanging from the rear-view mirror. The chairman unhooked it and began to pray in a loud sing-song voice.

'I know everything,' Carla screamed back. 'And I know about Andy and what he did. You're all the same. I've waited a long time but you're all going to get your come-uppance.'

Clive interrupted his prayer. 'Only the Lord can judge me,' he bellowed. 'He knows the sanctity of my love for Jenny.'

'You're her brother, for Christ's sake! You're no different from Andy. In fact you're far, far worse.'

The car picked up speed and Clive appeared to be paying no attention to where he was going. As he shot through the first red light, Carla began to panic.

'Let me out!' She gripped the door handle, prepared if she had to, to throw herself from the car. 'You're mad. Stop! Now!'

Clive appeared not to hear her. 'My poor Jenny,' he said, veering across the road, into oncoming traffic. 'I'll look after her and the baby. It'll be like before. No one to interfere with us. We'll be happy.'

Carla tried to grab the steering wheel. 'You're going to kill us.'

Clive knocked her away, a maniacal grin on his face. Carla held on to her seat in pure terror as they rounded the corner that led to the stadium. Up ahead she was relieved to see Andy stepping out of his car. Surely Clive would stop to face the man who had abused his beloved sister?

Instead he put his foot down hard on the accelerator. The car's powerful engine thrust them forward at an alarming speed.

'No!' Carla cried.

'You, me and him – we're going together!'

Carla's scream drowned out the sound of Clive's laughter as Andy's body hit the windscreen.

Chapter Forty-Nine

'Jenny, wake up.'

Jenny struggled for consciousness. The baby! 'Is she all right?'

'She's finding it easier to breathe. She made it through the night and that's a really good sign,' the doctor reassured her. 'We're very hopeful. Although it's still early days.'

Jenny smiled for the first time in what seemed like forever. Surrounding her were her friends who had spent their second all-night vigil on a collection of uncomfortable plastic chairs. How any of them had slept was a mystery, but from their yawning and stretching, sleep had won out eventually.

'She's a lot better,' Jenny said excitedly.

Her news was greeted by three smiling, tired faces.

'Can I see her now?'

'In a while. We just have to do some more tests.' He patted her hand before leaving.

Loulou was the first to speak. 'It must be me praying. I think God thought that if someone like me is prepared to pray then he damn well better make sure she's all right.'

'What's that quote about one sinner? My priest used to preach it all the time. I know,' Jenny said, laughing.

'"Joy shall be in heaven over one sinner that repenteth, more than over ninety and nine just persons, which need no repentance."'

The others joined in her laughter. The relief that the baby girl had made it through the night, coupled with the lack of sleep, made them all feel light-headed.

This snatched moment of joy proved to be short lived. A knock on the door was followed by two uniformed policemen entering the hospital room.

'Jenny Waite?' the older of the two men asked.

'Yes?'

'Sorry to impose on you but I'm afraid we have some bad news. Your—'

'My baby?' Why were the police there to tell her about her baby?

'No, no. There's been an accident. Your brother was involved. He's in hospital. It's nothing too serious, but—'

'An accident – where?' Loulou asked.

The younger policeman spoke, clearly recognising Loulou and wanting to impress her. 'Well, it wasn't so much an accident as attempted murder.'

'What?'

'There was a witness – Carla Ryman – who was in the car at the time. According to her statement your brother purposely drove into Andy McKay.'

'Andy? Is he dead?' Loulou asked, unable to believe her ears.

The startled look on the young policeman's face showed that he had forgotten about Loulou's relationship with the player.

'Of course, you're his girlfriend,' he said. 'I'm sorry,

Miss Lamb. Mr McKay is alive but he has sustained some serious injuries.'

Loulou looked at him wide-eyed. 'How serious?'

'Your boyfriend has broken his neck. If you'd like to come with us we can take you to him now.' He turned back to Jenny. 'We're very sorry to bring you this news, especially at a time like this. But, I'm afraid, your brother is under arrest for attempted murder.'

Jenny nodded automatically as the two policemen blustered on for a few more minutes. Finally they realised that the women were too shocked to be able to shed any further light on the situation at that particular time.

'We'll need to interview you. But it can wait. Miss Lamb?'

'Jenny needs me at the moment,' she said. 'I'll go later.'

The policemen seemed surprised at her response but nodded and left.

Tanya was the first to speak. 'He finally got his come-uppance – and from your brother of all people. But what was Carla doing in the car?'

'She told me she was going to sort it all out. But I don't think she meant like this,' Jenny replied.

'She's done us both a favour,' Loulou said bitterly.

'Do you want us to do anything?' Tanya asked. 'Contact Clive?'

'No.' Jenny paused, tempted to tell her friends the full horror of her brother's interference, but then she decided it was time to put it behind her. Two birds with one car, as it were. All she said was, 'Clive can rot in hell. He and Andy are two of a kind.'

'Jenny, we're ready. You'll be able to hold her today,' a nurse said, bustling into the room.

Forgetting about her wound, Jenny tried to leap out of the bed. As her stitches pulled against her skin she let out an agonised yell.

'Steady,' the nurse admonished.

'I'm fine. Honestly.' Not even the pain could ruin this moment. 'I've decided to name the baby Hope.'

'It's a beautiful name,' Rachel said.

Loulou and Tanya, with tears in their eyes, agreed.

Before Jenny left the room, she turned to her friends. 'I would never have got through this without you and I won't ever be able to show my appreciation . . .'

Her friends all shook their heads, making embarrassed noises.

'Never mind modesty,' Jenny continued. 'But now it's time to get back to your own lives. You know, the world outside these four walls.'

Tanya, Loulou and Rachel stood motionless, the same thought going through all their minds. What did their lives hold now? All had lost a battle but they had gained each other and found themselves. The future was as yet undecided, but all of them hoped that together they would win the war.

Chapter Fifty

Carla took the bank statement from her handbag and read it again. The cheque from the newspaper had cleared and there was now almost two hundred thousand pounds in her account. The bank manager had even asked her to go in and talk about investing some of it. Some chance.

'Are you ready to order, madam?' the waiter asked, his shirt quite the whitest Carla had ever seen.

'I'll have the salmon,' she said, not quite sure what everything on the menu actually was.

'And to drink?'

'A bottle of champagne.' She resisted adding 'the best' as she guessed that the best at the Palace Hotel might be a little too expensive, even for her.

The waiter nodded and walked away. Carla wanted to pinch herself. Here she was ordering salmon and champagne at the Palace – and paying for it herself. Nobody was trying to throw her out, nobody was thinking she was a prostitute. She'd made it.

With the attempted murder charge hanging over him, every paper in the country had been clamouring for stories on Clive, and Carla's tale and accompanying photographs had gone to the highest bidder.

Clive was in no position to keep up his end of the

bargain over the pictures, and anyway he deserved it after what he had done to Jenny. All men were pigs. And then there was the fact that he had tried to kill her. Her hand automatically went up to the wound on her forehead. It was healing nicely and the doctors had assured her there would be only a small scar. She had thought about suing Clive, but she wanted out, to move on. A new life where no one knew who Carla Ryman was.

With this money under her belt she was intending to go back to Berlin and maybe invest in a strip bar. Make some money from some other poor cow taking off her clothes.

Her name was mud here anyway. She'd never get within sniffing distance of another football club in this country again. And the best thing about it was that she didn't care. She'd seen what it was really like to be a Trophy Wife, and all the designer dresses in the world couldn't make up for the hell they had to go though.

The champagne arrived and the waiter poured her a glass.

'Cheers, gorgeous,' she said, giving him a wink.

David walked up to the clearing but Tanya was nowhere to be seen. She probably wasn't going to come. It had been silly to suggest meeting here at the forest. It was just that they'd spent some of their happiest times here.

Clive, in the light of his arrest and the Carla Ryman scandal, had announced his resignation that morning but the news brought David no comfort. Even Graham Leary calling him to offer him a place in

management at the new-look Notting Hill did nothing
to lift his spirits. As far as he was concerned he'd lost
everything.

'Tanya!' He spotted her walking slowly along the
path. She still looked very tired and weak. 'I didn't
think you'd come.'

She kissed him on the cheek. 'Of course you did.
When have I ever let you down?'

Never was the answer. If only she could have said
the same about him. 'How's Jenny?'

'She's fine. And the baby's beautiful.'

'And the others?'

'They're getting through it.'

'What about you?' Without thinking about it, he
had taken hold of her hand.

'I'm taking each day as it comes. Sometimes I feel
positive, other days it gets me down. I still don't think
I've quite come to terms with it.'

Mention of her illness reminded him once again
how much he had failed her. They walked in silence,
David growing more uncomfortable by the second.
At the far side of the clearing he stopped and faced
her.

'I just wanted to tell you how sorry I am. If there
is anything – anything – I can do to try to put things
right . . .'

'Let it go, David. It's all in the past.' Although
her voice was gentle, David could hear a note of
resignation too.

He wanted to find the right words, something that
would break through to Tanya and let her know he
meant everything he said. But words escaped him and
he lapsed into silence again.

They came to the stream, which had been replenished by the overnight rain. Standing on the bridge, they stared at the water.

'Was it worth it?' Tanya said, finally. 'So much pain. So many people hurt. All for what? A game.'

'No,' David said quietly.

'How could you stand by when Jenny was . . .' Tanya stopped herself. 'And there's me telling you to let it go.'

'You've got every right to be angry,' he said and then realised that he sounded incredibly patronising. He was making a complete mess of things. Yet again.

'Look at me, David. Do I seem angry? I'm not angry, I'm heartbroken. Don't you think I'd like to do or say something that would make everything all right? But life isn't like that. There aren't any easy answers.'

'If you told me that you still loved me – that would make everything all right with me.'

Tanya sighed. 'David, I do still love you.'

David's heart leaped. 'You do? Then maybe we could make a go of it. Take it slowly but—'

Tanya interrupted him. 'Me loving you doesn't make anything right. In fact, it does the complete opposite. We can't go back. Ever.'

'This is madness,' David said, panic stricken, aware that Tanya was slipping away from him. 'You say you love me and I know I love you more than anything in the world. There must be a way we can sort this out.'

'I'm sorry.' She kissed him on the cheek again. 'I've got to get off now.'

'I thought we could go for a meal somewhere,' he said, still clutching her hand.

There were tears in her eyes. 'I can't forgive you. It's

not about what you did to me. I know you were frightened. I know what you'd been through with your
mother. But you kept quiet about Jenny. You stood
by and did nothing. You condoned a woman being
raped. I can't forgive you for that. And so despite the
fact that I still love you with all of my heart, if I came
back to you I'd never be able to forgive myself.'

Tanya pulled her hand free and turned to leave.
David stood on the bridge and watched helplessly as
she disappeared through the trees, knowing that she
was walking out of his life forever.

Rachel flopped back on the pillow. 'Enough,' she
giggled. 'I need a rest.'

Chris kissed her nose. 'Just five minutes.'

Rachel smiled lazily. The more she and Chris made
love the better it got, if that were possible. It seemed
as if he knew, telepathically, what she wanted, where
and when.

'It's three o'clock,' she murmured, looking at the
clock. 'I feel so decadent. We've been in bed nearly
all day.'

'The kids won't be back for ages yet.'

The children were spending the day with Robbie.
Rachel had agreed that he could see them as long as
Zoë wasn't with him.

'Mmm I know,' she said, snuggling up to him. 'I've
been thinking. I'm not going to be able to be a lady
of leisure much longer. I need to get a job. Heaven
knows who would employ me, though.'

'Rachel, I'll look after you.'

'No,' she replied sharply. And then in a gentler
voice, 'Sorry, but I couldn't ever let a man look after

me again. I need my independence, to stand on my own two feet. And to tell you the truth, I think I'd go mad staying at home much longer.'

'I know I shouldn't have said that. I'm not Robbie, Rachel, I'm not looking for a little wifey who'll do everything I want and—'

'You're certainly not Robbie,' Rachel laughed, pulling him on top of her. 'One more time and then we're definitely getting up.'

Loulou got off the phone from Meret. Despite his injuries Andy had managed to tell reporters all about Loulou. And today, of all days, her photo and life story had been on the front page of several tabloids. There were also photos of both Dexter and Meret. She'd have thought Andy would have had more serious things to think about than her. As she'd read the stories, she could feel his bitterness towards her, and all women, seeping off the page.

When she'd warned Meret of what had happened, the singer just laughed.

'As they say,' she drawled, 'all publicity is good publicity.'

Loulou had tried to join in her laughter but it wasn't the effect the story would have on her that mattered, it was how it would affect her son. She thought how awful it all sounded. 'Oh, by the way, I'm your mother and I'm a dyke.' It was enough to send him into therapy for the rest of his life.

And, of course, the papers had been hounding her. She was so heavily disguised that she hardly recognised herself. But the last thing she needed was a press welcoming party for Dexter.

As she paced up and down she found it hard to accept that all around her normal life went on. How could the rushing businessmen and the excited holidaymakers act like they hadn't a care in the world, when any minute she could lose the one person she had ever truly loved? How she wanted to be one of these happy-go-lucky people who weren't about to confess their darkest secret.

She looked up at the arrivals board. The plane had just landed and her stomach churned and twisted in response. She went to wait by the gates, part of her tempted to turn round and run in the other direction and never stop. But she knew that there was no turning back now.

Time passed slowly before the passengers finally made it out of the luggage hall and through customs. Almost at the end of the raggedy crowd came Dexter. He looked smaller than she remembered and much more vulnerable. Loulou thought her heart was going to break. Sniffing, she managed a wave and a smile. Dexter's trusting face lit up immediately. This was going to be the hardest thing she'd ever had to do.

To give herself courage as she watched her son get ever nearer to the truth, she thought about what her friends had been through: Tanya alone with breast cancer; Jenny raped, her baby just holding on to life; and Rachel, publicly humiliated by a husband who was hardly better than a rapist. They were coping. Thinking of Tanya, who was fighting her disease with a bravery that Loulou found astounding, made her feel stronger. As the song said, she would survive.

They would all survive.

Epilogue

It was a beautiful, warm, mellow summer's day, and the only sound, apart from the children playing in the pool, was the lazy hum of the bees. Jenny lifted her daughter towards her and kissed her tiny nose. The baby gurgled in response. Jenny could still barely believe that so much happiness could come from so much misery.

Her daughter, Hope, was the most beautiful baby in the world and Jenny found it hard to put her down. The comfort of holding Hope's warm little body and smelling her innocence was something she still hadn't got used to.

In all of Jenny's life she had never experienced love like it: an unconditional love, an untainted love, a love that made her get up in the morning with a smile and fall asleep at night content with her lot. She no longer suffered from nightmares.

Her happiness showed physically. When she stood in front of the mirror, still surprised to see a brown-haired bob, the only lines she now noticed were laughter lines. Looking after Hope meant never having the time to slap on the make-up or wear anything that couldn't immediately be washed but she had to admit to herself that she looked great.

Even her need to drink had disappeared. Now she could drink like others, for enjoyment not obliteration.

And she had been extra blessed with the friendship of the three women who now sat around in her garden, lazily enjoying the good weather.

Such was her joy that even seeing the solicitor the day before to start divorce proceedings against Michael had not marred her happiness. It was a new start for her and her daughter. She had finally learned that having a bad man wasn't better than having no man at all. Jenny was, at long last, at peace with herself and the world.

Which was probably more than could be said of Michael. Through the grapevine she'd heard that Sharon had thrown him out after several turbulent months of living together, and from the whispering it wouldn't be long before Notting Hill, under its new chairman, followed suit.

Rachel watched Demi and Robbie Jnr as they splashed each other in the pool. She hoped it wasn't her imagination but her children appeared to be finally getting on with each other. It had been several days since they had had a cross word.

How this had happened, she wasn't quite sure. There had been nights of bad dreams and crying for Daddy but it seemed like they were beginning to accept that he would never live with them again.

The weekend before, when she had dropped the children off at Robbie's, he had passed her a scrap of paper. In a scrawly, childish hand, with nearly every word misspelled, he had told her that he loved her and wanted to come back. When she returned for the children she simply shook her head in response. There was no going back.

When Rachel's thoughts turned to her previous life she was shocked at how acquiescent she had been. How could she have put her own needs so far below those of Robbie? She would never look after a man like that again.

She had even given up her romances, no longer needing or wanting fantasy. With Chris she had what she believed to be the real thing, but only time would tell and she was determined to take it slowly.

Rachel felt like she was being given a chance to have her youth again. Part of this included the frivolous pursuit of make-up and clothes. Her friends were constantly amused by her questions about what lipstick she should wear or if her newest dress showed off her figure to its best advantage. She had just had her hair cut short and highlighted, just like she would have had done when she was sixteen if she'd had the courage. Well, she did now.

And then there was her job. She had put to use the two things she was good at – children and reading – and had started teaching literacy to young teenagers.

Tanya pointed out something to Dexter and Loulou's heart contracted. Since she had told him the truth about his birth he had hardly spoken. The only thing he did was paint and the only person he even half connected with was Tanya. Loulou spent her days hoping for a reconciliation. Her friends constantly reassured her that any day now her son would begin to forgive her. In the meantime, she tried desperately hard to forgive herself.

When she read about Andy, who would be confined to a wheelchair forever, she felt as if her relationship with him had been in another lifetime. She could feel no pity for him. He had brought his punishment on himself. Clive hadn't told the papers about Andy raping Jenny but he had told them about another woman, who had since come forward. The police were still investigating.

Loulou knew that she had changed so much that sometimes even she didn't recognise herself. The only thing that had remained a constant was how she looked. Still immaculate and, as ever, on top of what one should and shouldn't be wearing, she hid her sadness behind the façade.

Meret had stuck by her but wanted to return to America. She had asked Loulou and Dexter to join her. But Loulou didn't know whether she could leave her friends and her new business partnership with Tanya. They were going to put Tanya's strange designs into production as jewellery. All Loulou could offer was her faith in Tanya and her ability to cajole people into buying her friend's work.

For once Loulou wanted to stand still, to stay put, to plant some roots for both herself and her son.

Tanya finished helping Dexter with his picture and then lay back on the lounger. She felt happy. Happy that she was alive, happy that she had these friends, happy that she had found something she believed in. Now in remission, she had recently been nominated to be the spokesperson for a cancer charity. Tanya had taken up the post with relish. For the first time she was getting column inches for what she said rather than what she looked like.

Not that she looked bad. Released from the constrictions of a Page Three girl, Tanya had taken up the natural look that she was born to have. Her hair had returned to its light brown shade and a style that didn't require a hairdryer. Her clothes were more conservative and she knew that she probably wouldn't feel completely comfortable until she had reconstructive surgery.

But, in the meantime, there were more important things to think about. Only that morning she and Loulou had signed their business agreement. Even now, with the sun making her sleepy, hundreds of jewellery ideas floated through her mind. The only sorrow on the horizon was David, but she knew that in time even that pain would fade.

Jenny placed Hope in her Moses basket and went back up to the house. She returned with a bottle of champagne and four glasses. After a brief struggle, the cork rocketed into the air.

As the overflowing glasses clinked together, Jenny said simply, 'To friendship.'

Warner Books now offers an exciting range of quality titles by both established and new authors. All of the books in this series are available from:

Little, Brown and Company (UK),
P.O. Box 11,
Falmouth,
Cornwall TR10 9EN.

Fax No: 01326 317444.
Telephone No: 01326 372400
E-mail: books@barni.avel.co.uk

Payments can be made as follows: cheque, postal order (payable to Little, Brown and Company) or by credit cards, Visa/Access. Do not send cash or currency. UK customers and B.F.P.O. please allow £1.00 for postage and packing for the first book, plus 50p for the second book, plus 30p for each additional book up to a maximum charge of £3.00 (7 books plus).

Overseas customers including Ireland, please allow £2.00 for the first book plus £1.00 for the second book, plus 50p for each additional book.

NAME (Block Letters) ....

....

ADDRESS ....

....

....

☐ I enclose my remittance for ....

☐ I wish to pay by Access/Visa Card

Number | | | | | | | | | | | | | | | | |

Card Expiry Date | | | | |